AN UNOFFICIAL GRAPHIC NOVEL

GAME OF THE GUARDIANS

THE S.Q.U.I.D. SQUAD #3

MEGAN MILLER

D0963612

SKY PONY PRESS
New York

Copyright © 2020 by Hollan Publishing, Inc.

Minecraft® is a registered trademark of Notch Development AB.
The Minecraft game is copyright © Mojang AB.

Sky Pony Press books may be purchased in bulk at special discounts for sales promotion, corporate gifts, fund-raising, or educational purposes. Special editions can also be created to specifications. For details, contact the Special Sales Department, Sky Pony Press, 307 West 36th Street, 11th Floor, New York, NY 10018 or info@skyhorsepublishing.com.

Sky Pony® is a registered trademark of Skyhorse Publishing, Inc.®, a Delaware corporation.

Minecraft® is a registered trademark of Notch Development AB.

The Minecraft game is copyright © Mojang AB.

Visit our website at www.skyponypress.com.

10 9 8 7 6 5 4 3 2 1

Library of Congress Cataloging-in-Publication Data is available on file.

Cover design by Kai Texel
Cover and interior art by Megan Miller

Print ISBN: 978-1-5107-5986-2
Ebook ISBN: 978-1-5107-6540-5

Printed in China

Introduction

It is a dire time in the world. The Evil Pillagers are conquering villages and destroying the villagers' culture and libraries. But far out at sea live the Book Guardians, a secret group of miners and villagers helping to save the libraries' precious books. The Book Guardians bring chests of books, before they can be destroyed by Pillagers, to the Book Guardians' hidden underwater ravine headquarters. Here a small group of three families collects the books and stores them for better times—for when the Pillagers are defeated.

While the grownups are checking deliveries, securing books, making plans, and double-checking those plans, the children—Inky, Luke, and Max—are meeting new friends and solving mysteries! And that's not all. The Dolphins were so happy for the trio's help, they gave them the GOLDEN DUST MAGIC OF SPEAKING TO CREATURES. So, yes, the children can talk to their underwater neighbors, the underwater creatures, fish, and squid they share their new home with. And now the intrepid three, the "S.Q.U.I.D. Squad," are ready to take on any undersea mystery, no matter how deep or treacherous!

Meet the S.Q.U.I.D. Squad

INKY

Clever. Enjoys organizing stuff. Faced too many squid to count. Knows what words like *acronym* mean. Mostly likes to play by the rules.

LUKE

A little rebellious. Enjoys delivering a good speech. He sees himself as the leader, but Inky and Max have other ideas.

MAX

Brave. Leaves Inky and Luke in the dust when it comes to crafting stuff really, really fast. Their secret club name was his idea—the Super Qualified Underwater Investigation Detective ... er ... Squad. Just say "S.Q.U.I.D. Squad," it's easier.

And also, meet ...

EMI

Special friend to the squad, she also fled to the oceans to escape the Pillagers. She lives secretly in a cottage on the other side of the coral reef.

SOFI

Inky's mom. Redstone engineer in charge of the book delivery system. And she has ALREADY figured out that Inky, Luke, and Max have made their OWN secret underwater cave headquarters INSIDE OF the Book Guardian's own secret underwater ravine headquarters. She hasn't even told anyone else about it!

ABS

Sofi's brother. He can haul chests of books like you wouldn't believe.

ZANE

Max's dad. He goes on a lot of secret missions to find new villages that want to save their books.

NEHA

This is Zane's sister. She's learning the art of potions!

PER AND JUN

Luke's mom and dad. Per is fond of speeches and Jun tries to let him know when they go on too long. They go out on secret missions, too.

MABEL

Friend to the Squad, unafraid to say what she thinks!

Chapter 1
Return to Turtle Egg Island

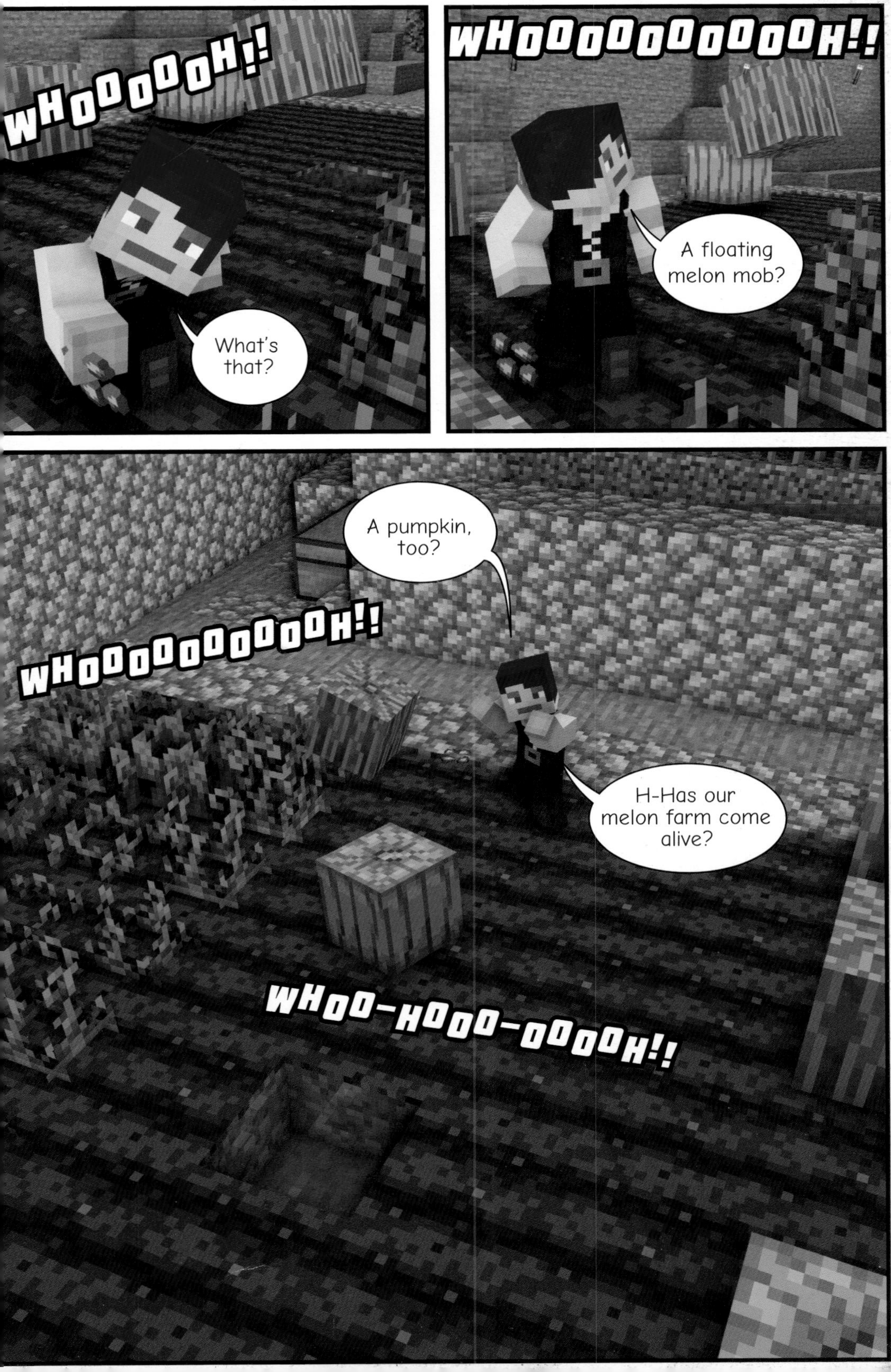
WHOOOOOH!!
What's that?
WHOOOOOOOOOOOH!!
A floating melon mob?
A pumpkin, too?
WHOOOOOOOOOOOH!!
H-Has our melon farm come alive?
WHOO-HOOO-OOOOH!!

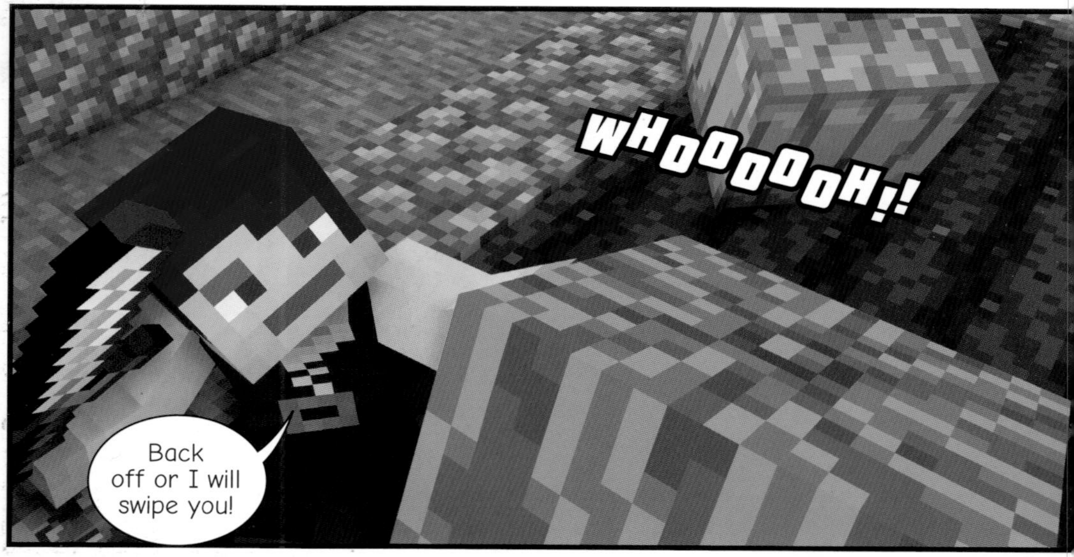
WHOOOOOOH!!
Back off or I will swipe you!

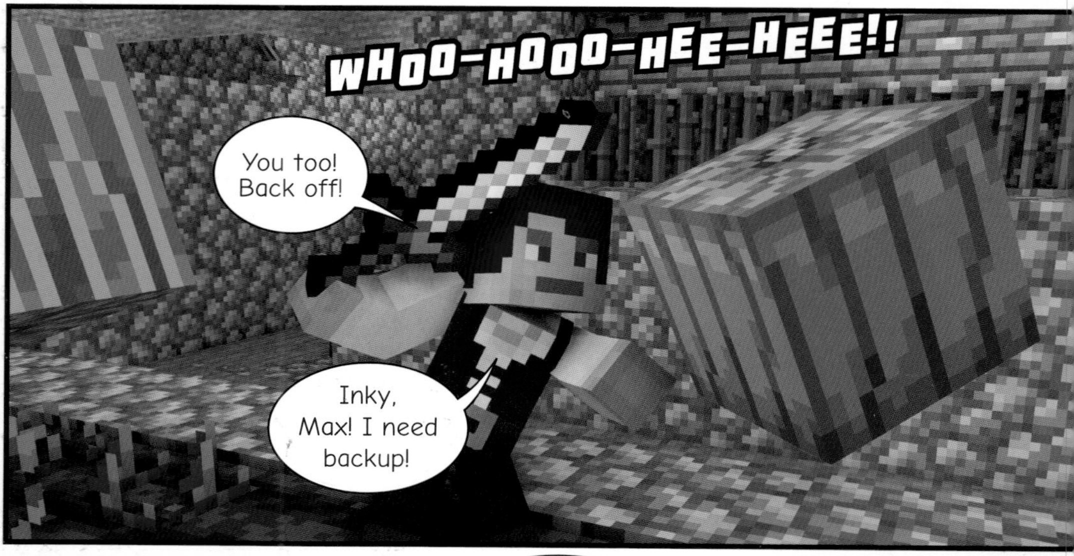
WHOO-HOOO-HEE-HEEE!!
You too! Back off!
Inky, Max! I need backup!

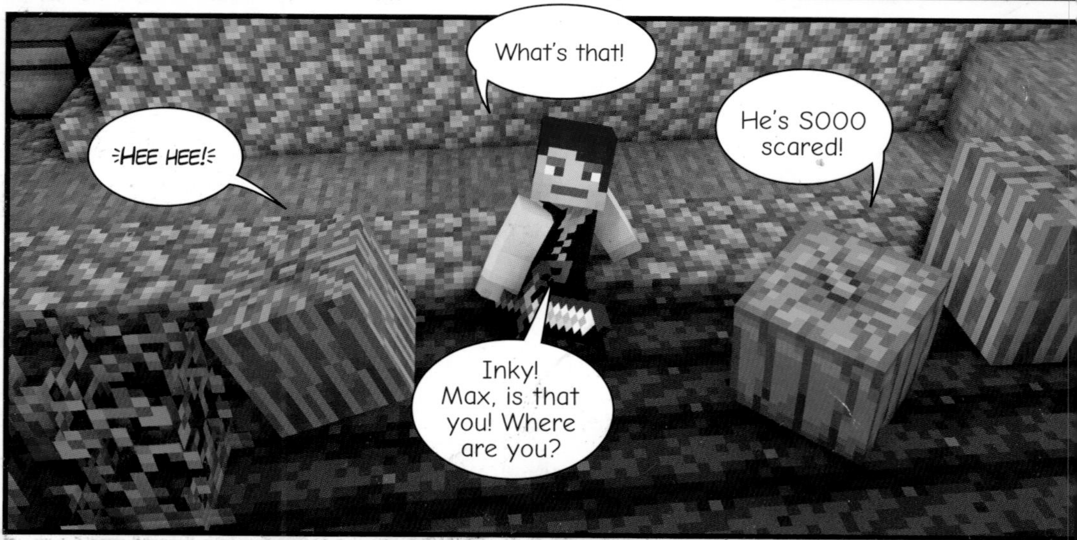
HEE HEE!
What's that!
He's SOOO scared!
Inky! Max, is that you! Where are you?

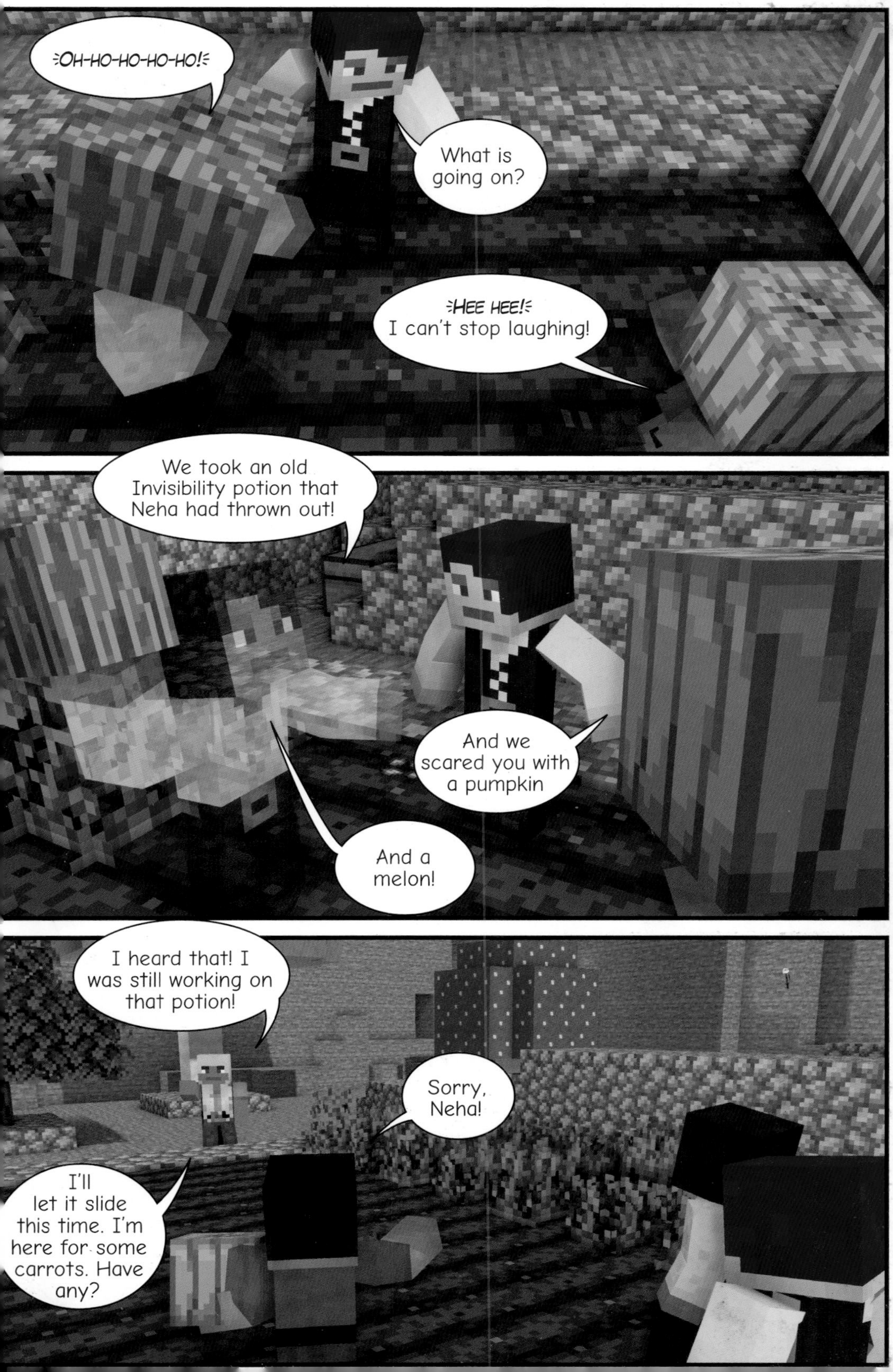
OH-HO-HO-HO-HO!
What is going on?
HEE HEE! I can't stop laughing!
We took an old Invisibility potion that Neha had thrown out!
And we scared you with a pumpkin
And a melon!
I heard that! I was still working on that potion!
Sorry, Neha!
I'll let it slide this time. I'm here for some carrots. Have any?

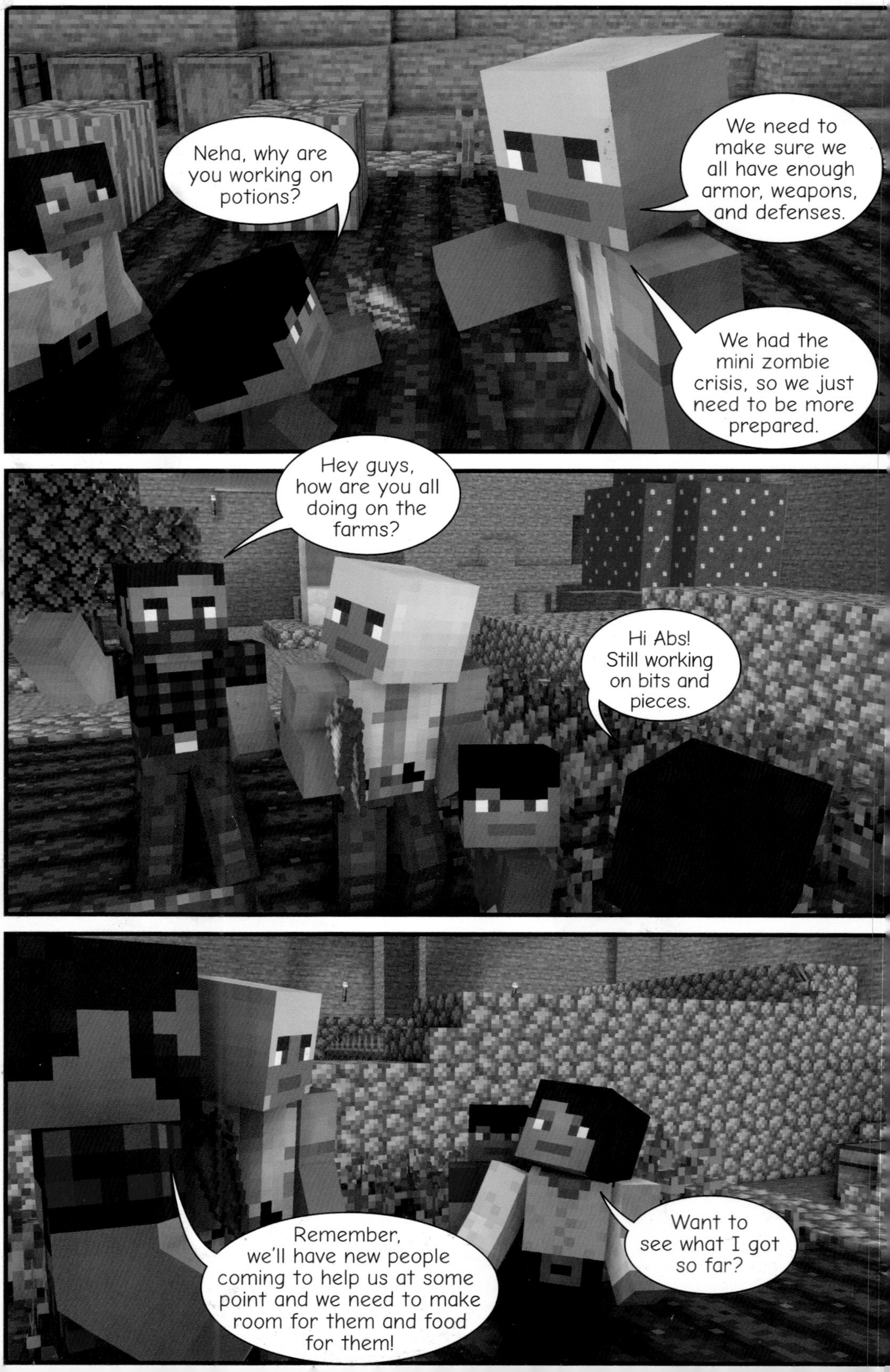
Neha, why are you working on potions?
We need to make sure we all have enough armor, weapons, and defenses.
We had the mini zombie crisis, so we just need to be more prepared.
Hey guys, how are you all doing on the farms?
Hi Abs! Still working on bits and pieces.
Remember, we'll have new people coming to help us at some point and we need to make room for them and food for them!
Want to see what I got so far?

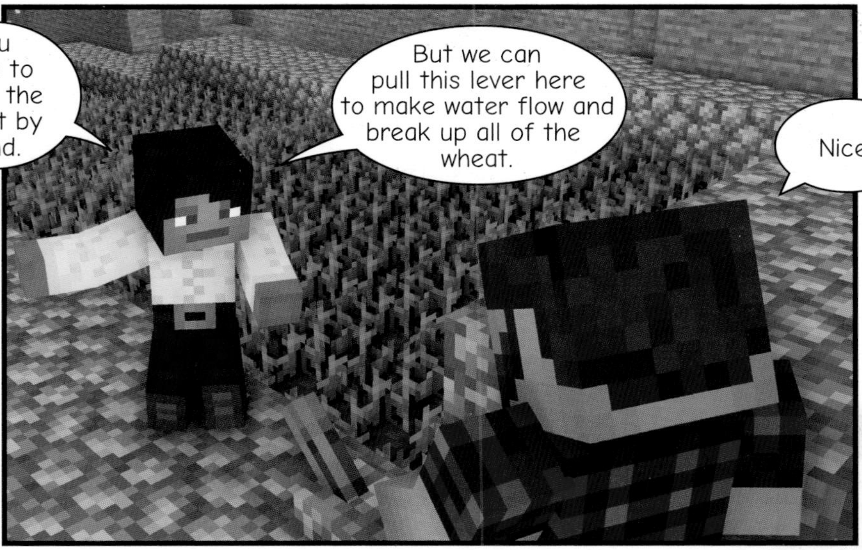
You have to plant the wheat by hand.
But we can pull this lever here to make water flow and break up all of the wheat.
Nice.

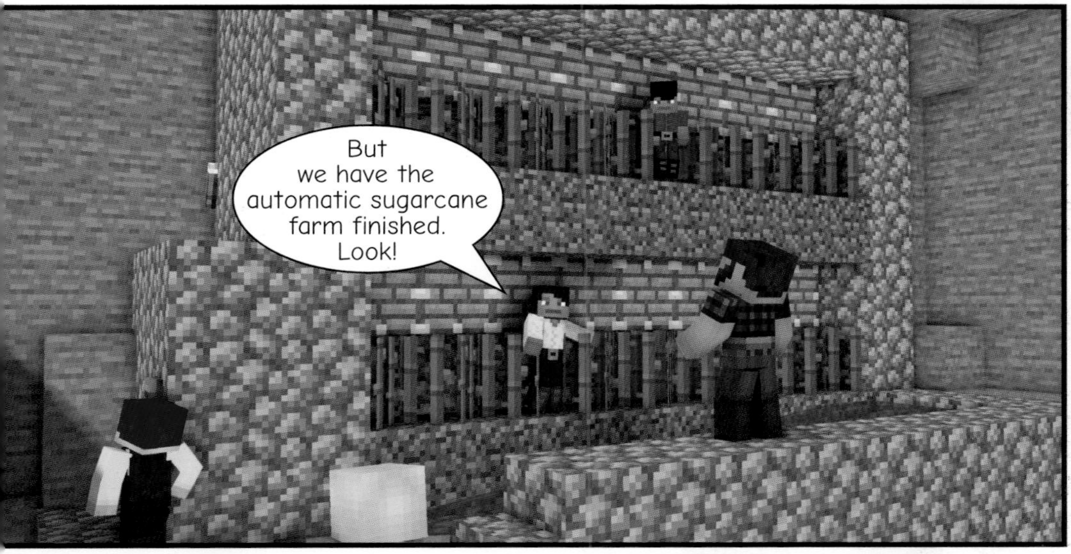
But we have the automatic sugarcane farm finished. Look!

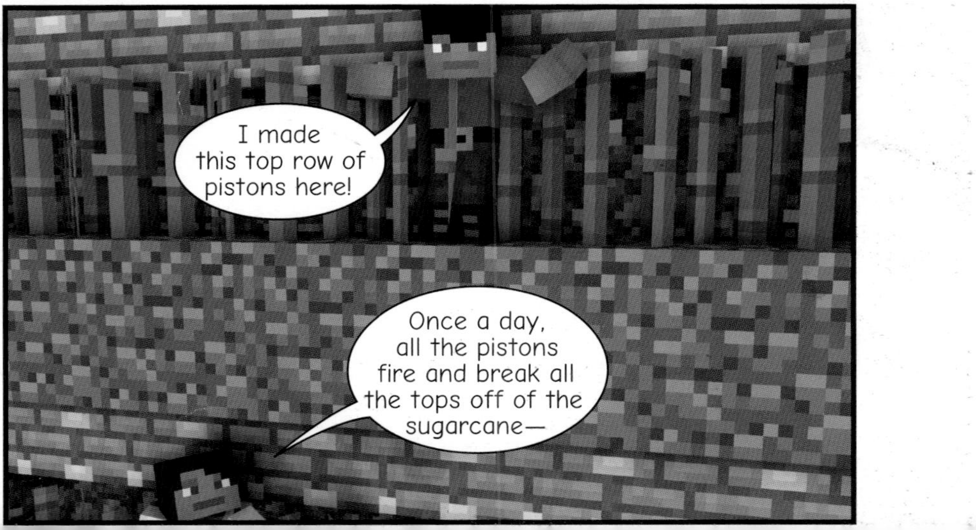
I made this top row of pistons here!
Once a day, all the pistons fire and break all the tops off of the sugarcane—

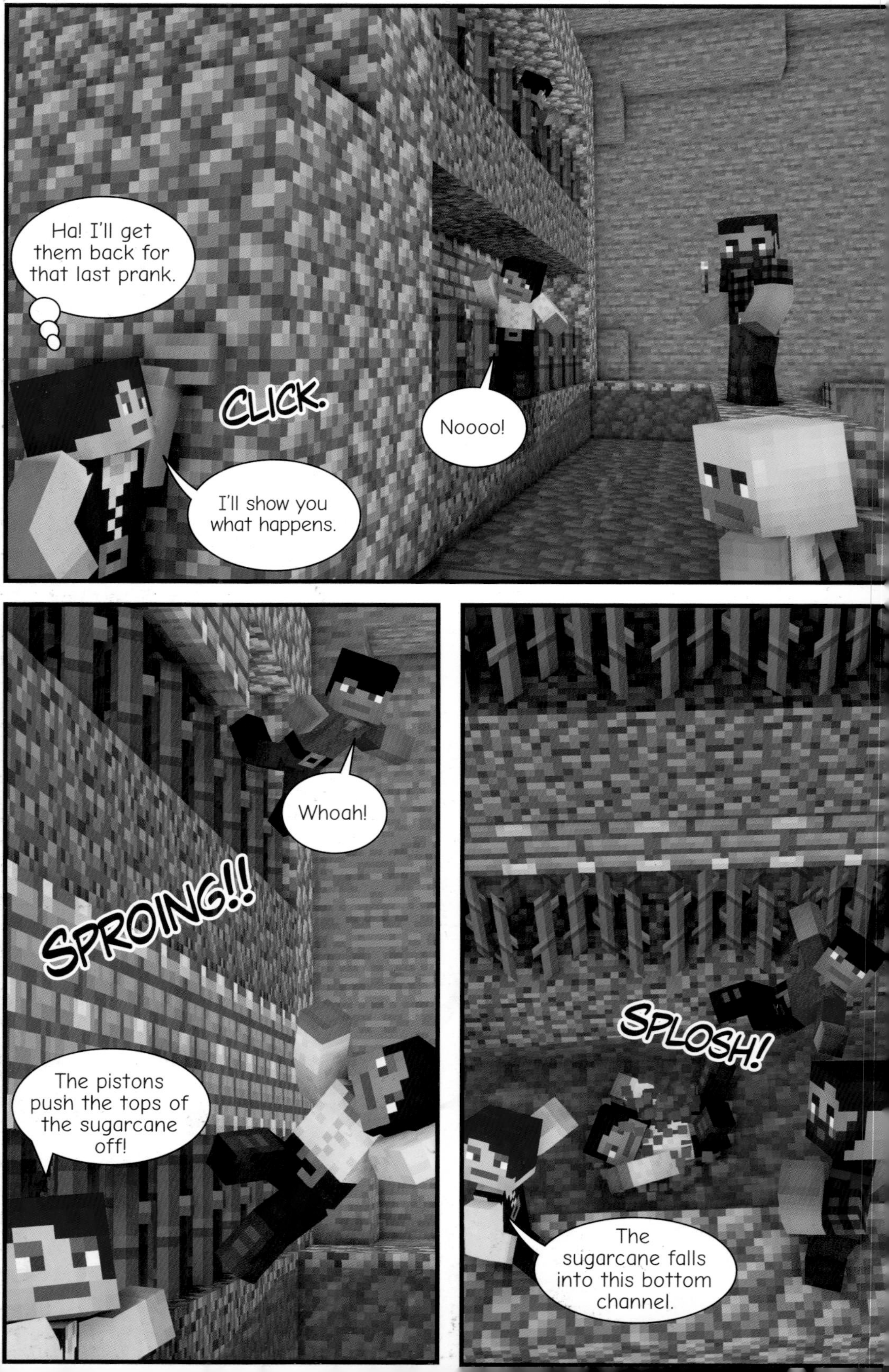
Ha! I'll get them back for that last prank.
CLICK.
I'll show you what happens.
Noooo!
Whoah!
SPROING!!
The pistons push the tops of the sugarcane off!
SPLOSH!
The sugarcane falls into this bottom channel.

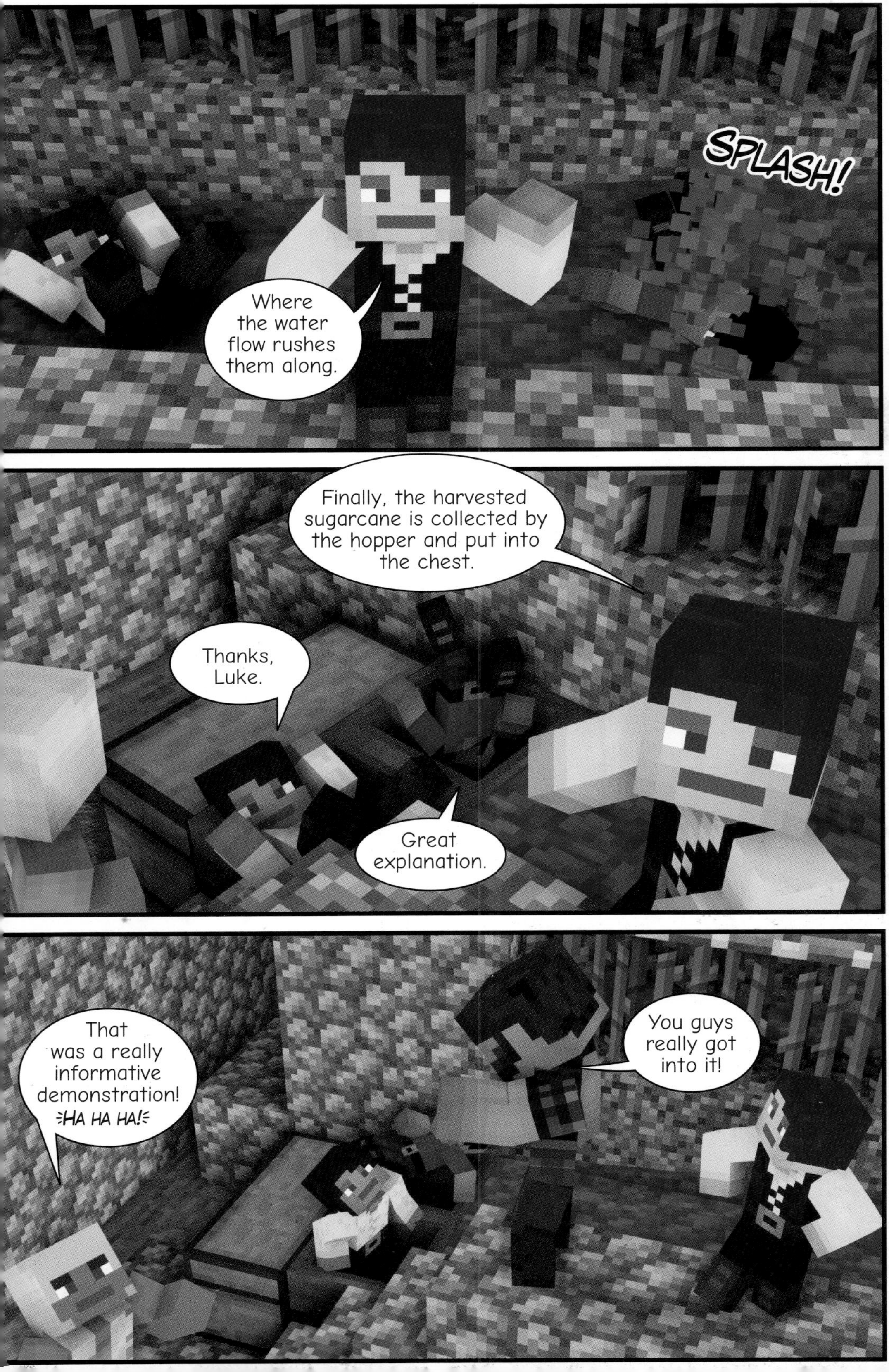
SPLASH!
Where the water flow rushes them along.
Finally, the harvested sugarcane is collected by the hopper and put into the chest.
Thanks, Luke.
Great explanation.
That was a really informative demonstration! HA HA HA!
You guys really got into it!

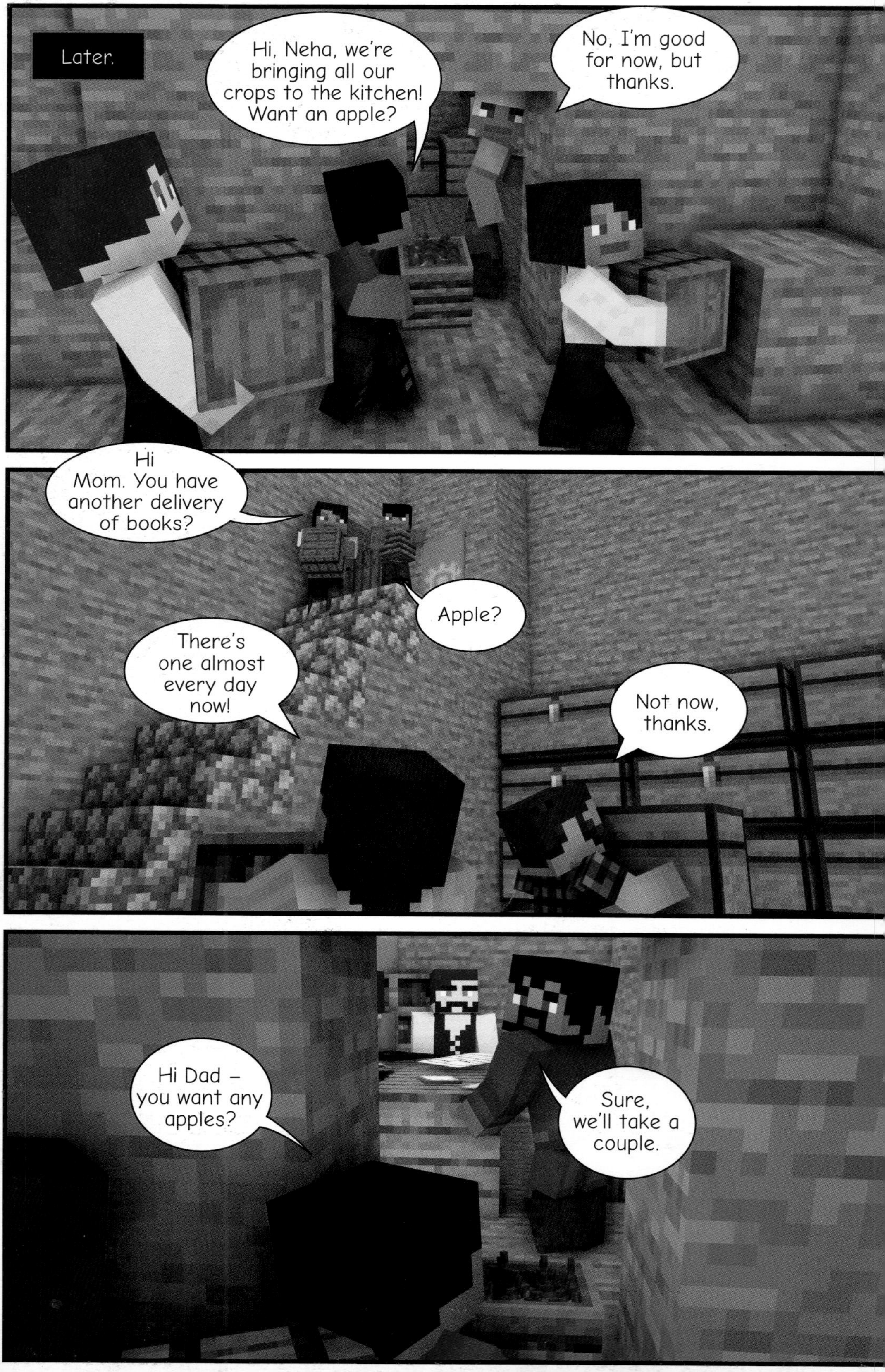
Later.
Hi, Neha, we're bringing all our crops to the kitchen! Want an apple?
No, I'm good for now, but thanks.
Hi Mom. You have another delivery of books?
There's one almost every day now!
Apple?
Not now, thanks.
Hi Dad – you want any apples?
Sure, we'll take a couple.

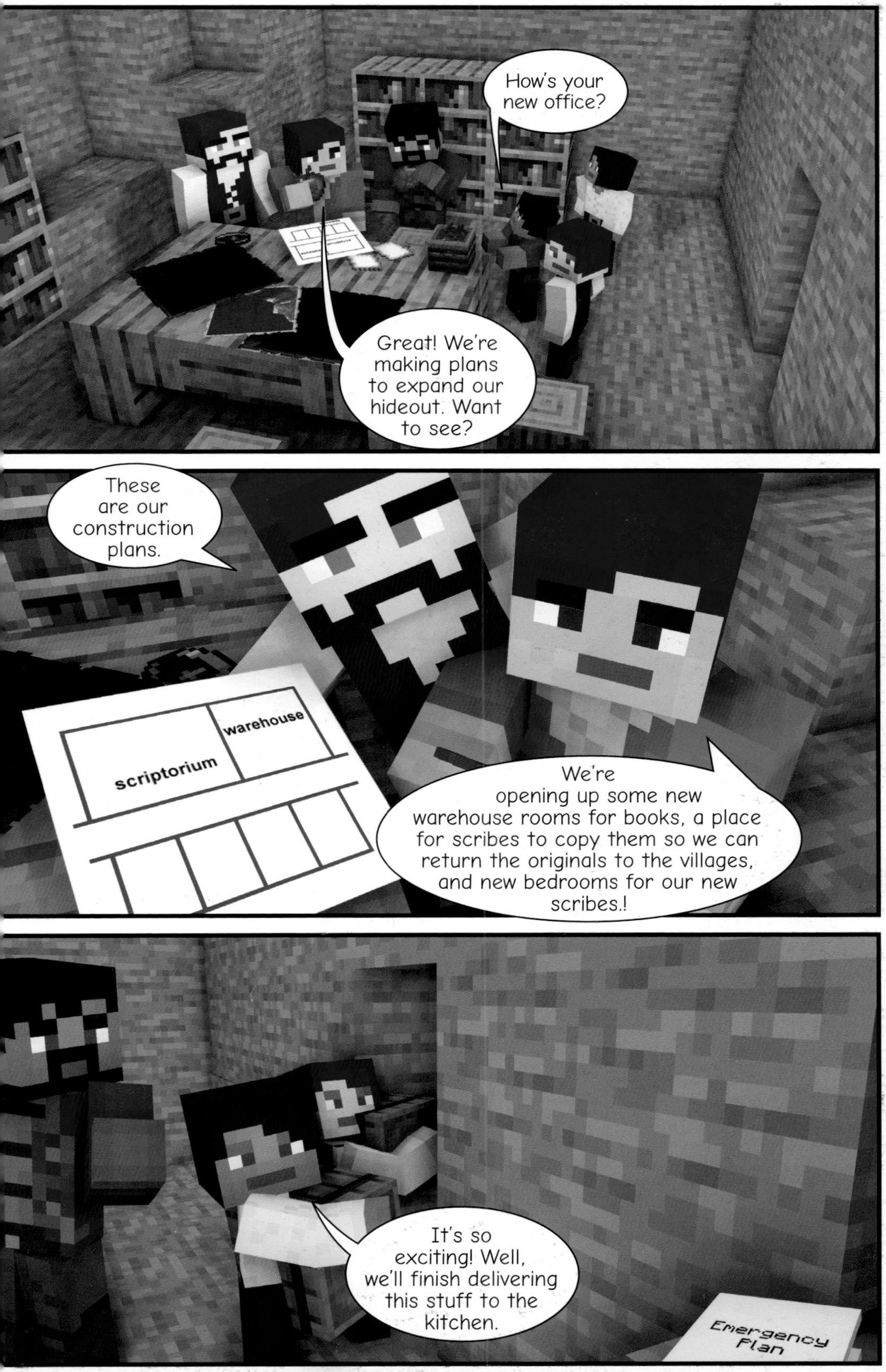
How's your new office?
Great! We're making plans to expand our hideout. Want to see?
These are our construction plans.
warehouse
scriptorium
We're opening up some new warehouse rooms for books, a place for scribes to copy them so we can return the originals to the villages, and new bedrooms for our new scribes.!
It's so exciting! Well, we'll finish delivering this stuff to the kitchen.
Emergency Plan

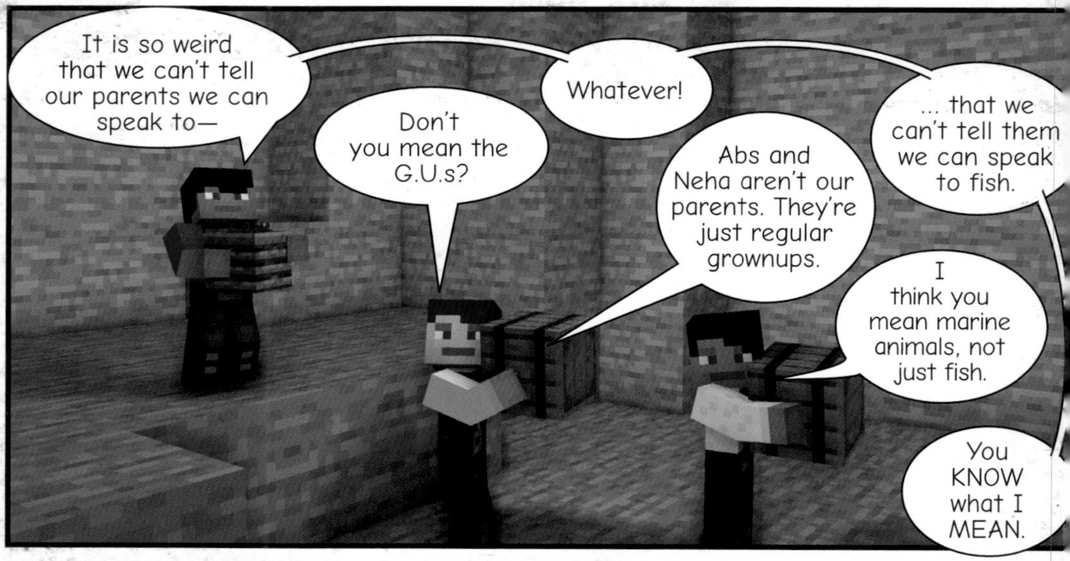
It is so weird that we can't tell our parents we can speak to—
Don't you mean the G.U.s?
Whatever!
... that we can't tell them we can speak to fish.
Abs and Neha aren't our parents. They're just regular grownups.
I think you mean marine animals, not just fish.
You KNOW what I MEAN.

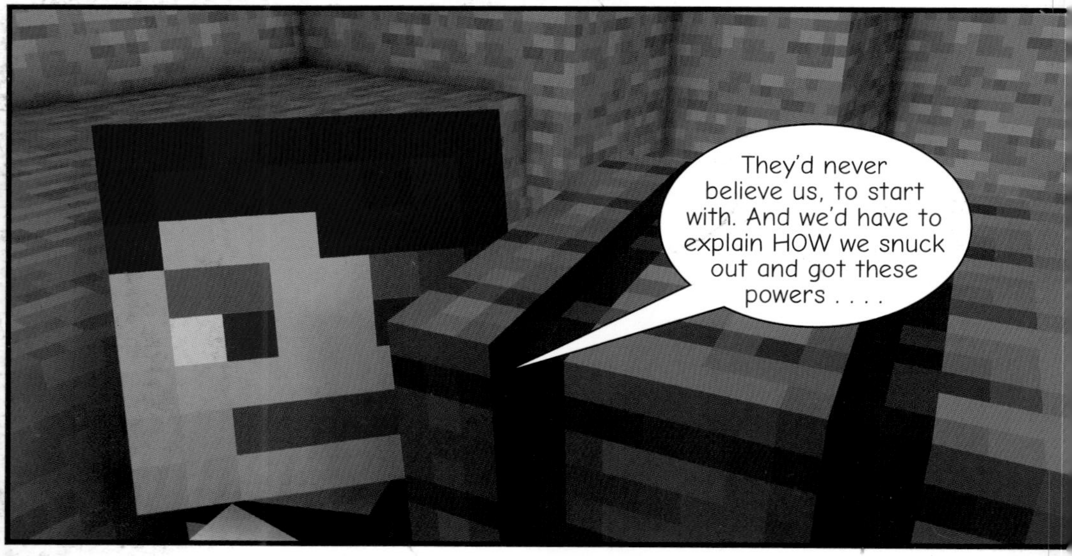
They'd never believe us, to start with. And we'd have to explain HOW we snuck out and got these powers . . . .

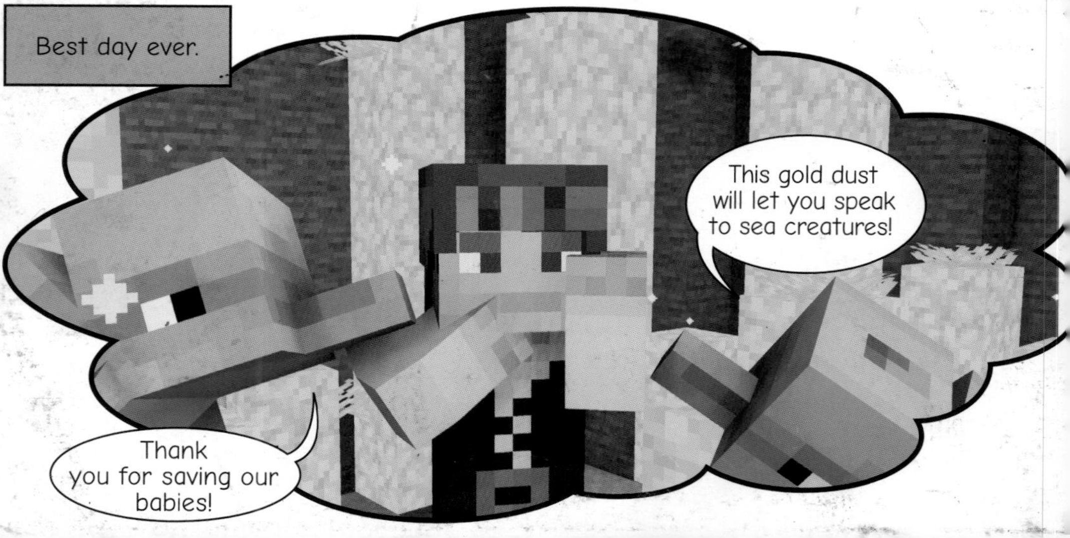
Best day ever.
This gold dust will let you speak to sea creatures!
Thank you for saving our babies!

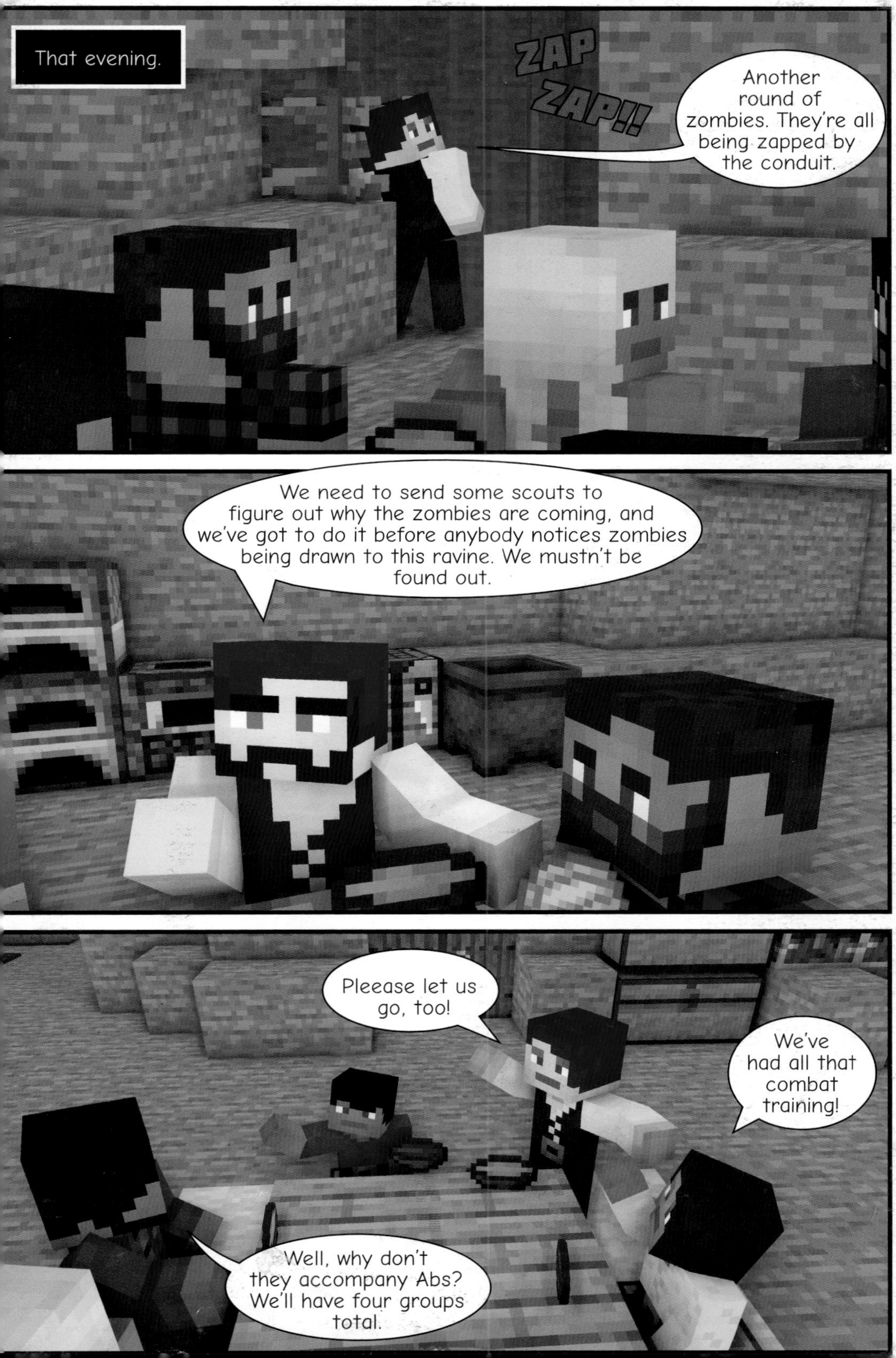
That evening.
ZAP
ZAP!!
Another round of zombies. They're all being zapped by the conduit.
We need to send some scouts to figure out why the zombies are coming, and we've got to do it before anybody notices zombies being drawn to this ravine. We mustn't be found out.
Pleease let us go, too!
We've had all that combat training!
Well, why don't they accompany Abs? We'll have four groups total.

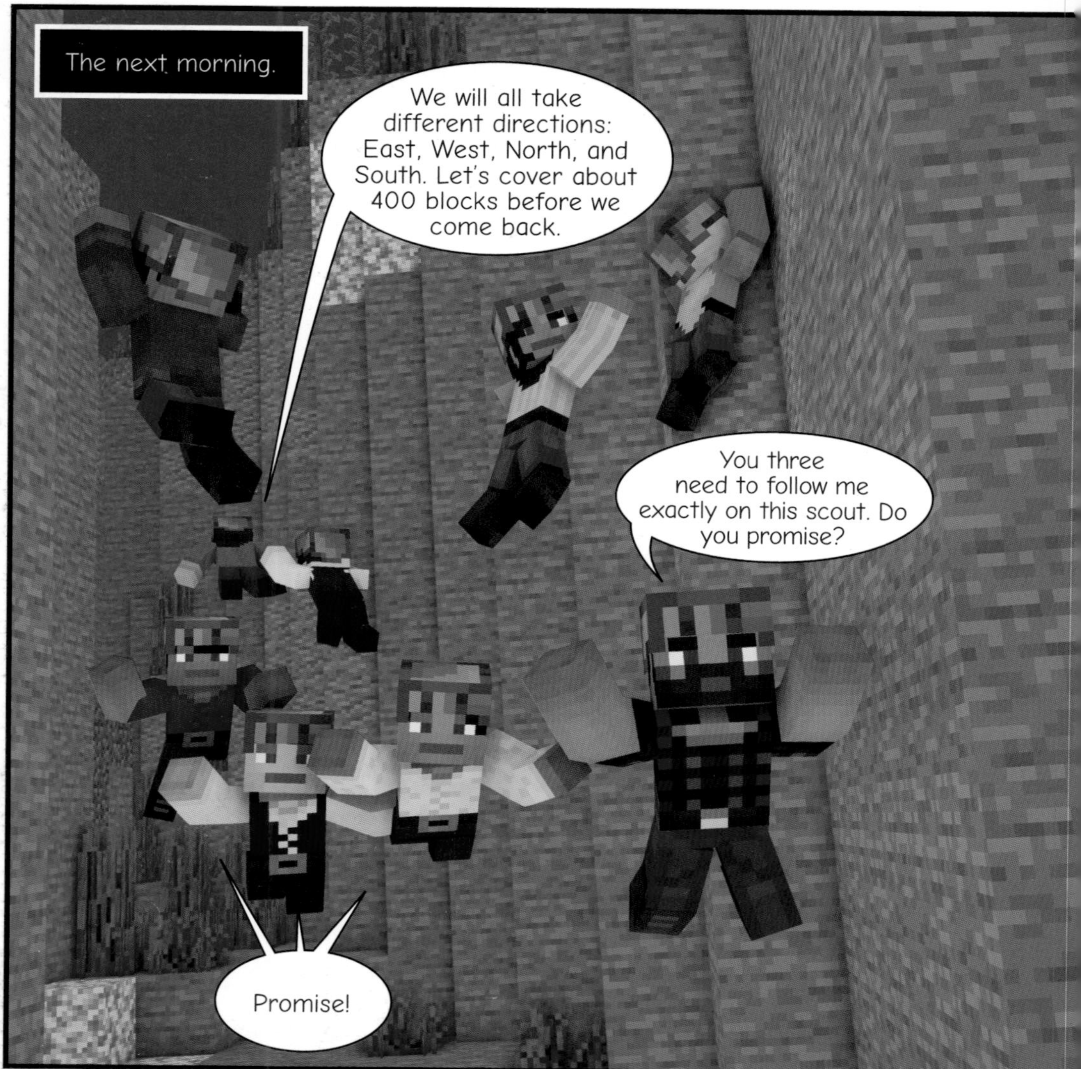
The next morning.
We will all take different directions: East, West, North, and South. Let's cover about 400 blocks before we come back.
You three need to follow me exactly on this scout. Do you promise?
Promise!

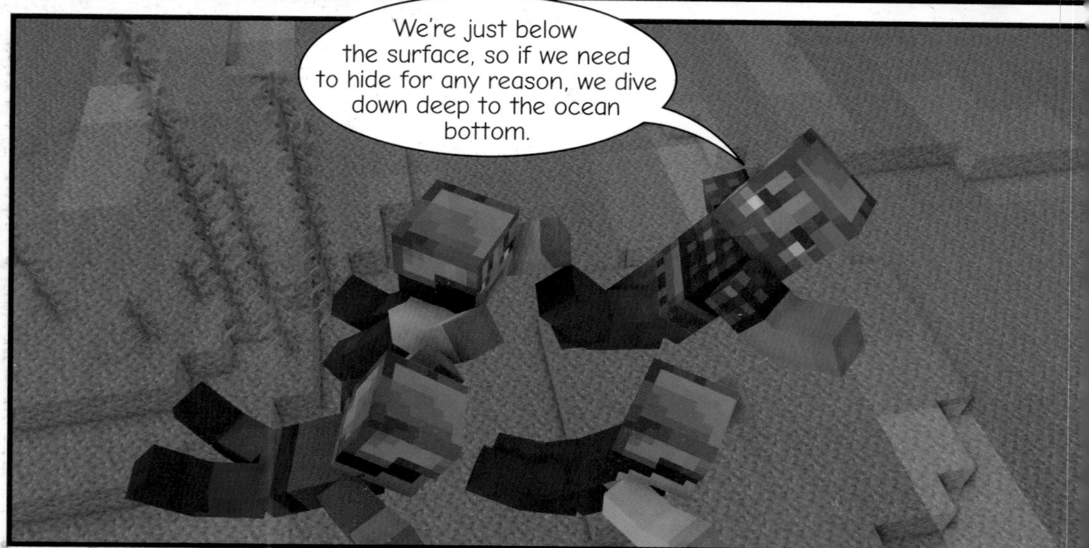
We're just below the surface, so if we need to hide for any reason, we dive down deep to the ocean bottom.

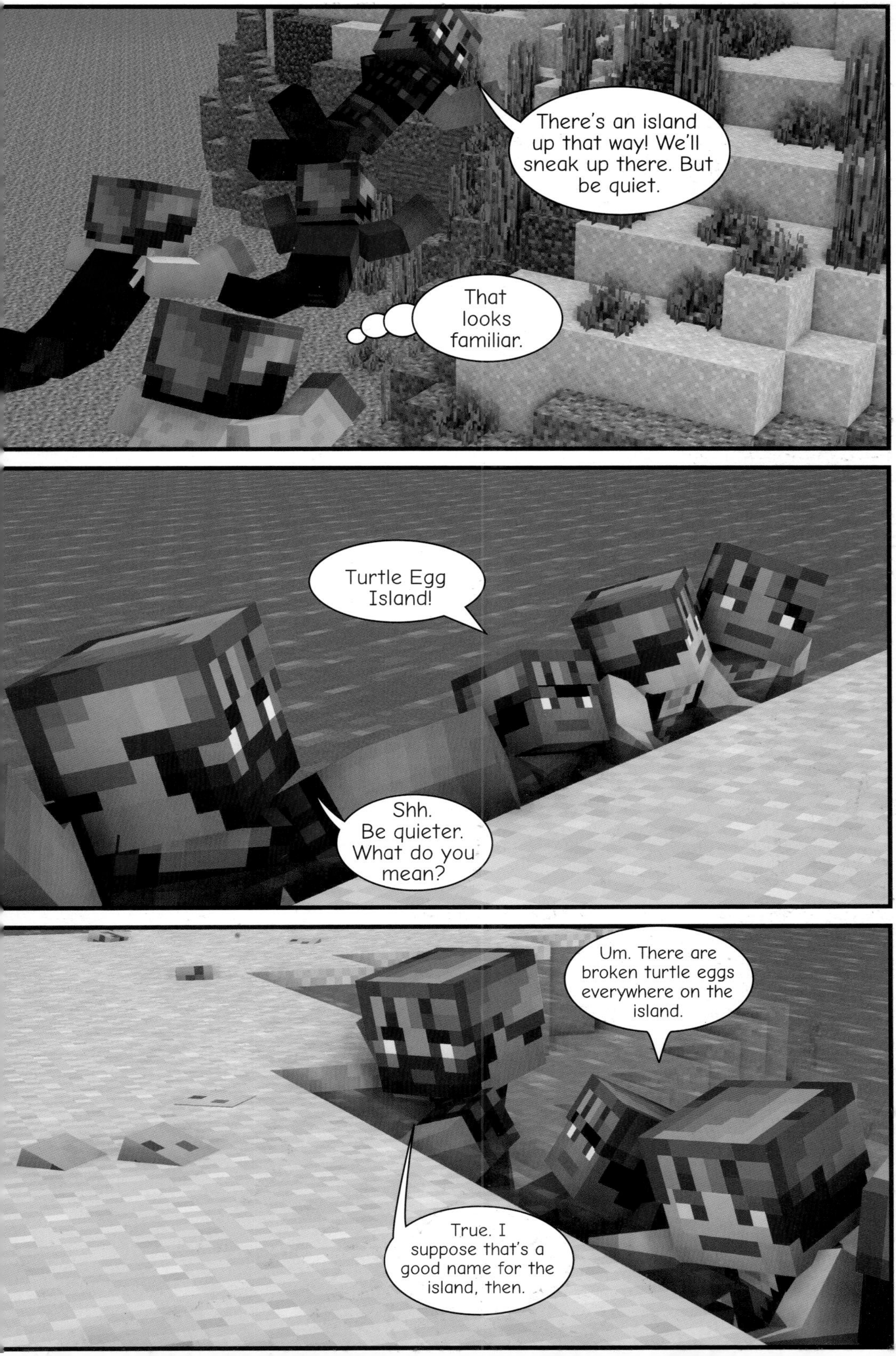
There's an island up that way! We'll sneak up there. But be quiet.
That looks familiar.
Turtle Egg Island!
Shh. Be quieter. What do you mean?
Um. There are broken turtle eggs everywhere on the island.
True. I suppose that's a good name for the island, then.

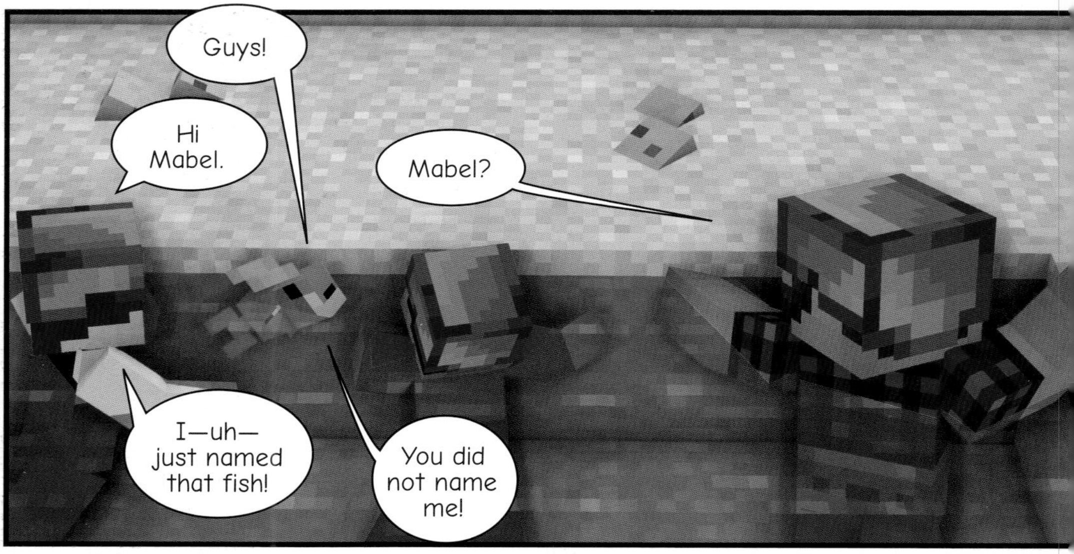
Guys!
Hi Mabel.
Mabel?
I—uh—just named that fish!
You did not name me!

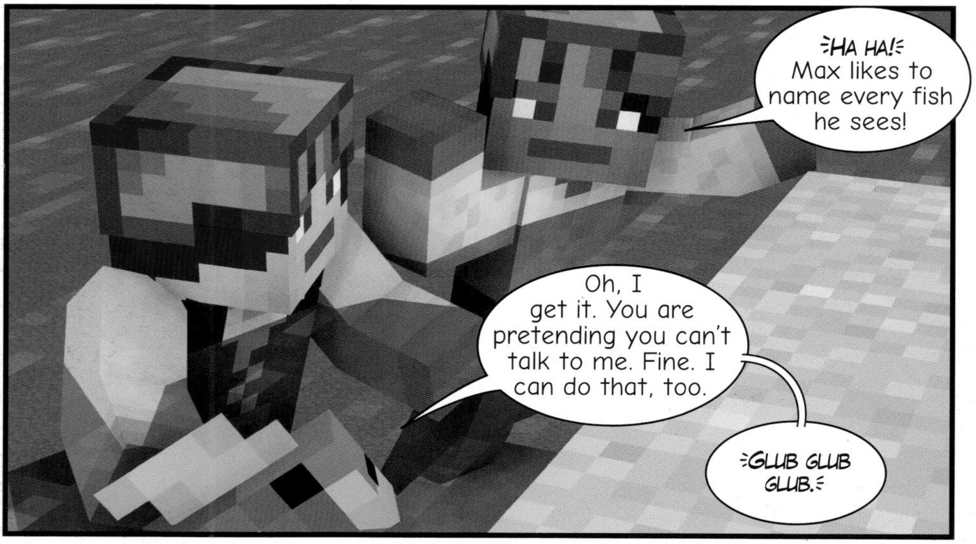
HA HA! Max likes to name every fish he sees!
Oh, I get it. You are pretending you can't talk to me. Fine. I can do that, too.
GLUB GLUB GLUB.

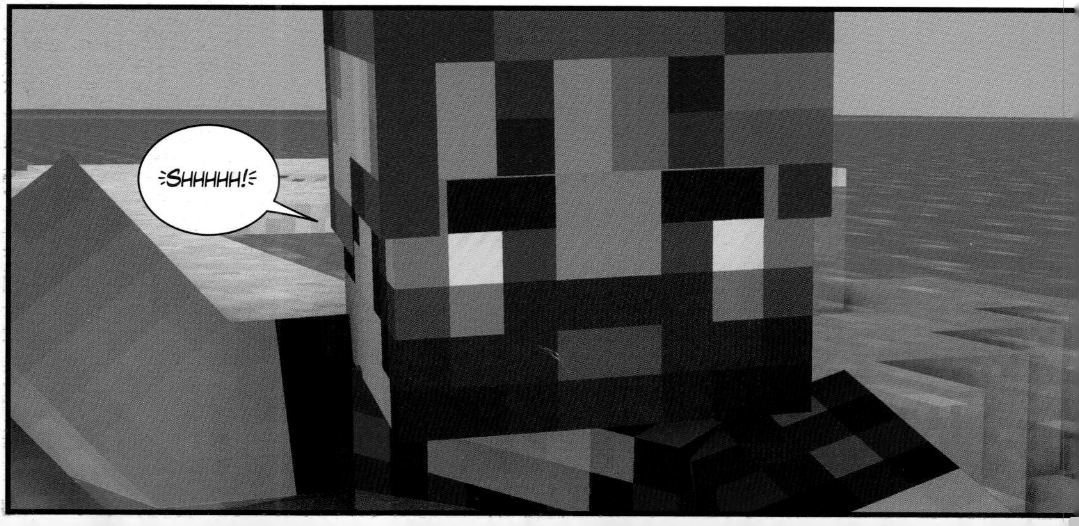
SHHHHH!

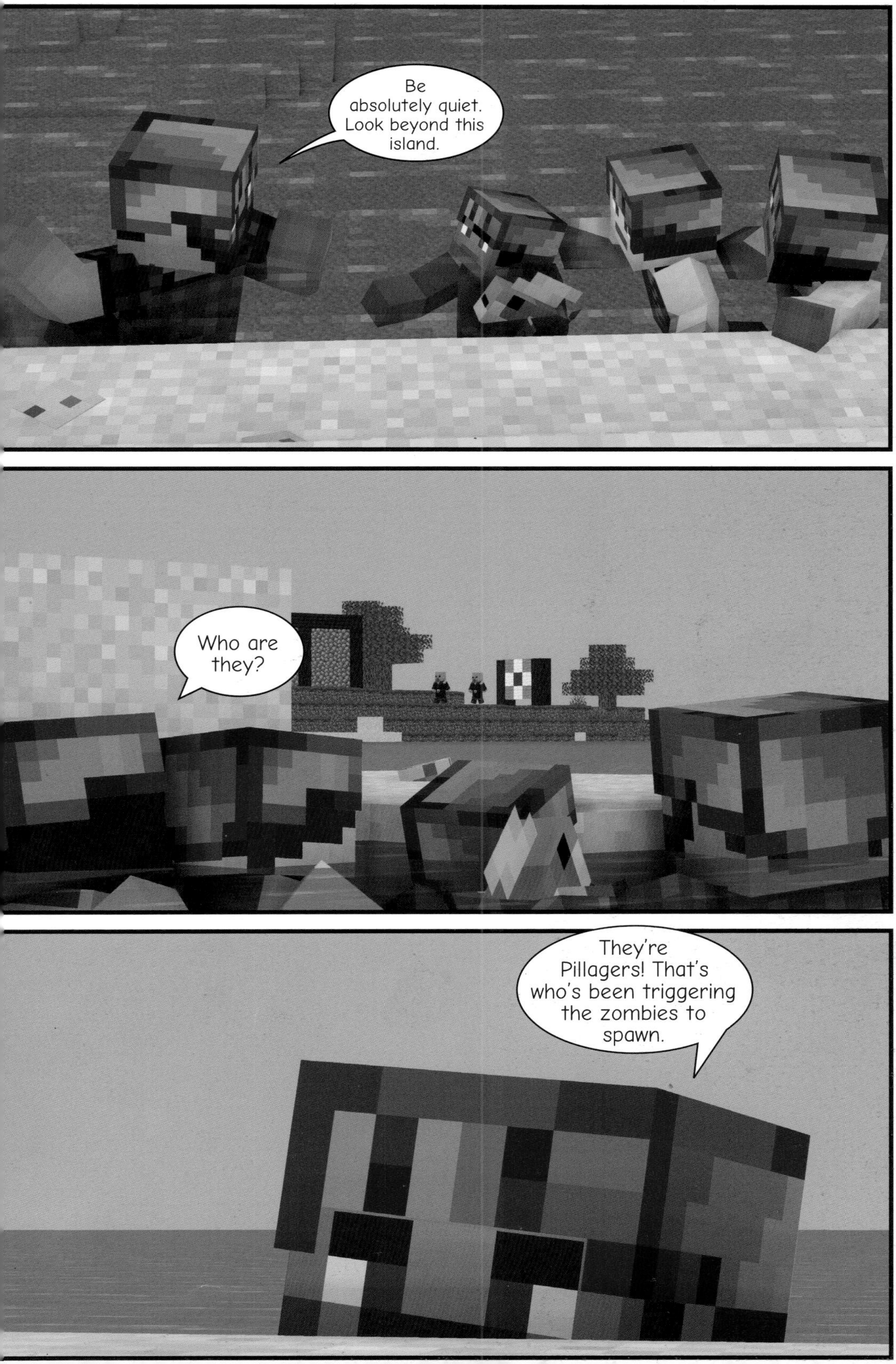
Be absolutely quiet. Look beyond this island.
Who are they?
They're Pillagers! That's who's been triggering the zombies to spawn.

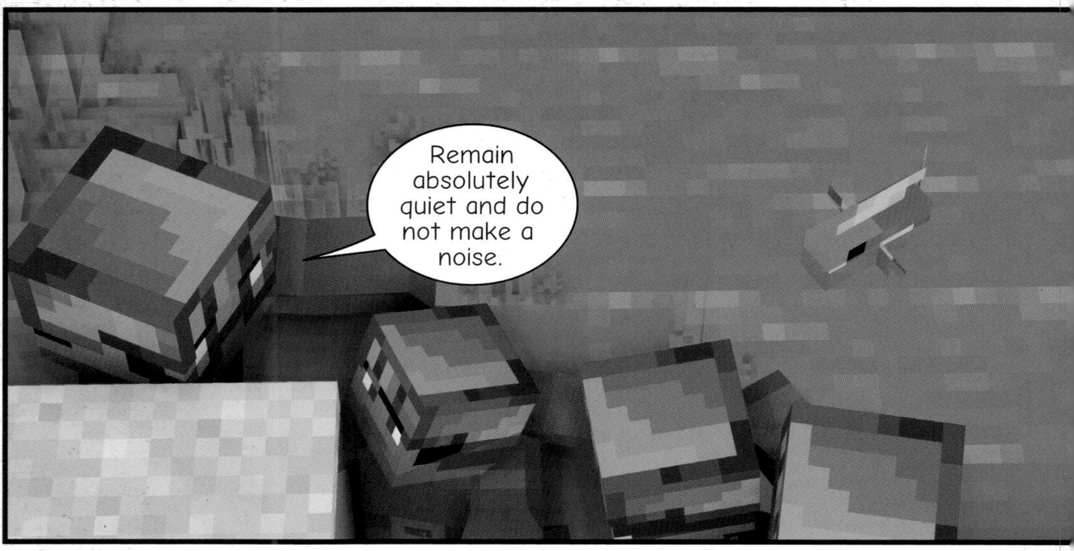
Remain absolutely quiet and do not make a noise.

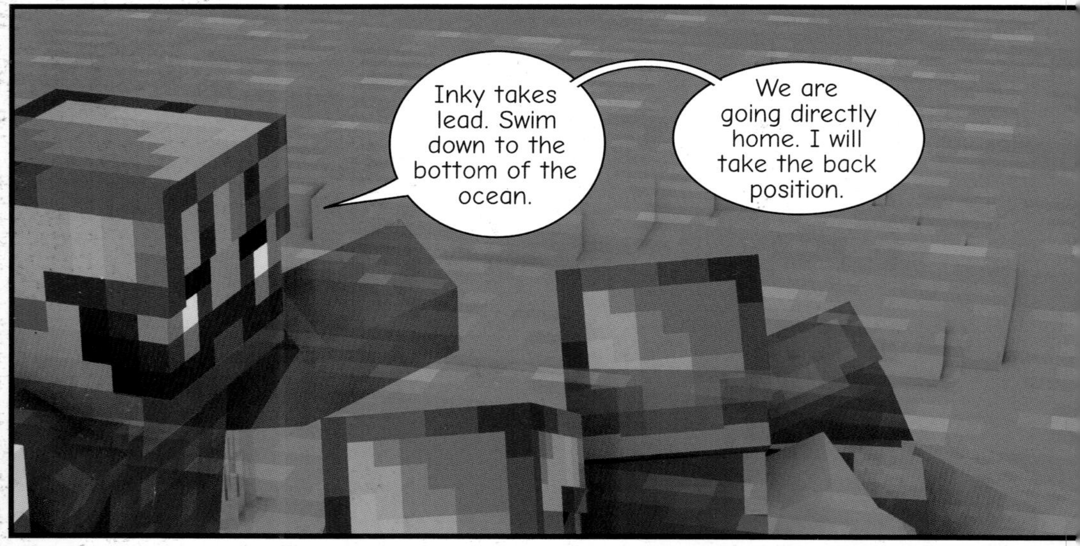
Inky takes lead. Swim down to the bottom of the ocean.
We are going directly home. I will take the back position.

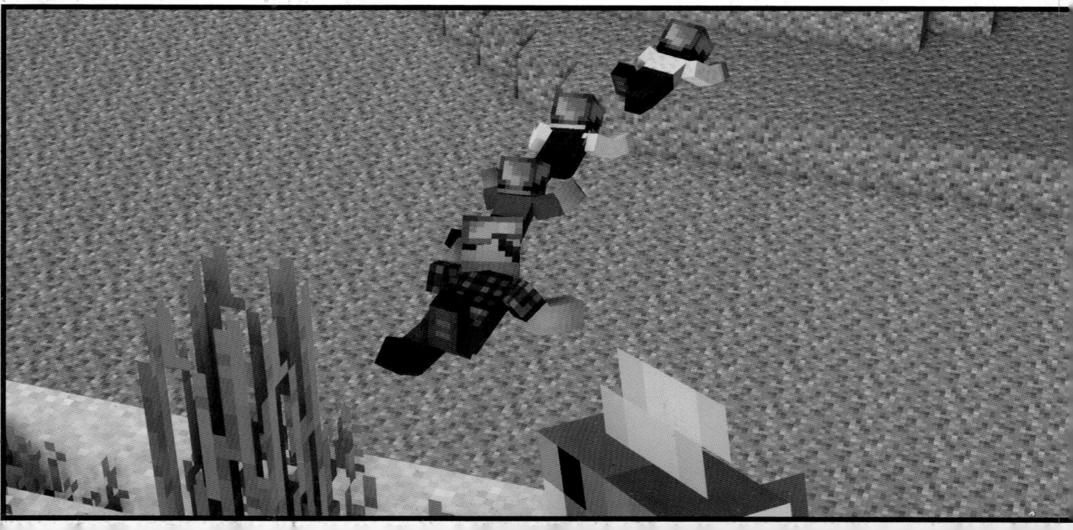

Chapter 2
Hide and Seek

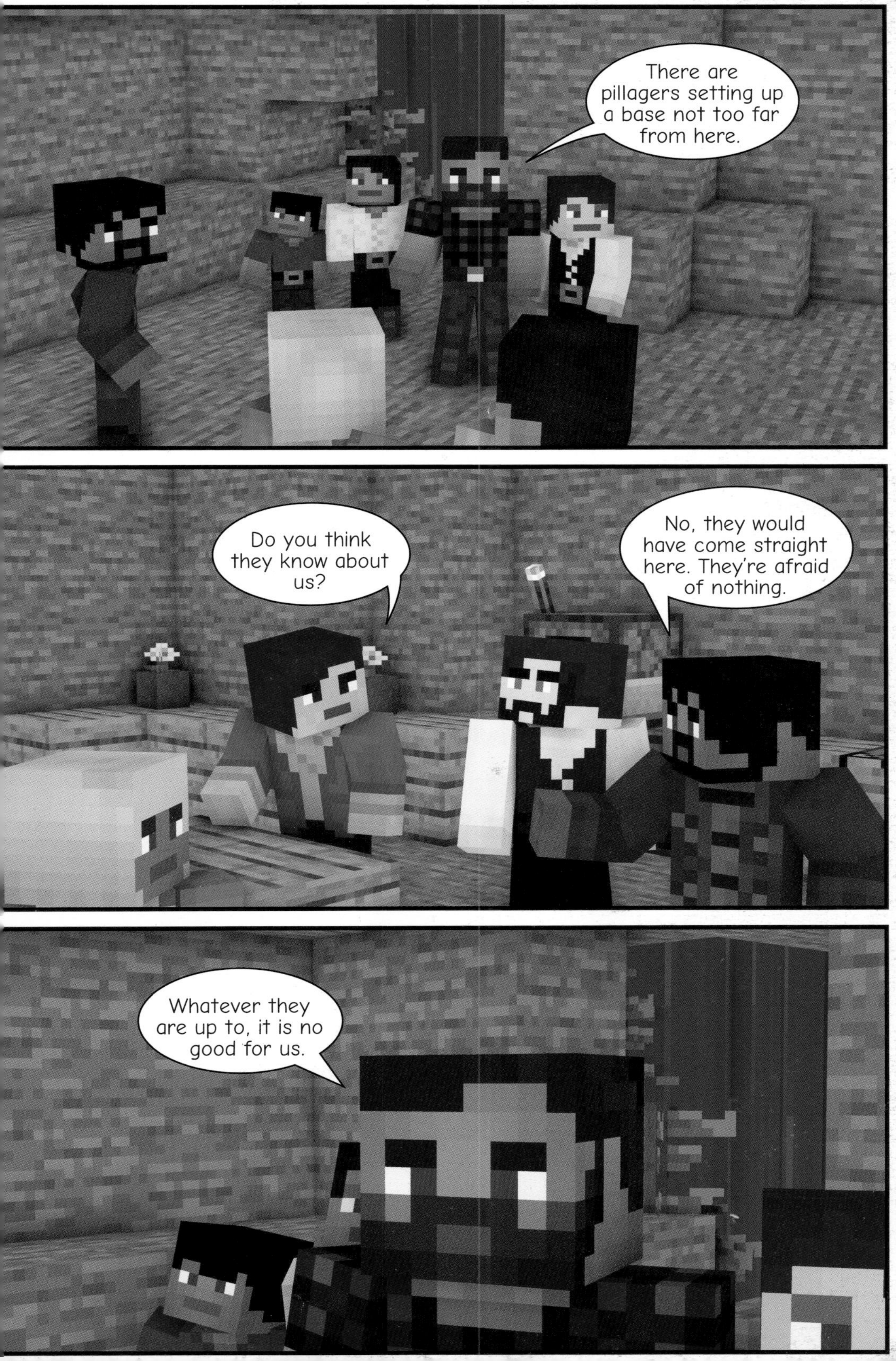
There are pillagers setting up a base not too far from here.
Do you think they know about us?
No, they would have come straight here. They're afraid of nothing.
Whatever they are up to, it is no good for us.

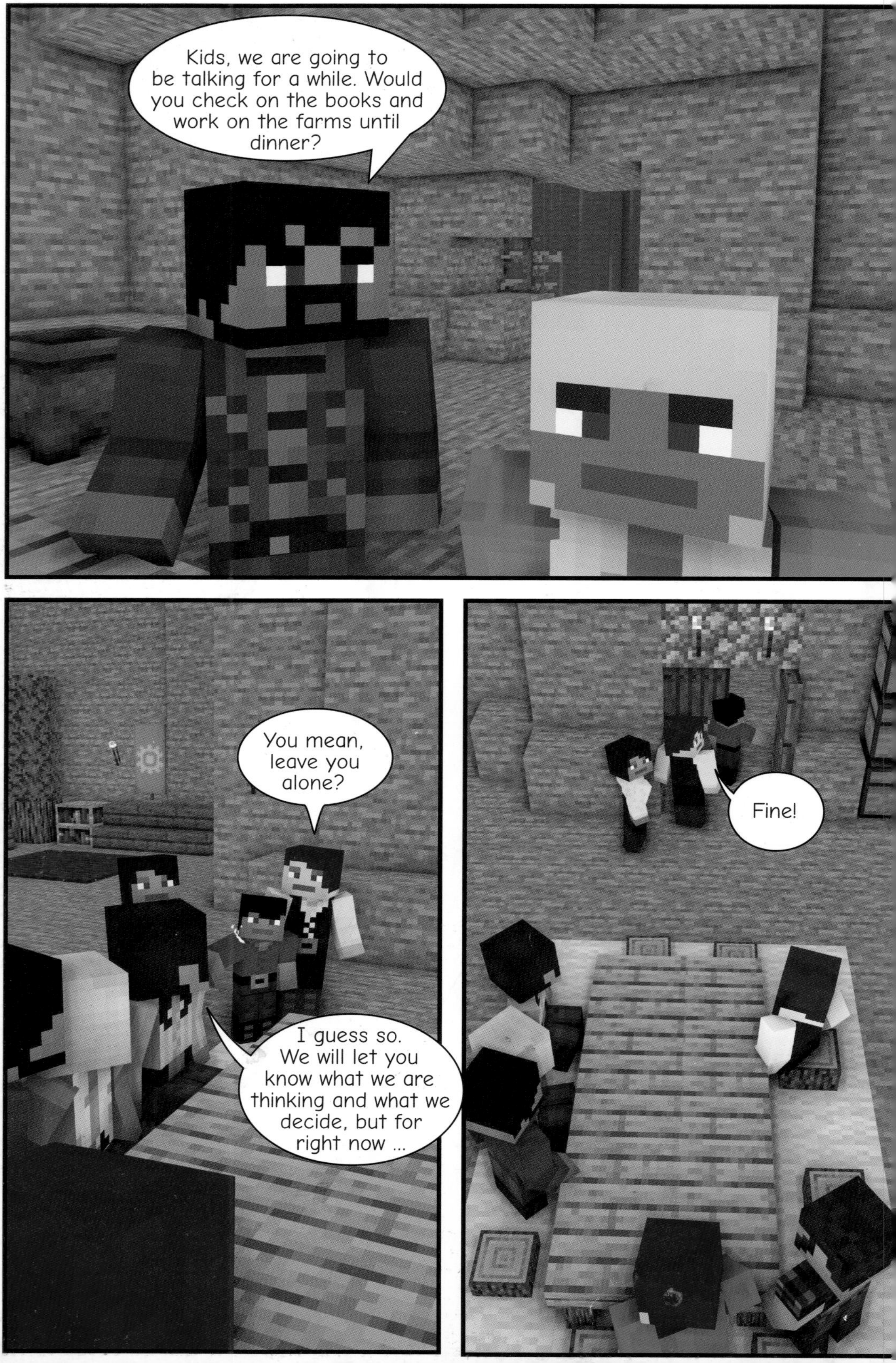
Kids, we are going to be talking for a while. Would you check on the books and work on the farms until dinner?
You mean, leave you alone?
I guess so. We will let you know what we are thinking and what we decide, but for right now ...
Fine!

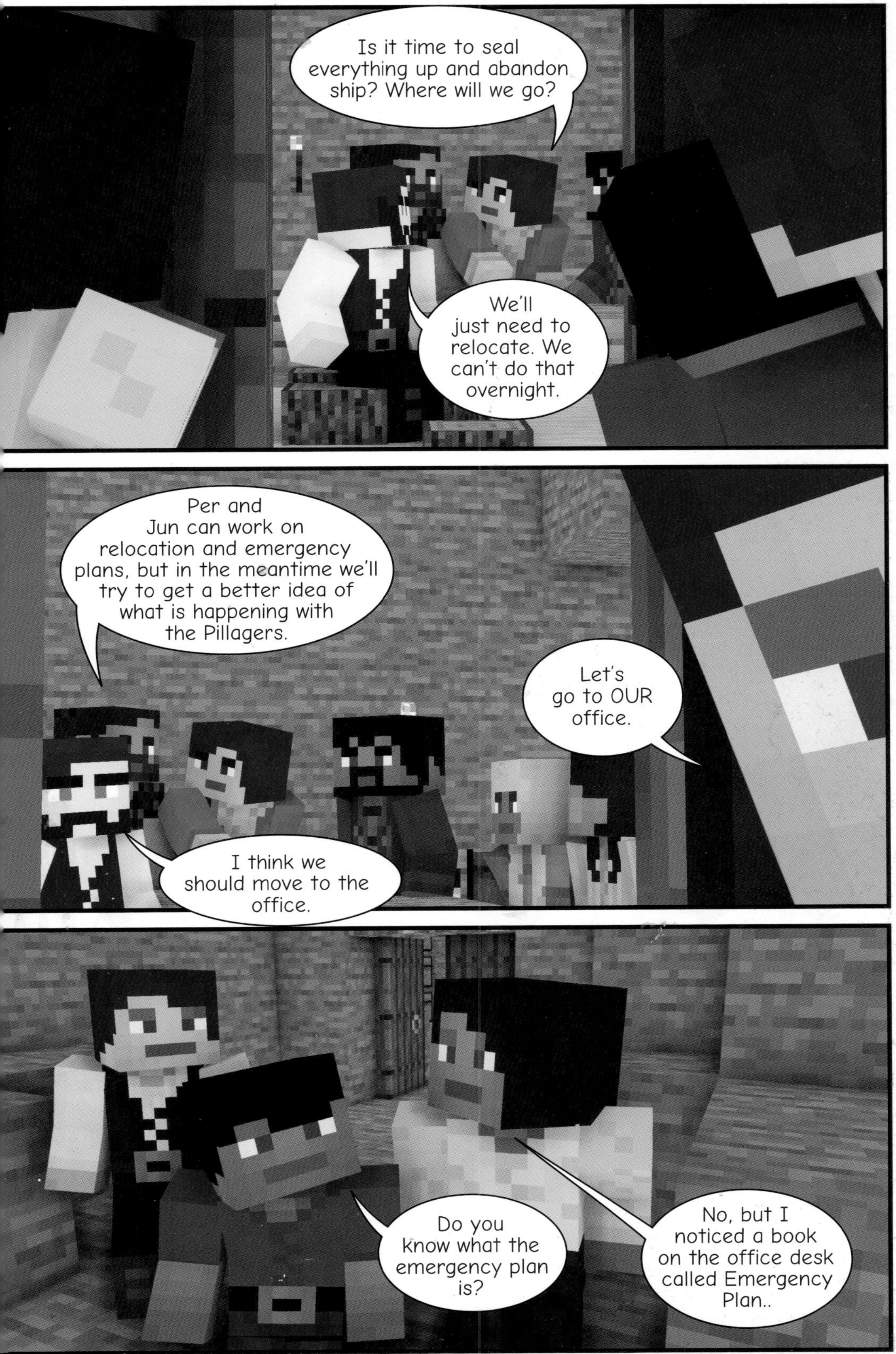
Is it time to seal everything up and abandon ship? Where will we go?
We'll just need to relocate. We can't do that overnight.
Per and Jun can work on relocation and emergency plans, but in the meantime we'll try to get a better idea of what is happening with the Pillagers.
I think we should move to the office.
Let's go to OUR office.
Do you know what the emergency plan is?
No, but I noticed a book on the office desk called Emergency Plan..

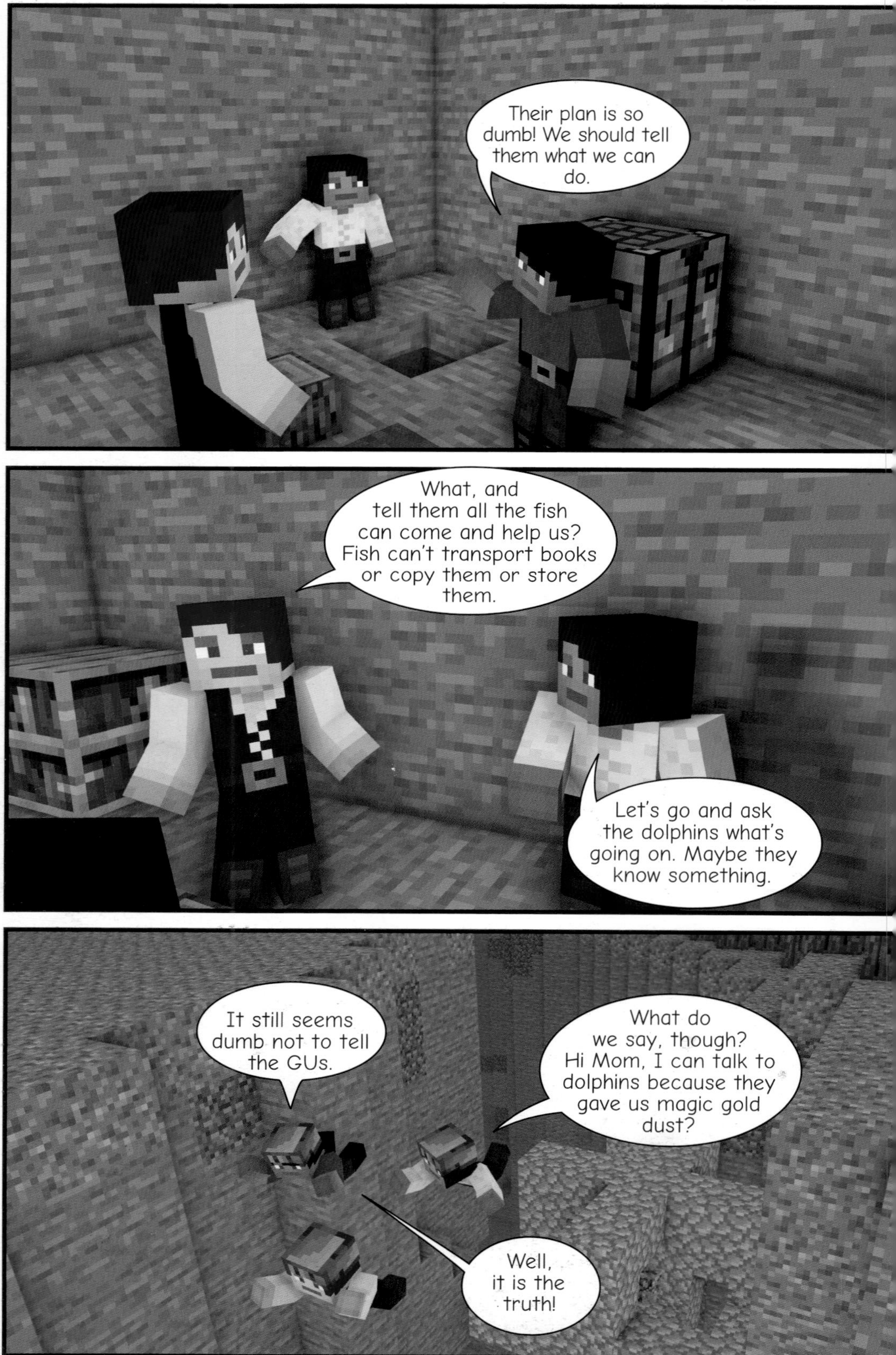
Their plan is so dumb! We should tell them what we can do.
What, and tell them all the fish can come and help us? Fish can't transport books or copy them or store them.
Let's go and ask the dolphins what's going on. Maybe they know something.
It still seems dumb not to tell the GUs.
What do we say, though? Hi Mom, I can talk to dolphins because they gave us magic gold dust?
Well, it is the truth!

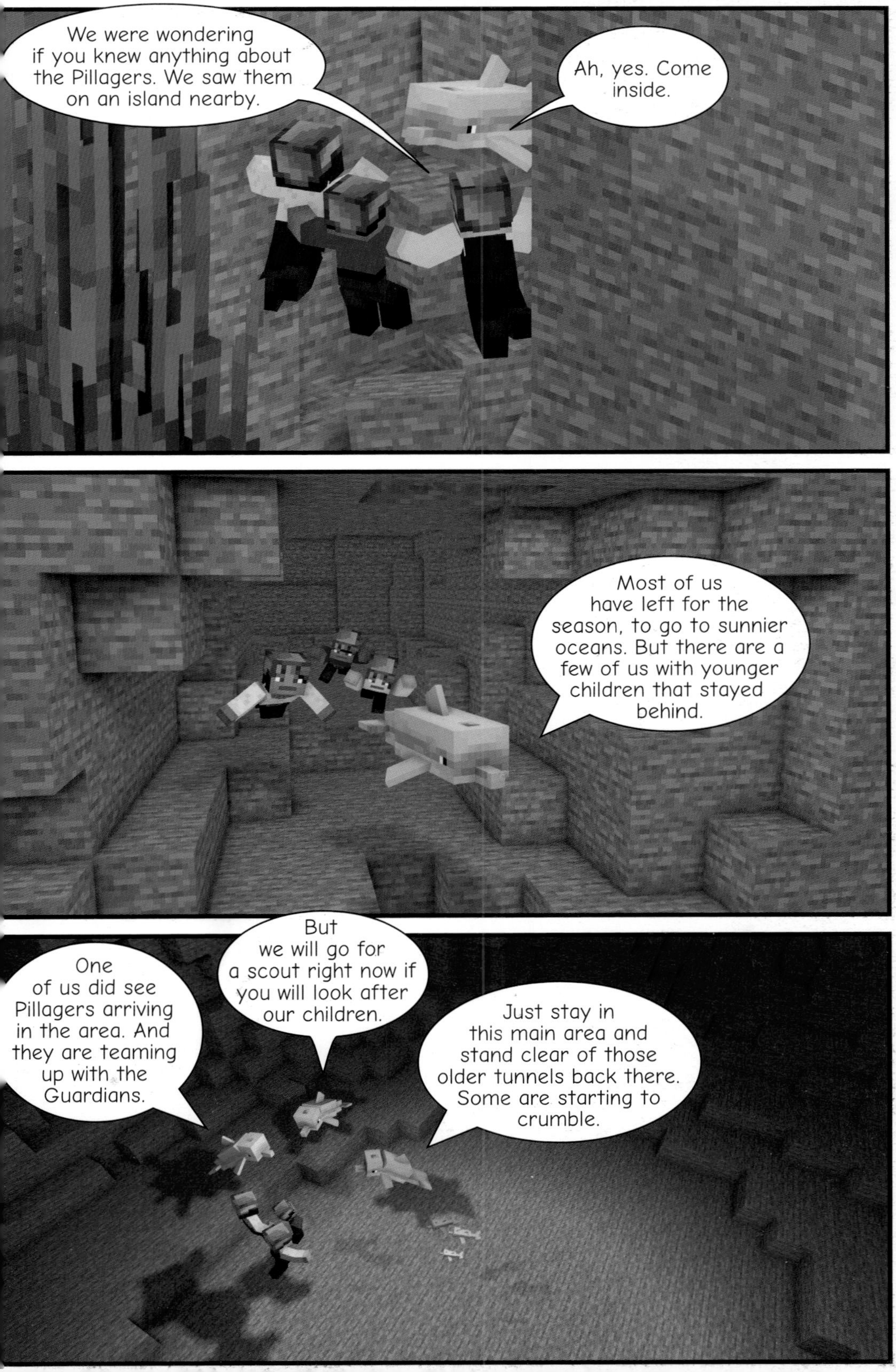
We were wondering if you knew anything about the Pillagers. We saw them on an island nearby.
Ah, yes. Come inside.
Most of us have left for the season, to go to sunnier oceans. But there are a few of us with younger children that stayed behind.
One of us did see Pillagers arriving in the area. And they are teaming up with the Guardians.
But we will go for a scout right now if you will look after our children.
Just stay in this main area and stand clear of those older tunnels back there. Some are starting to crumble.

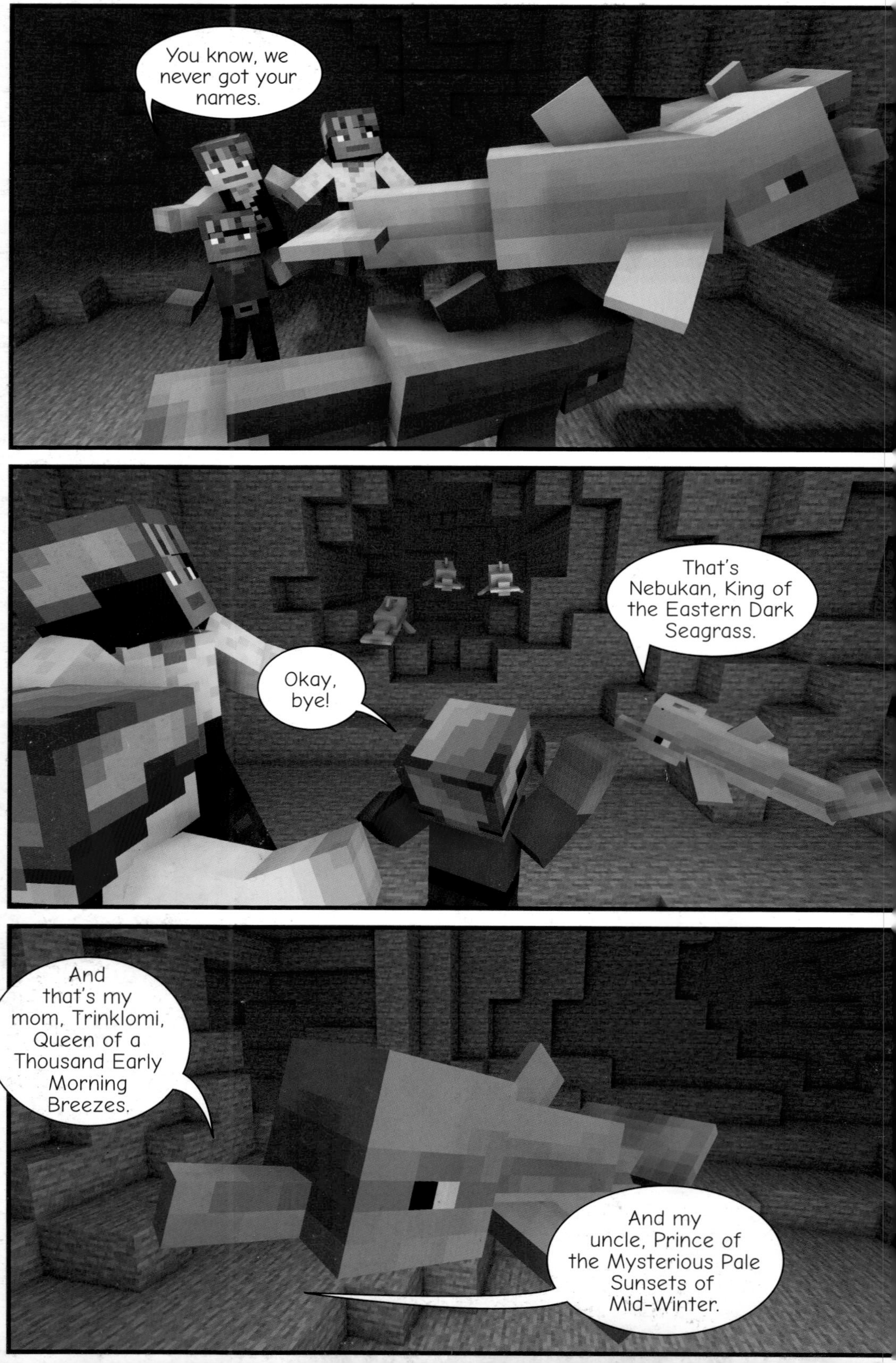
You know, we never got your names.
That's Nebukan, King of the Eastern Dark Seagrass.
Okay, bye!
And that's my mom, Trinklomi, Queen of a Thousand Early Morning Breezes.
And my uncle, Prince of the Mysterious Pale Sunsets of Mid-Winter.

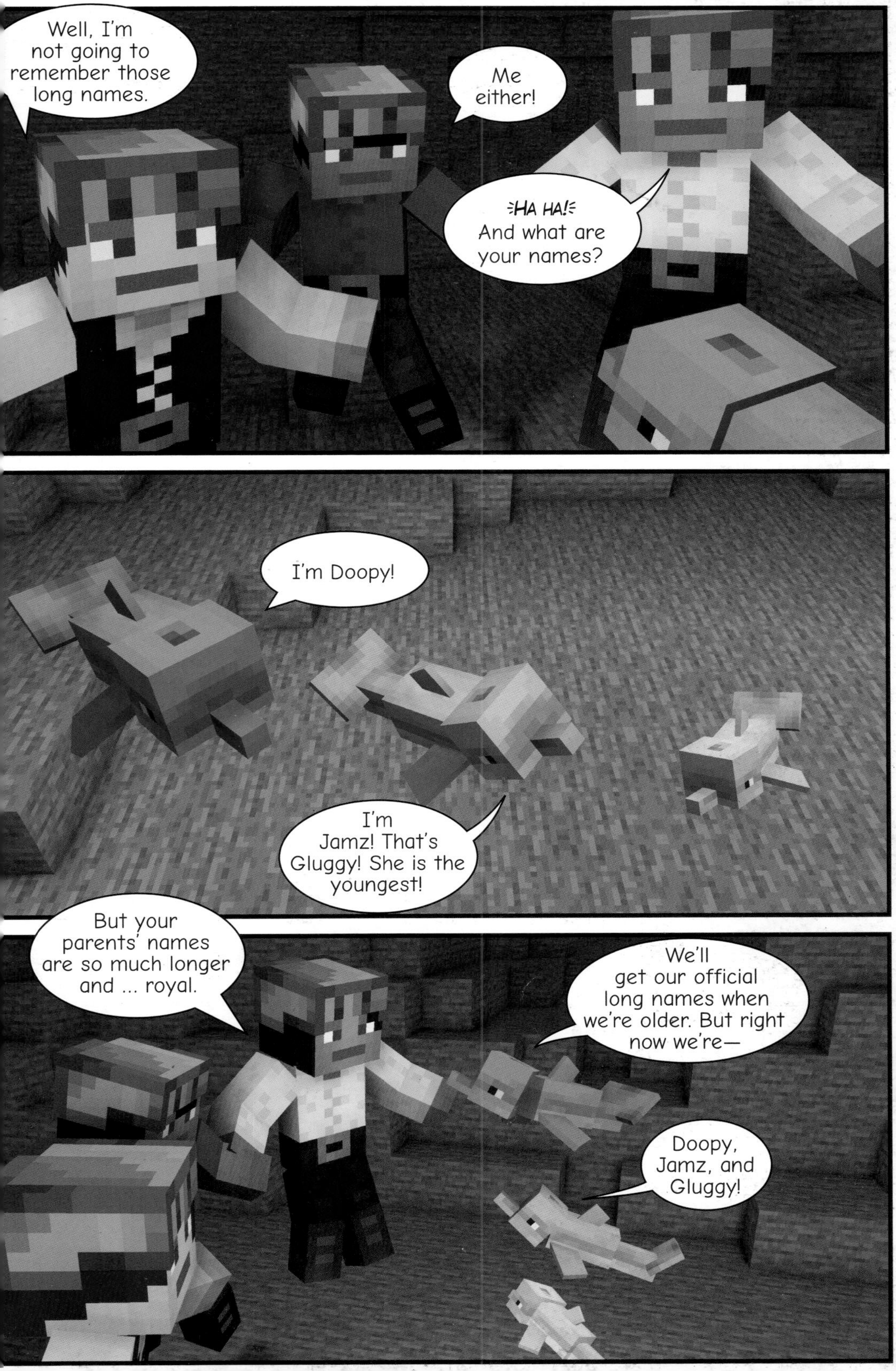
Well, I'm not going to remember those long names.
Me either!
HA HA! And what are your names?
I'm Doopy!
I'm Jamz! That's Gluggy! She is the youngest!
But your parents' names are so much longer and ... royal.
We'll get our official long names when we're older. But right now we're—
Doopy, Jamz, and Gluggy!

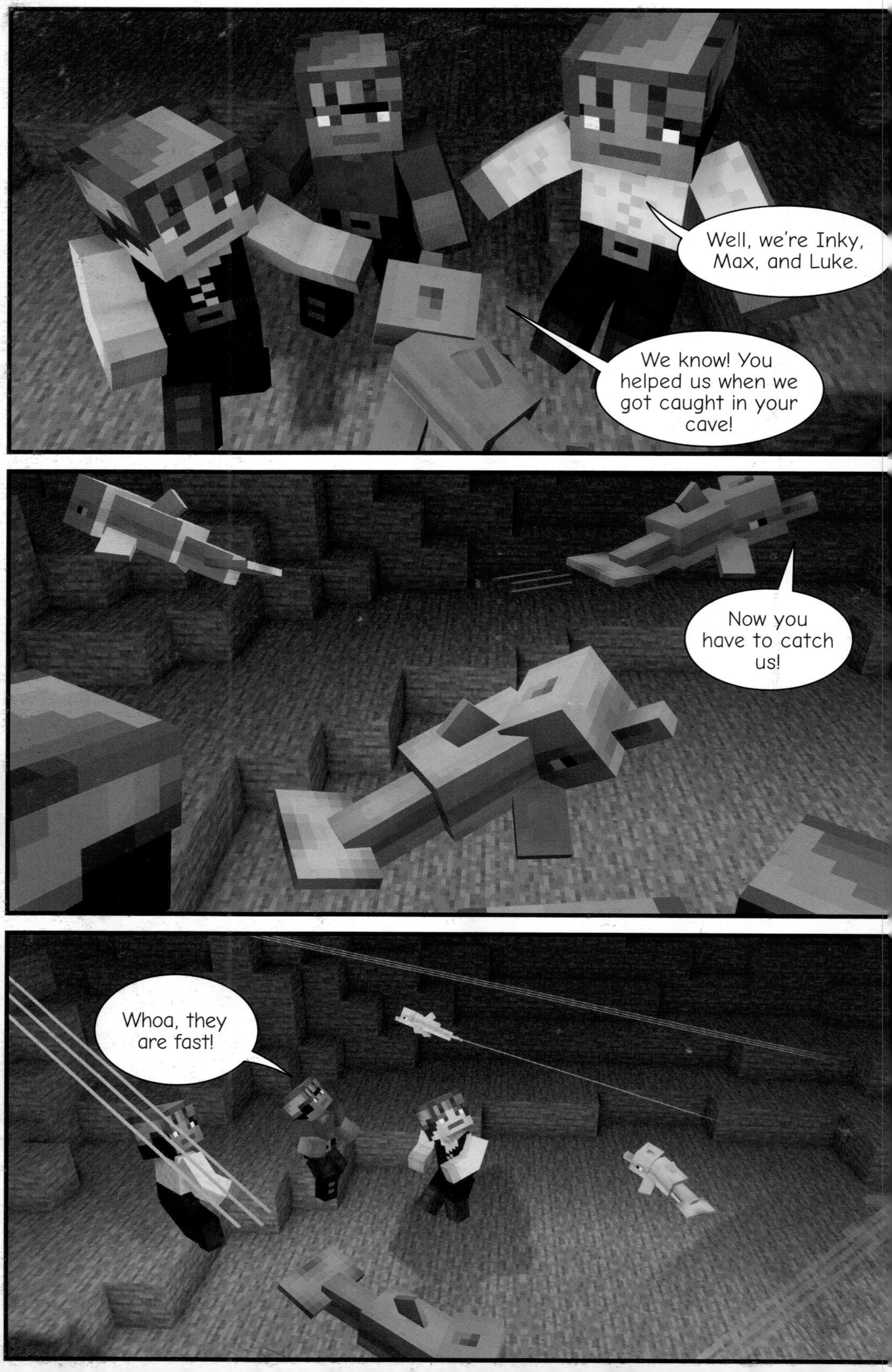
Well, we're Inky, Max, and Luke.
We know! You helped us when we got caught in your cave!
Now you have to catch us!
Whoa, they are fast!

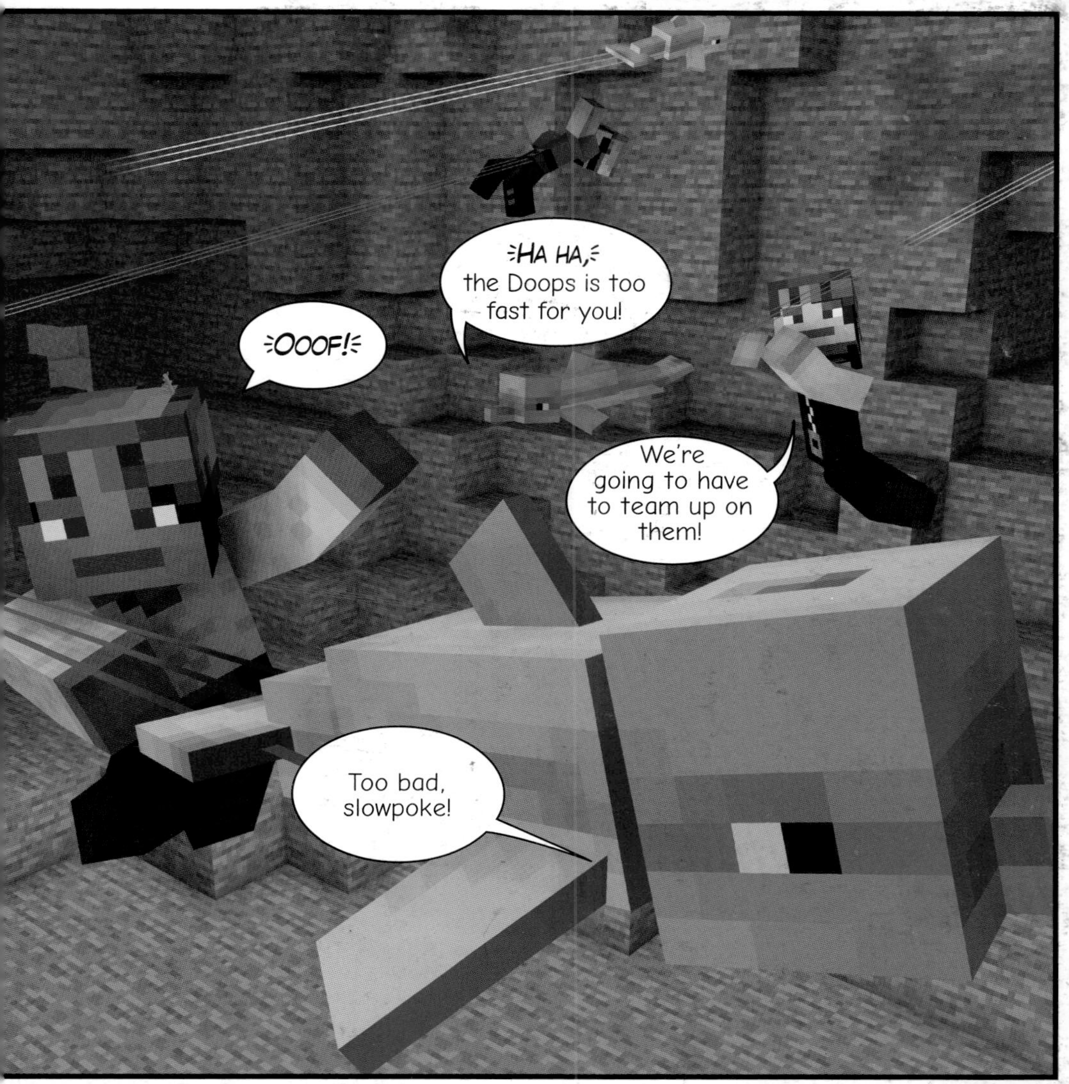
OOOF!
HA HA, the Doops is too fast for you!
We're going to have to team up on them!
Too bad, slowpoke!

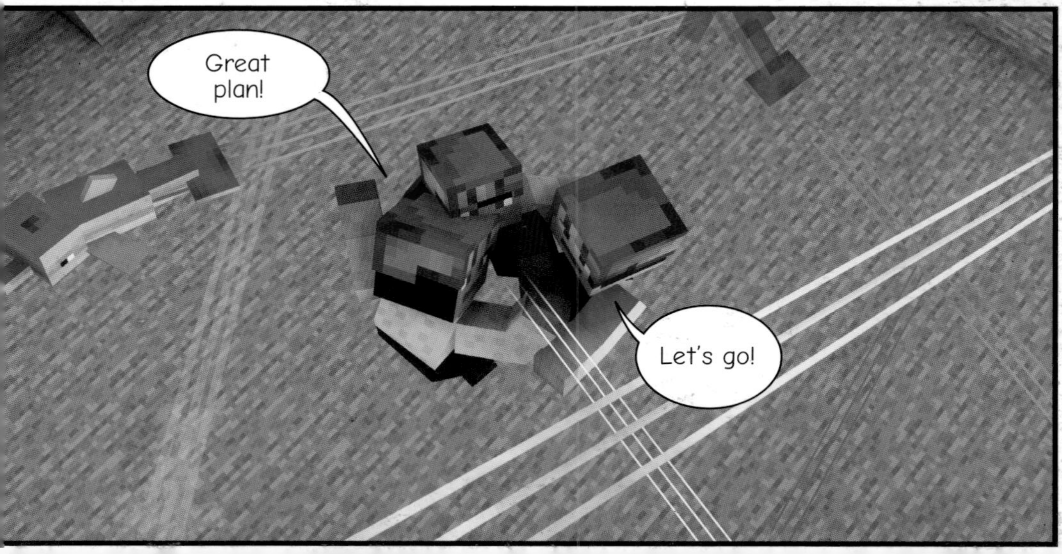
Great plan!
Let's go!

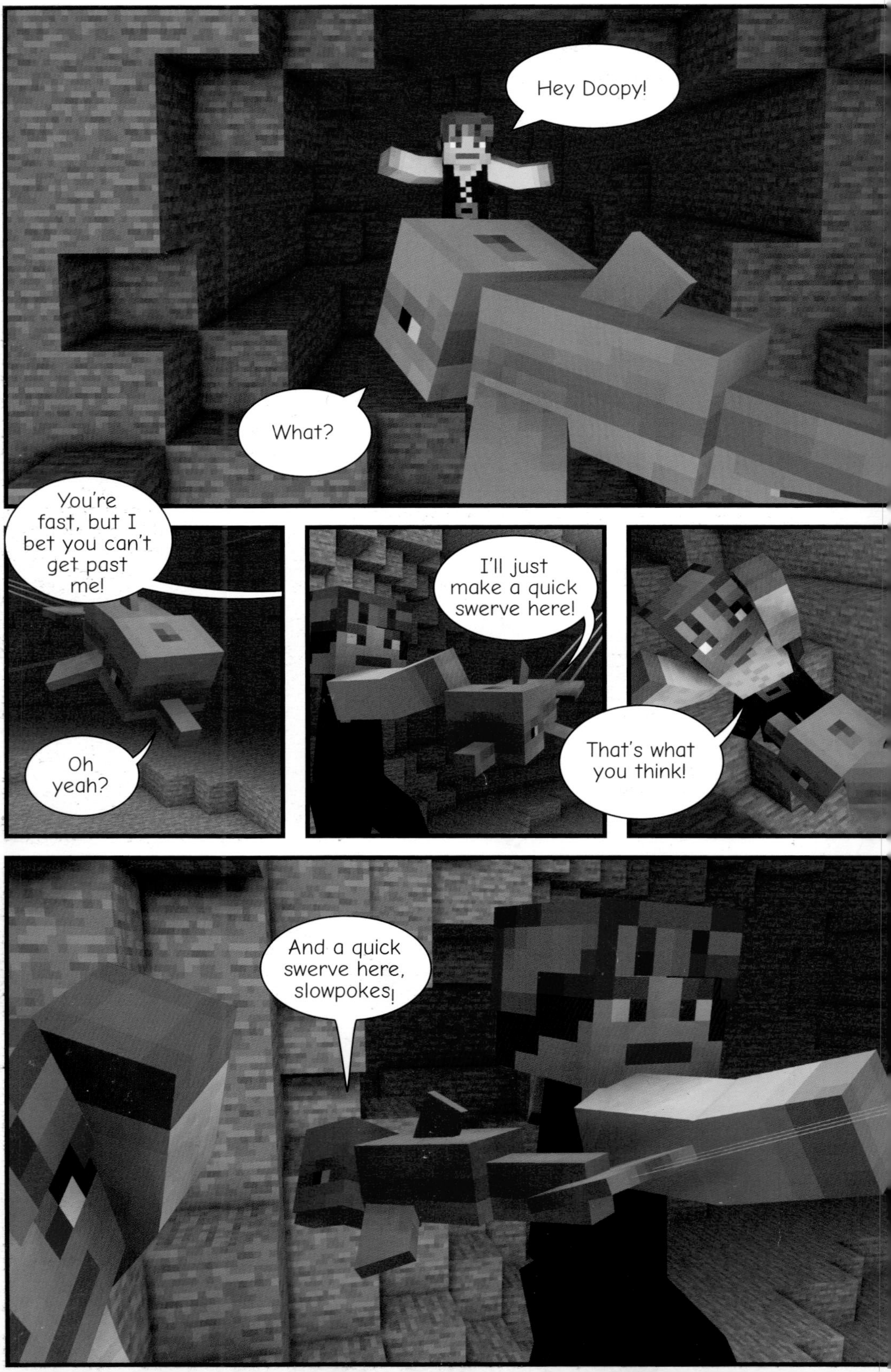

Hey Doopy!
What?
You're fast, but I bet you can't get past me!
Oh yeah?
I'll just make a quick swerve here!
That's what you think!
And a quick swerve here, slowpokes!

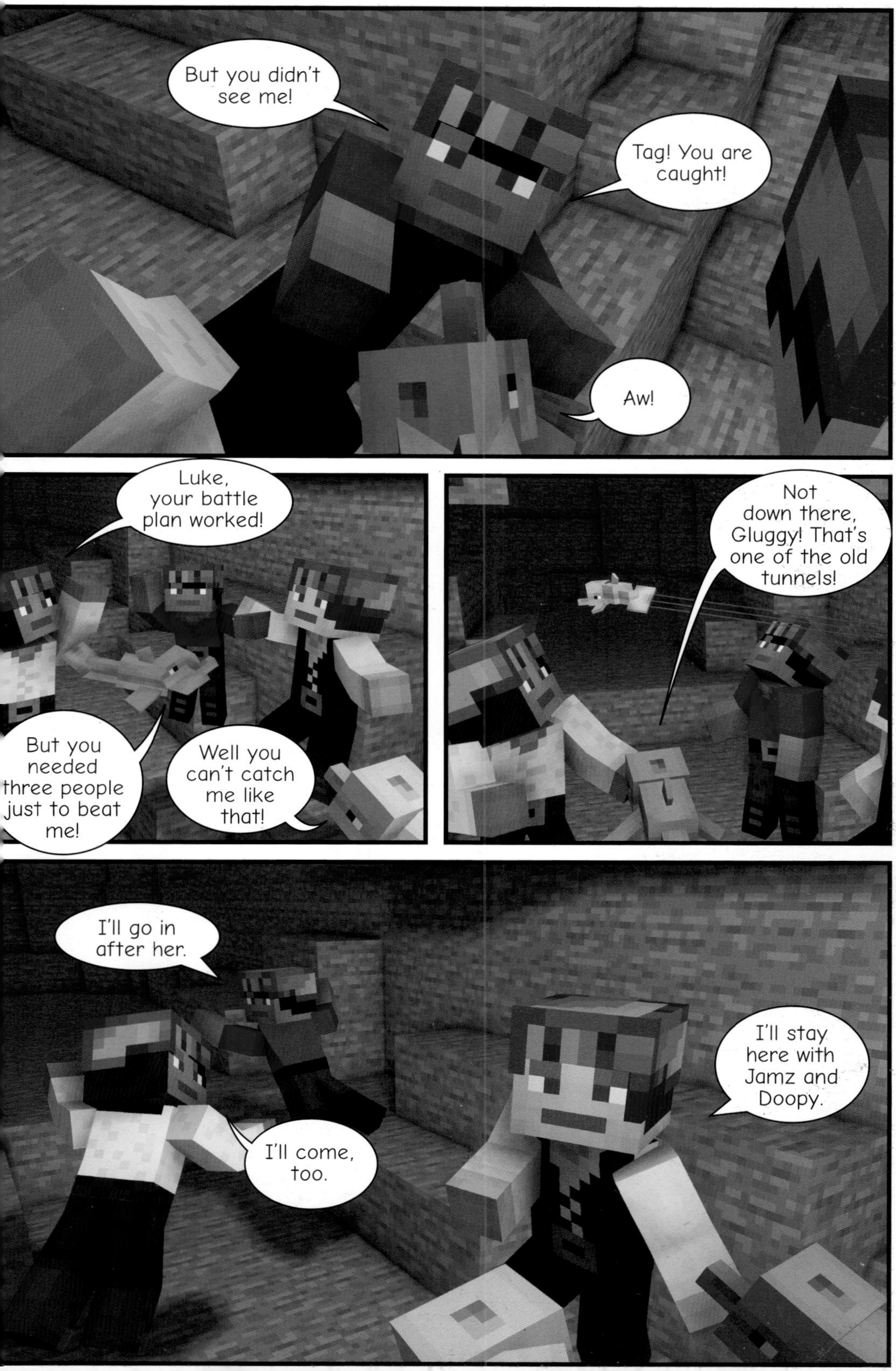
But you didn't see me!
Tag! You are caught!
Aw!
Luke, your battle plan worked!
But you needed three people just to beat me!
Well you can't catch me like that!
Not down there, Gluggy! That's one of the old tunnels!
I'll go in after her.
I'll come, too.
I'll stay here with Jamz and Doopy.

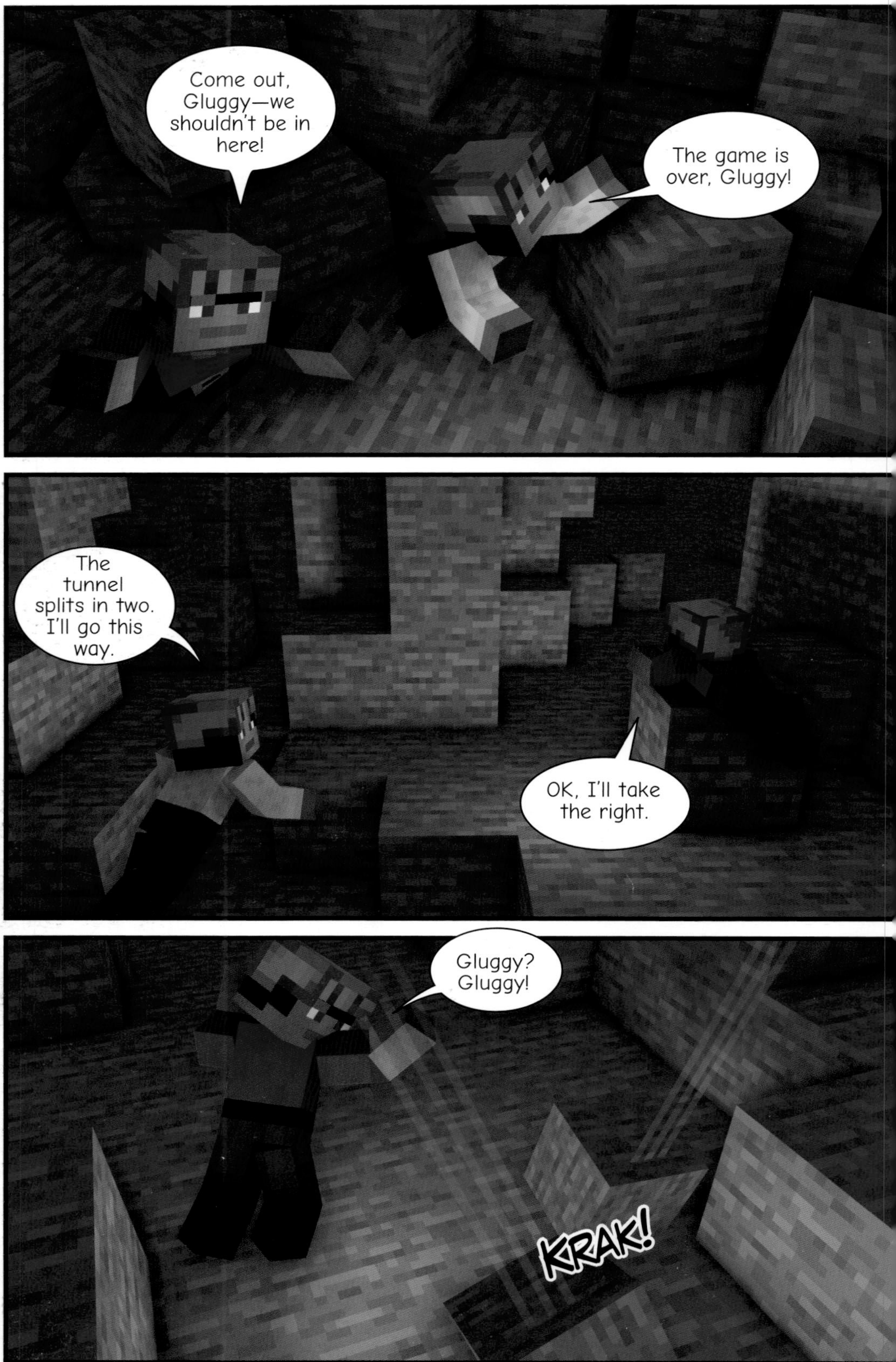
Come out, Gluggy—we shouldn't be in here!
The game is over, Gluggy!
The tunnel splits in two. I'll go this way.
OK, I'll take the right.
Gluggy? Gluggy!
KRAK!

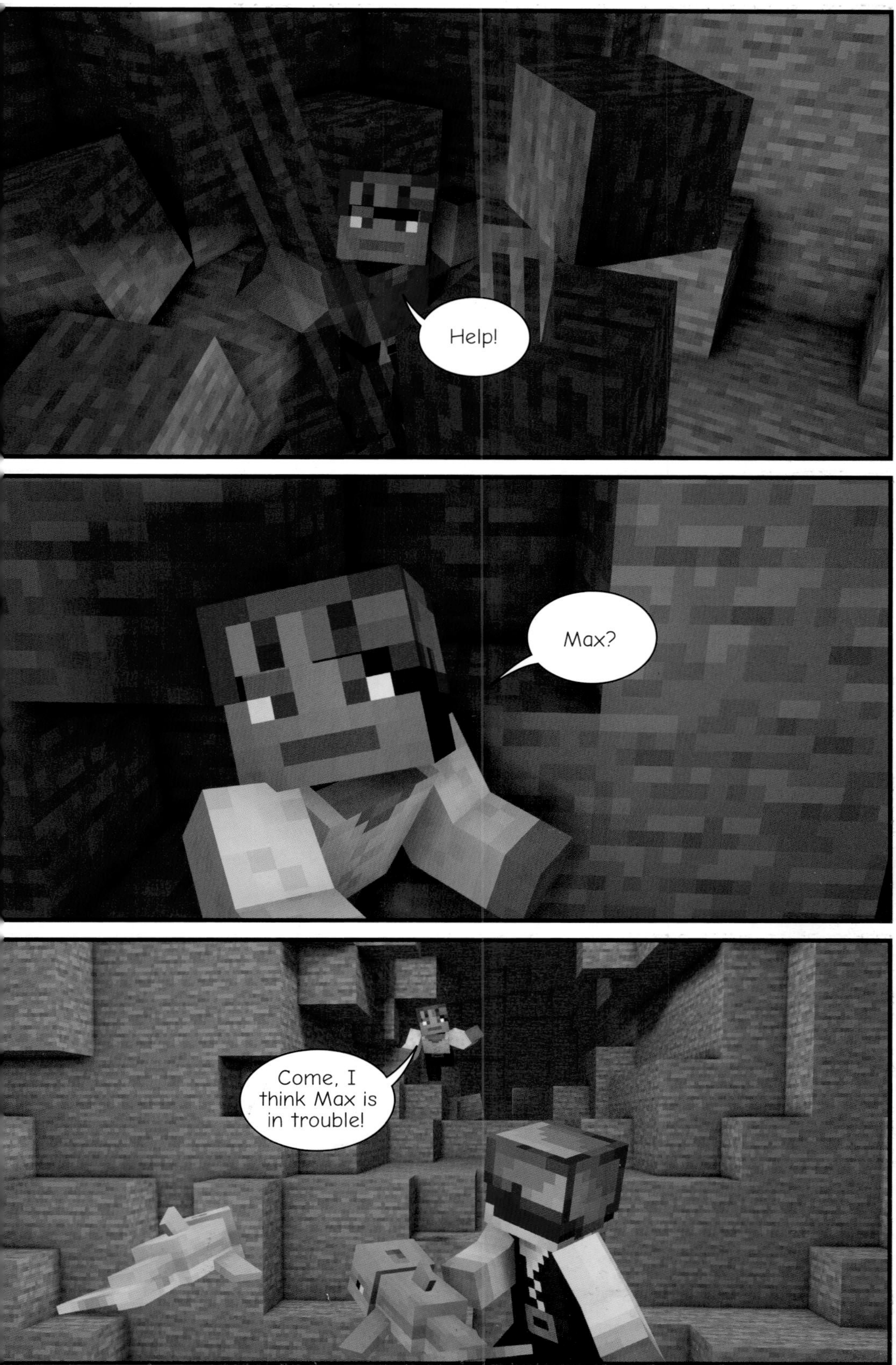
Help!
Max?
Come, I think Max is in trouble!

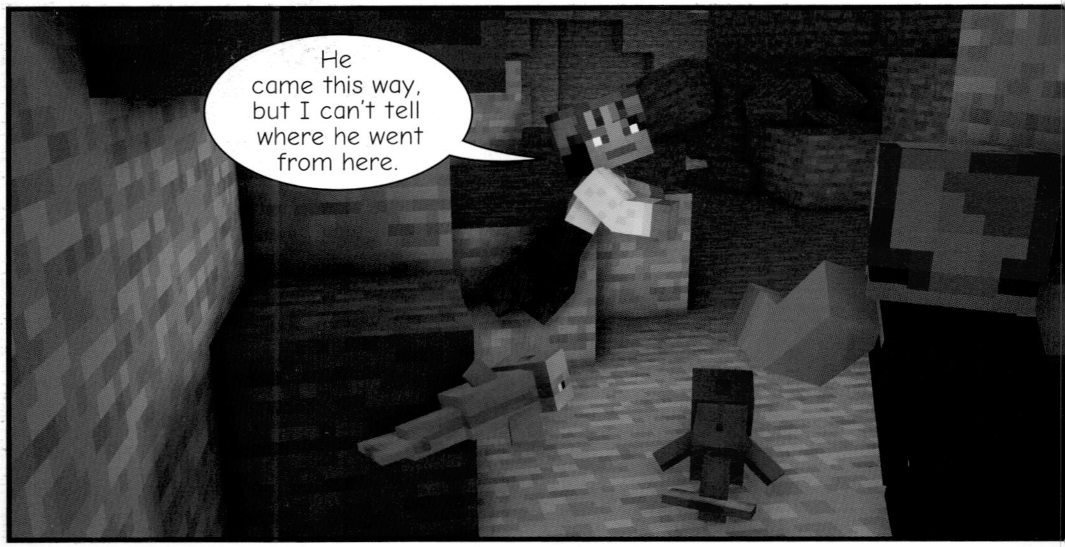
He came this way, but I can't tell where he went from here.

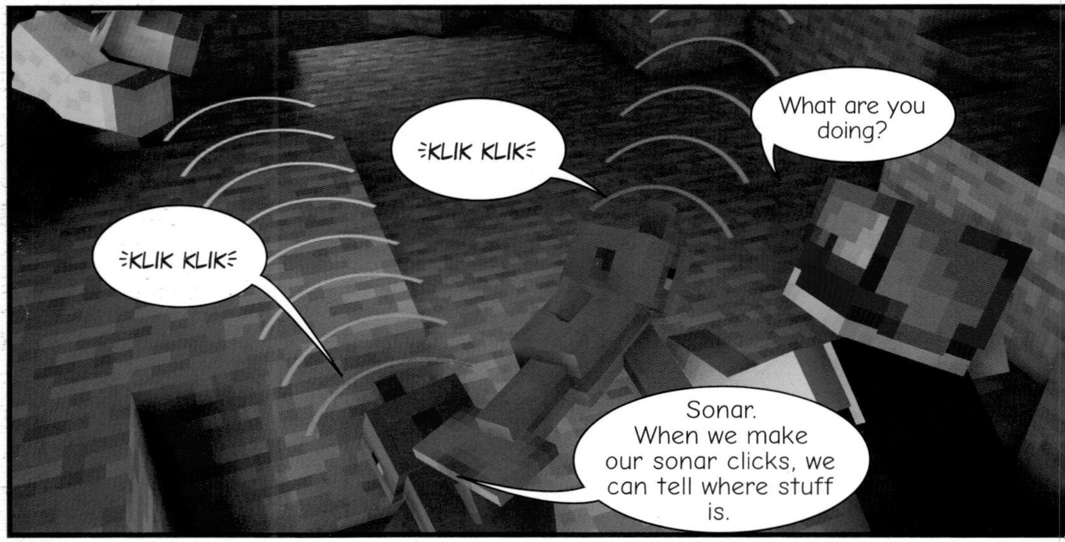
KLIK KLIK
KLIK KLIK
What are you doing?
Sonar. When we make our sonar clicks, we can tell where stuff is.

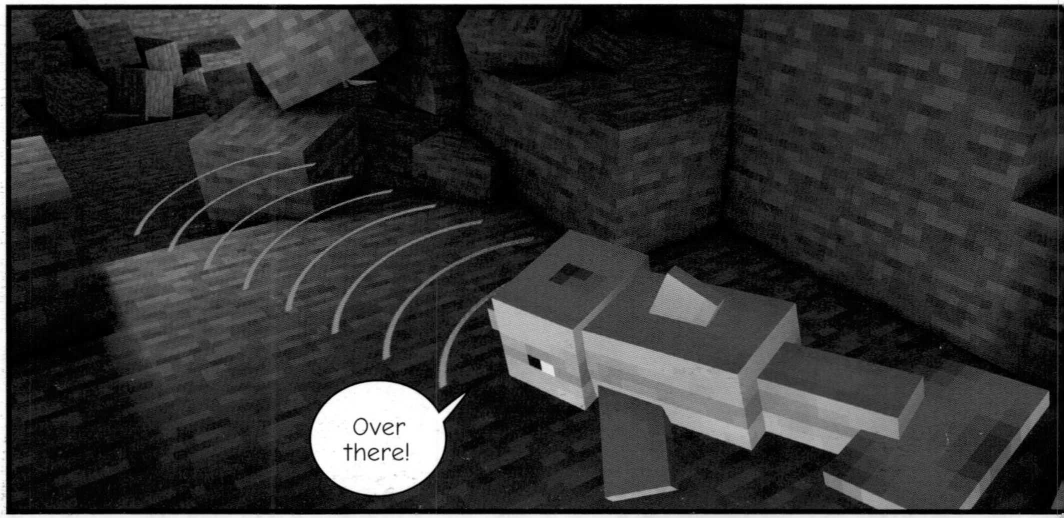
Over there!

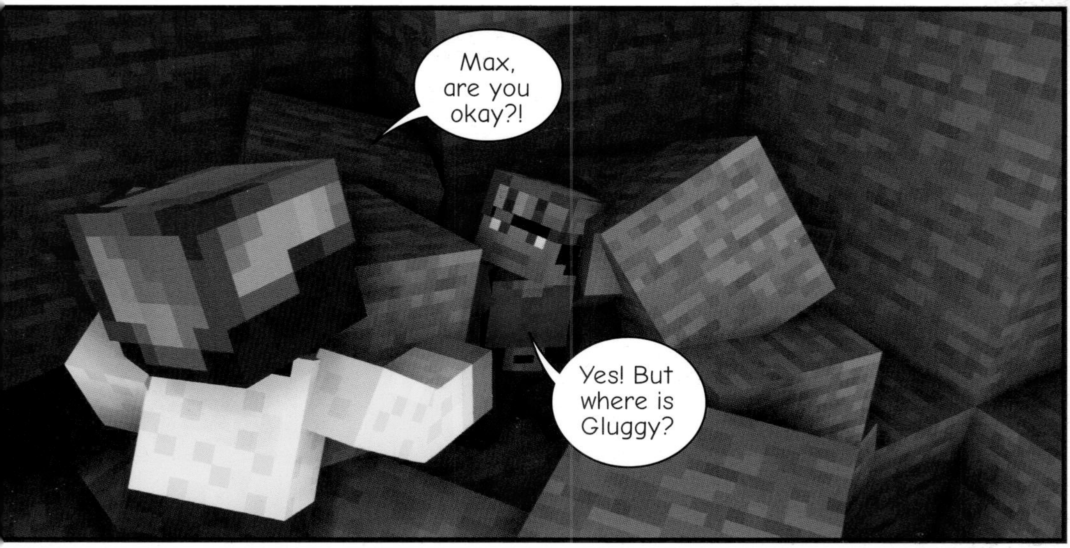
Max, are you okay?!
Yes! But where is Gluggy?

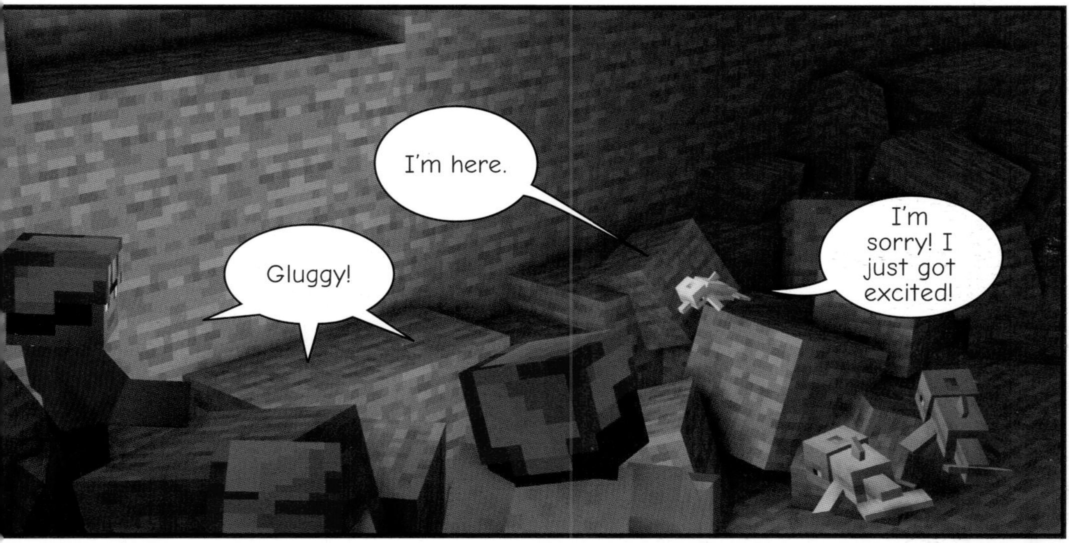
I'm here.
Gluggy!
I'm sorry! I just got excited!

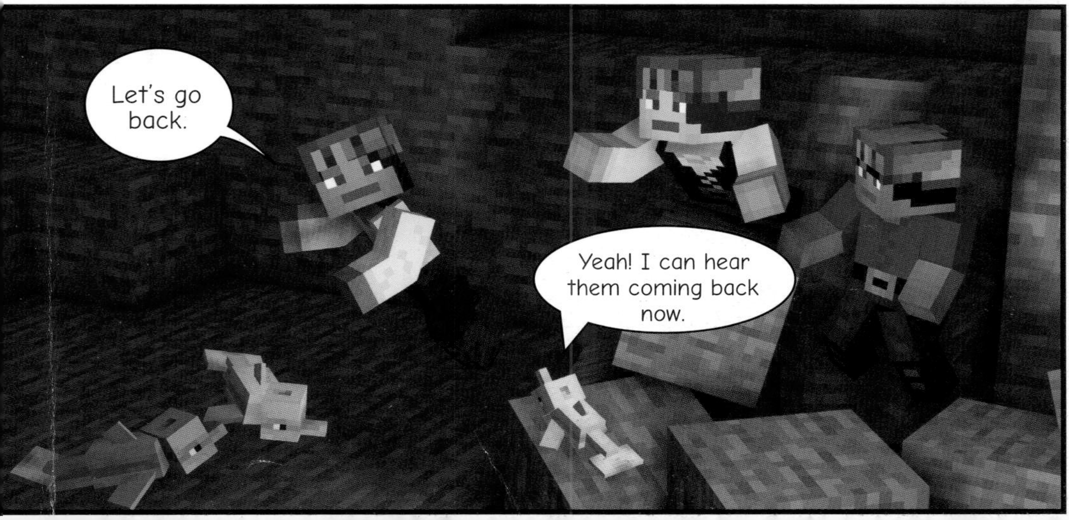
Let's go back.
Yeah! I can hear them coming back now.

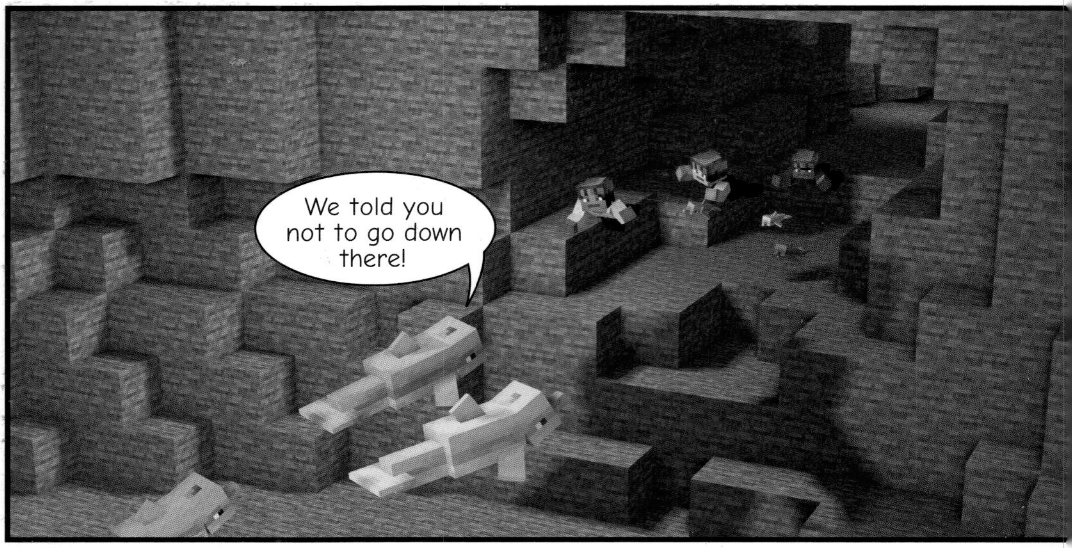
We told you not to go down there!

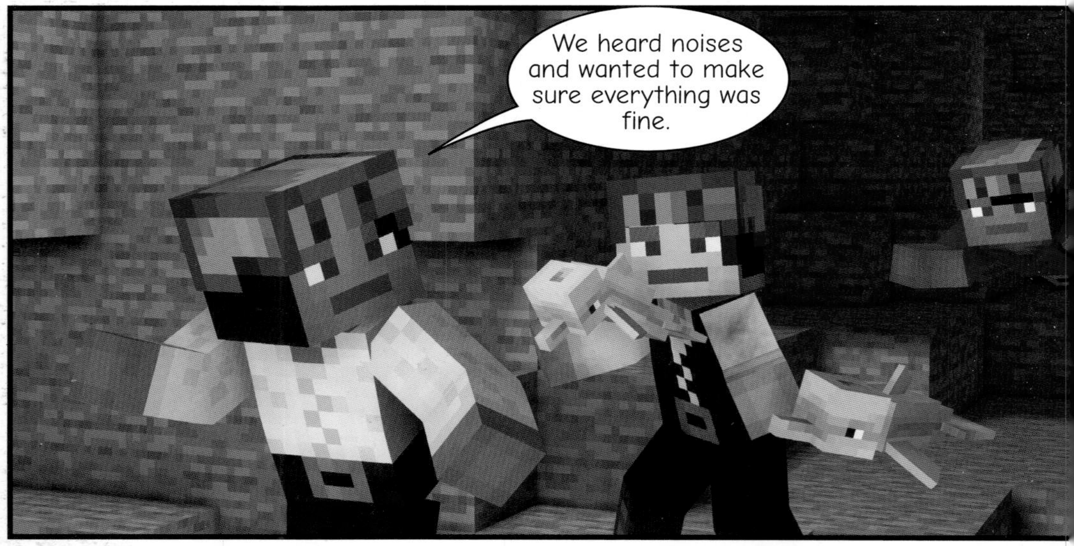
We heard noises and wanted to make sure everything was fine.

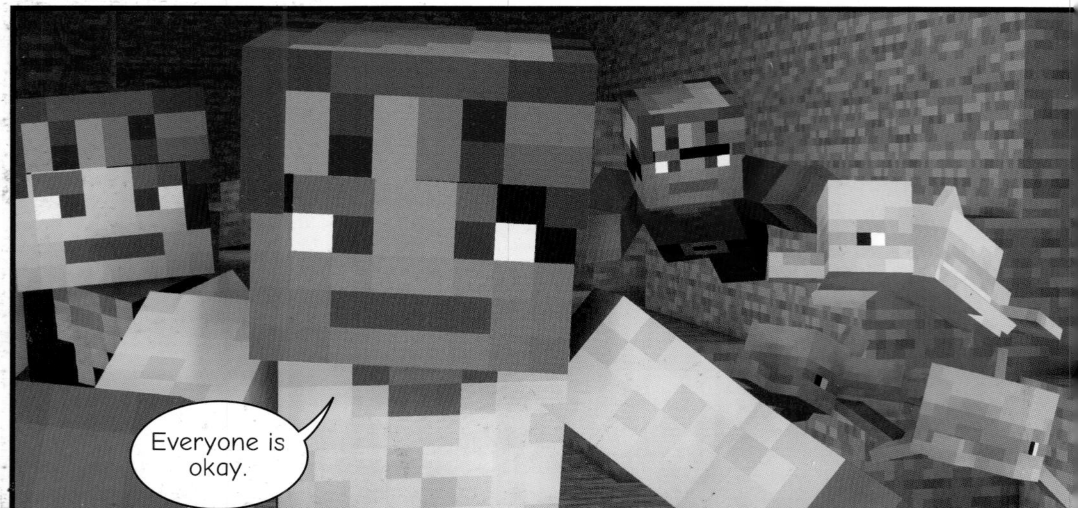
Everyone is okay.

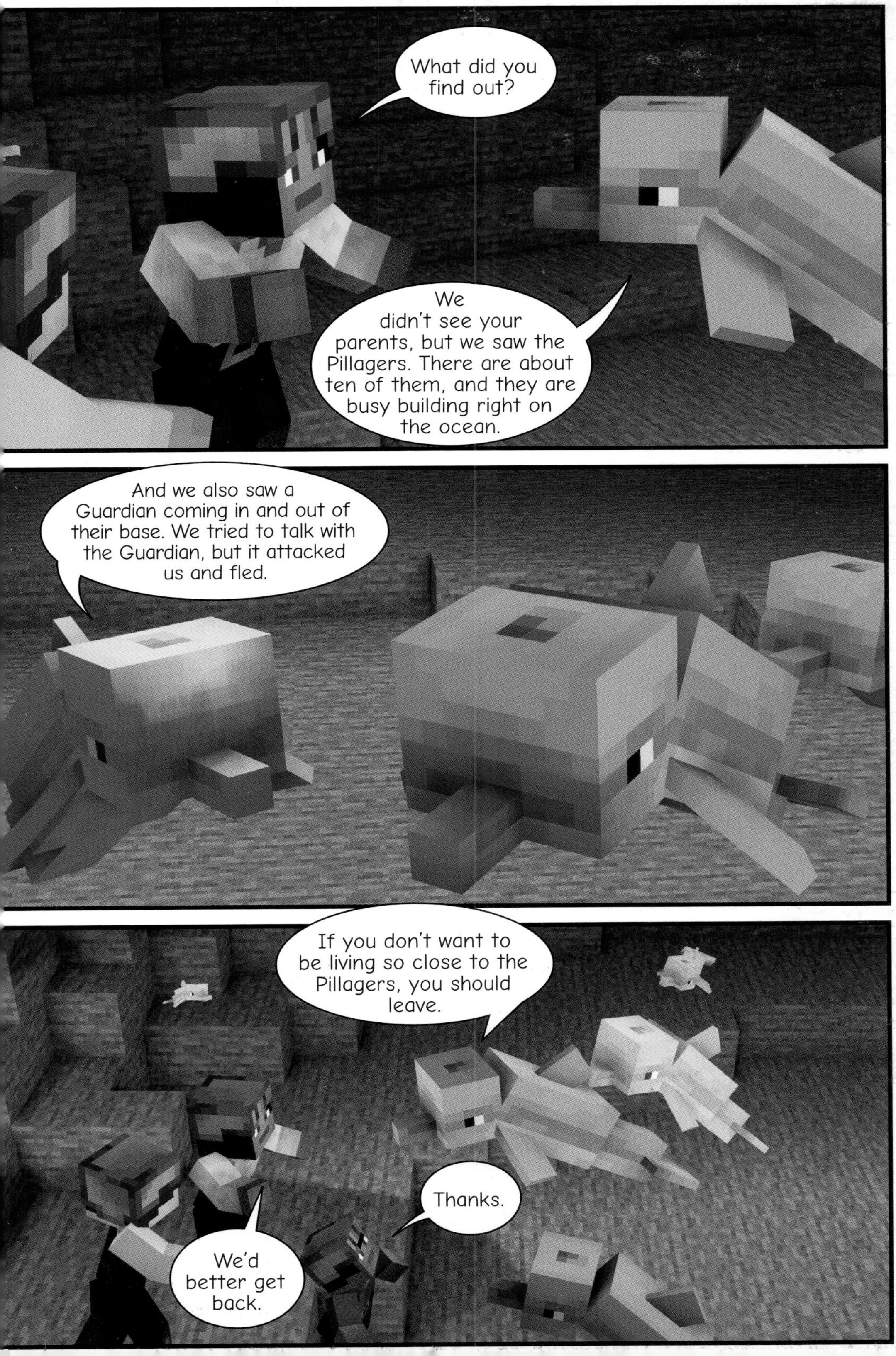

What did you find out?
We didn't see your parents, but we saw the Pillagers. There are about ten of them, and they are busy building right on the ocean.
And we also saw a Guardian coming in and out of their base. We tried to talk with the Guardian, but it attacked us and fled.
If you don't want to be living so close to the Pillagers, you should leave.
Thanks.
We'd better get back.

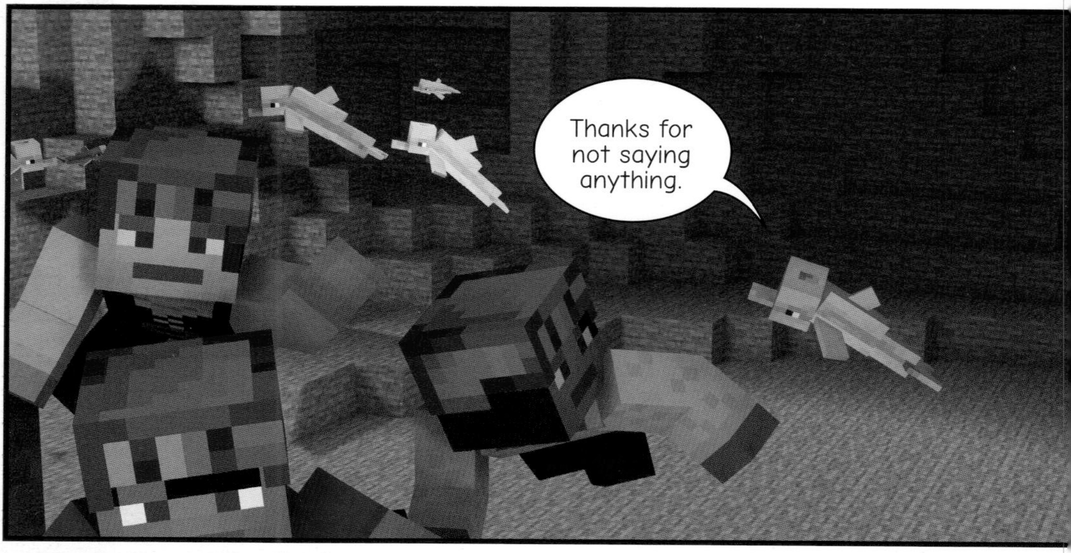
Thanks for not saying anything.

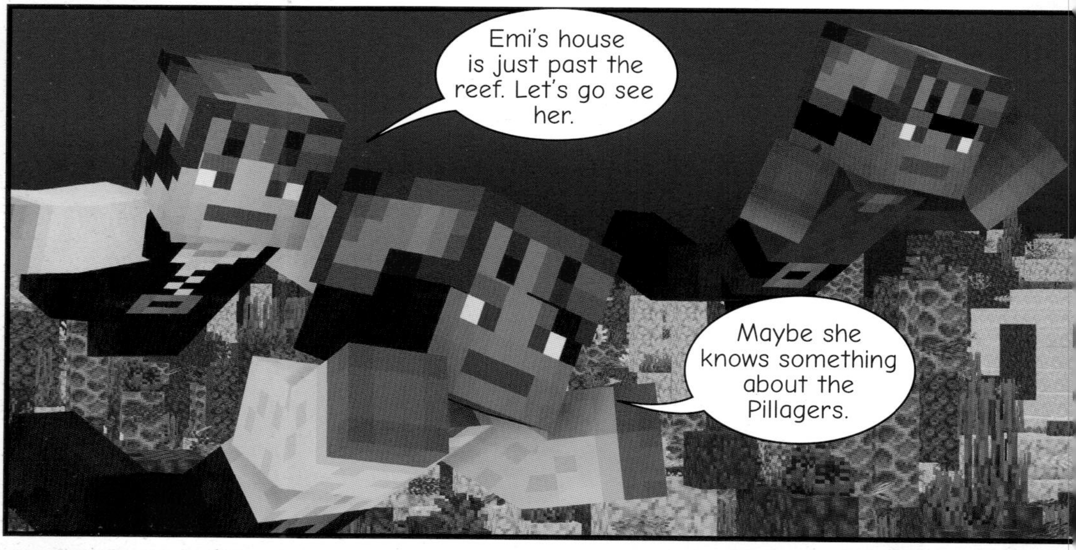
Emi's house is just past the reef. Let's go see her.
Maybe she knows something about the Pillagers.

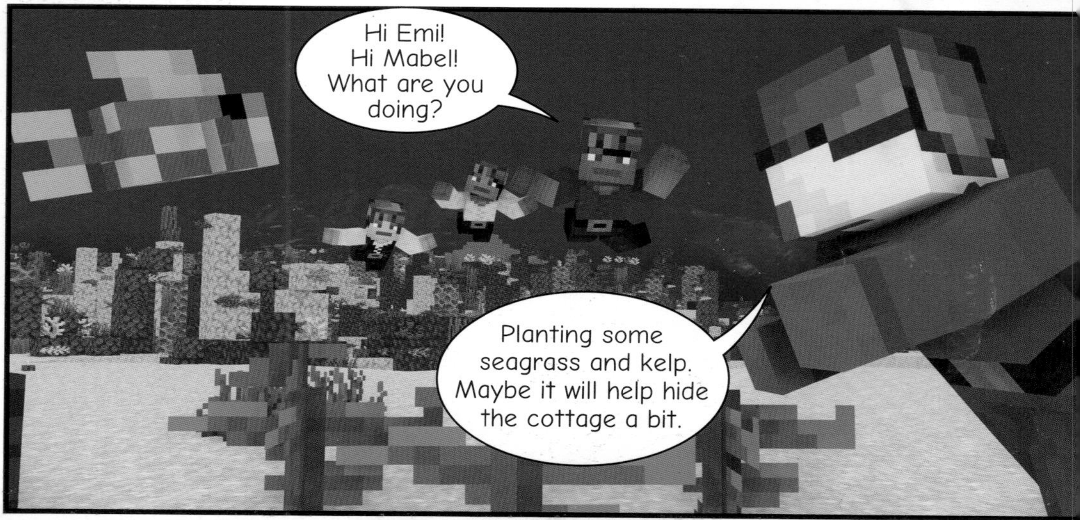
Hi Emi! Hi Mabel! What are you doing?
Planting some seagrass and kelp. Maybe it will help hide the cottage a bit.

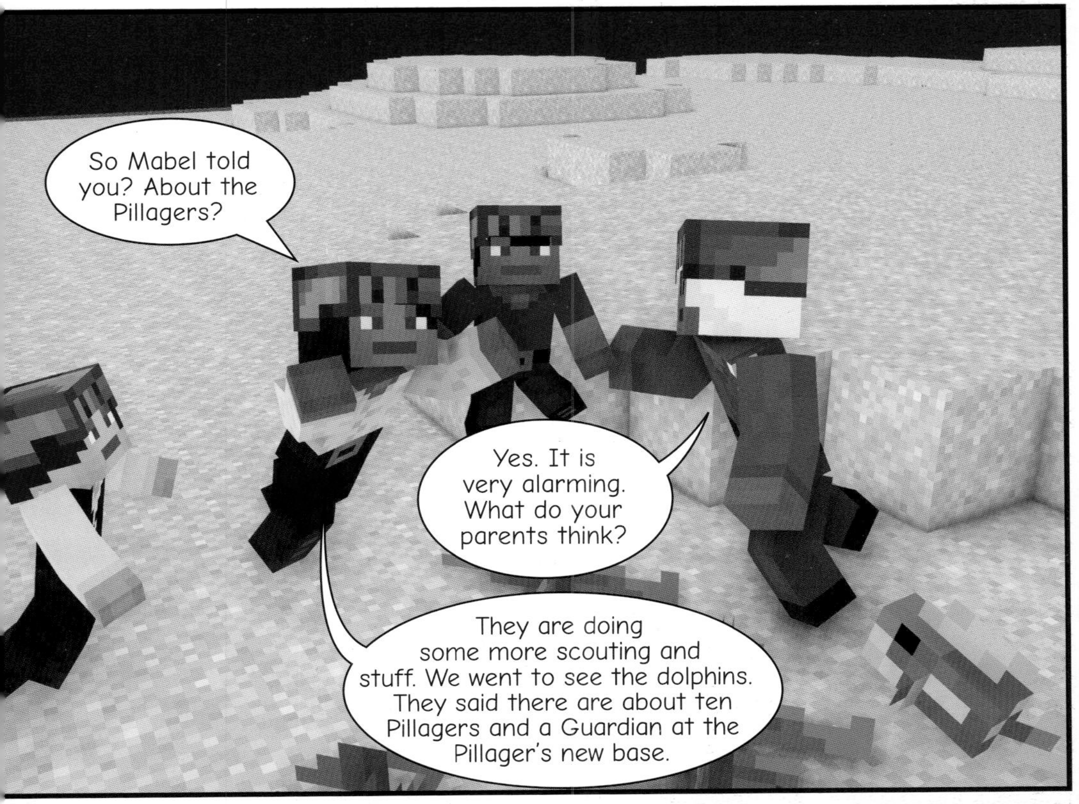
So Mabel told you? About the Pillagers?
Yes. It is very alarming. What do your parents think?
They are doing some more scouting and stuff. We went to see the dolphins. They said there are about ten Pillagers and a Guardian at the Pillager's new base.

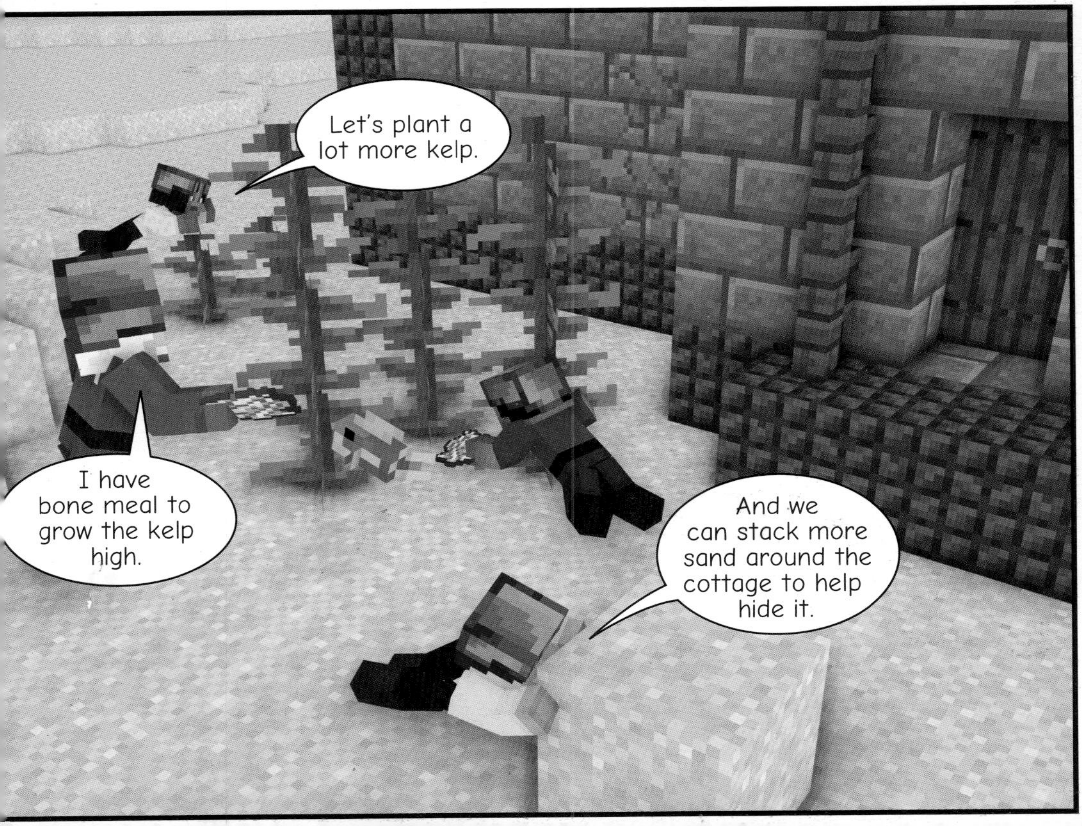
Let's plant a lot more kelp.
I have bone meal to grow the kelp high.
And we can stack more sand around the cottage to help hide it.

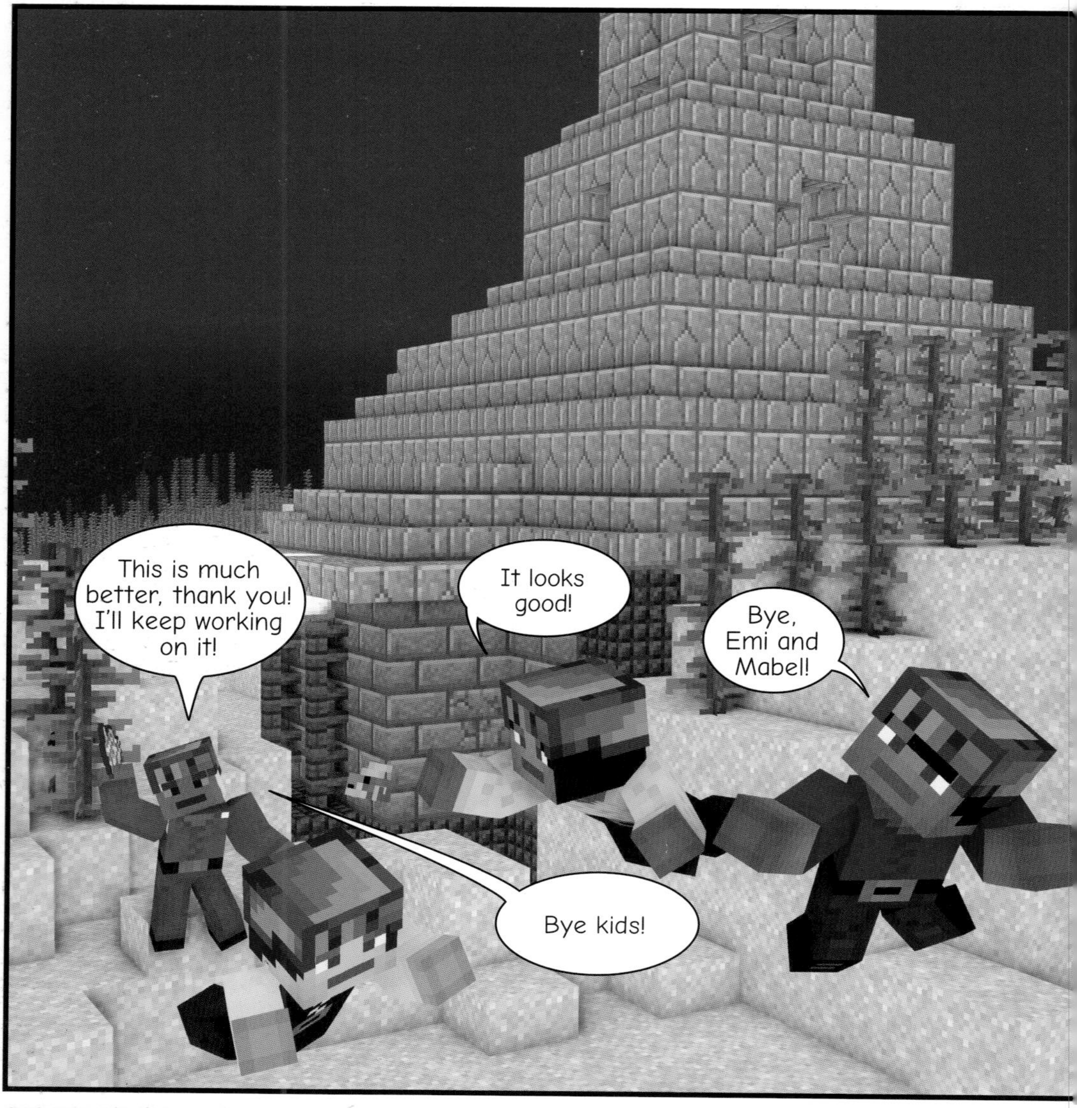
This is much better, thank you! I'll keep working on it!
It looks good!
Bye, Emi and Mabel!
Bye kids!

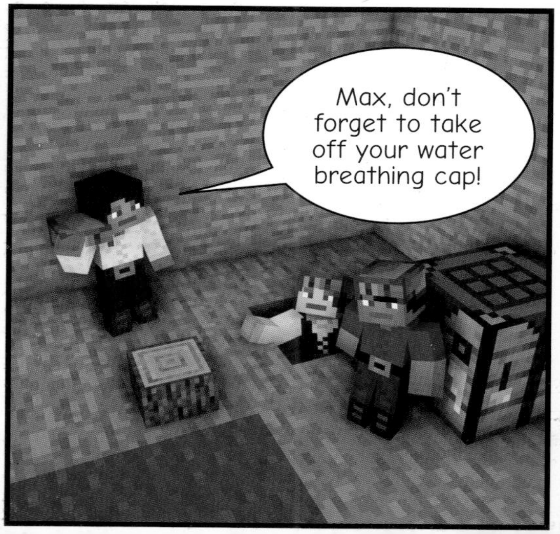
Max, don't forget to take off your water breathing cap!

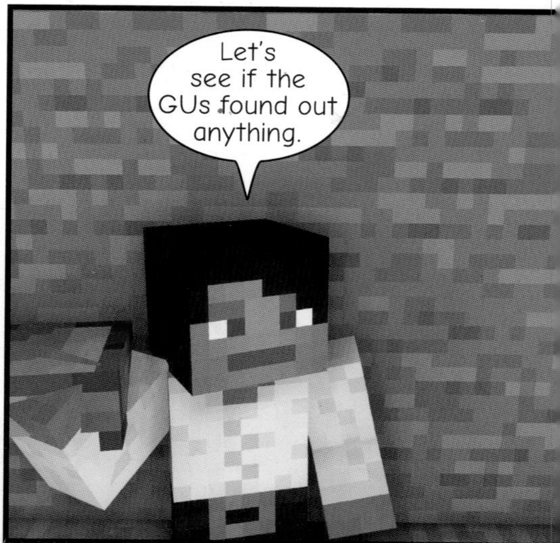
Let's see if the GUs found out anything.

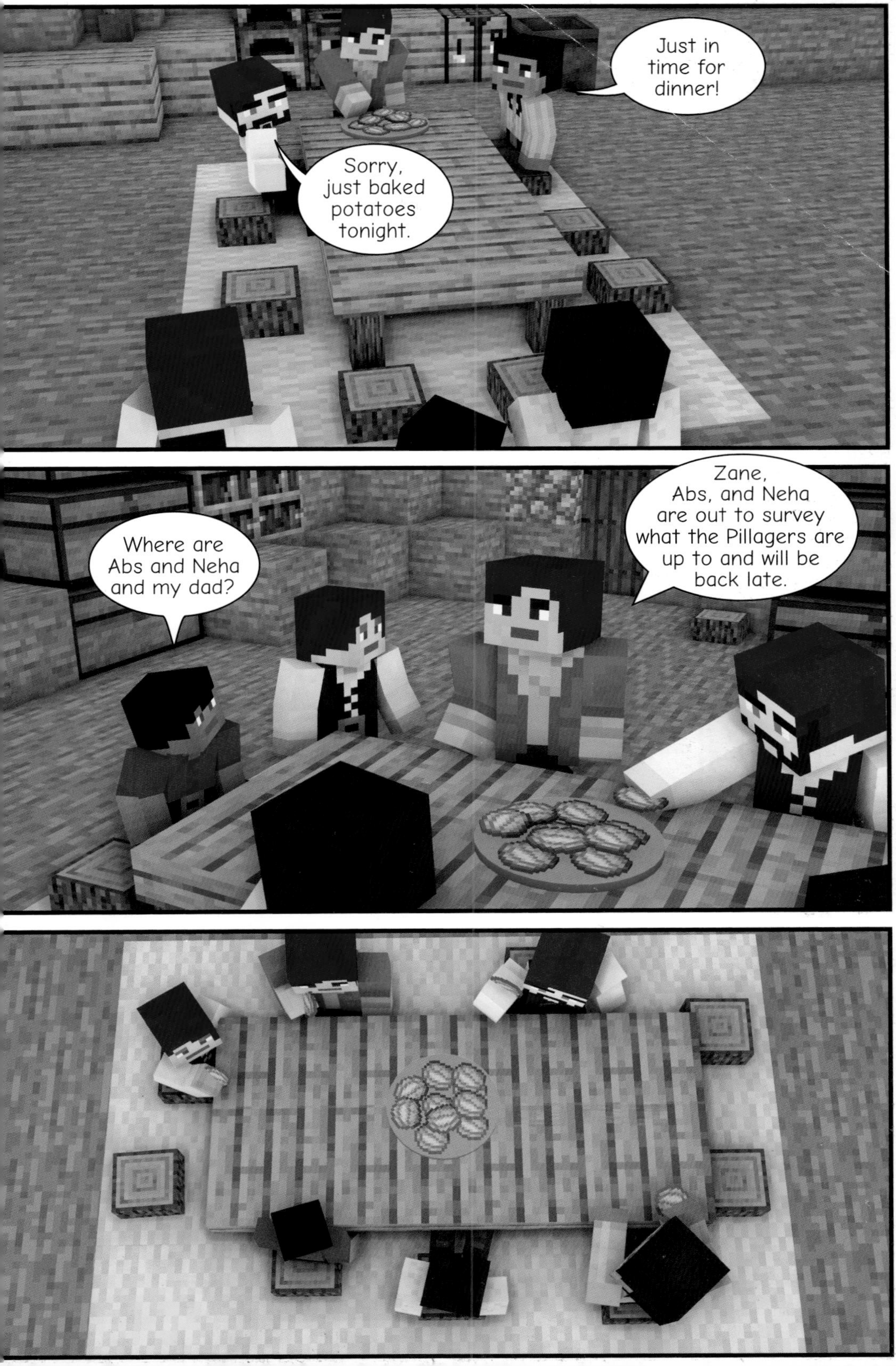
Just in time for dinner!
Sorry, just baked potatoes tonight.
Where are Abs and Neha and my dad?
Zane, Abs, and Neha are out to survey what the Pillagers are up to and will be back late.

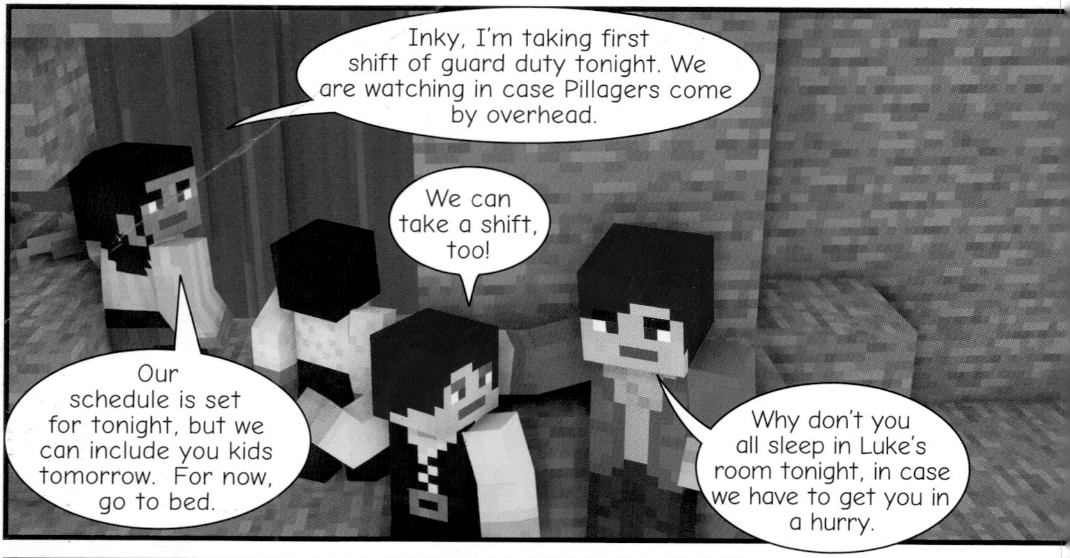
Inky, I'm taking first shift of guard duty tonight. We are watching in case Pillagers come by overhead.
We can take a shift, too!
Our schedule is set for tonight, but we can include you kids tomorrow. For now, go to bed.
Why don't you all sleep in Luke's room tonight, in case we have to get you in a hurry.

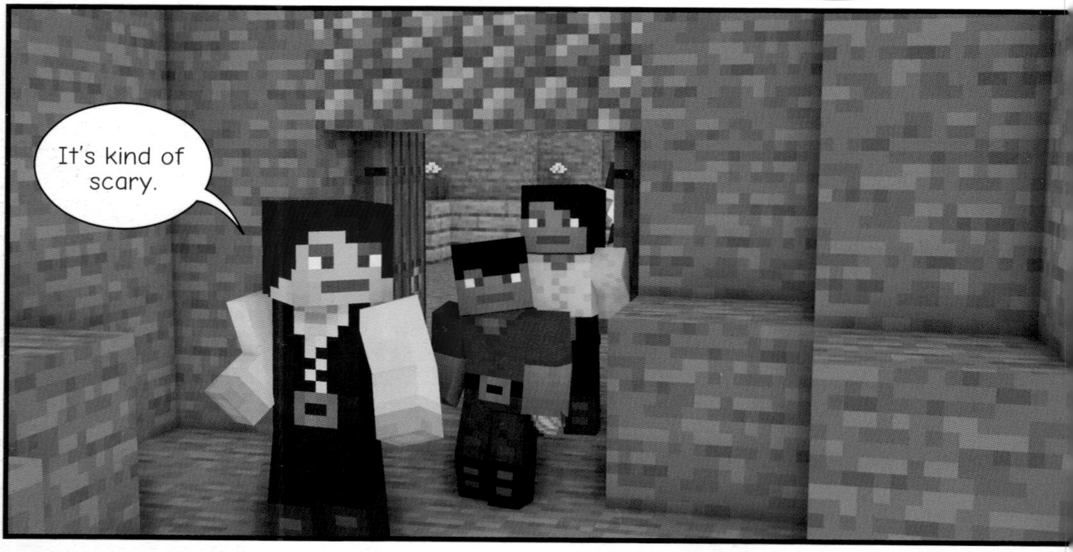
It's kind of scary.

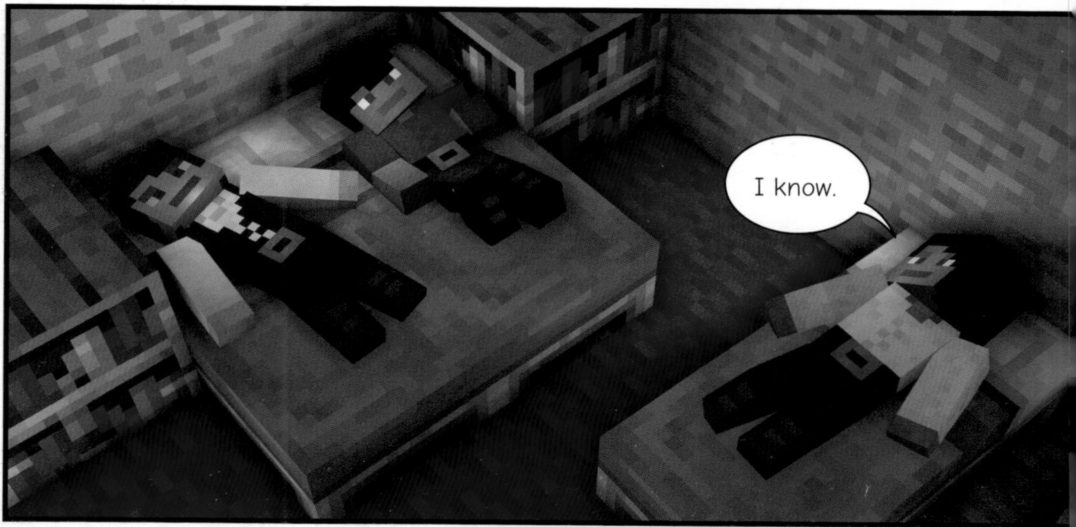
I know.

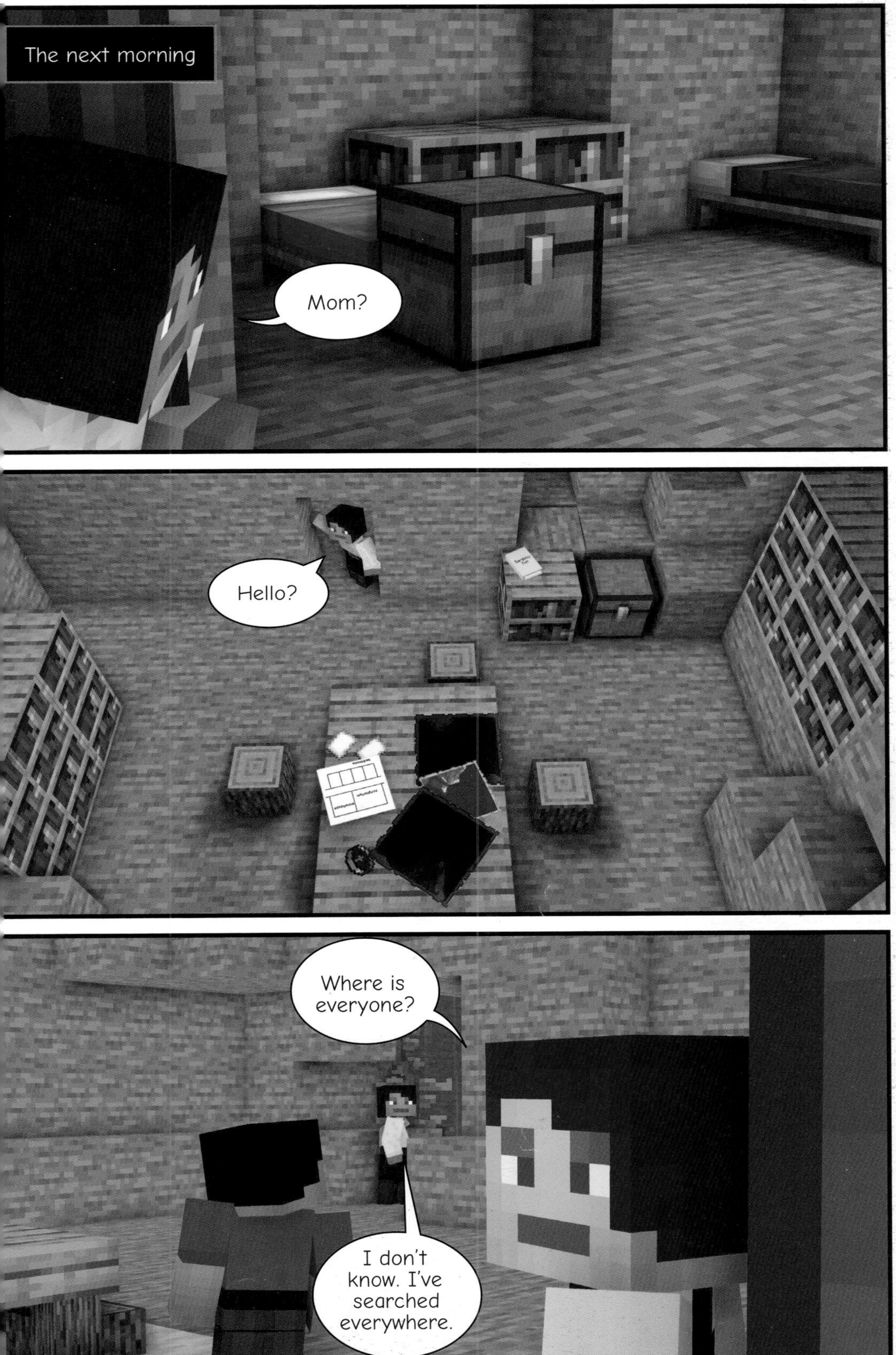
The next morning
Mom?
Hello?
Where is everyone?
I don't know. I've searched everywhere.

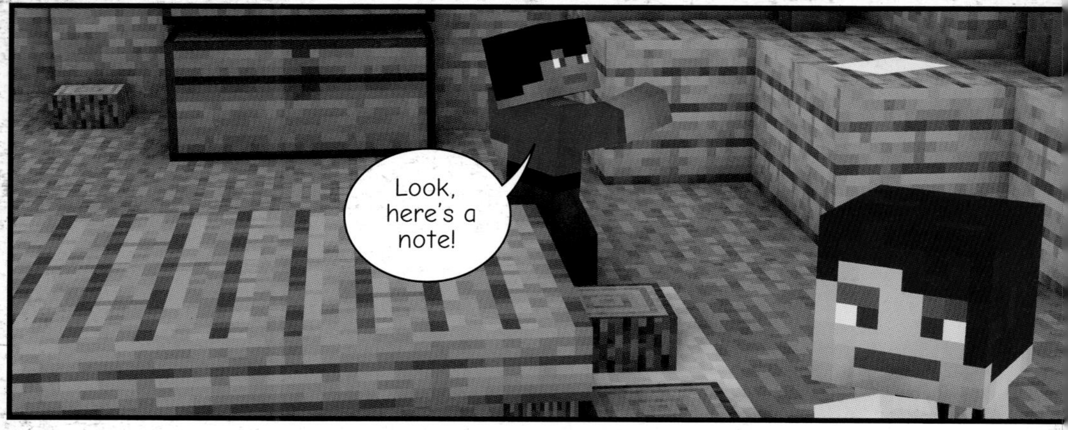
Look, here's a note!

Abs, Neha, and Zane haven't come back from their scout. We're going to look for them. Meanwhile, keep a sharp lookout at the ravine.

If we are not back by tomorrow night, open the emergency plan in the office and follow instructions.

Love,

Sofi, Per, and Jun

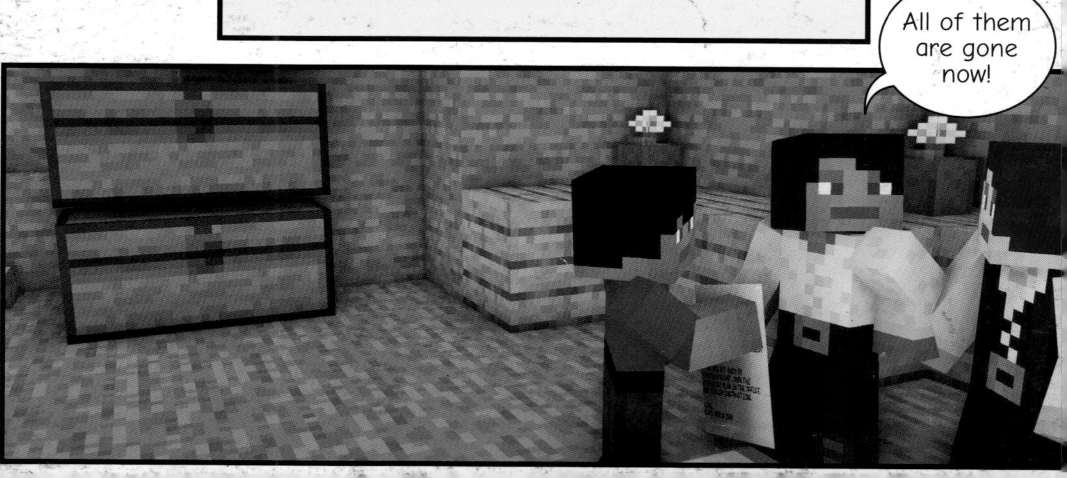
All of them are gone now!

Chapter 3
Gone

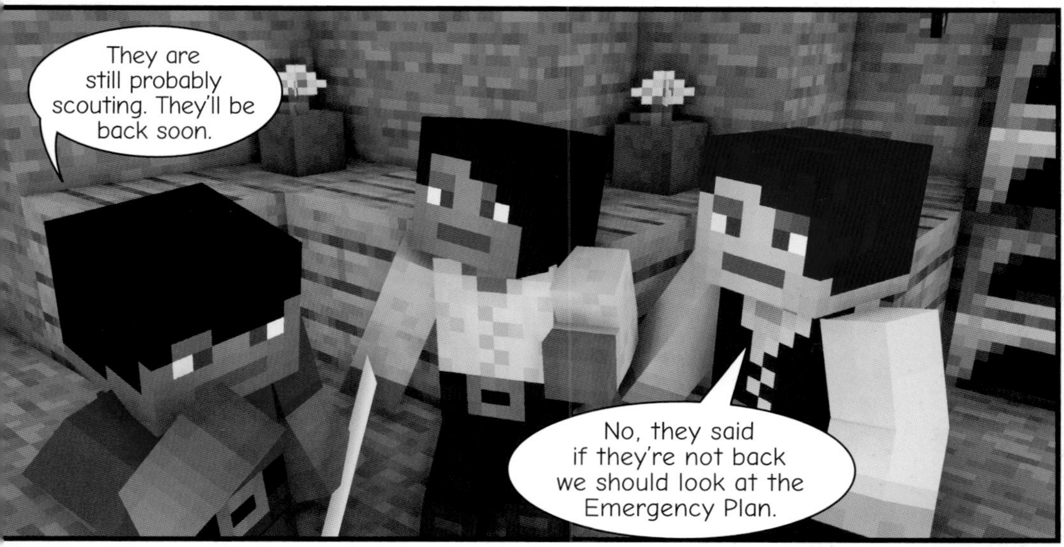
They are still probably scouting. They'll be back soon.
No, they said if they're not back we should look at the Emergency Plan.

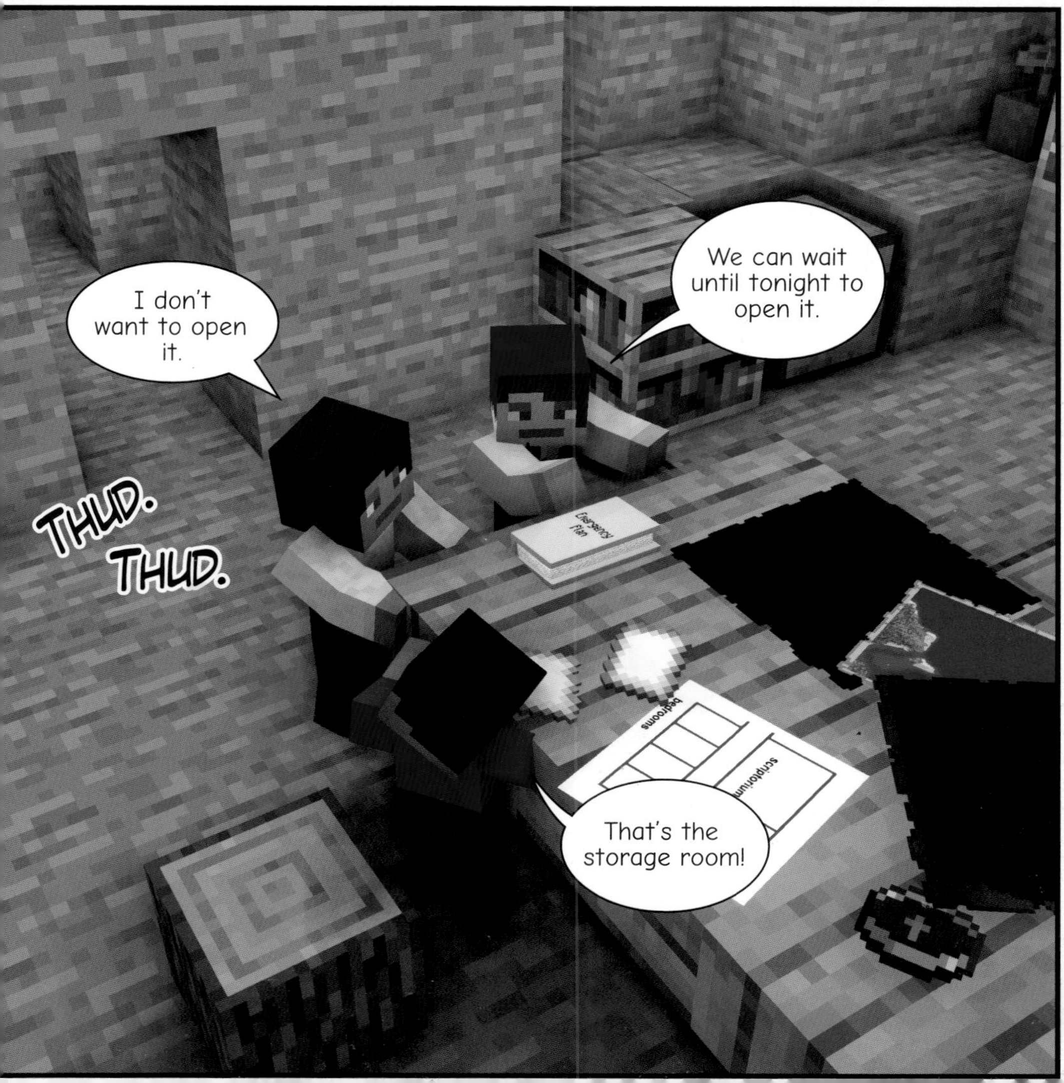
I don't want to open it.
We can wait until tonight to open it.
Emergency Plan
THUD.
THUD.
bedrooms
scriptorium
That's the storage room!

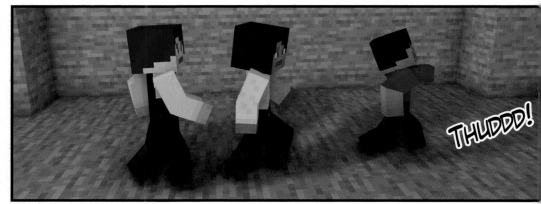

THUDDD!

It's just another shipment of books.

But Abs and Sofi would come back for the books arriving.

The Pillagers are more important. Abs and Sofi know we can take care of the deliveries.

The Pillagers must have caught them.

We have to go find them!

If they all got caught, then they were caught by surprise somehow. We need to figure out how to be even more careful.

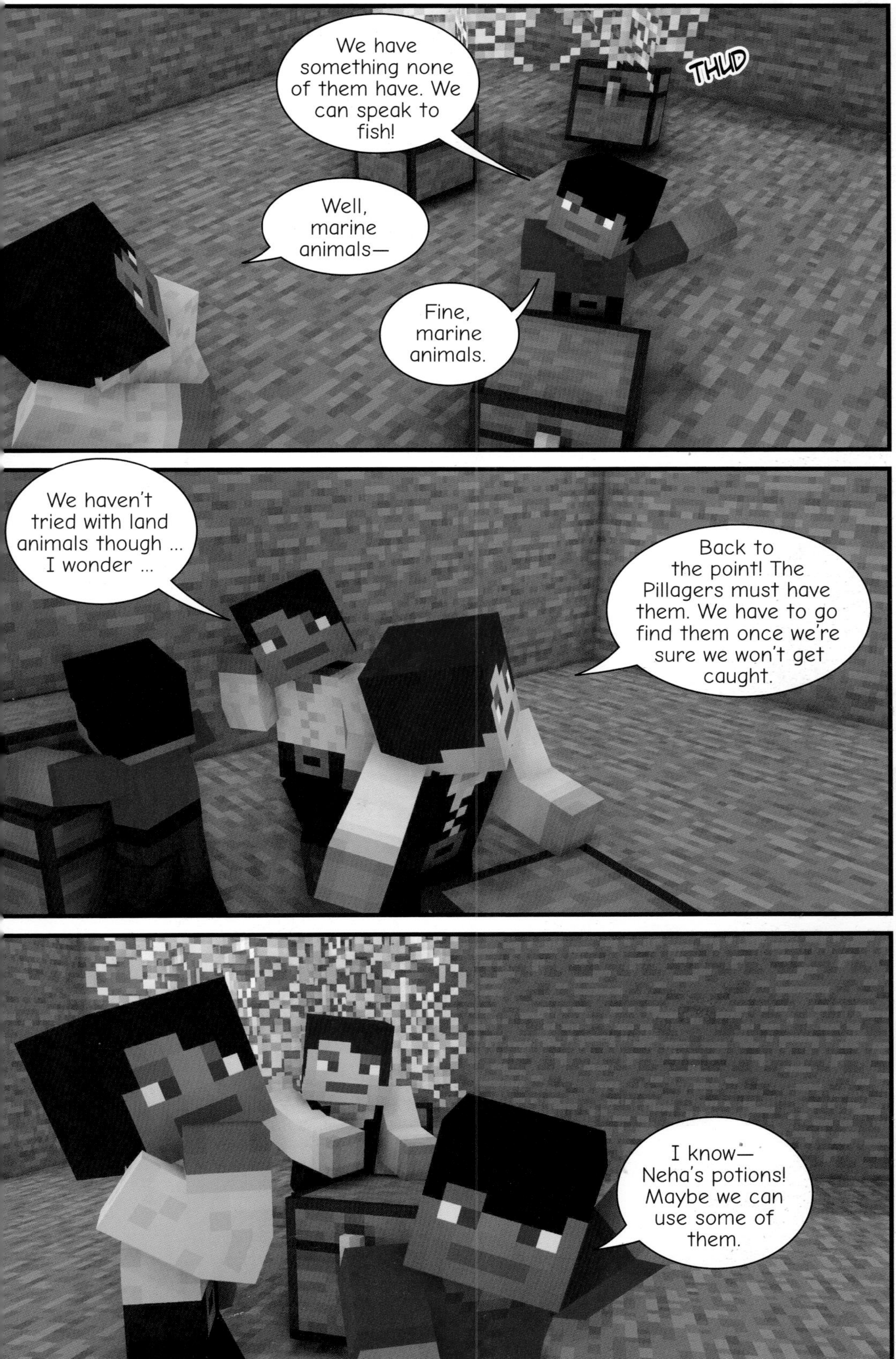
We have something none of them have. We can speak to fish!
THUD
Well, marine animals—
Fine, marine animals.
We haven't tried with land animals though ... I wonder ...
Back to the point! The Pillagers must have them. We have to go find them once we're sure we won't get caught.
I know— Neha's potions! Maybe we can use some of them.

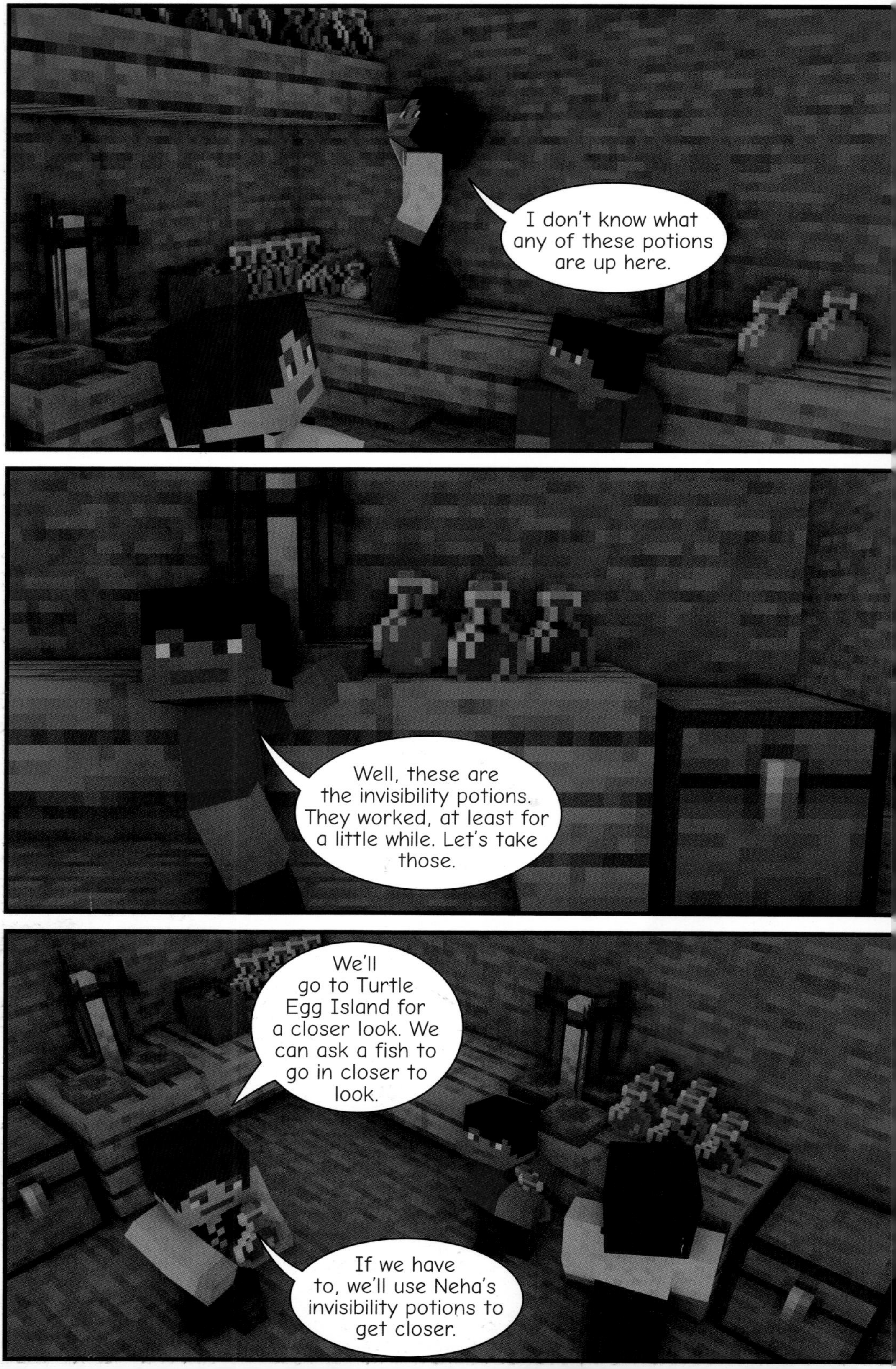
I don't know what any of these potions are up here.
Well, these are the invisibility potions. They worked, at least for a little while. Let's take those.
We'll go to Turtle Egg Island for a closer look. We can ask a fish to go in closer to look.
If we have to, we'll use Neha's invisibility potions to get closer.

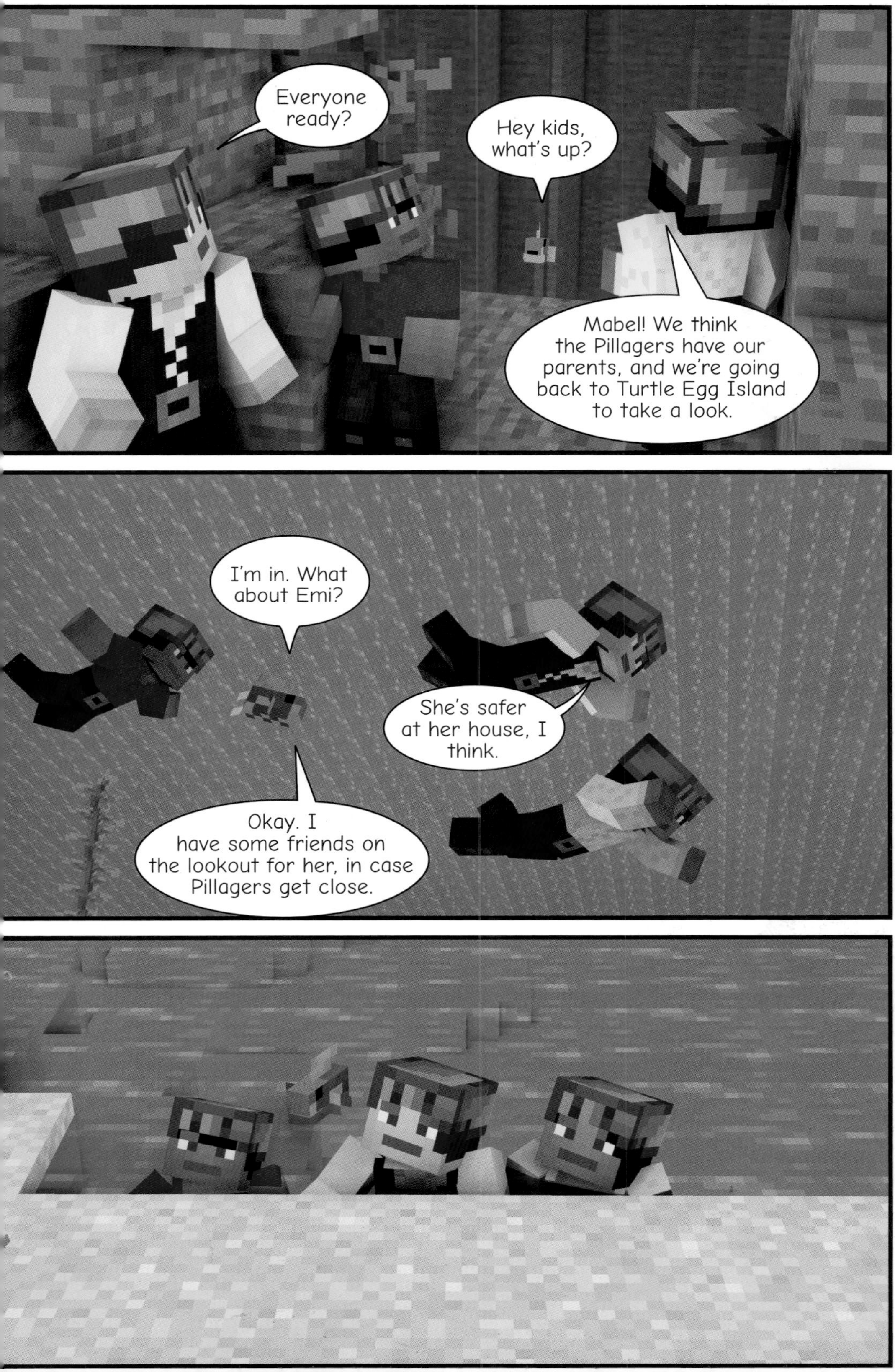
Everyone ready?
Hey kids, what's up?
Mabel! We think the Pillagers have our parents, and we're going back to Turtle Egg Island to take a look.
I'm in. What about Emi?
She's safer at her house, I think.
Okay. I have some friends on the lookout for her, in case Pillagers get close.

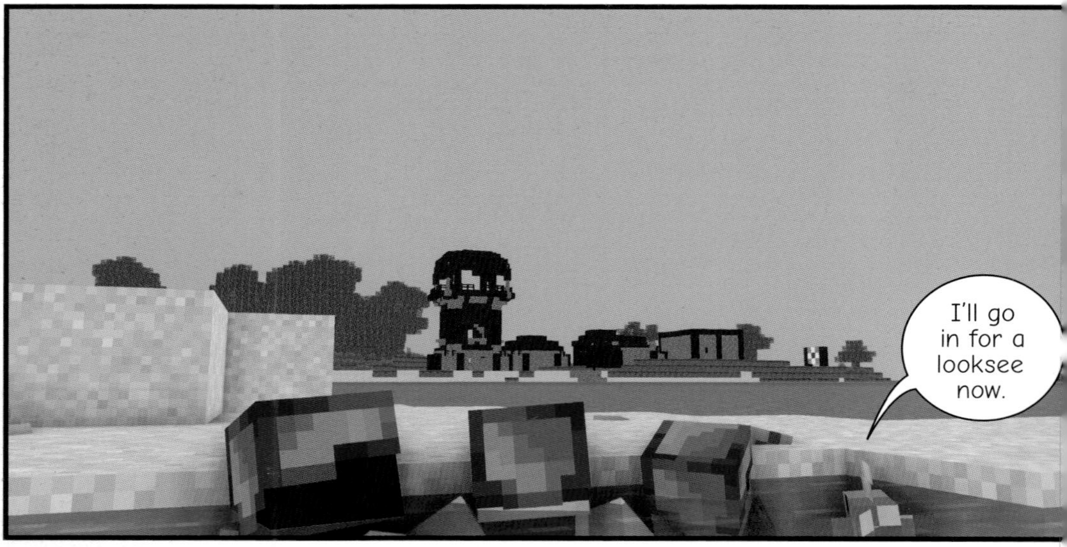
I'll go in for a looksee now.

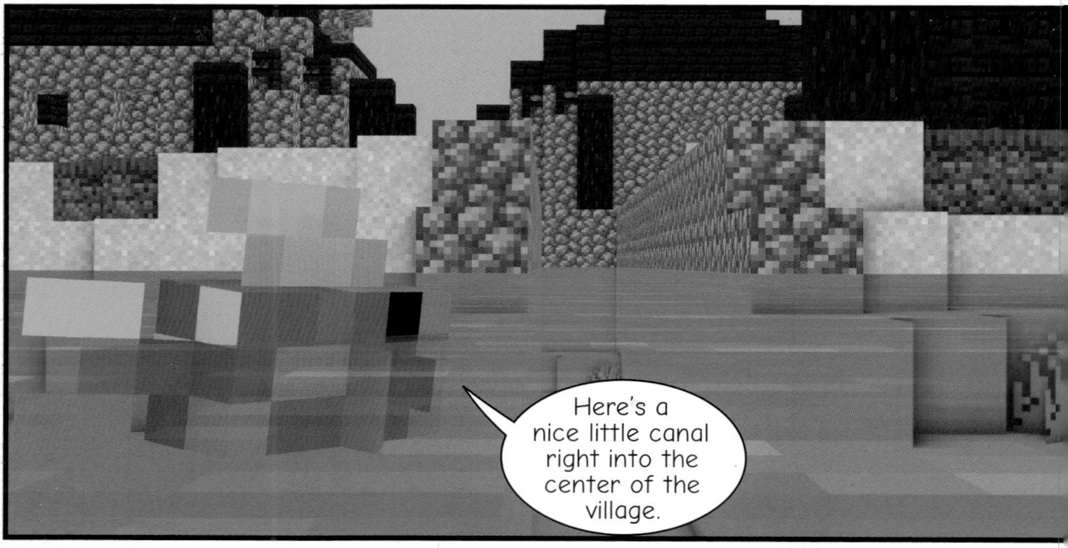
Here's a nice little canal right into the center of the village.

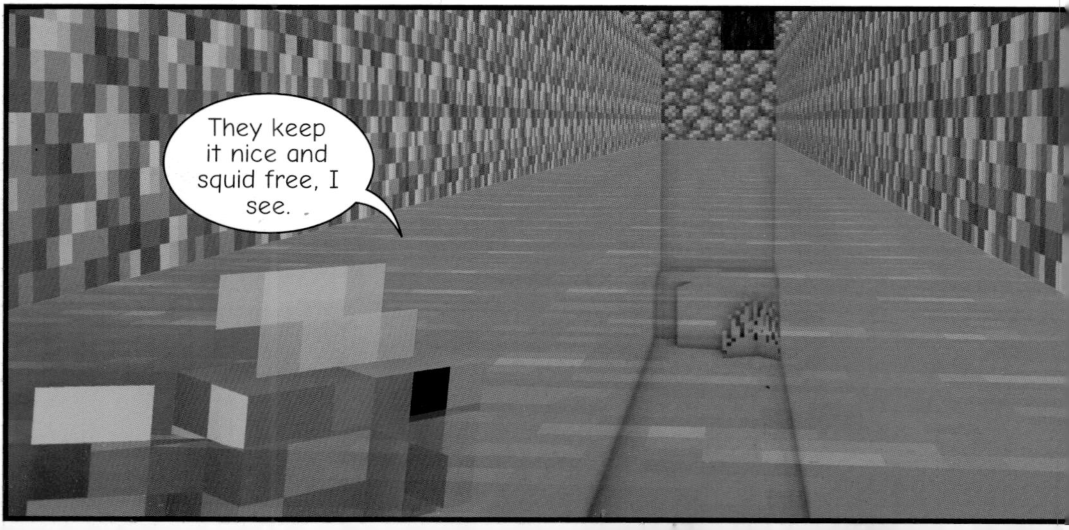
They keep it nice and squid free, I see.

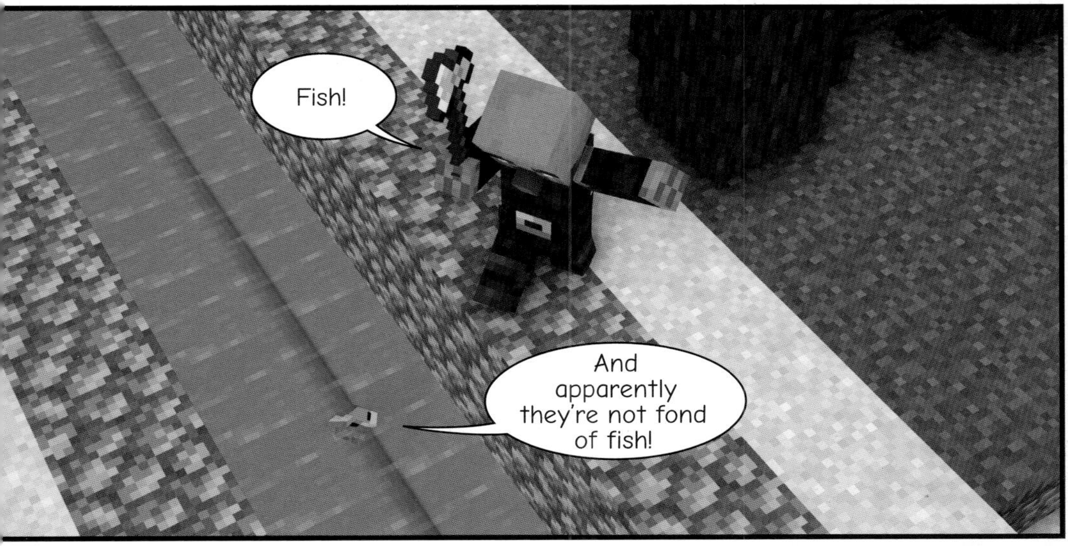
Fish!
And apparently they're not fond of fish!

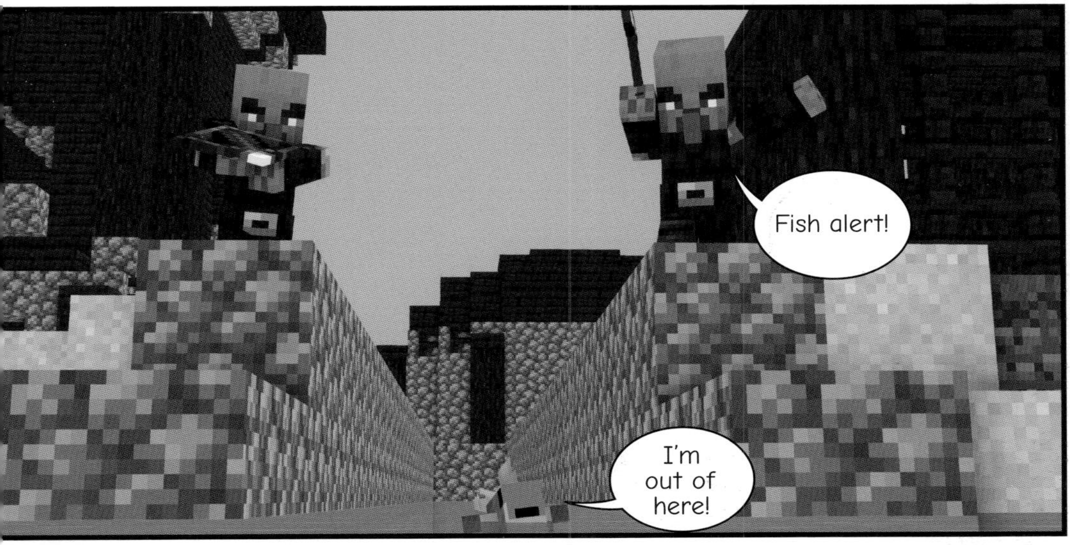
Fish alert!
I'm out of here!

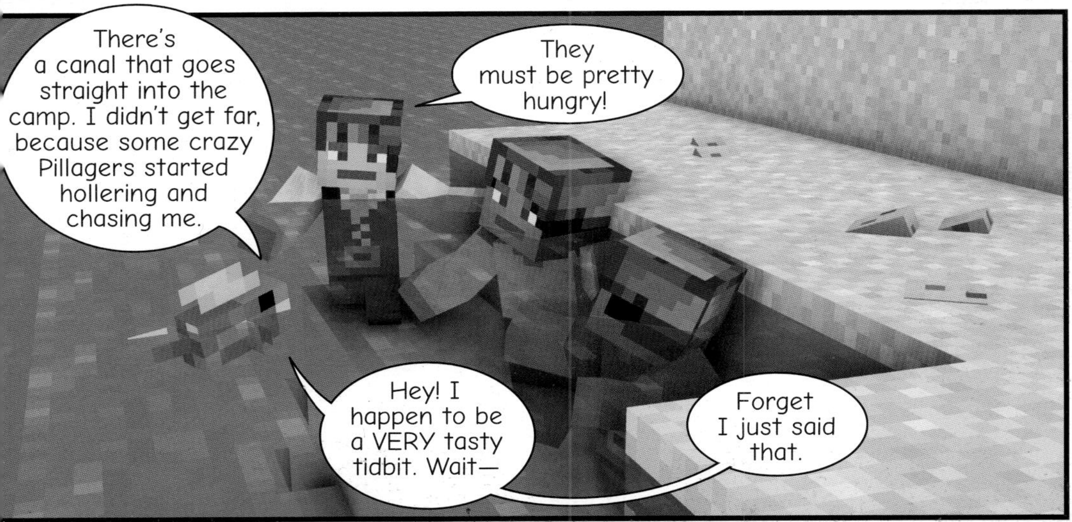
There's a canal that goes straight into the camp. I didn't get far, because some crazy Pillagers started hollering and chasing me.
They must be pretty hungry!
Hey! I happen to be a VERY tasty tidbit. Wait—
Forget I just said that.

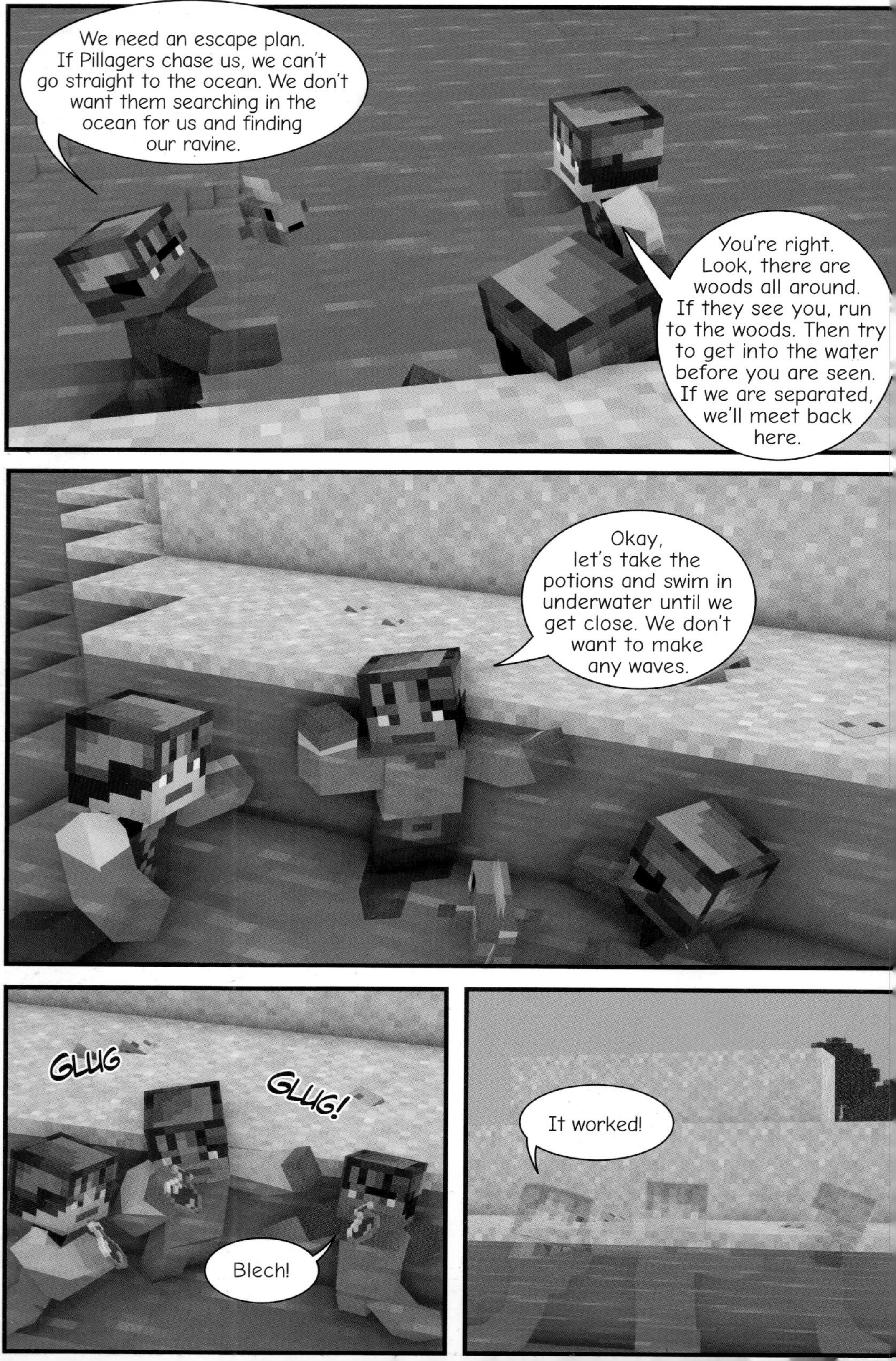
We need an escape plan. If Pillagers chase us, we can't go straight to the ocean. We don't want them searching in the ocean for us and finding our ravine.
You're right. Look, there are woods all around. If they see you, run to the woods. Then try to get into the water before you are seen. If we are separated, we'll meet back here.
Okay, let's take the potions and swim in underwater until we get close. We don't want to make any waves.
GLUG
GLUG!
Blech!
It worked!

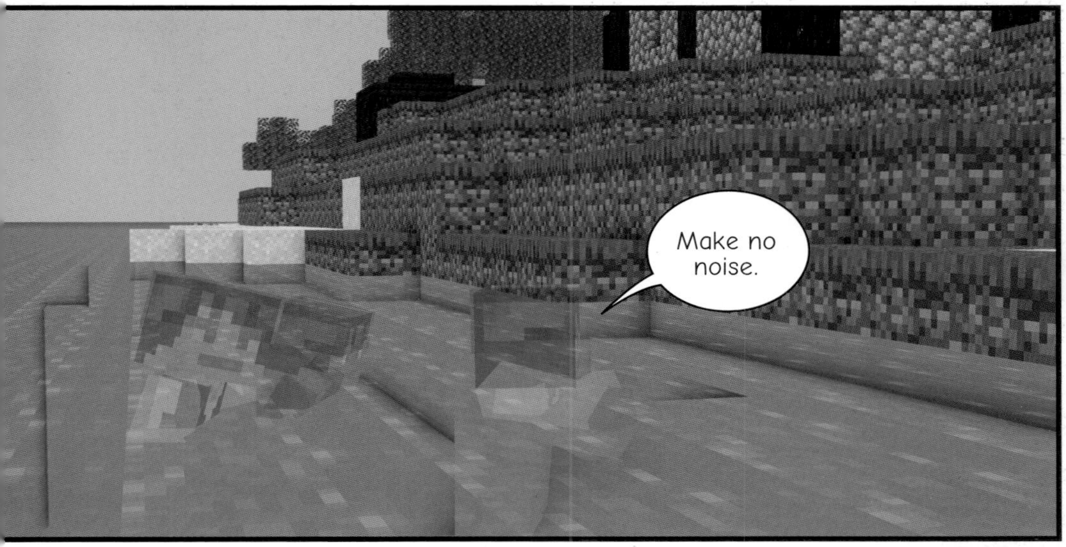
Make no noise.

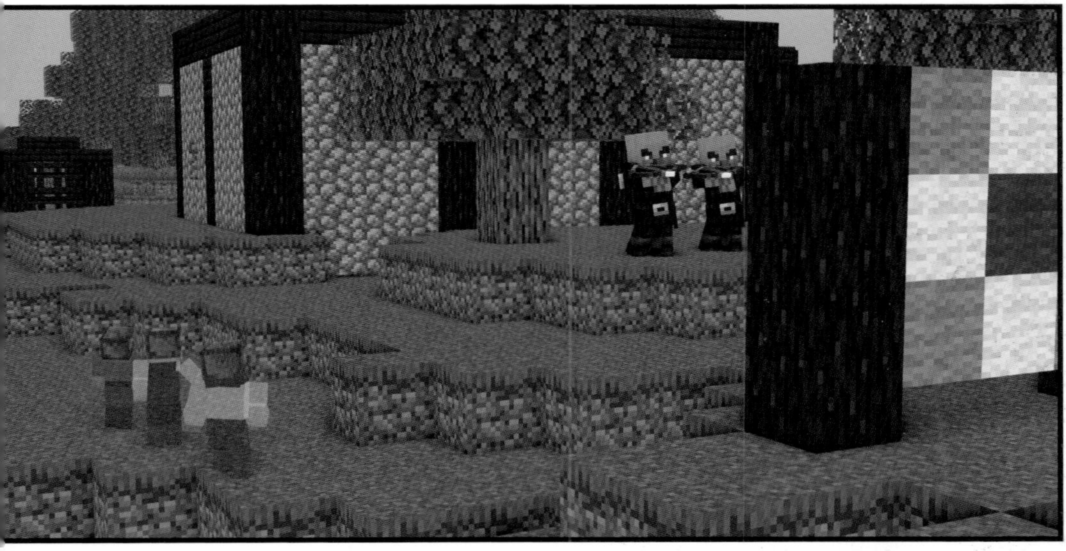

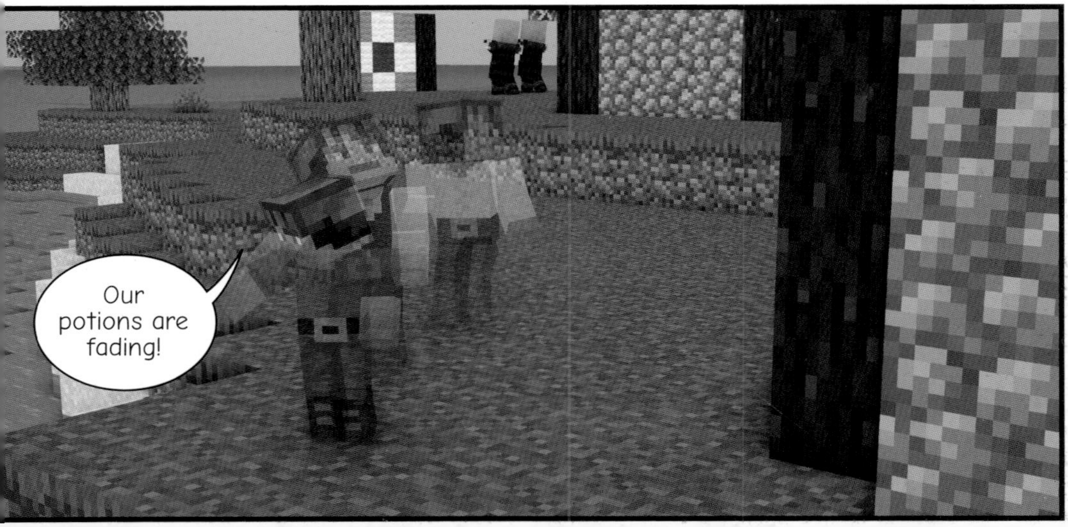
Our potions are fading!

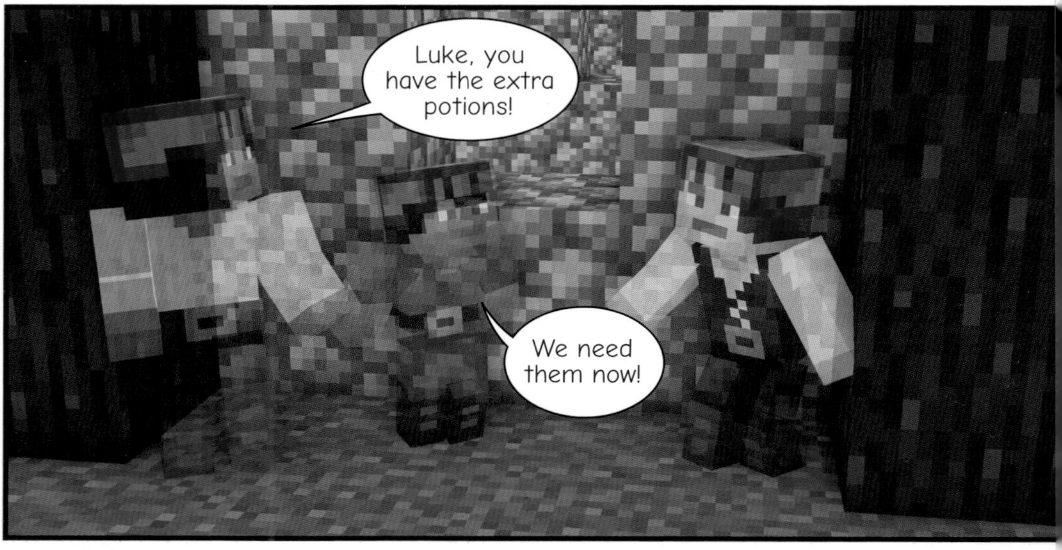
Luke, you have the extra potions!
We need them now!

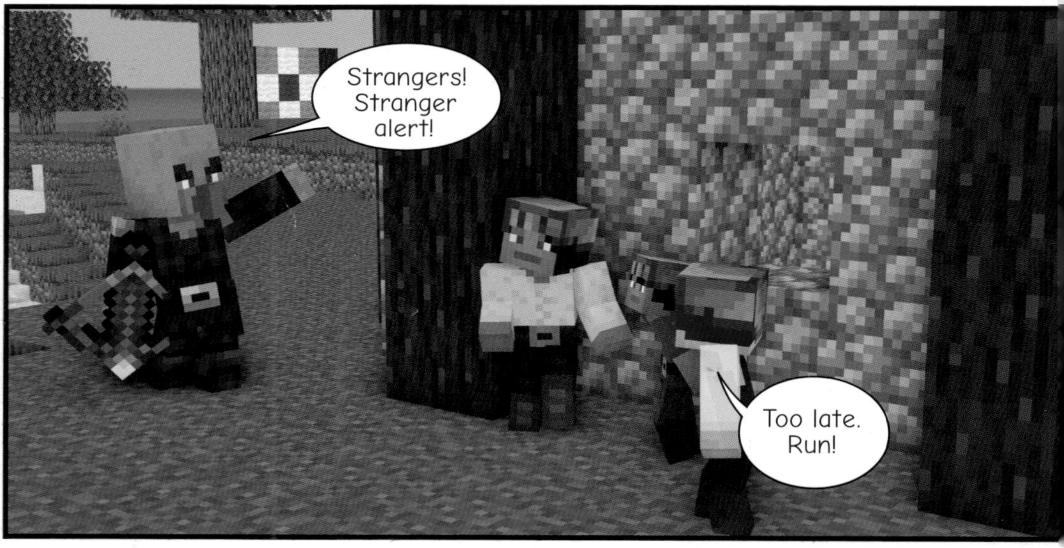
Strangers! Stranger alert!
Too late. Run!

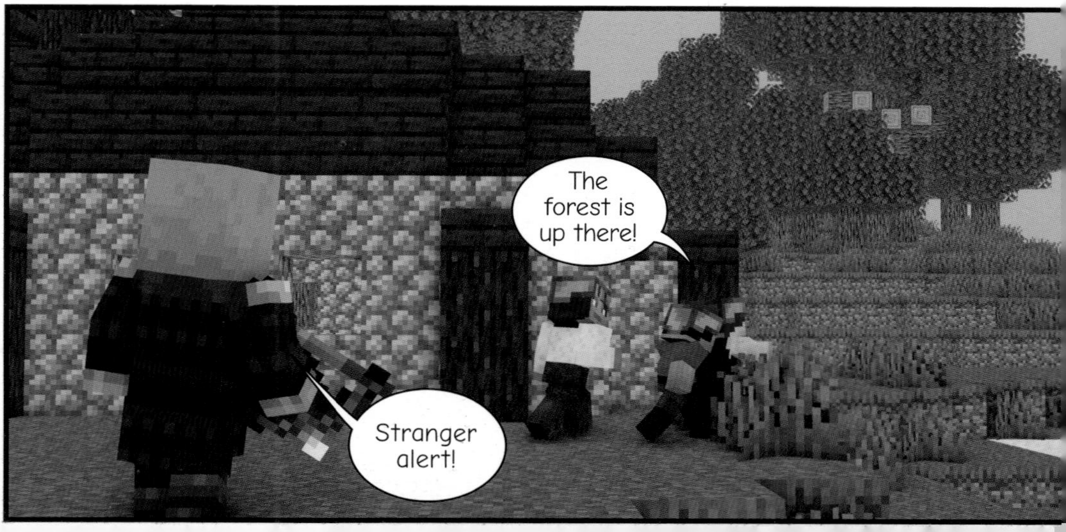
The forest is up there!
Stranger alert!

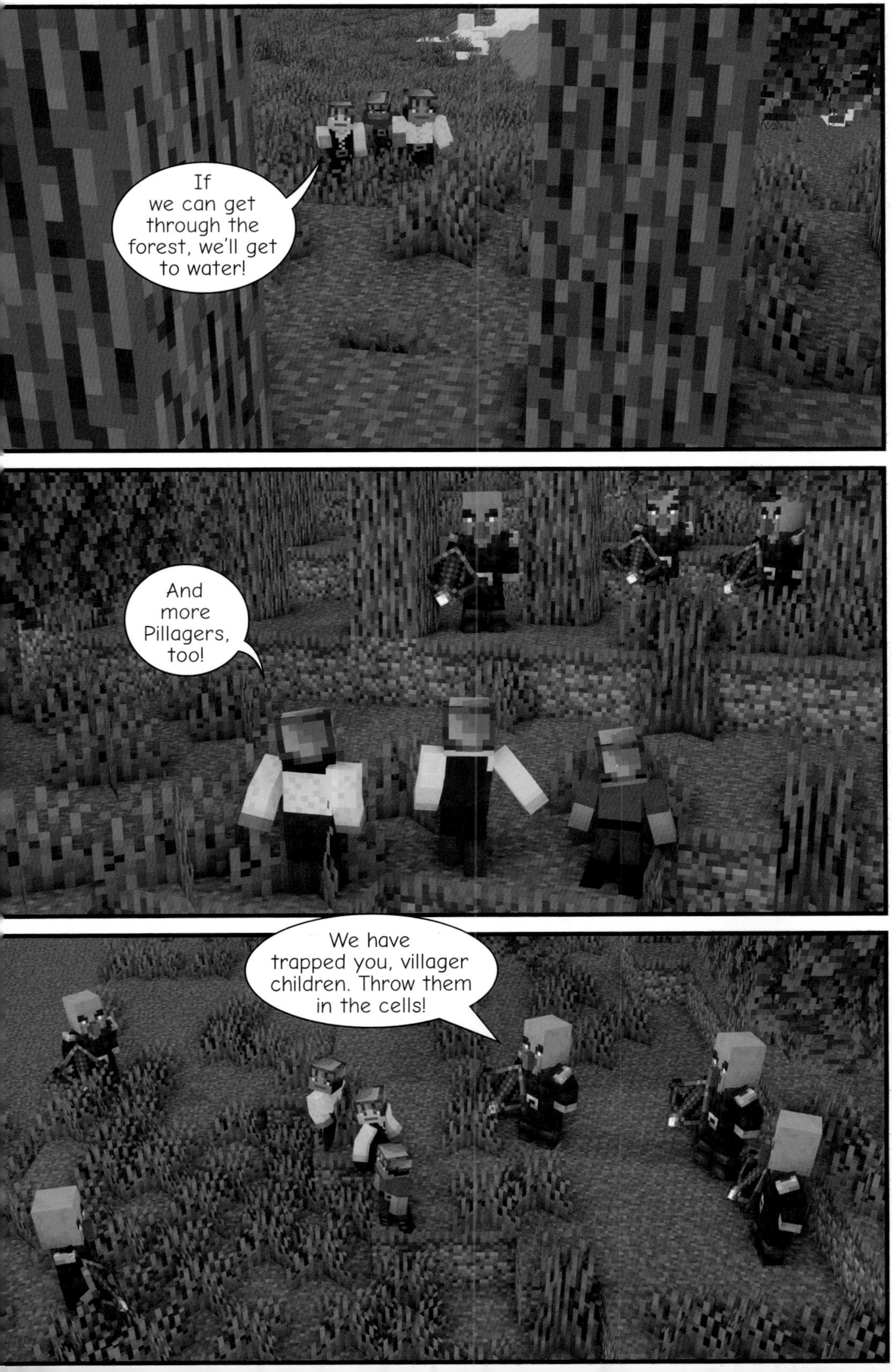
If we can get through the forest, we'll get to water!
And more Pillagers, too!
We have trapped you, villager children. Throw them in the cells!

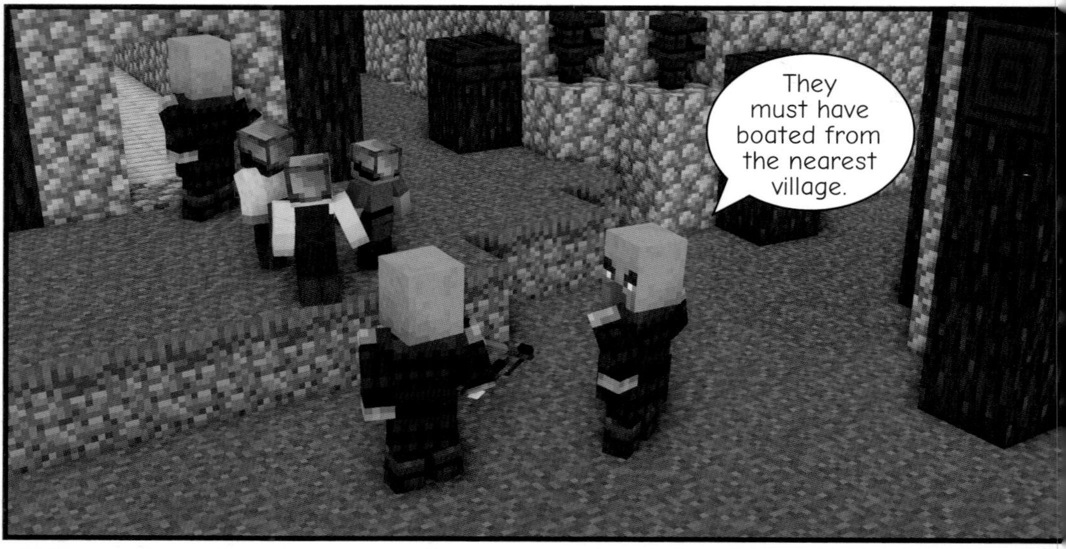
They must have boated from the nearest village.

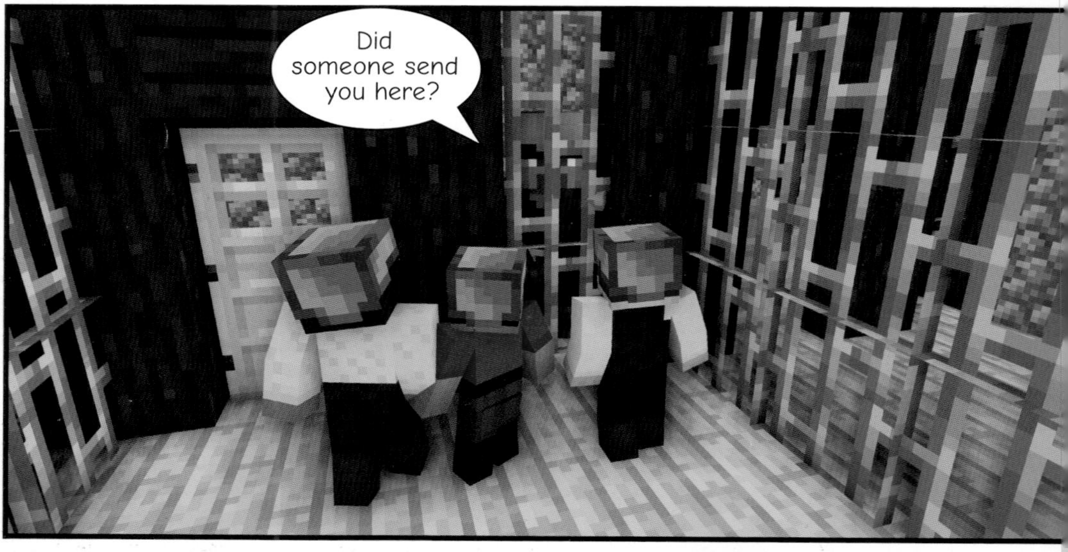
Did someone send you here?

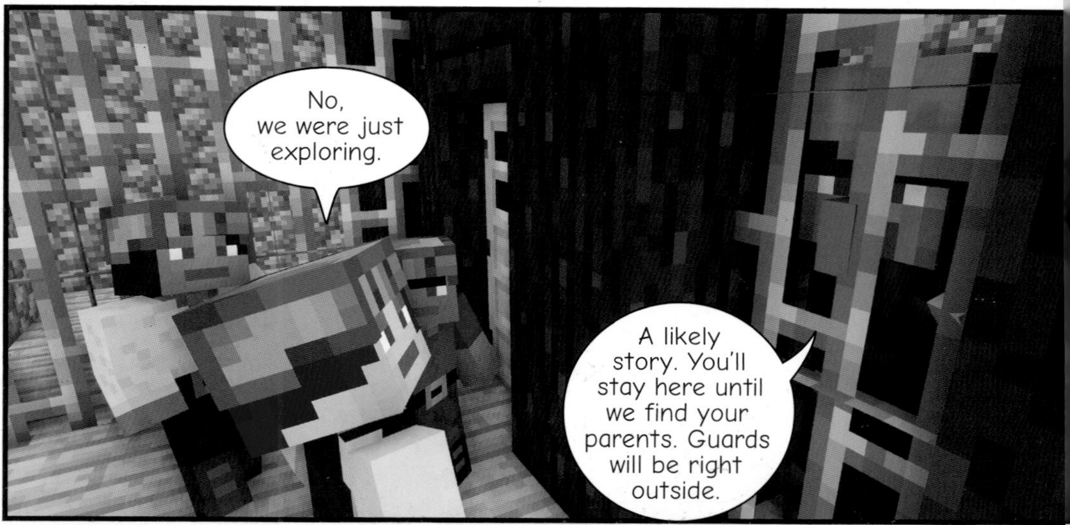
No, we were just exploring.
A likely story. You'll stay here until we find your parents. Guards will be right outside.

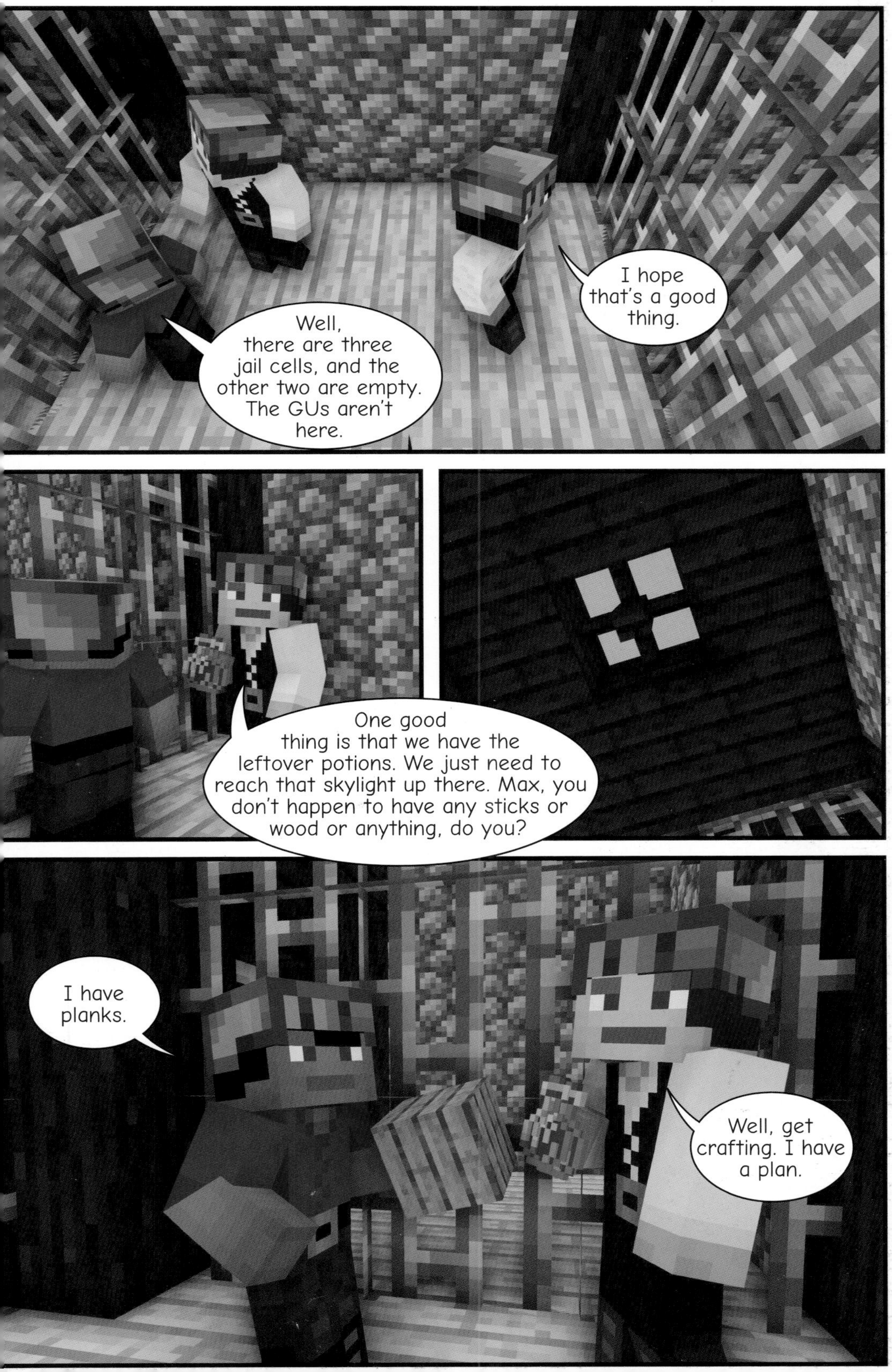
Well, there are three jail cells, and the other two are empty. The GUs aren't here.
I hope that's a good thing.
One good thing is that we have the leftover potions. We just need to reach that skylight up there. Max, you don't happen to have any sticks or wood or anything, do you?
I have planks.
Well, get crafting. I have a plan.

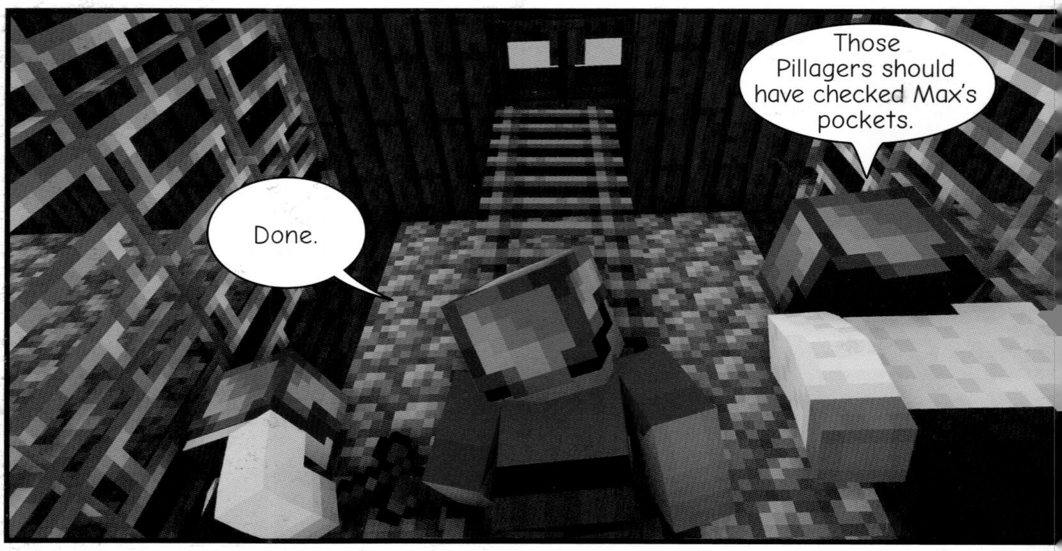
Those Pillagers should have checked Max's pockets.
Done.

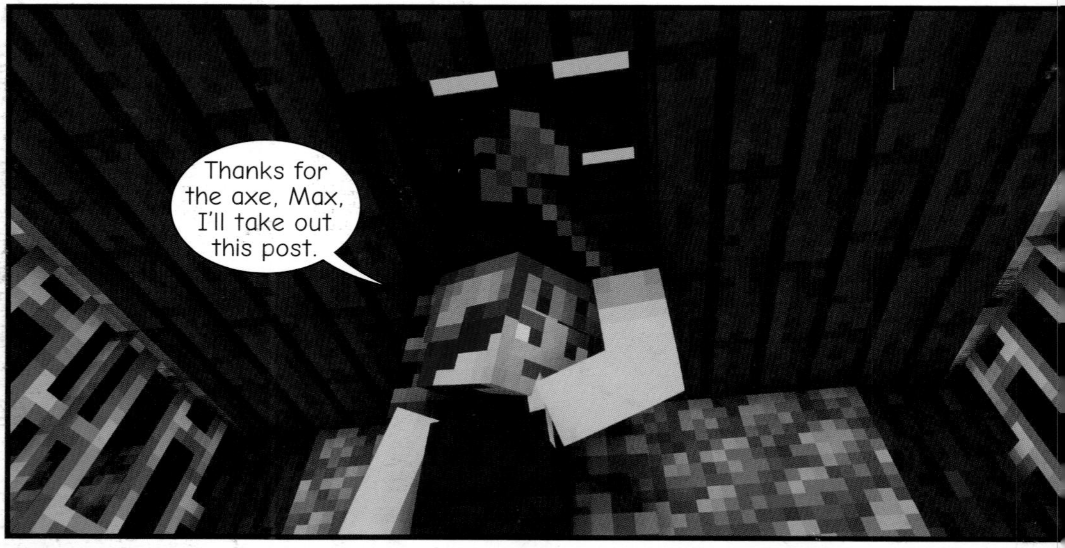
Thanks for the axe, Max, I'll take out this post.

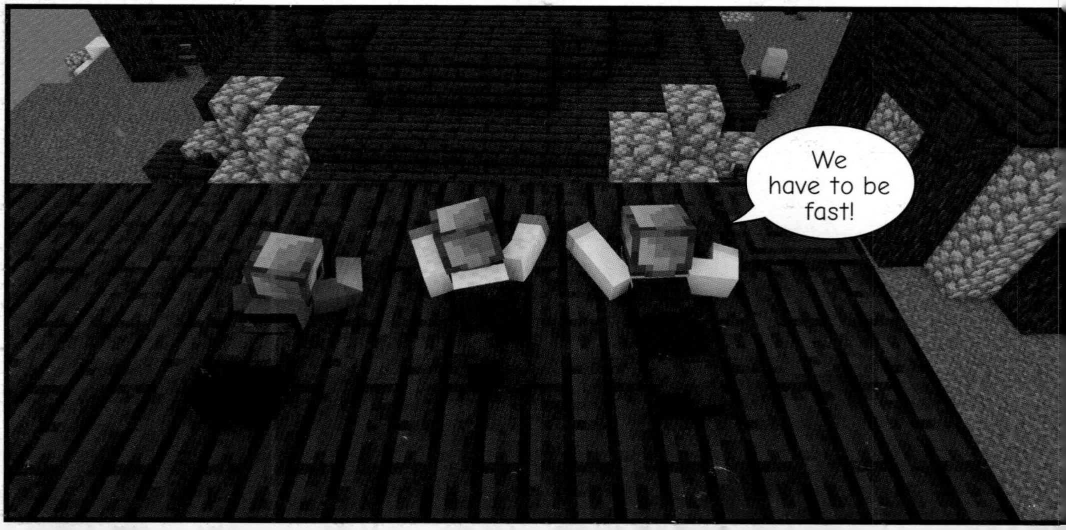
We have to be fast!

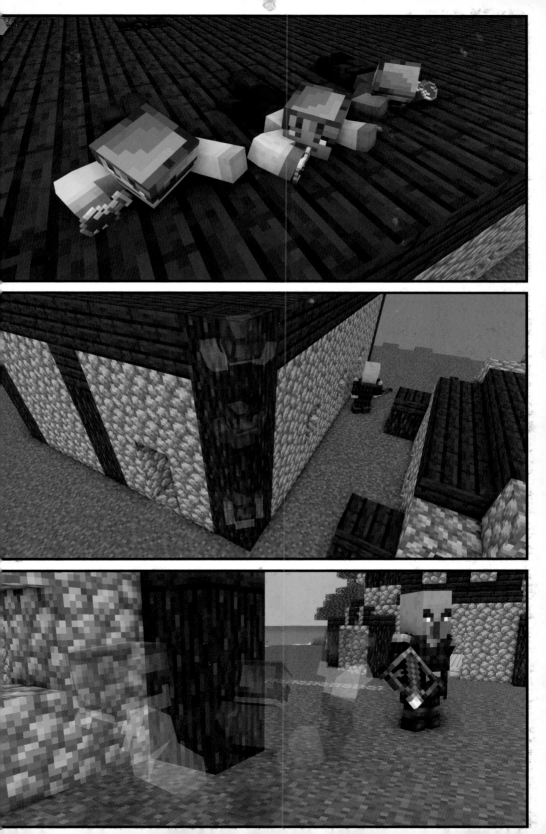

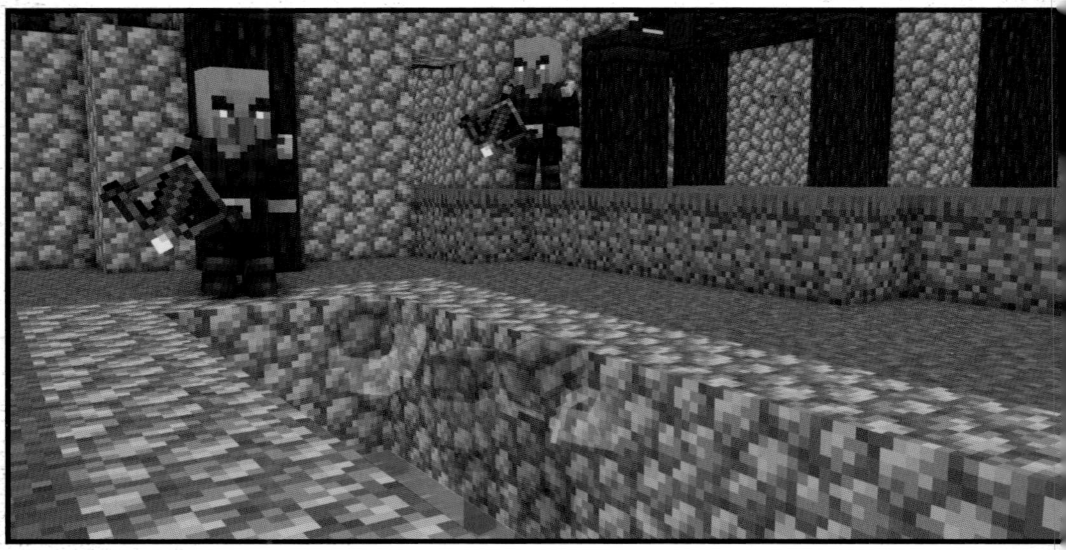

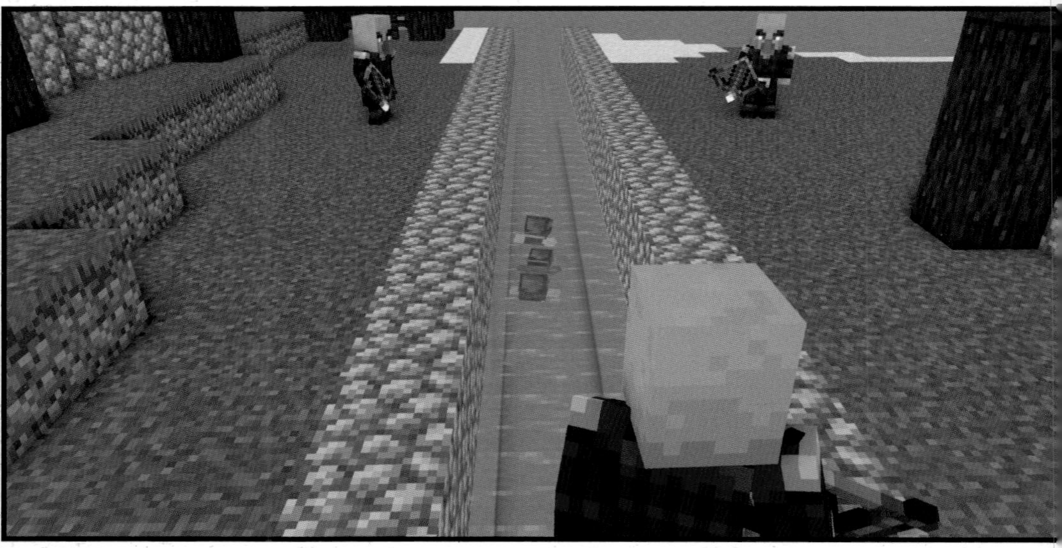

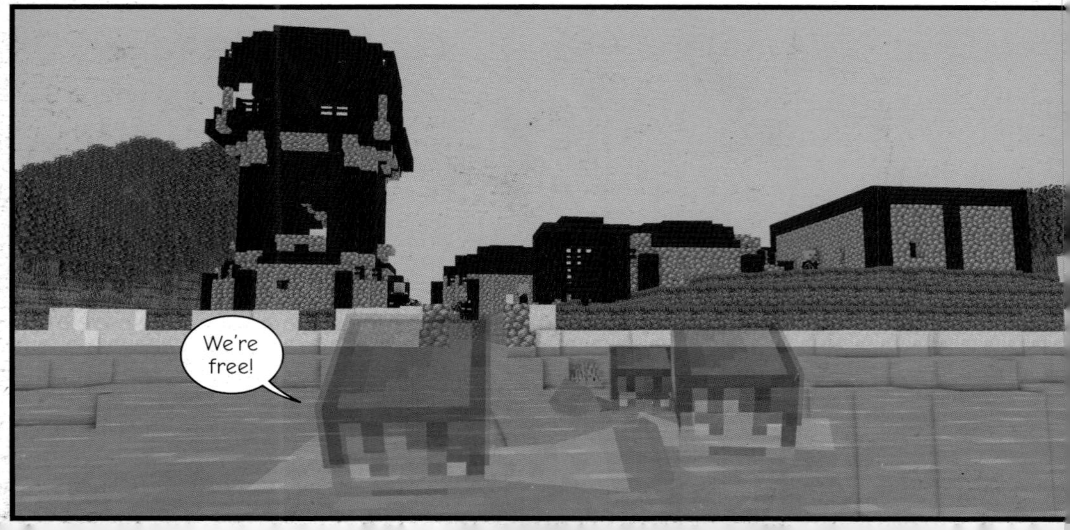
We're free!

Chapter 4
Signs of a
Struggle

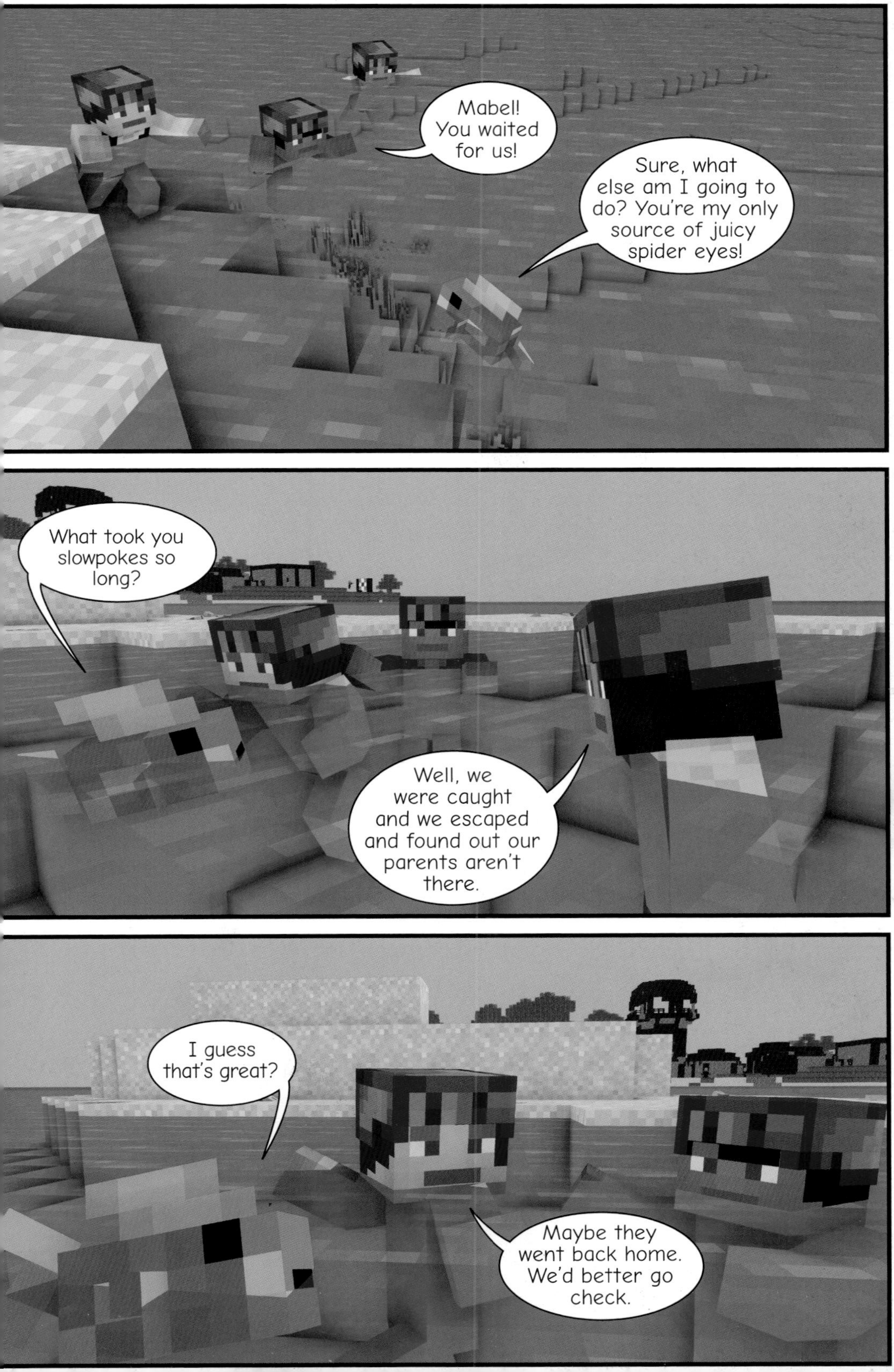
Mabel! You waited for us!
Sure, what else am I going to do? You're my only source of juicy spider eyes!
What took you slowpokes so long?
Well, we were caught and we escaped and found out our parents aren't there.
I guess that's great?
Maybe they went back home. We'd better go check.

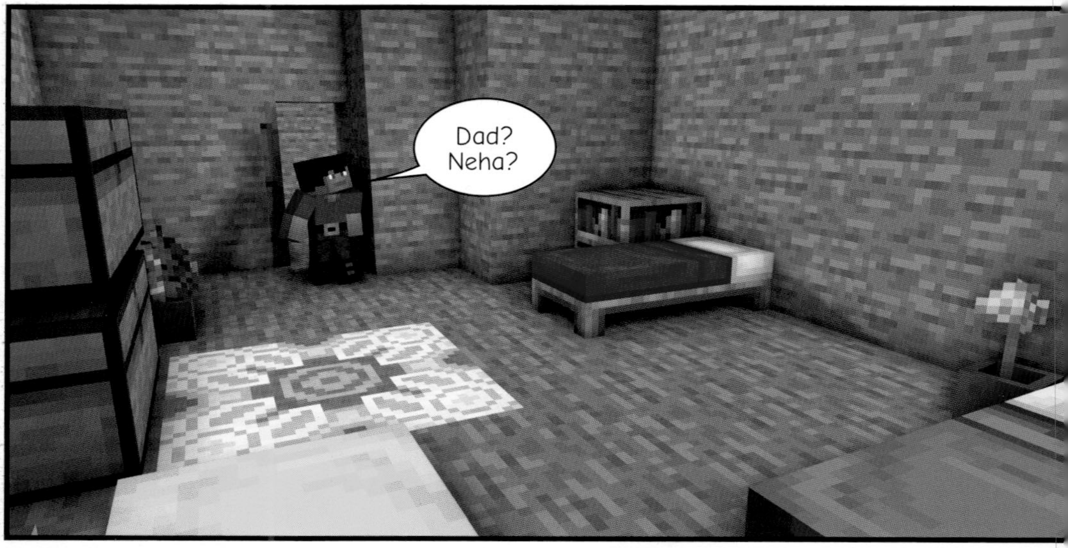
Dad?
Neha?

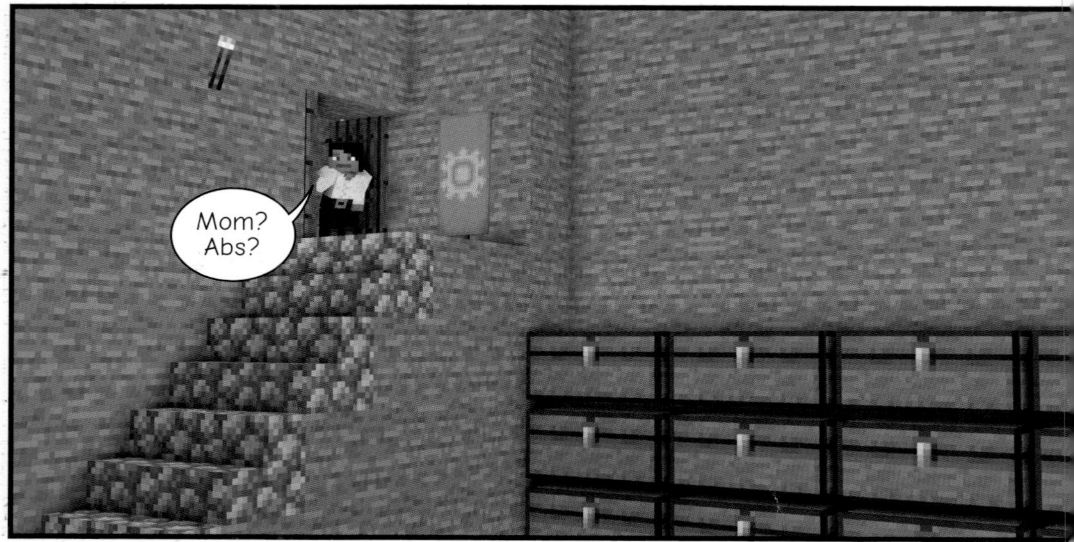
Mom?
Abs?

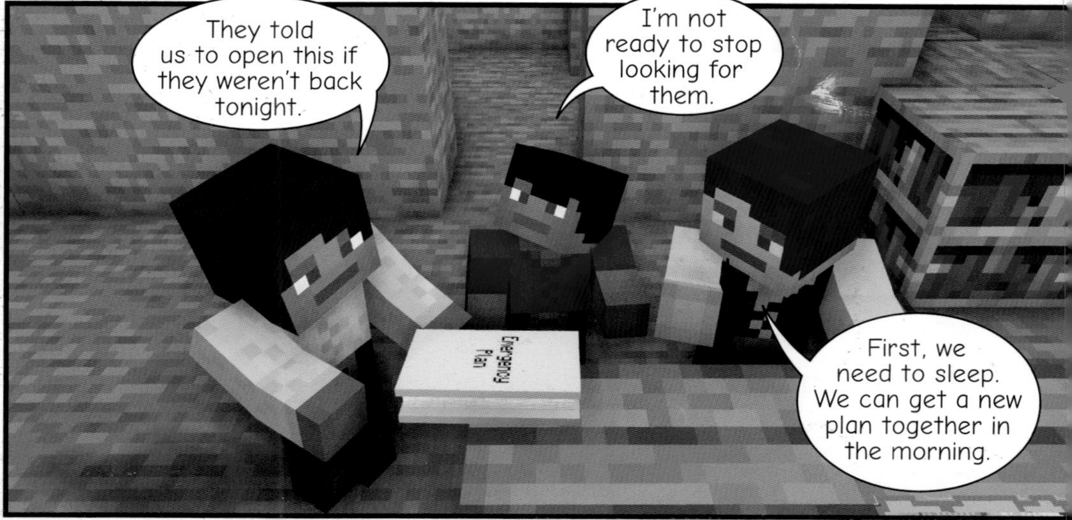
They told us to open this if they weren't back tonight.
I'm not ready to stop looking for them.
Emergency Plan
First, we need to sleep. We can get a new plan together in the morning.

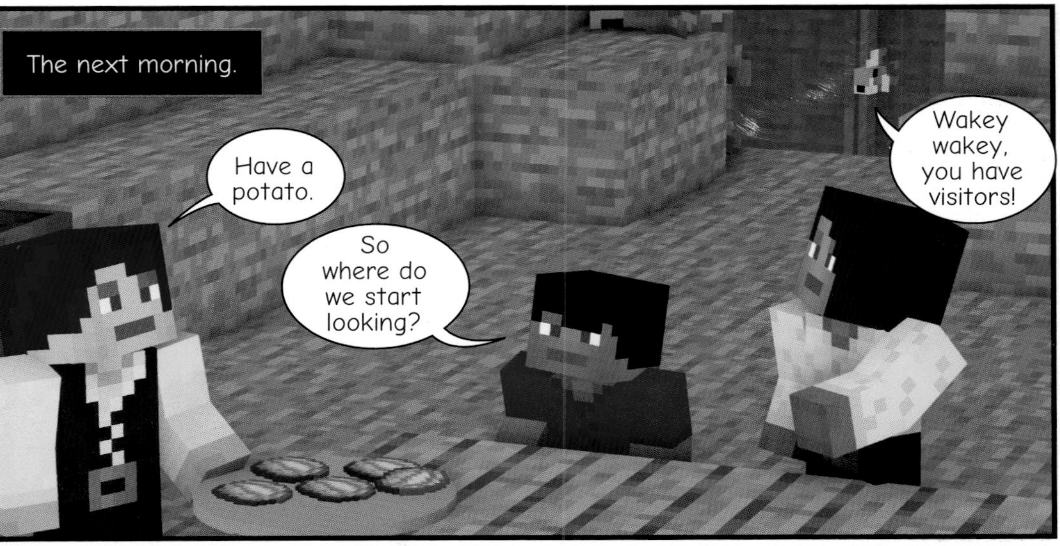
The next morning.
Have a potato.
So where do we start looking?
Wakey wakey, you have visitors!

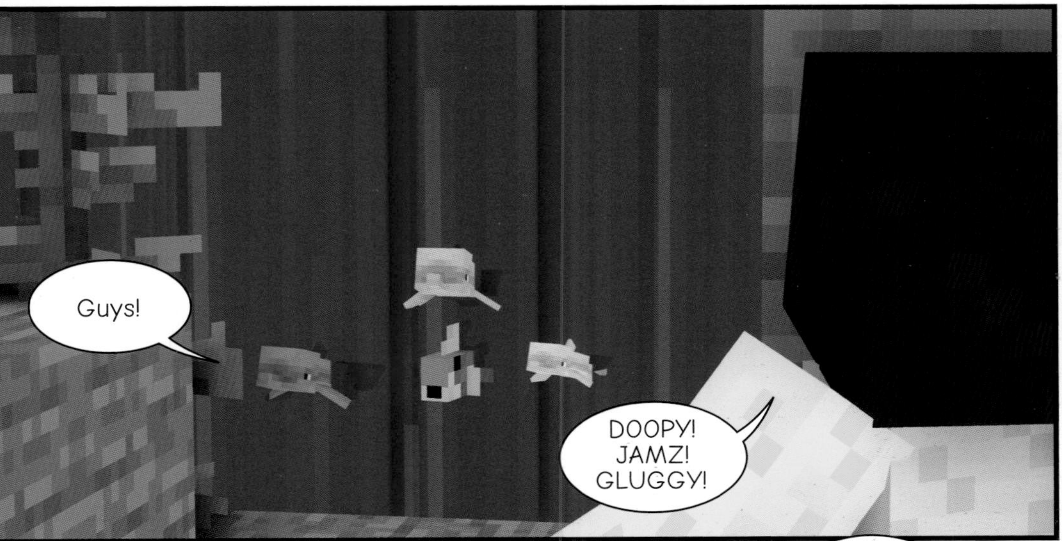
Guys!
DOOPY! JAMZ! GLUGGY!

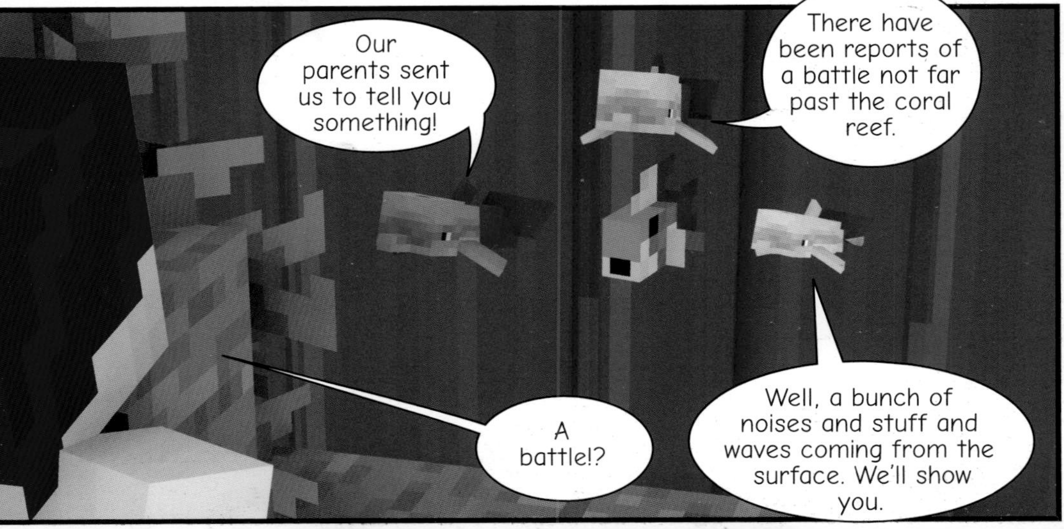
Our parents sent us to tell you something!
There have been reports of a battle not far past the coral reef.
A battle!?
Well, a bunch of noises and stuff and waves coming from the surface. We'll show you.

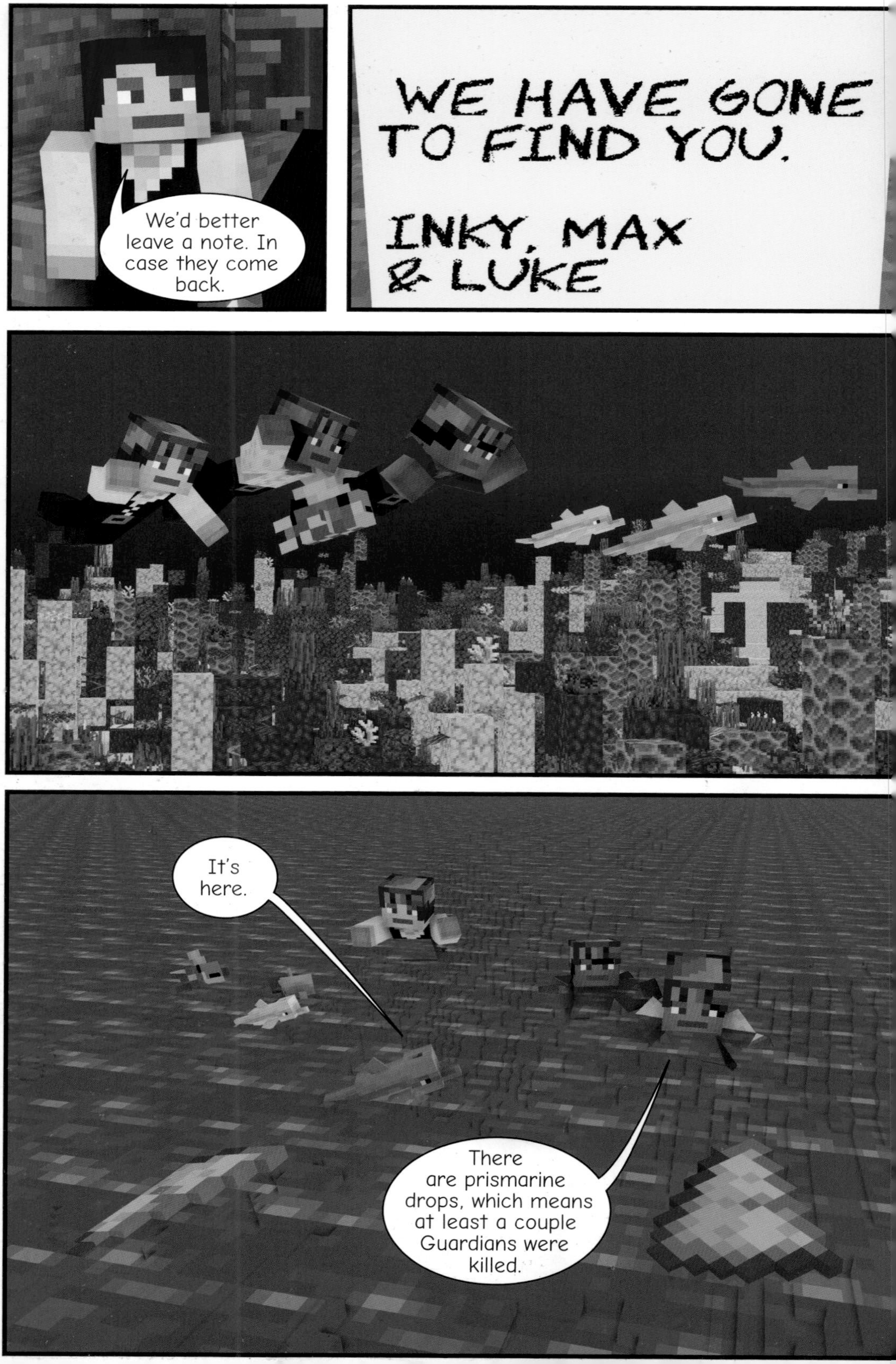
We'd better leave a note. In case they come back.
WE HAVE GONE TO FIND YOU.
INKY, MAX & LUKE
It's here.
There are prismarine drops, which means at least a couple Guardians were killed.

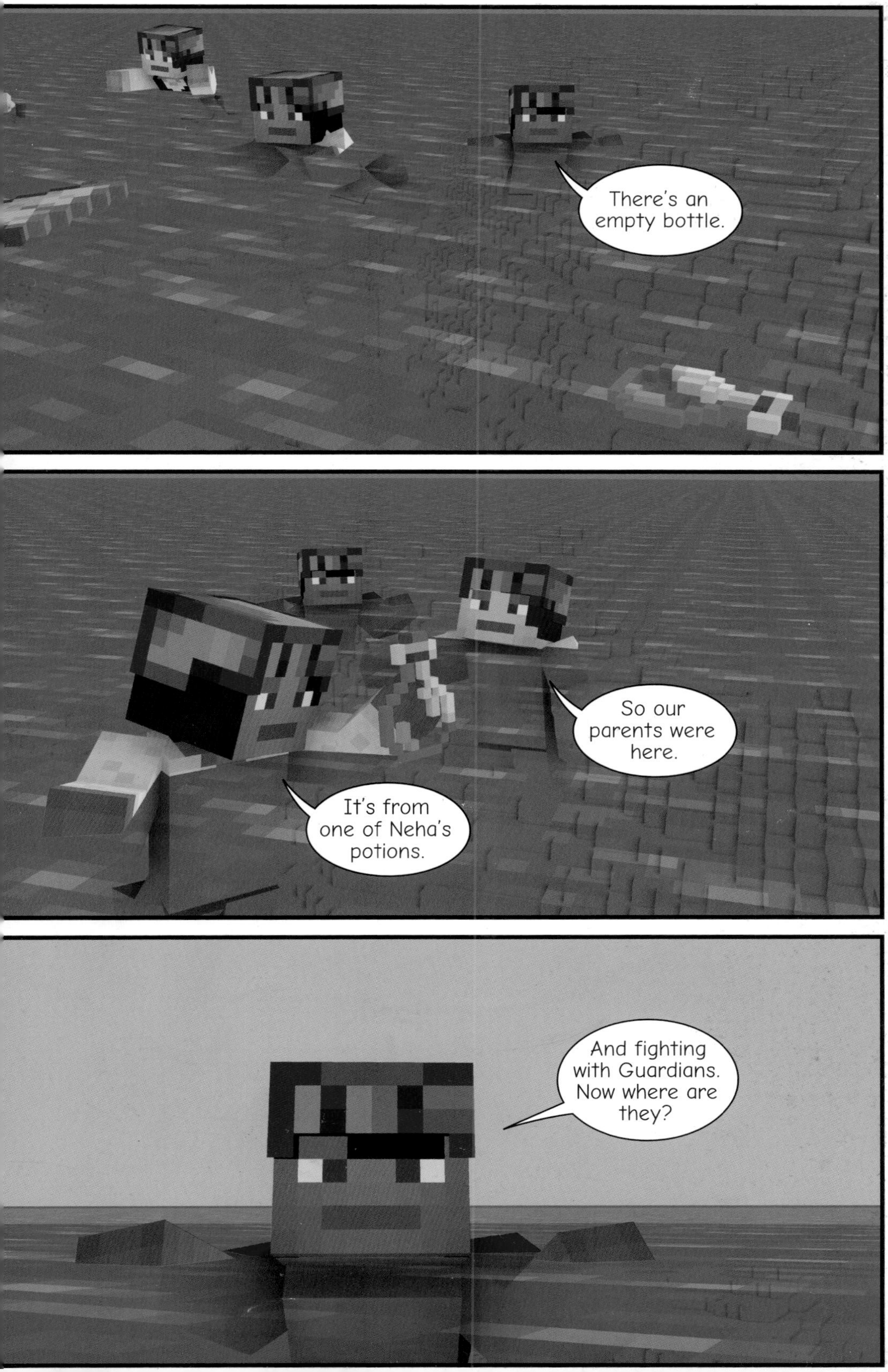

There's an empty bottle.
So our parents were here.
It's from one of Neha's potions.
And fighting with Guardians. Now where are they?

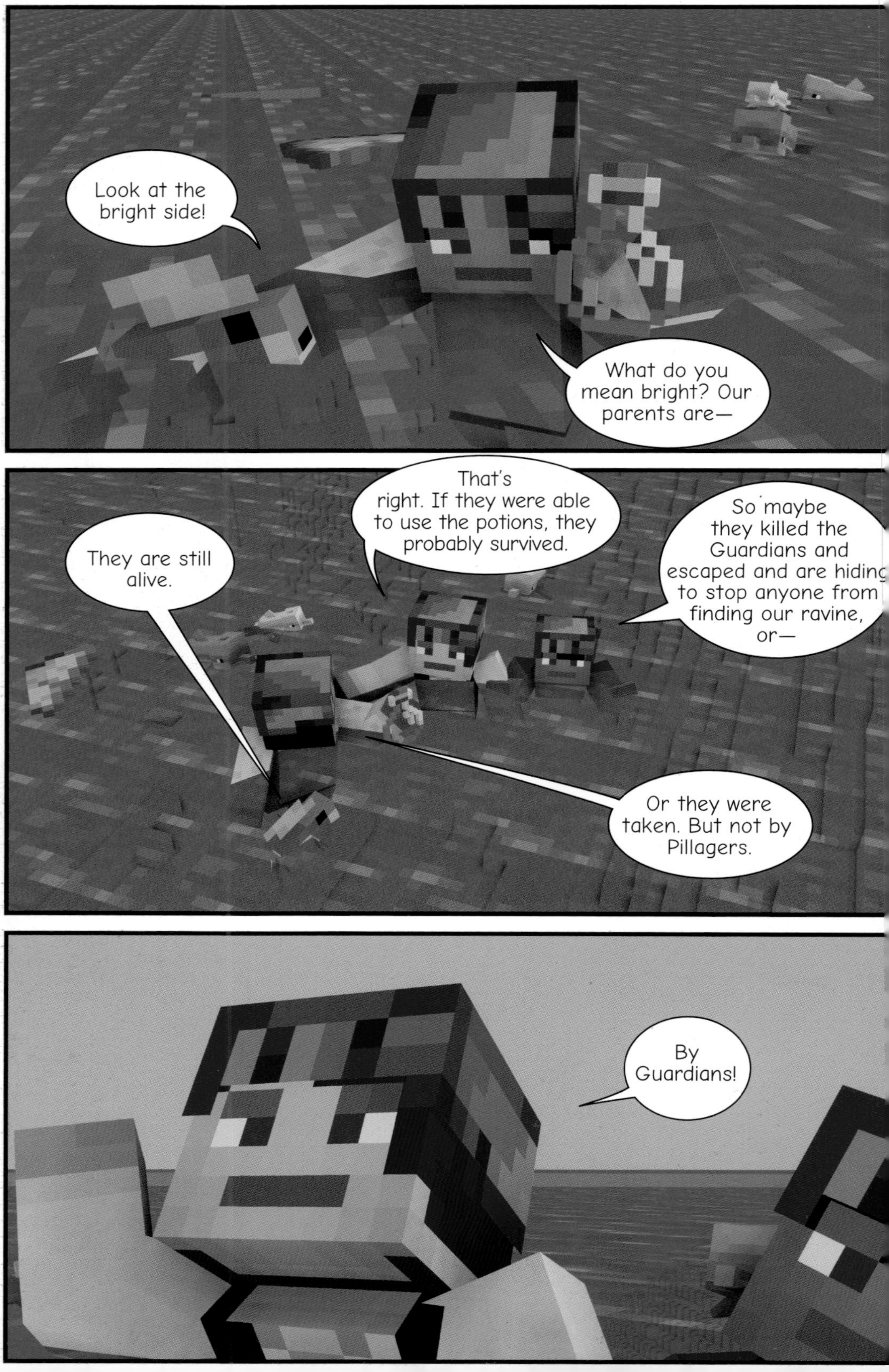
Look at the bright side!
What do you mean bright? Our parents are—
They are still alive.
That's right. If they were able to use the potions, they probably survived.
So maybe they killed the Guardians and escaped and are hiding to stop anyone from finding our ravine, or—
Or they were taken. But not by Pillagers.
By Guardians!

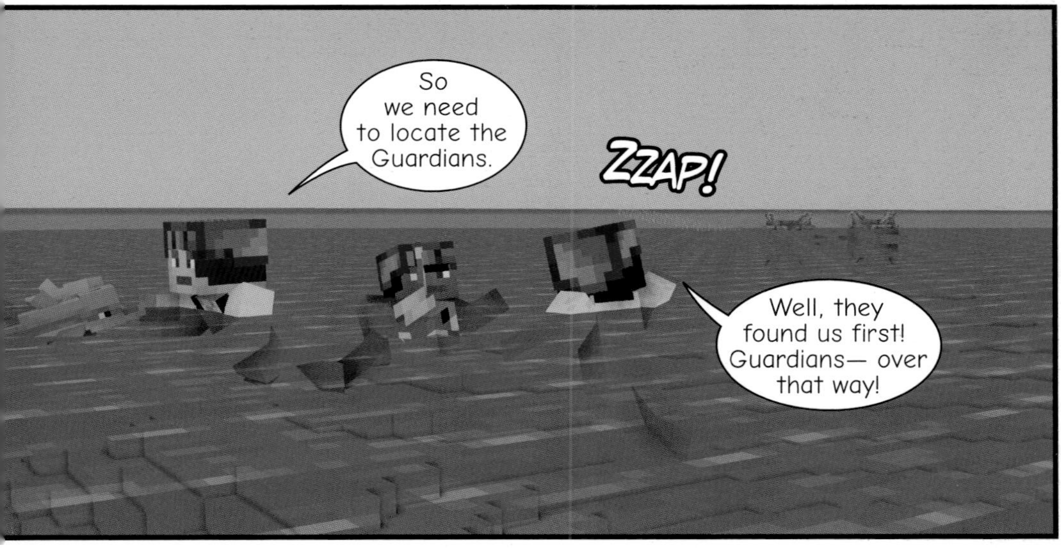
So we need to locate the Guardians.
ZZAP!
Well, they found us first! Guardians— over that way!

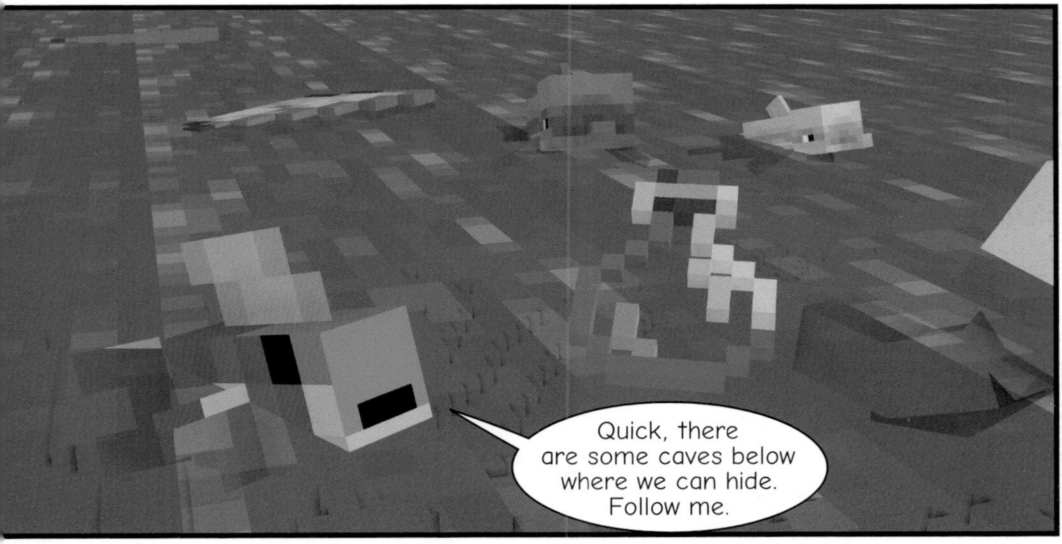
Quick, there are some caves below where we can hide. Follow me.

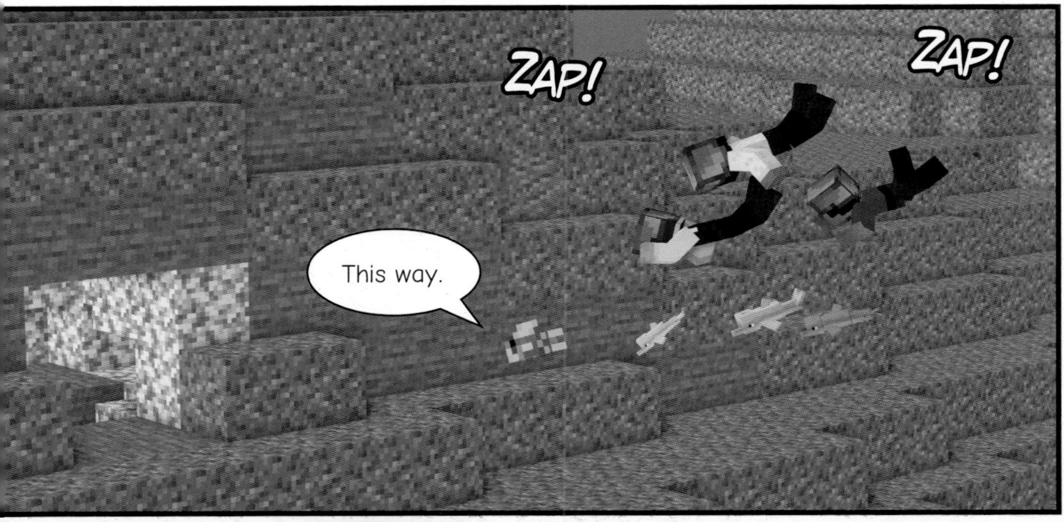
ZAP!
ZAP!
This way.

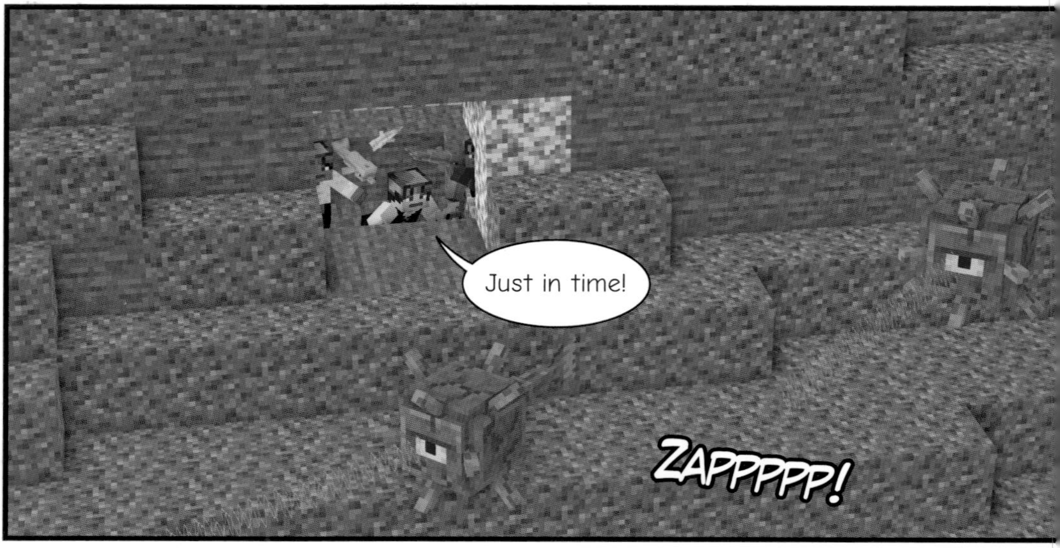
Just in time!
ZAPPPPPP!

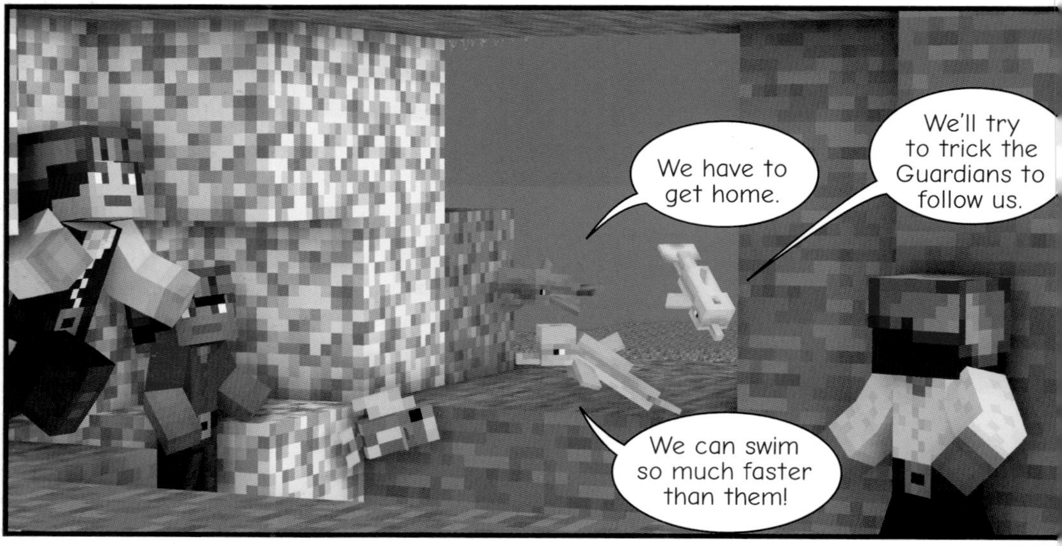
We have to get home.
We'll try to trick the Guardians to follow us.
We can swim so much faster than them!

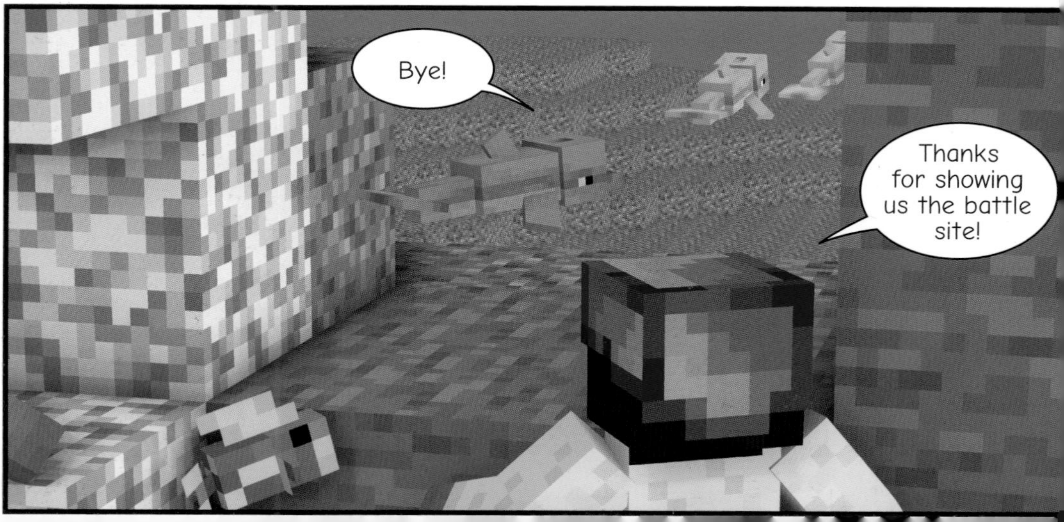
Bye!
Thanks for showing us the battle site!

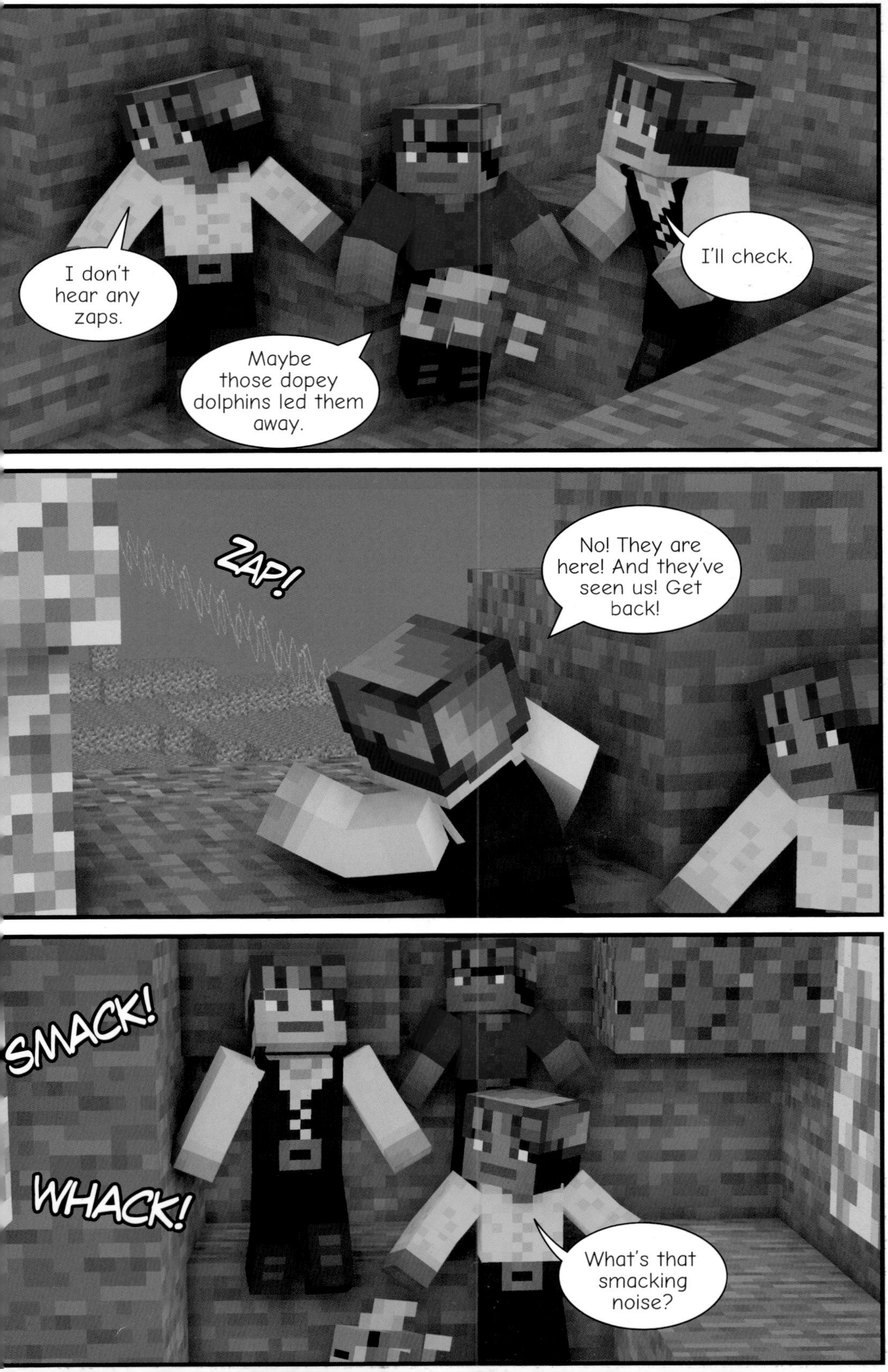
I don't hear any zaps.
Maybe those dopey dolphins led them away.
I'll check.
ZAP!
No! They are here! And they've seen us! Get back!
SMACK!
WHACK!
What's that smacking noise?

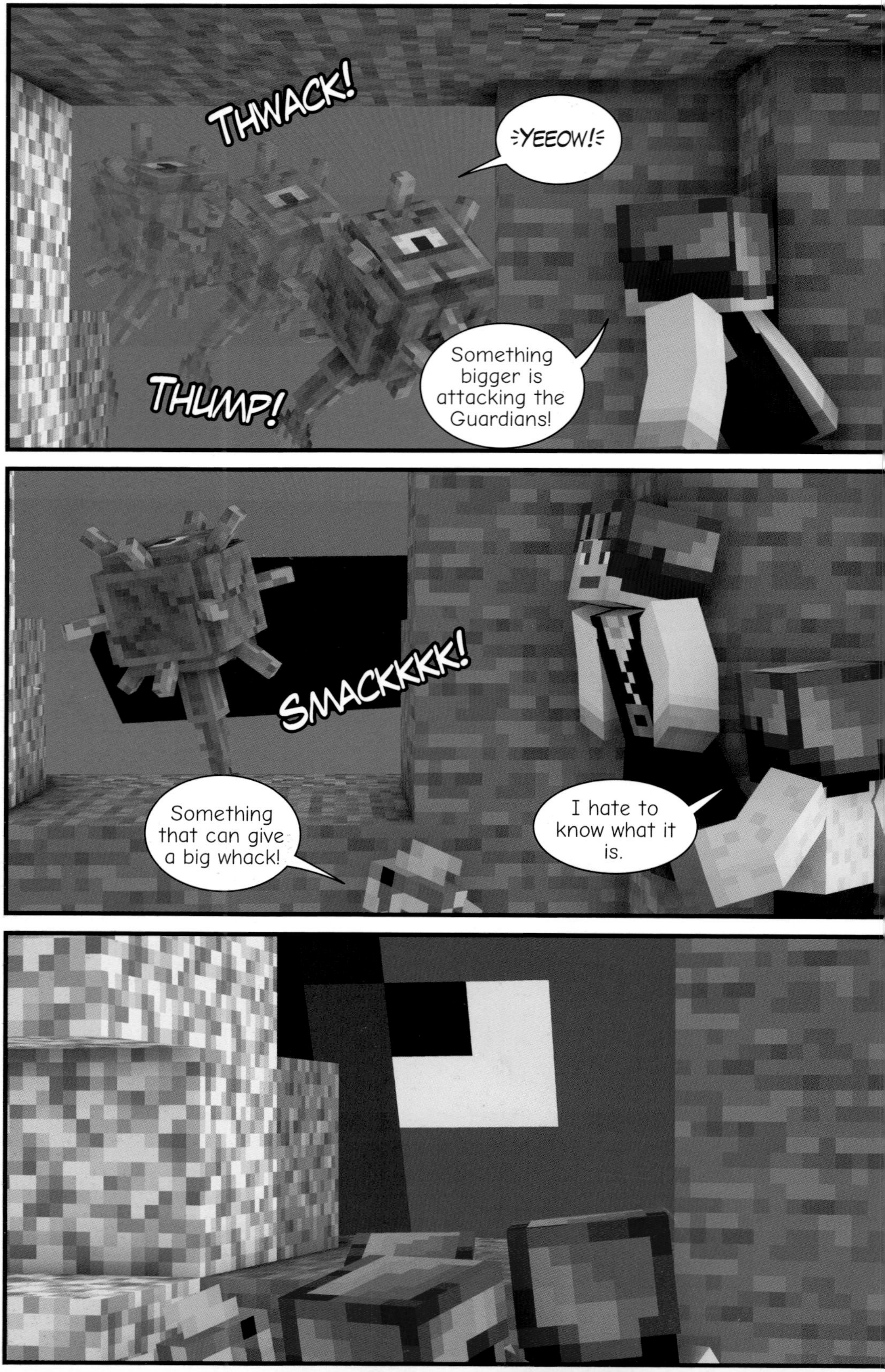
THWACK!
YEEOW!
THUMP!
Something bigger is attacking the Guardians!
SMACKKKK!
Something that can give a big whack!
I hate to know what it is.

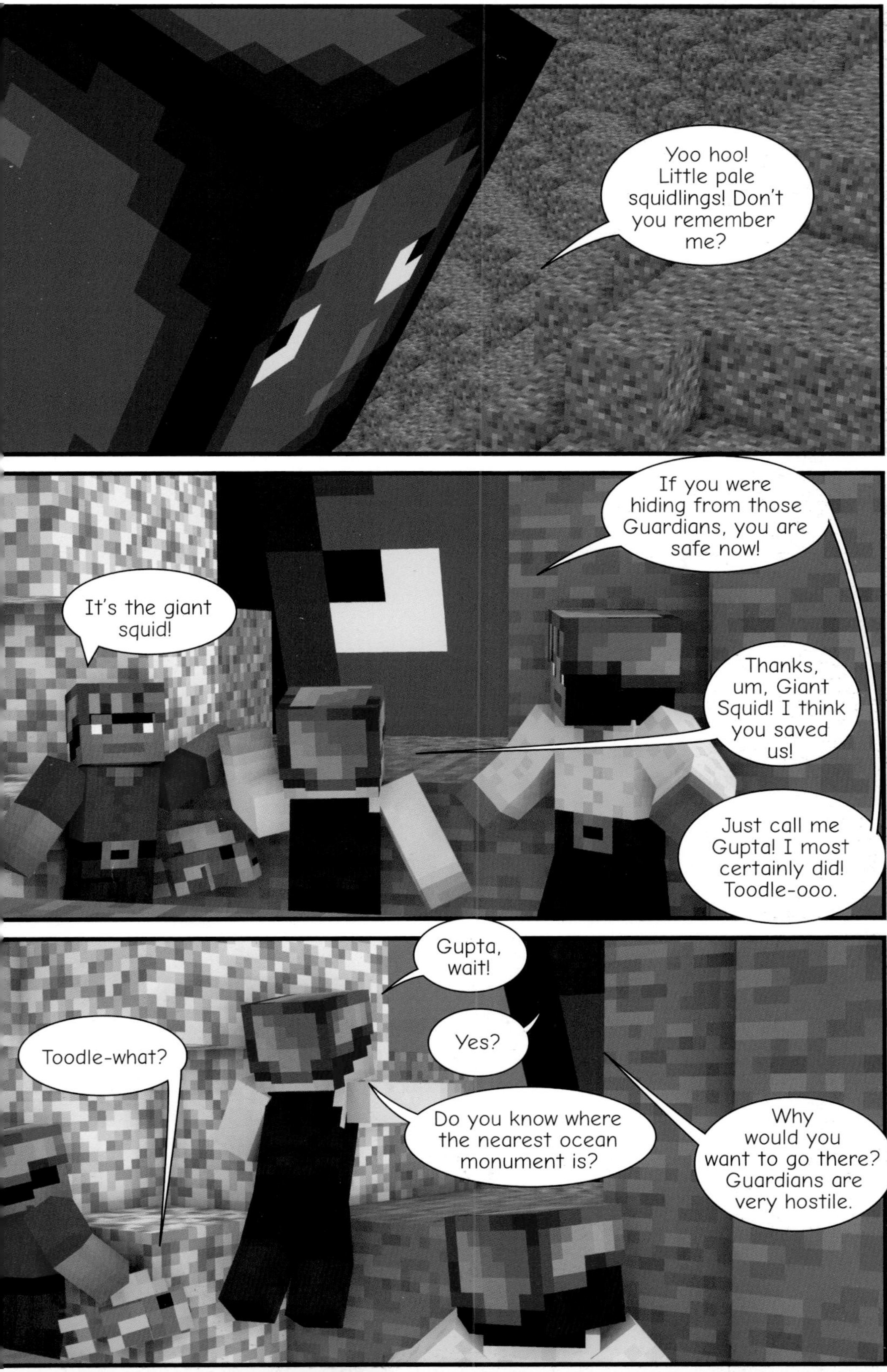
Yoo hoo! Little pale squidlings! Don't you remember me?
It's the giant squid!
If you were hiding from those Guardians, you are safe now!
Thanks, um, Giant Squid! I think you saved us!
Just call me Gupta! I most certainly did! Toodle-ooo.
Toodle-what?
Gupta, wait!
Yes?
Do you know where the nearest ocean monument is?
Why would you want to go there? Guardians are very hostile.

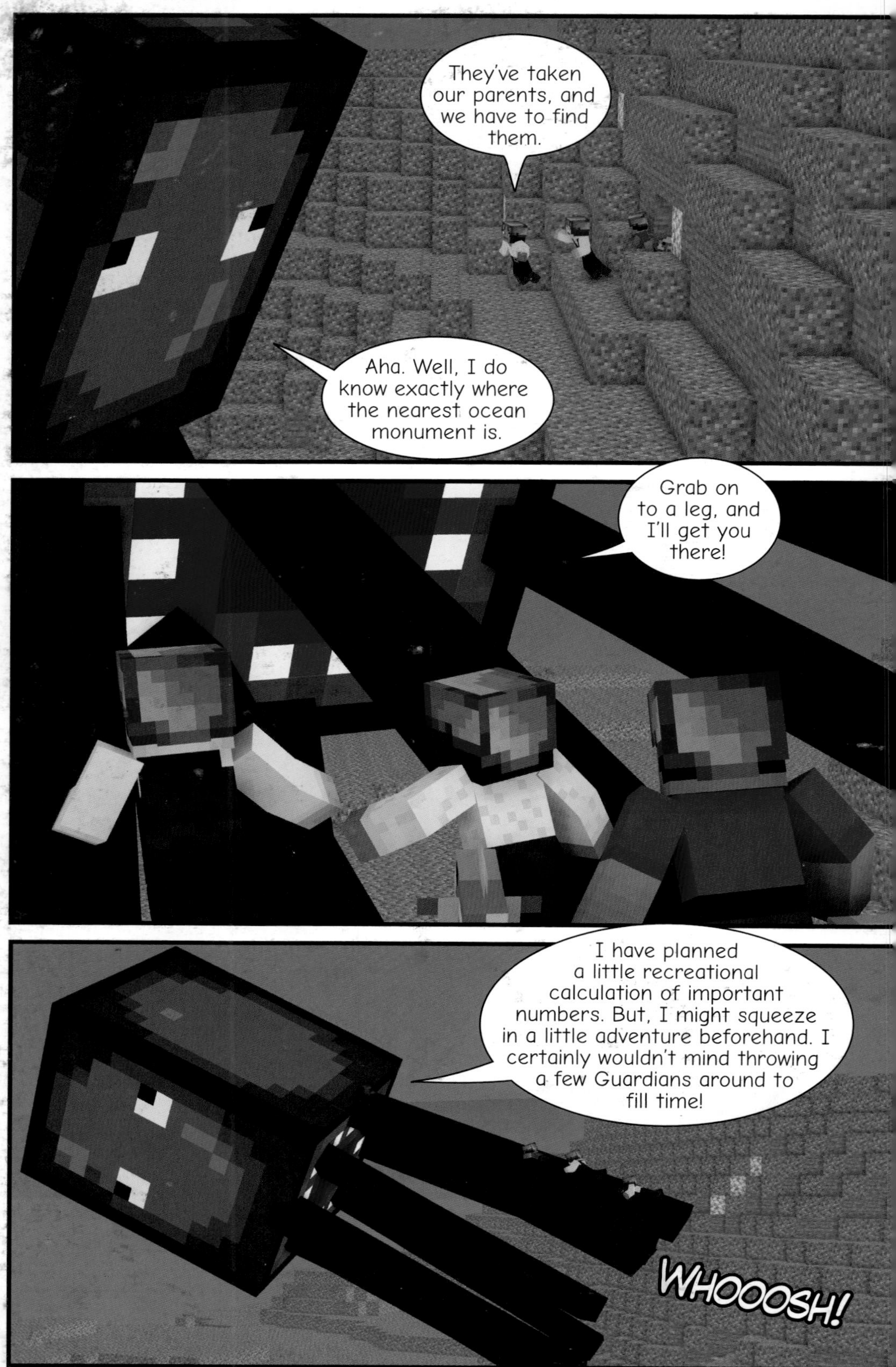
They've taken our parents, and we have to find them.
Aha. Well, I do know exactly where the nearest ocean monument is.
Grab on to a leg, and I'll get you there!
I have planned a little recreational calculation of important numbers. But, I might squeeze in a little adventure beforehand. I certainly wouldn't mind throwing a few Guardians around to fill time!
WHOOOSH!

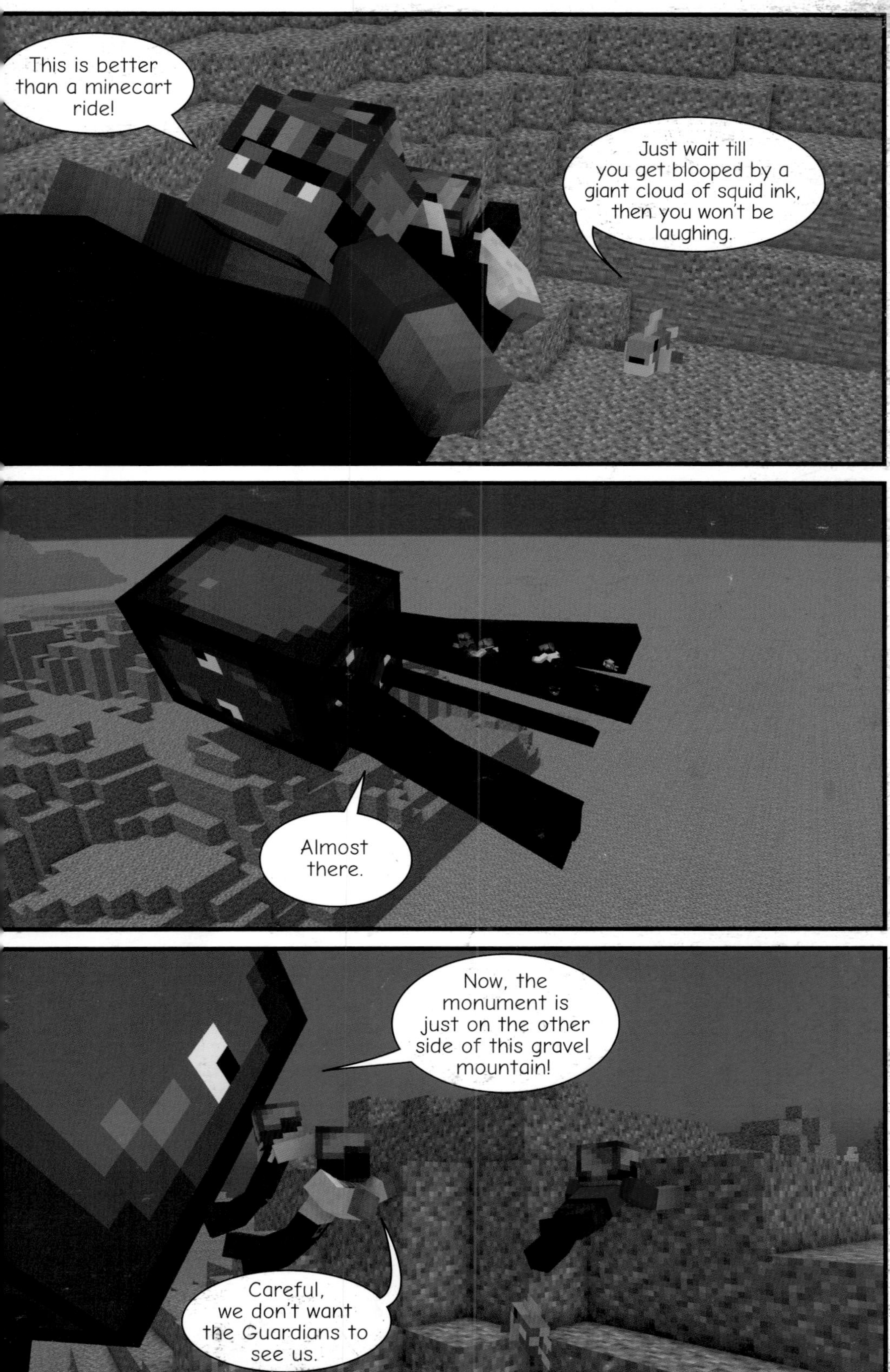
This is better than a minecart ride!
Just wait till you get blooped by a giant cloud of squid ink, then you won't be laughing.
Almost there.
Now, the monument is just on the other side of this gravel mountain!
Careful, we don't want the Guardians to see us.

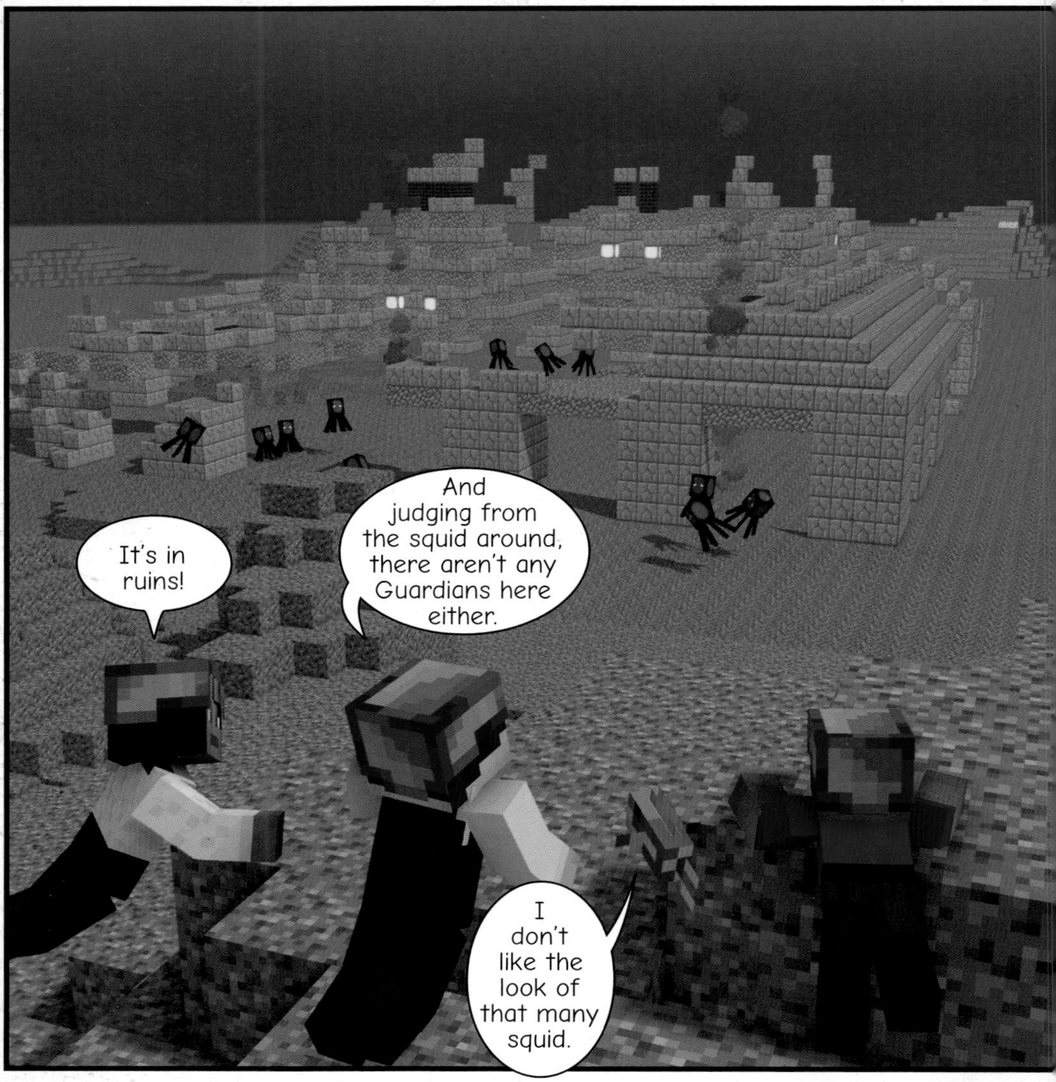

It's in ruins!
And judging from the squid around, there aren't any Guardians here either.
I don't like the look of that many squid.

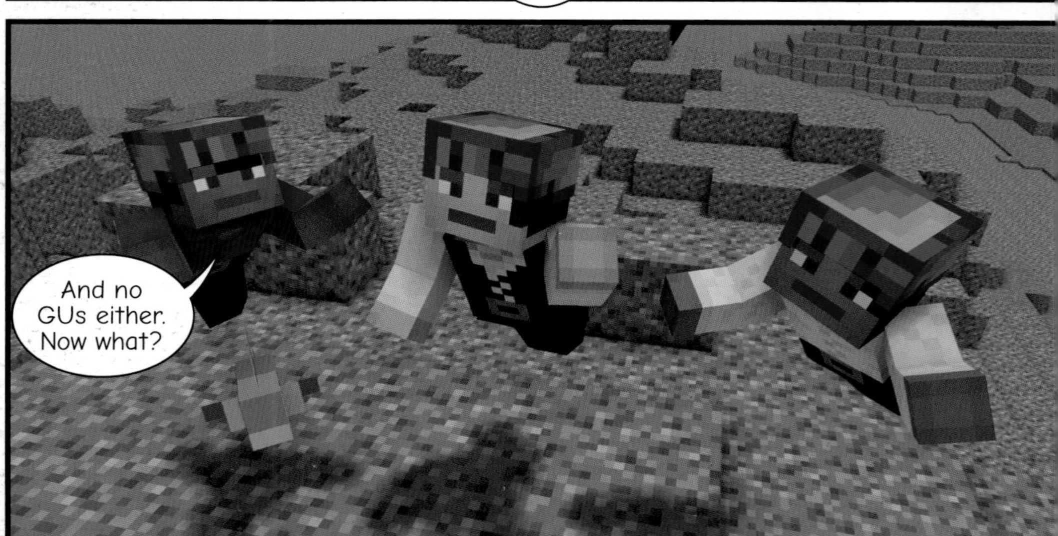

And no GUs either. Now what?

Chapter 5
Squid Pro Quo

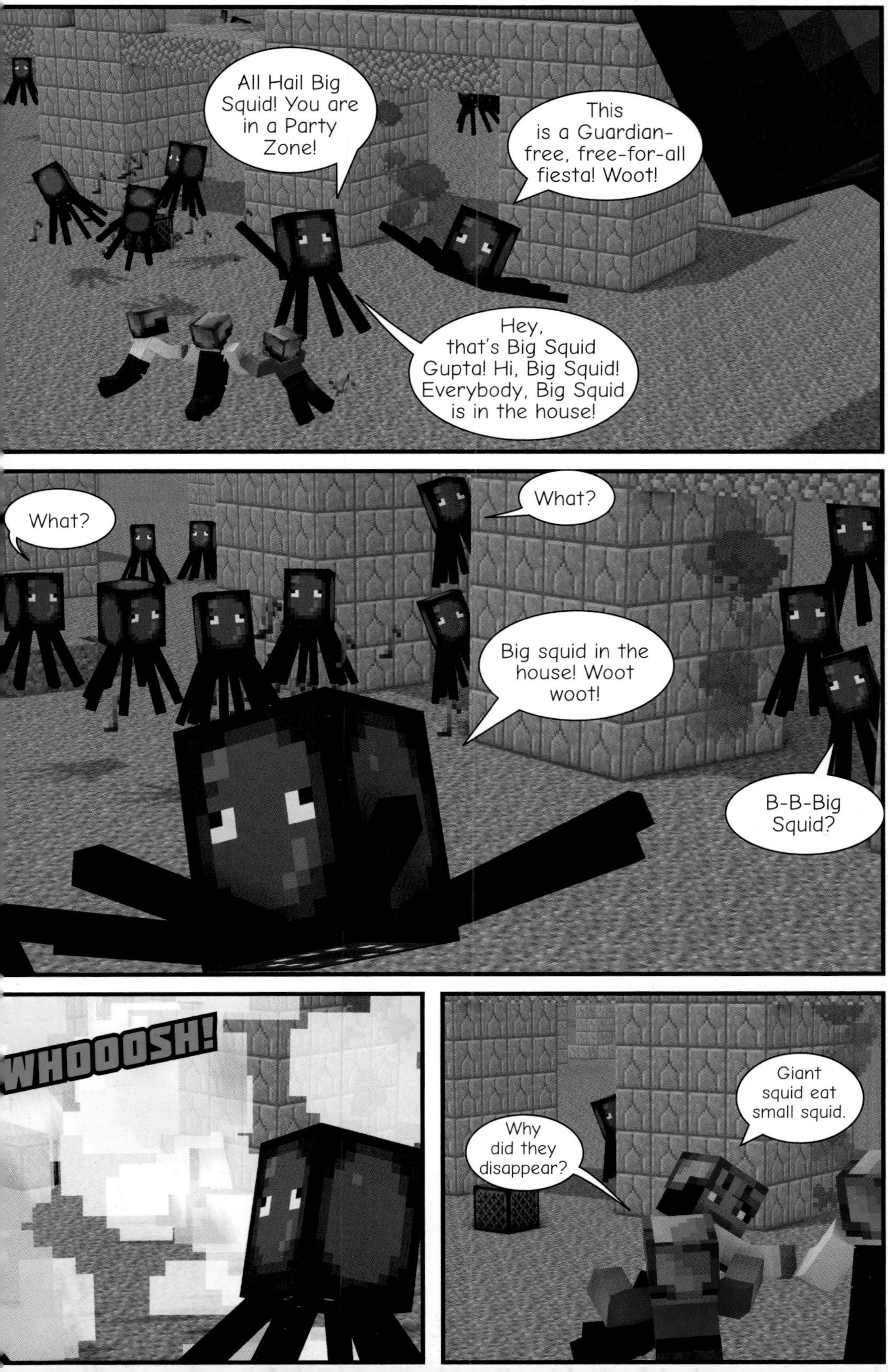

All Hail Big Squid! You are in a Party Zone!
This is a Guardian-free, free-for-all fiesta! Woot!
Hey, that's Big Squid Gupta! Hi, Big Squid! Everybody, Big Squid is in the house!
What?
What?
Big squid in the house! Woot woot!
B-B-Big Squid?
WHOOOSH!
Giant squid eat small squid.
Why did they disappear?

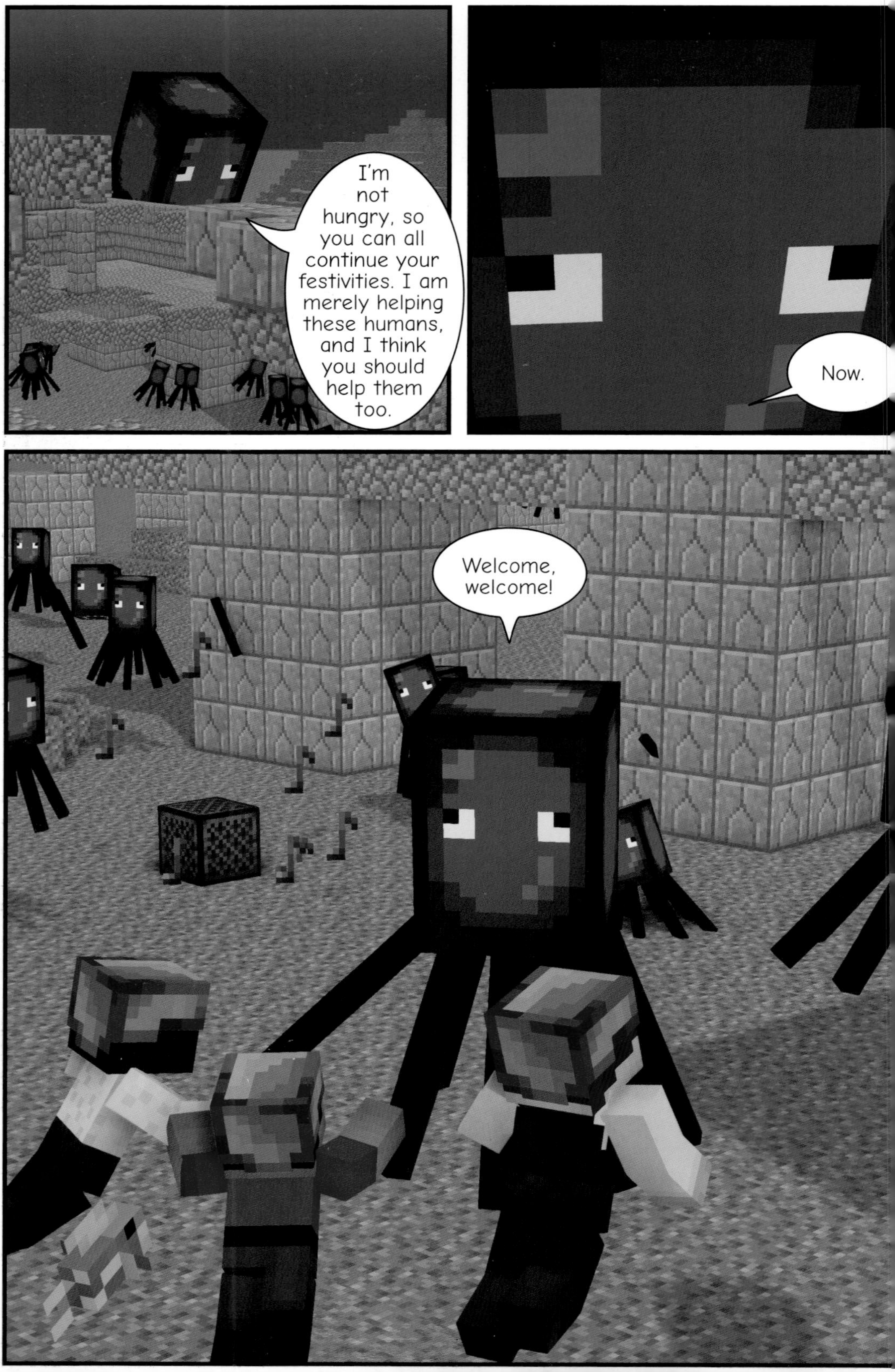
I'm not hungry, so you can all continue your festivities. I am merely helping these humans, and I think you should help them too.
Now.
Welcome, welcome!

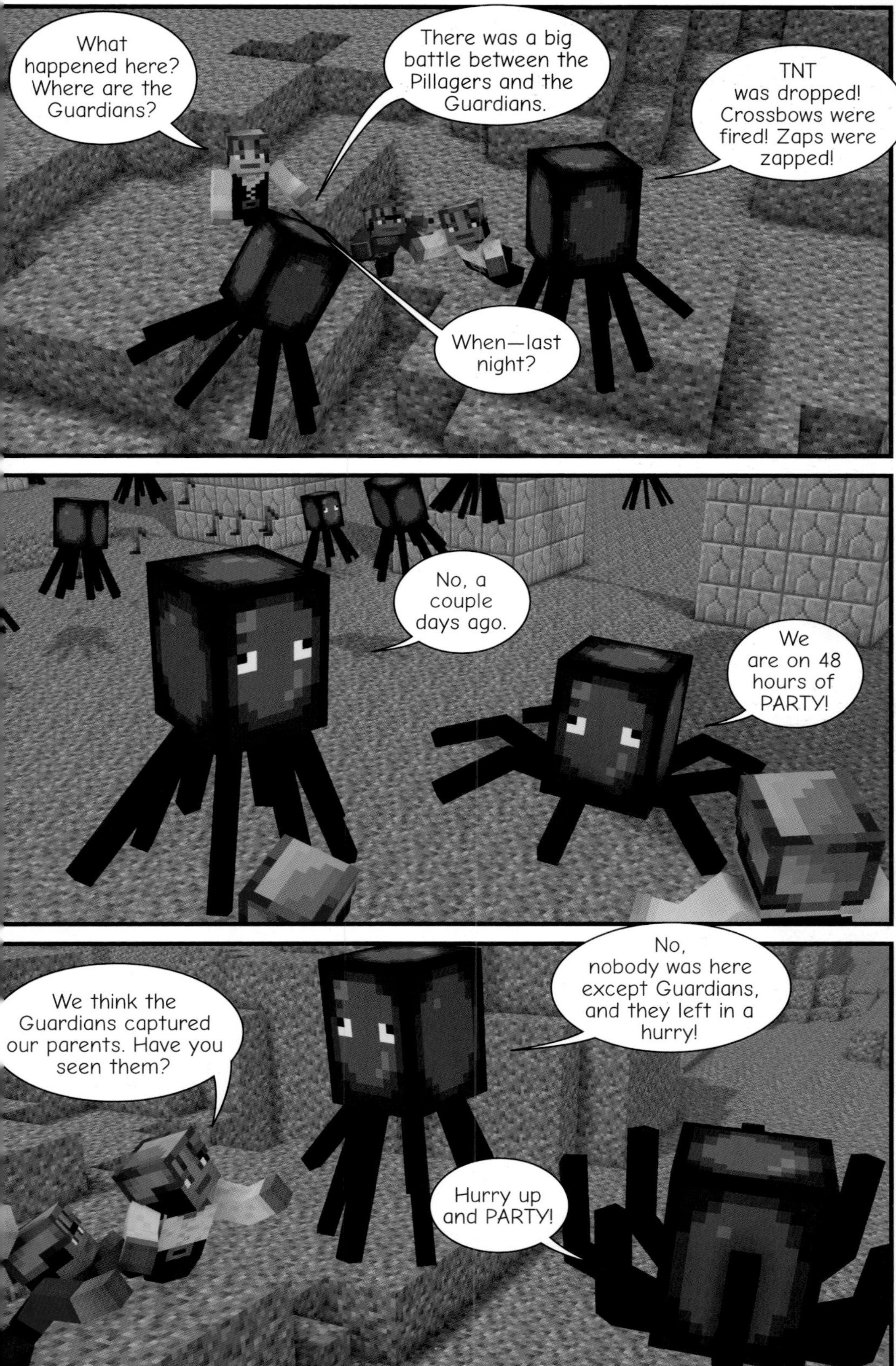

What happened here? Where are the Guardians?
There was a big battle between the Pillagers and the Guardians.
TNT was dropped! Crossbows were fired! Zaps were zapped!
When—last night?
No, a couple days ago.
We are on 48 hours of PARTY!
We think the Guardians captured our parents. Have you seen them?
No, nobody was here except Guardians, and they left in a hurry!
Hurry up and PARTY!

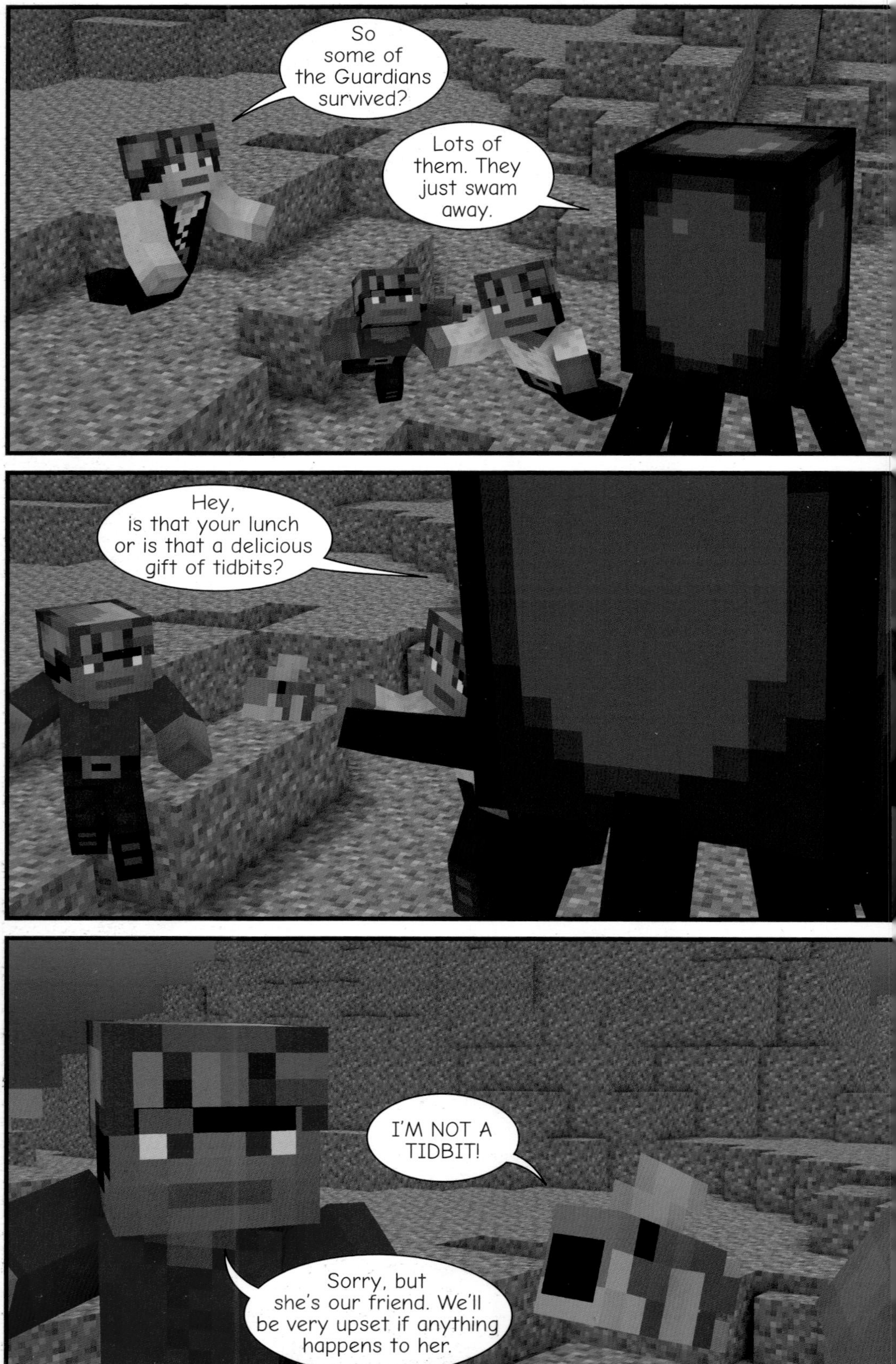

So some of the Guardians survived?
Lots of them. They just swam away.
Hey, is that your lunch or is that a delicious gift of tidbits?
I'M NOT A TIDBIT!
Sorry, but she's our friend. We'll be very upset if anything happens to her.

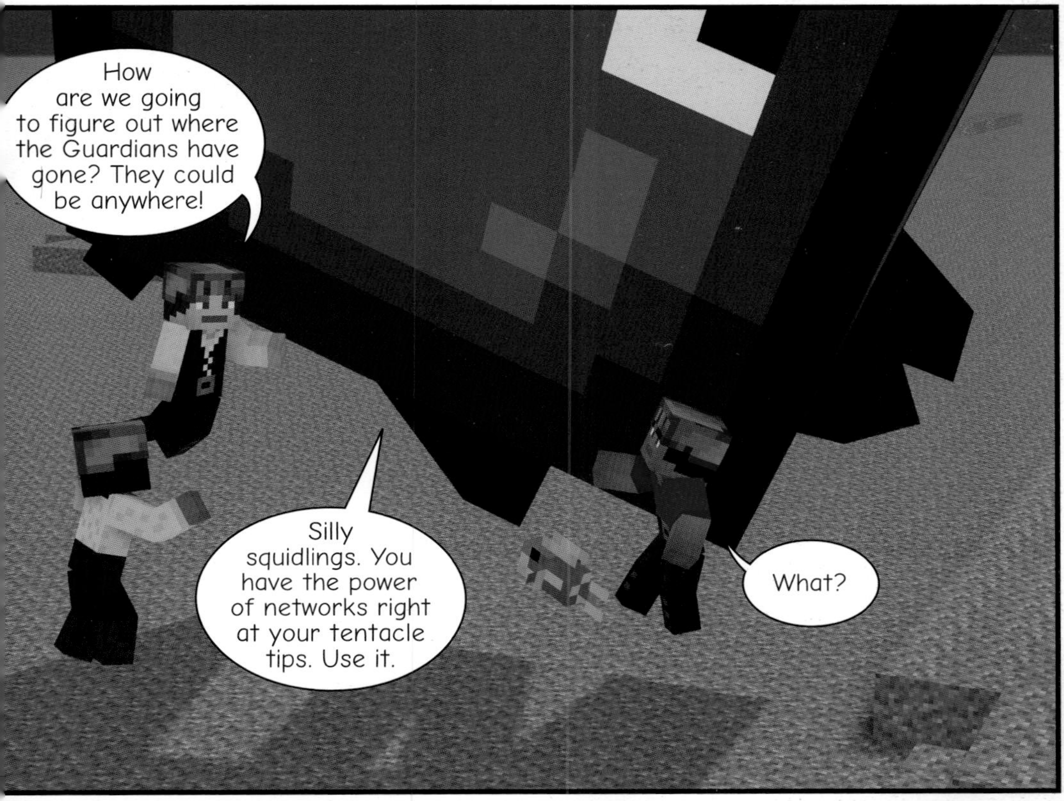
How are we going to figure out where the Guardians have gone? They could be anywhere!
Silly squidlings. You have the power of networks right at your tentacle tips. Use it.
What?

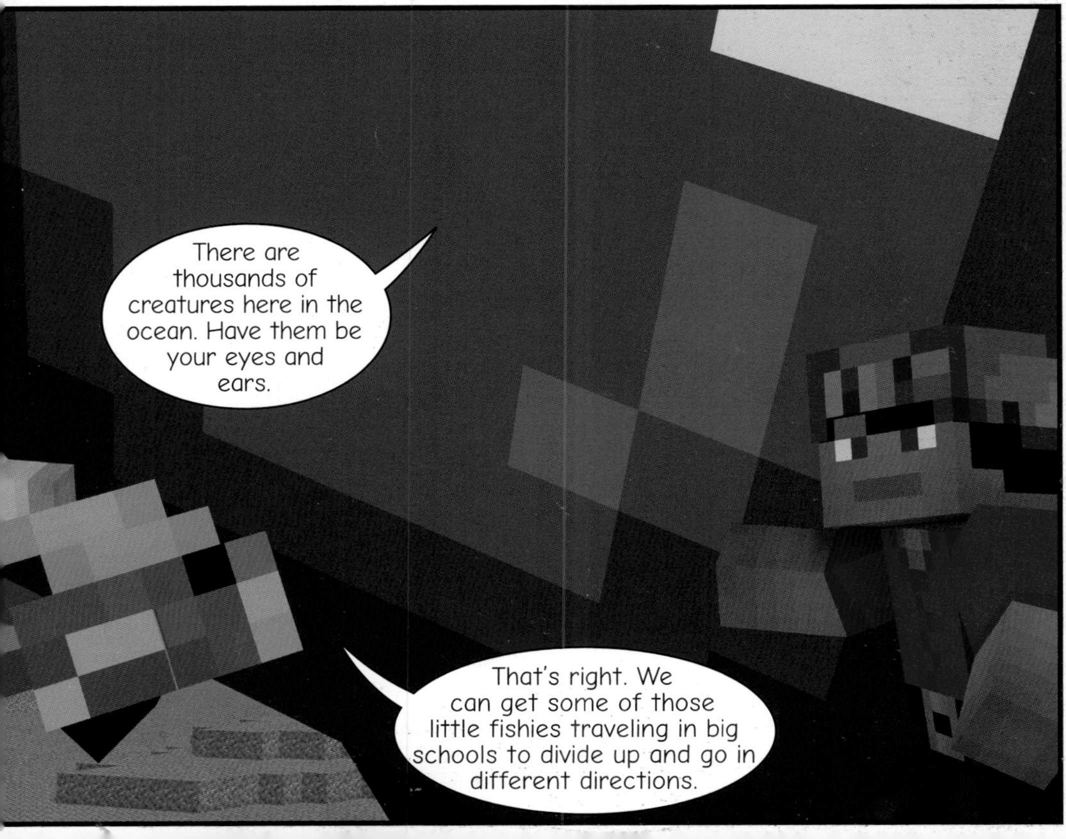
There are thousands of creatures here in the ocean. Have them be your eyes and ears.
That's right. We can get some of those little fishies traveling in big schools to divide up and go in different directions.

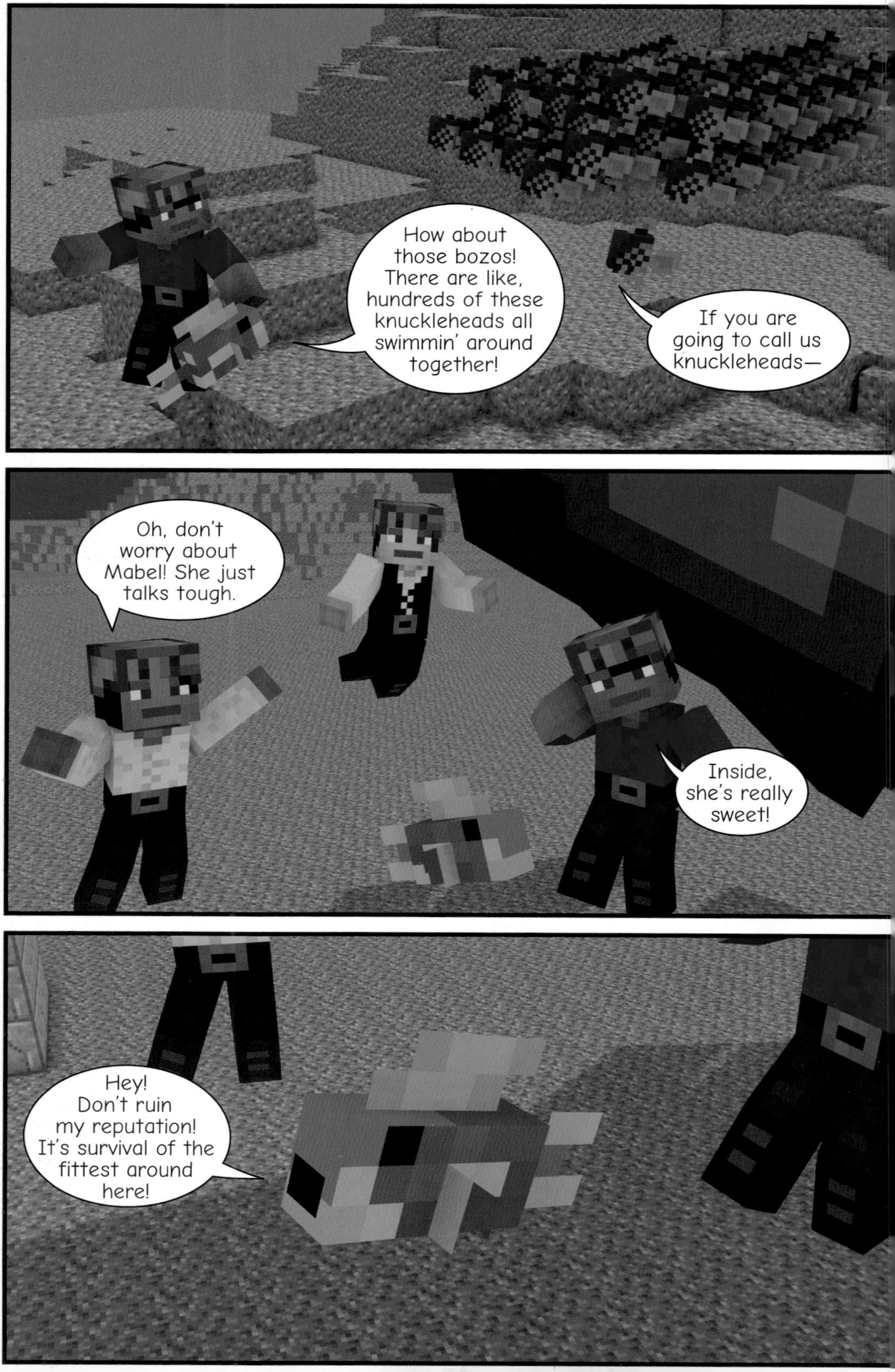
How about those bozos! There are like, hundreds of these knuckleheads all swimmin' around together!
If you are going to call us knuckleheads—
Oh, don't worry about Mabel! She just talks tough.
Inside, she's really sweet!
Hey! Don't ruin my reputation! It's survival of the fittest around here!

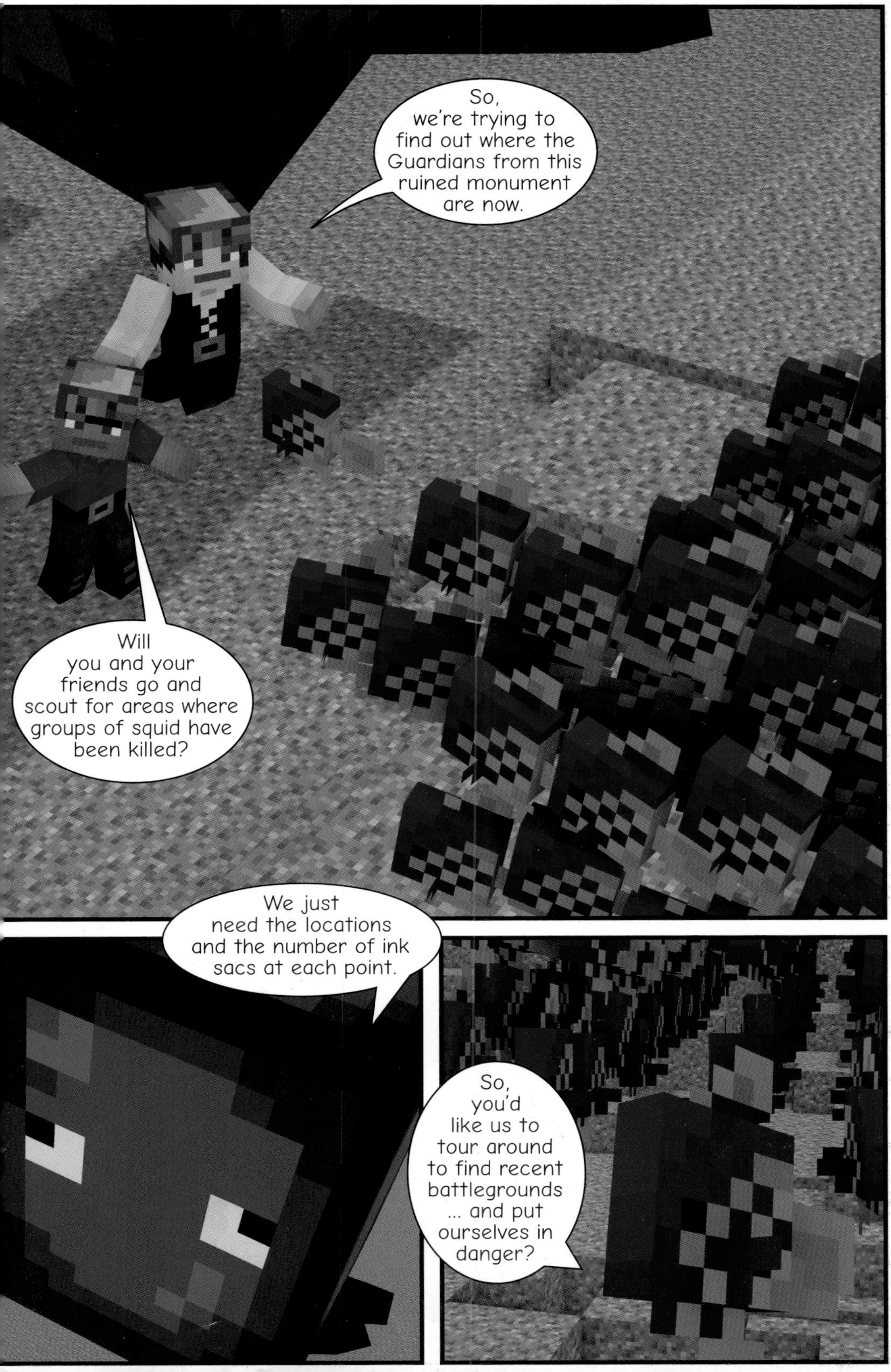
So, we're trying to find out where the Guardians from this ruined monument are now.
Will you and your friends go and scout for areas where groups of squid have been killed?
We just need the locations and the number of ink sacs at each point.
So, you'd like us to tour around to find recent battlegrounds ... and put ourselves in danger?

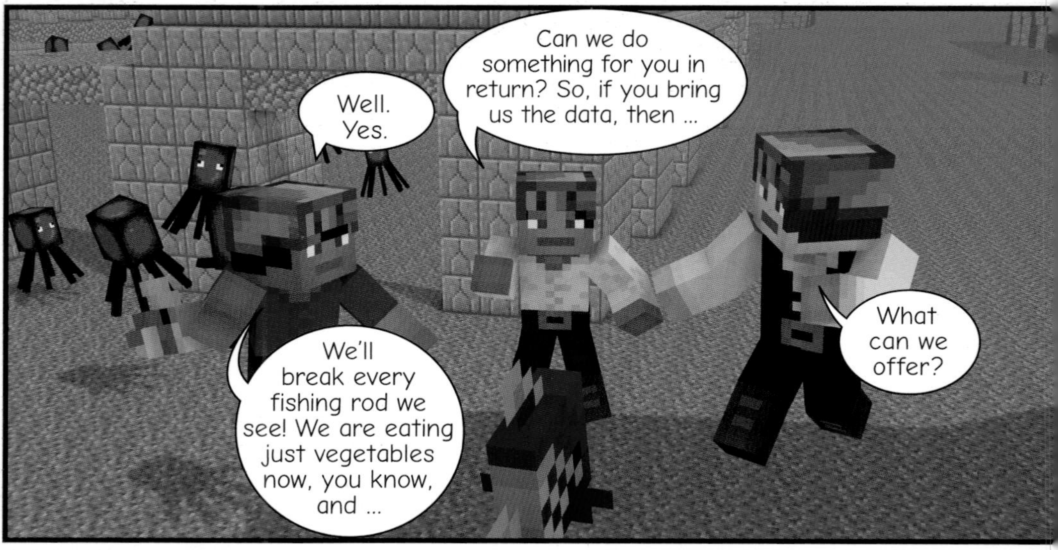
Well. Yes.
Can we do something for you in return? So, if you bring us the data, then ...
What can we offer?
We'll break every fishing rod we see! We are eating just vegetables now, you know, and ...

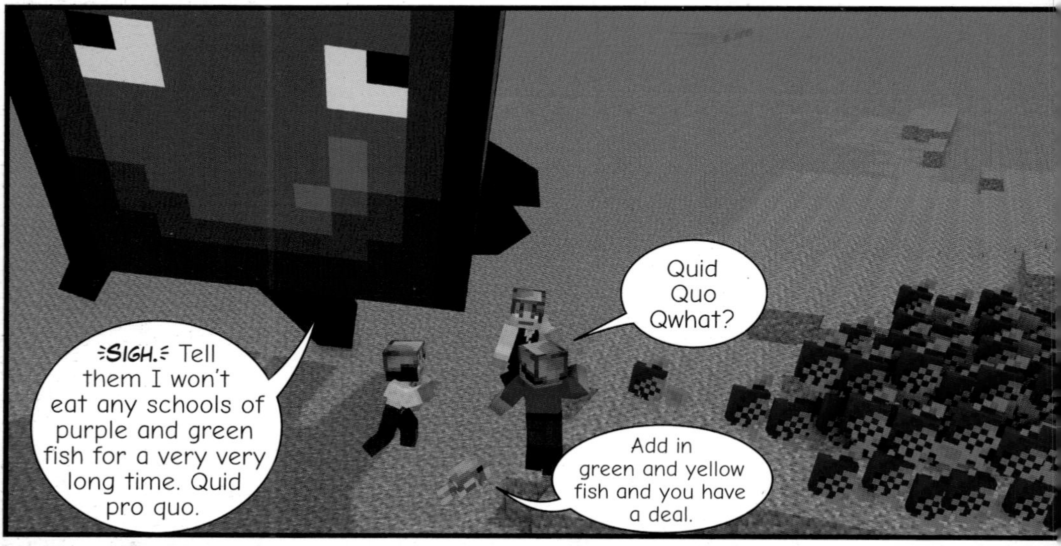
Quid Quo Qwhat?
SIGH. Tell them I won't eat any schools of purple and green fish for a very very long time. Quid pro quo.
Add in green and yellow fish and you have a deal.

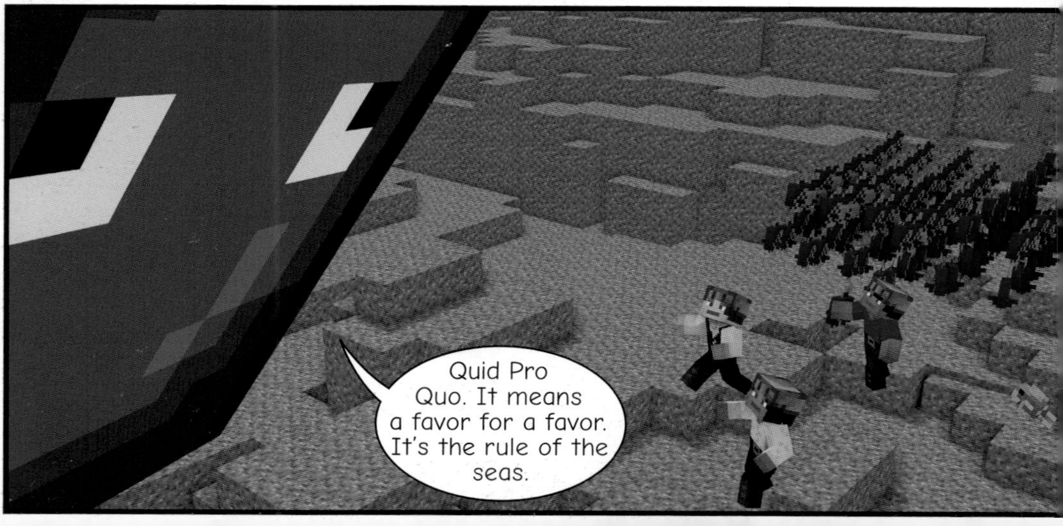
Quid Pro Quo. It means a favor for a favor. It's the rule of the seas.

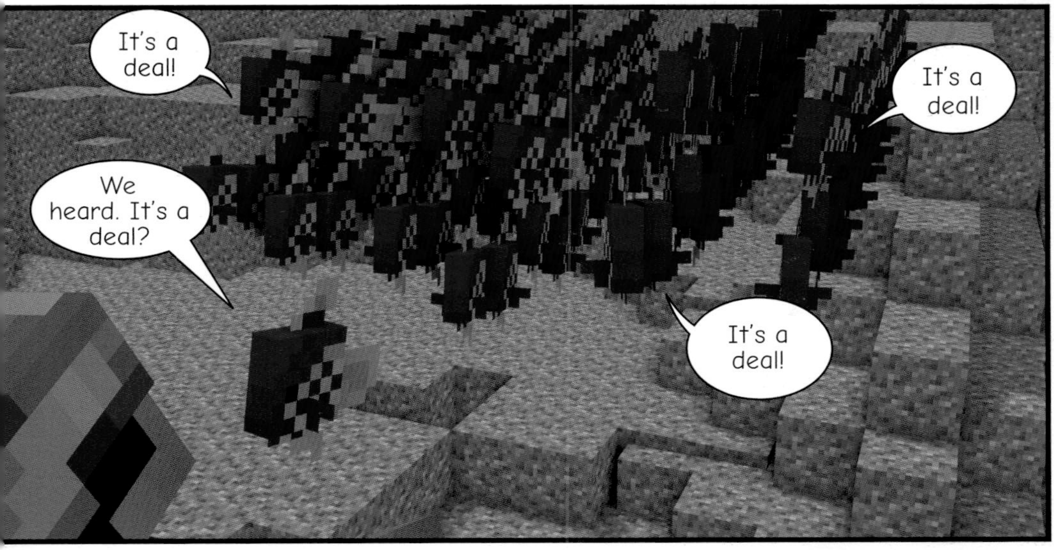
It's a deal!
We heard. It's a deal?
It's a deal!
It's a deal!
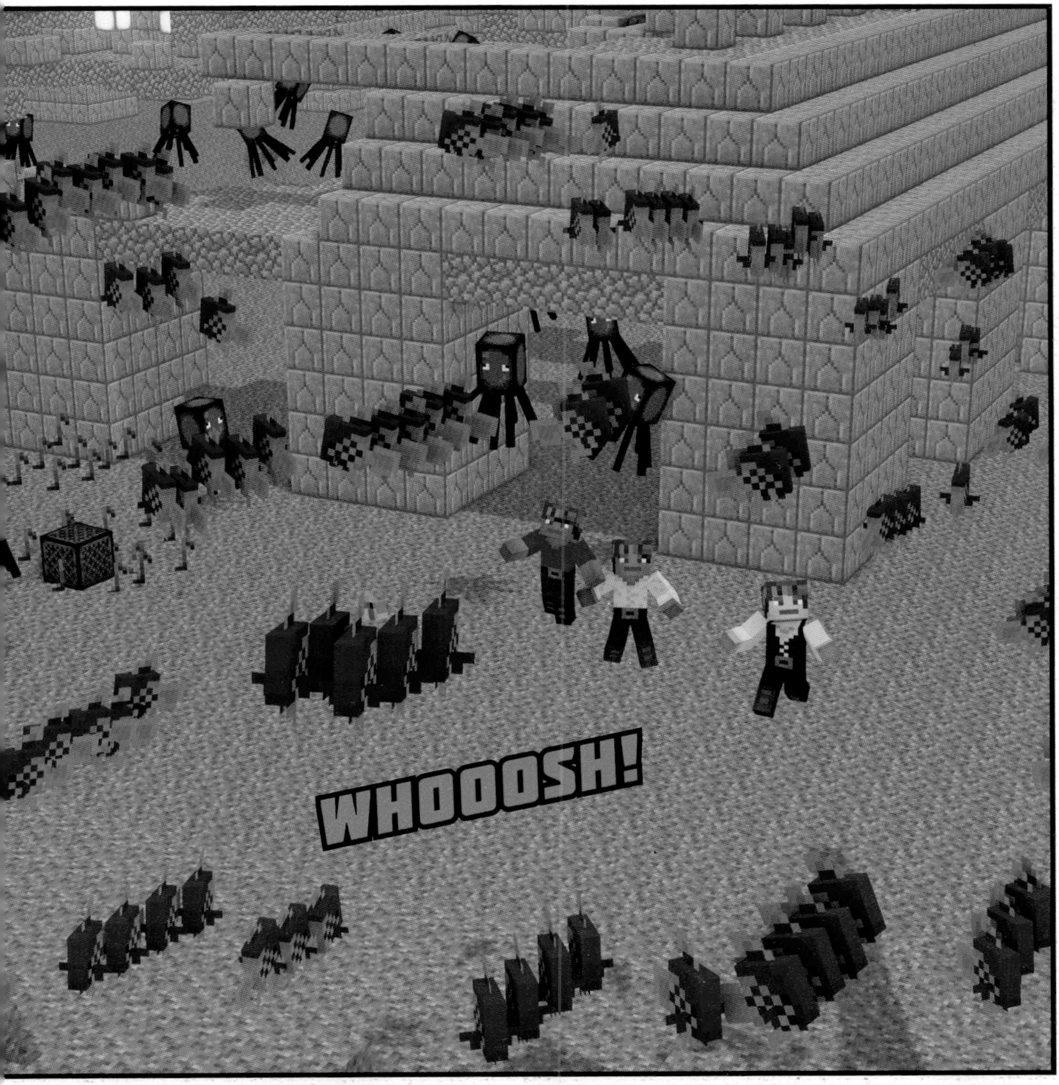
WHOOOOSH!

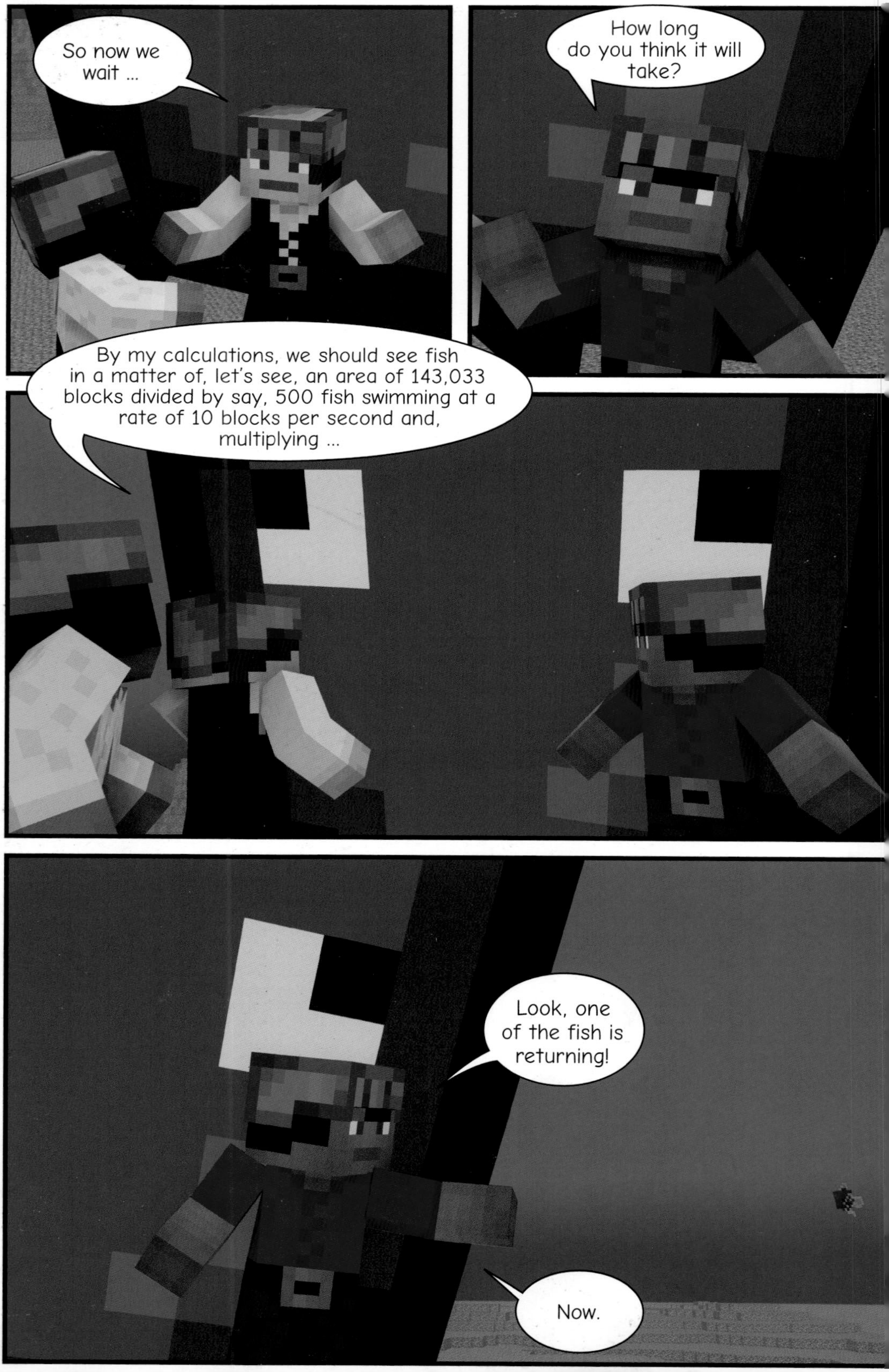

So now we wait ...
How long do you think it will take?
By my calculations, we should see fish in a matter of, let's see, an area of 143,033 blocks divided by say, 500 fish swimming at a rate of 10 blocks per second and, multiplying ...
Look, one of the fish is returning!
Now.

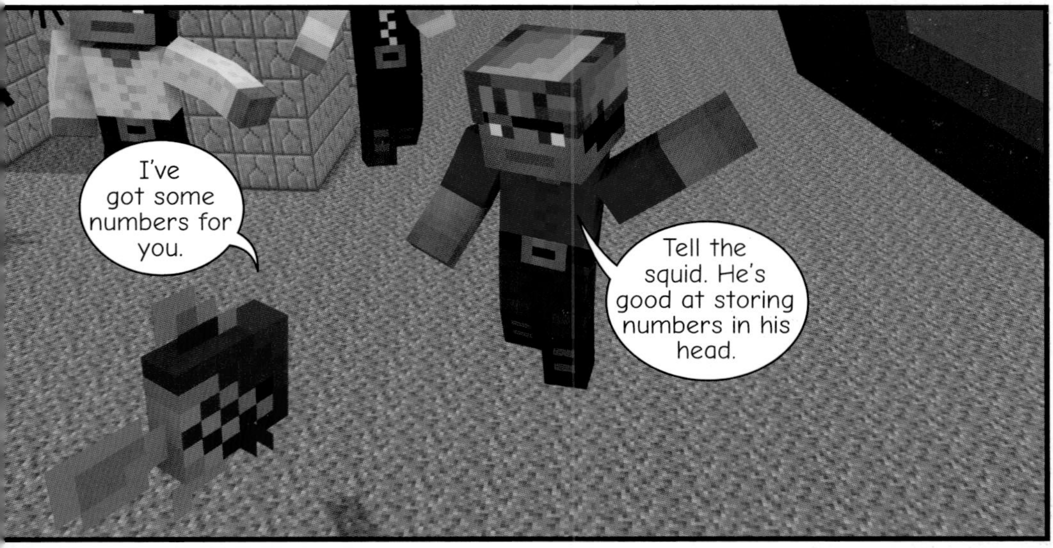
I've got some numbers for you.
Tell the squid. He's good at storing numbers in his head.

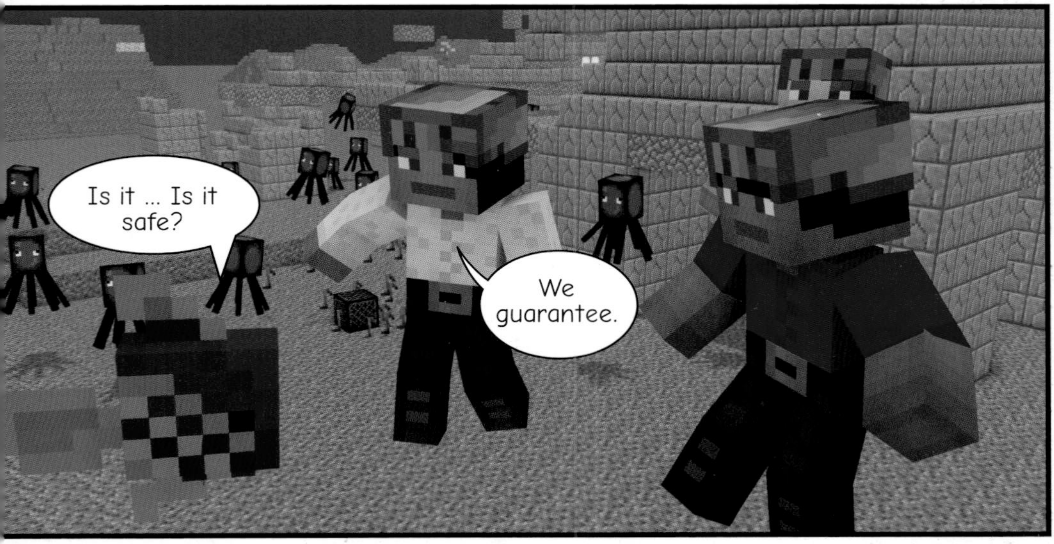
Is it ... Is it safe?
We guarantee.

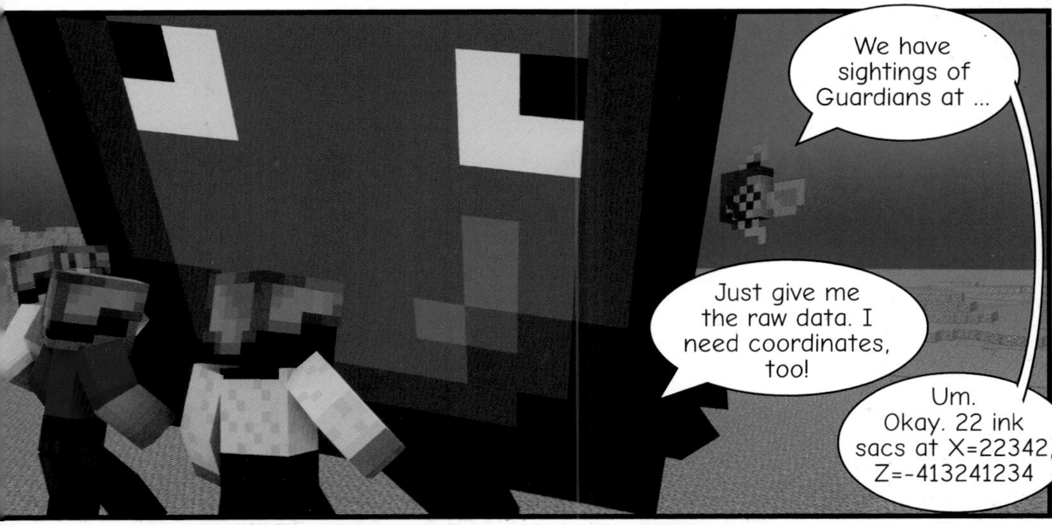
We have sightings of Guardians at ...
Just give me the raw data. I need coordinates, too!
Um. Okay. 22 ink sacs at X=22342, Z=-413241234

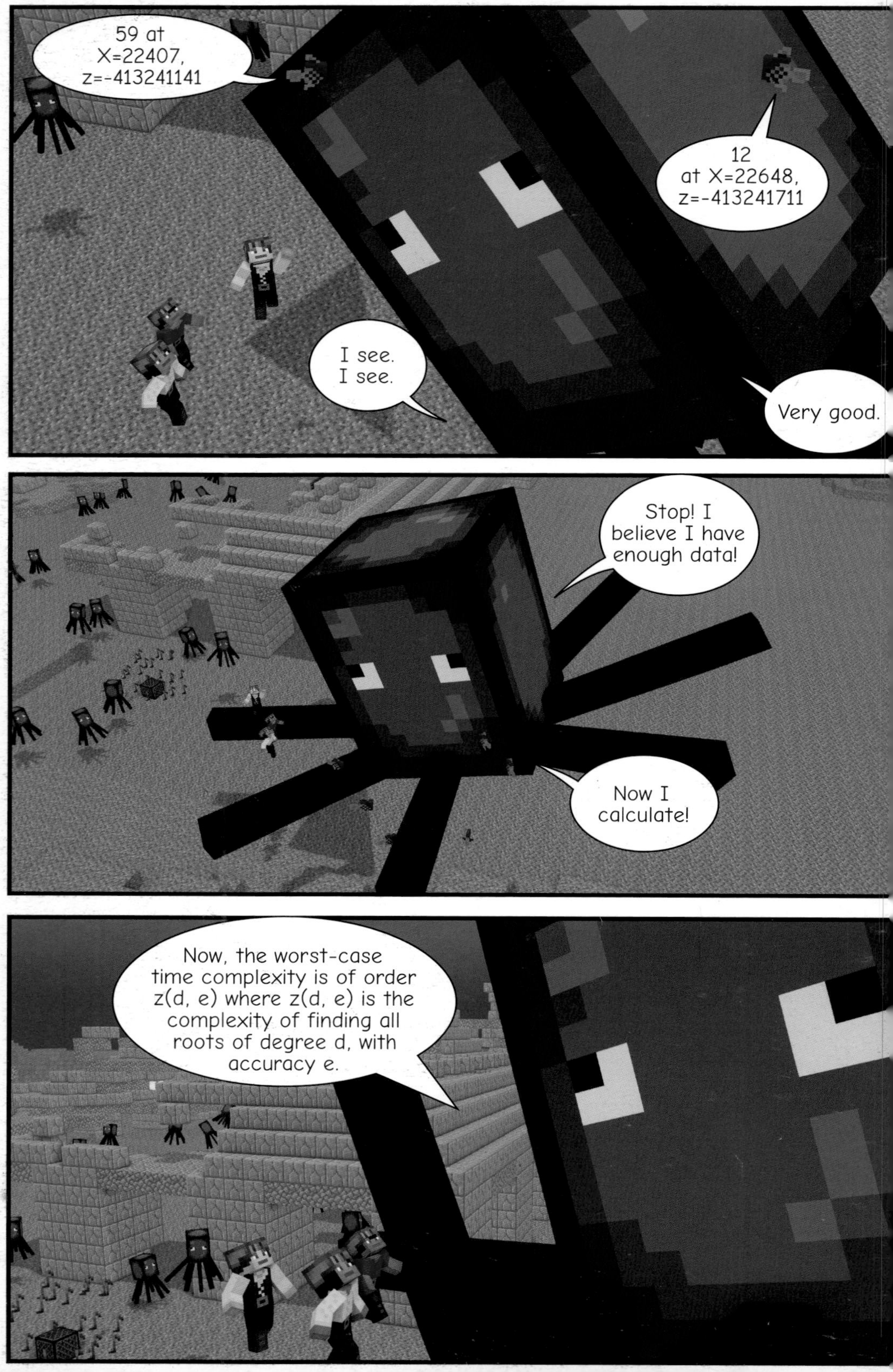
59 at X=22407, z=-413241141
12 at X=22648, z=-413241711
I see. I see.
Very good.
Stop! I believe I have enough data!
Now I calculate!
Now, the worst-case time complexity is of order z(d, e) where z(d, e) is the complexity of finding all roots of degree d, with accuracy e.

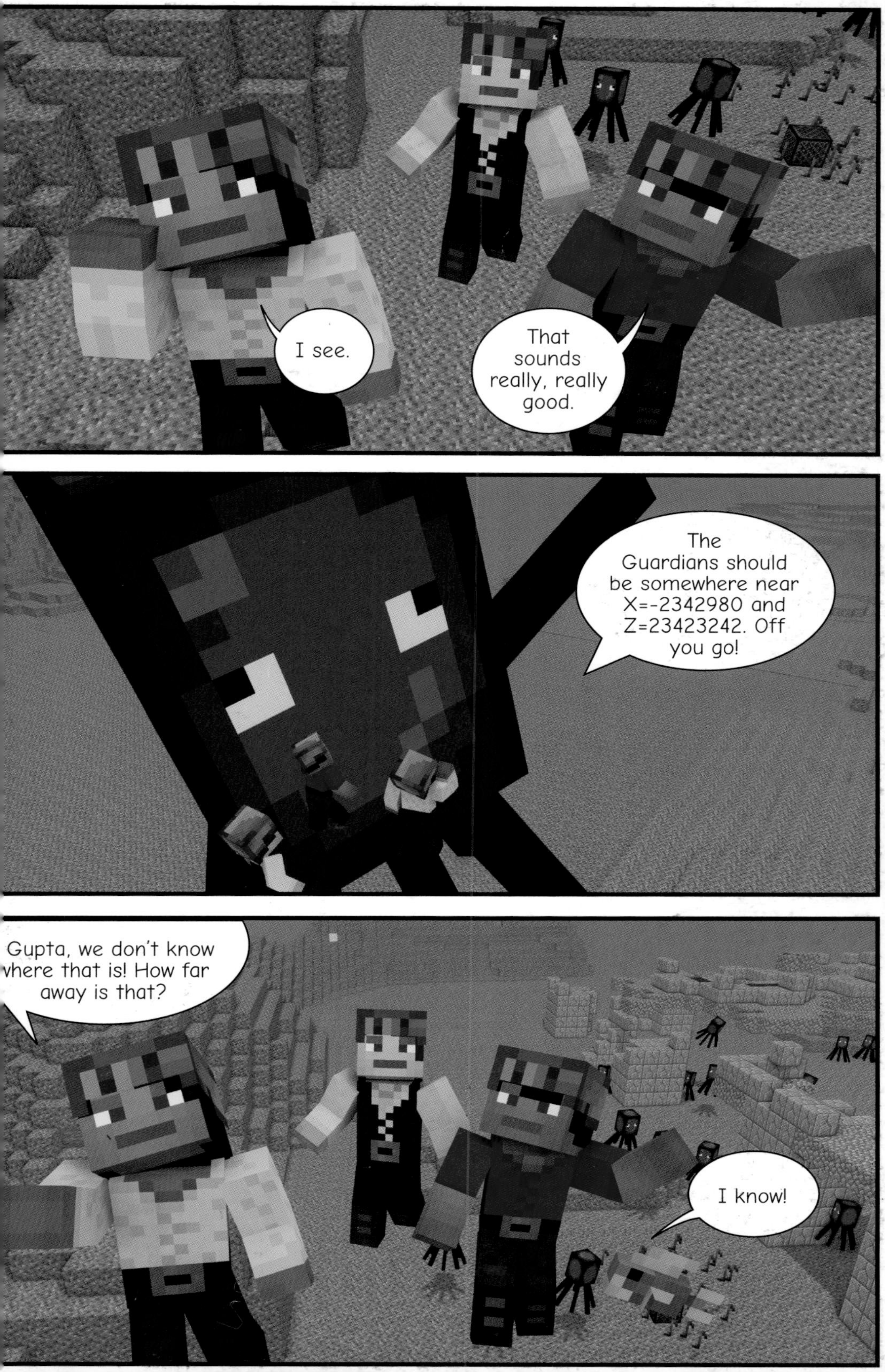
I see.
That sounds really, really good.
The Guardians should be somewhere near X=-2342980 and Z=23423242. Off you go!
Gupta, we don't know
here that is! How far away is that?
I know!

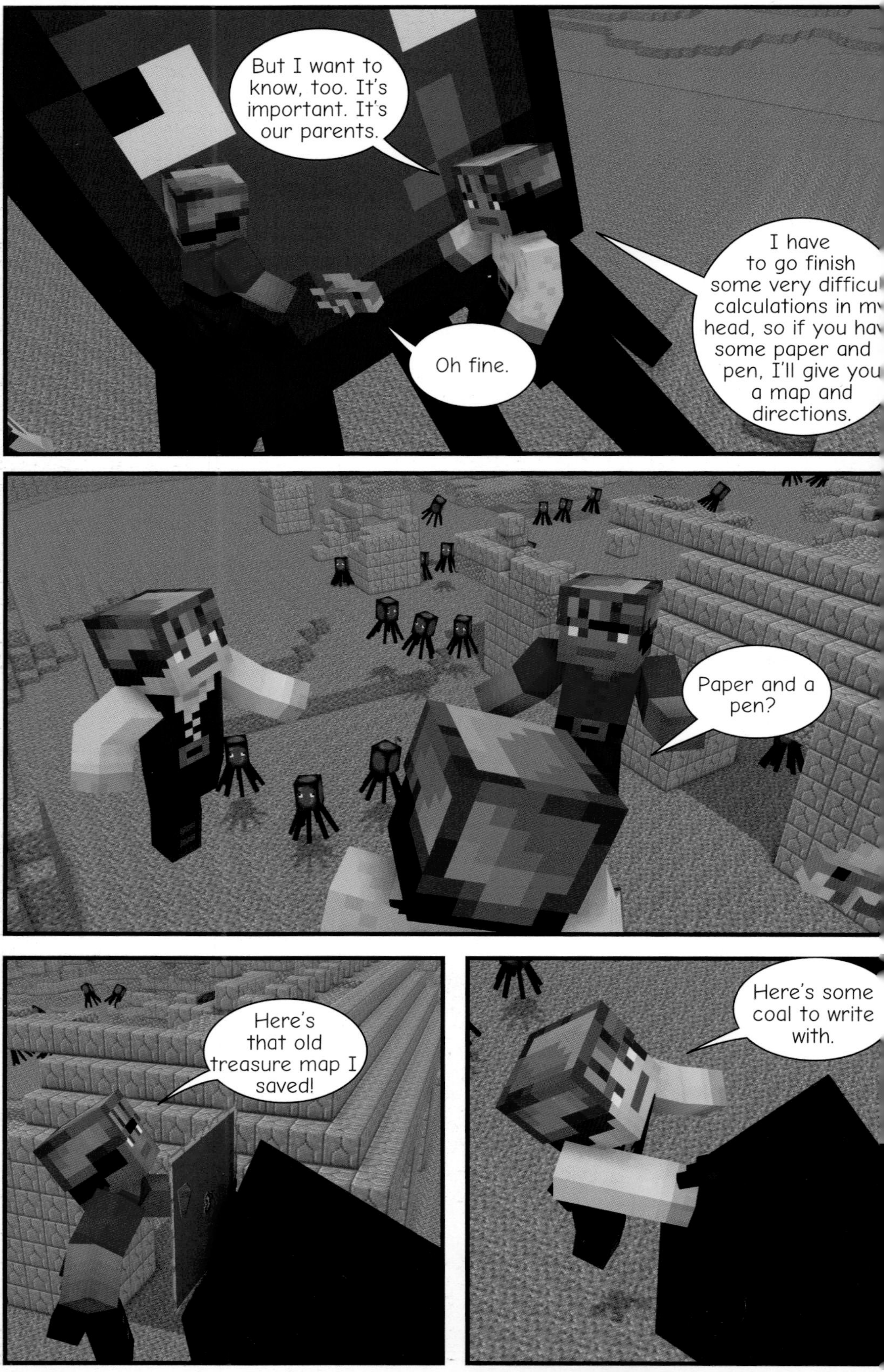
But I want to know, too. It's important. It's our parents.
Oh fine.
I have to go finish some very difficu calculations in m head, so if you ha some paper and pen, I'll give you a map and directions.
Paper and a pen?
Here's that old treasure map I saved!
Here's some coal to write with.

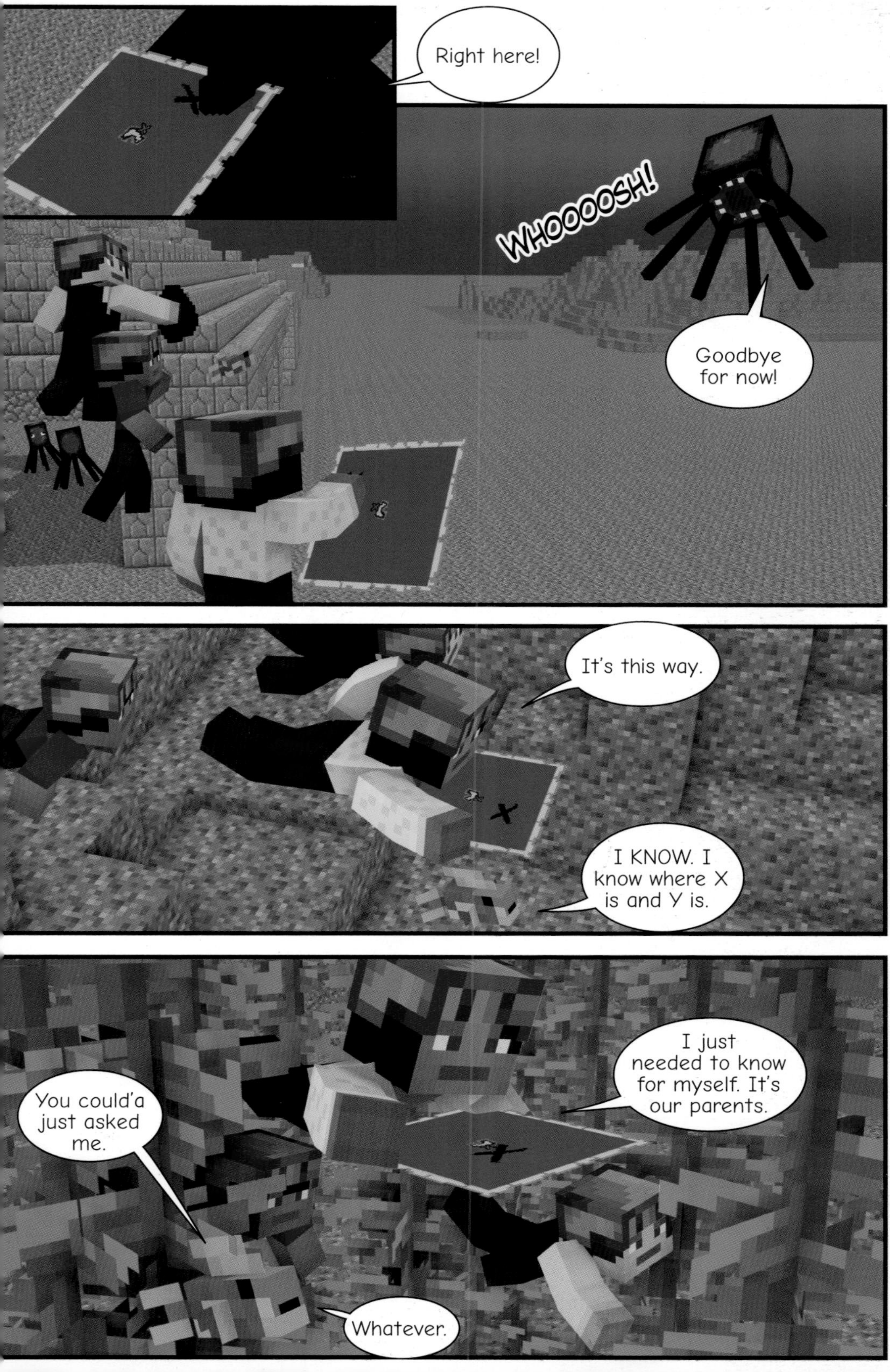
Right here!
WHOOOOOSH!
Goodbye for now!
It's this way.
I KNOW. I know where X is and Y is.
I just needed to know for myself. It's our parents.
You could'a just asked me.
Whatever.

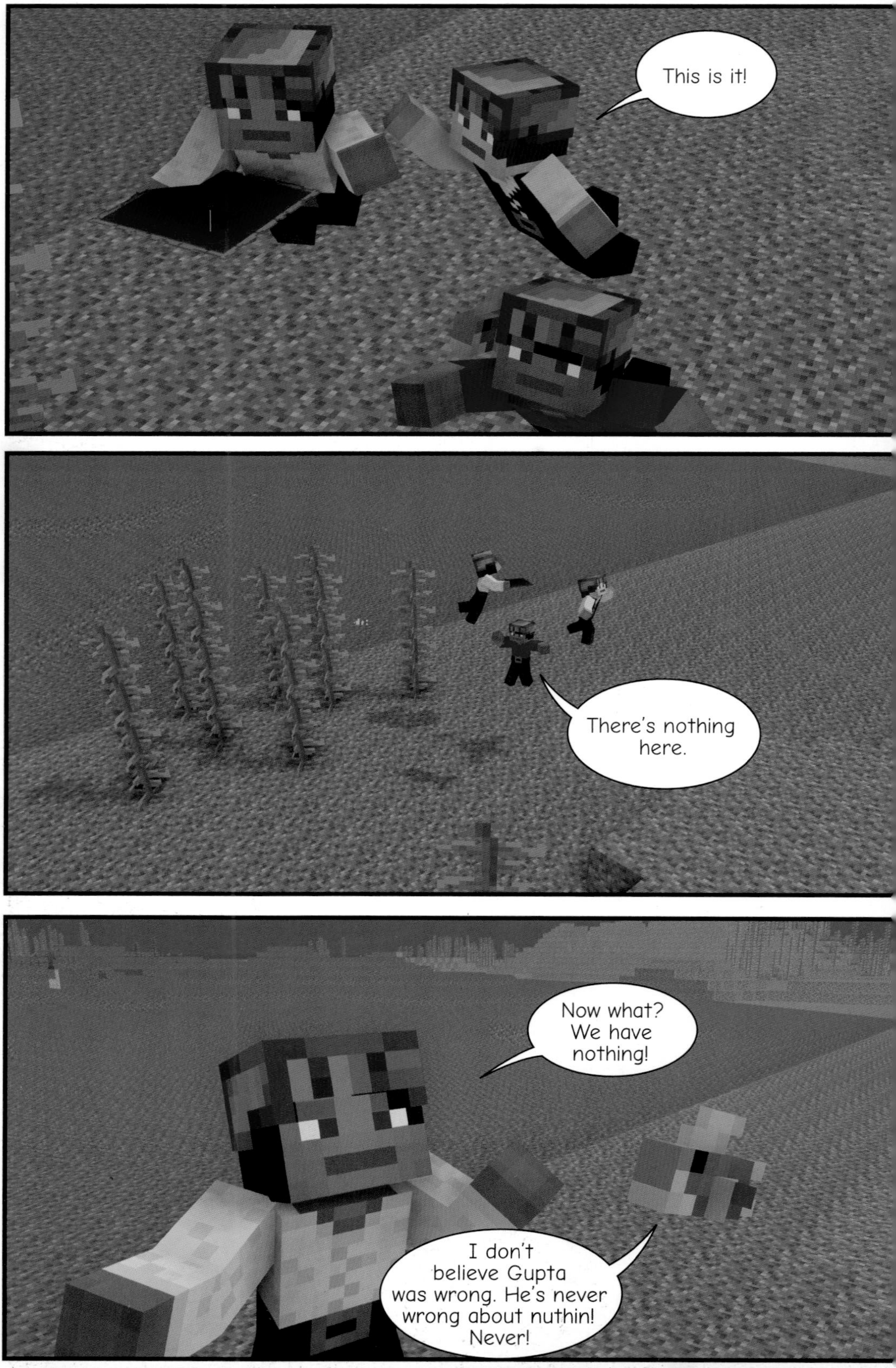
This is it!
There's nothing here.
Now what? We have nothing!
I don't believe Gupta was wrong. He's never wrong about nuthin! Never!

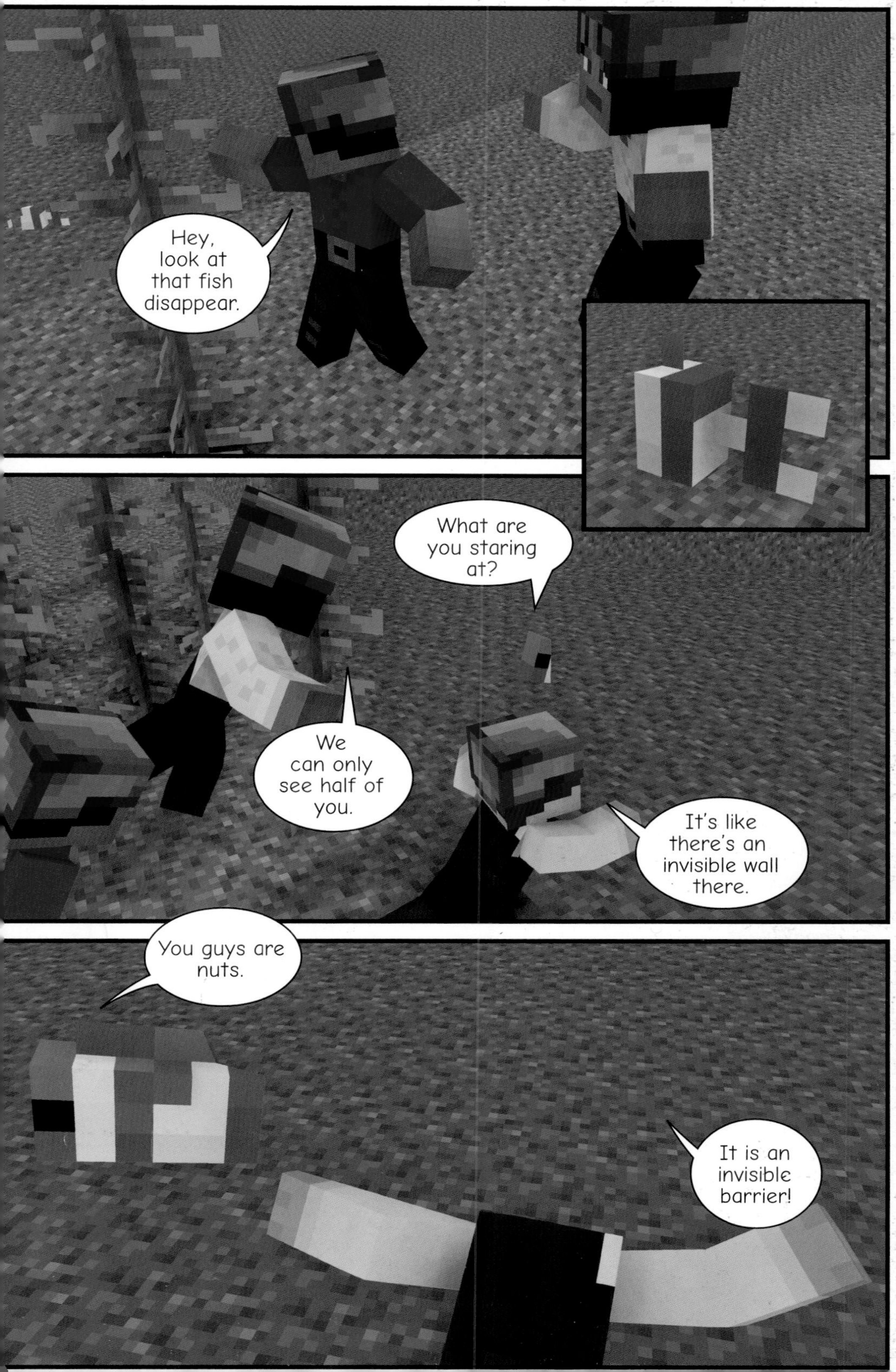
Hey, look at that fish disappear.
What are you staring at?
We can only see half of you.
It's like there's an invisible wall there.
You guys are nuts.
It is an invisible barrier!

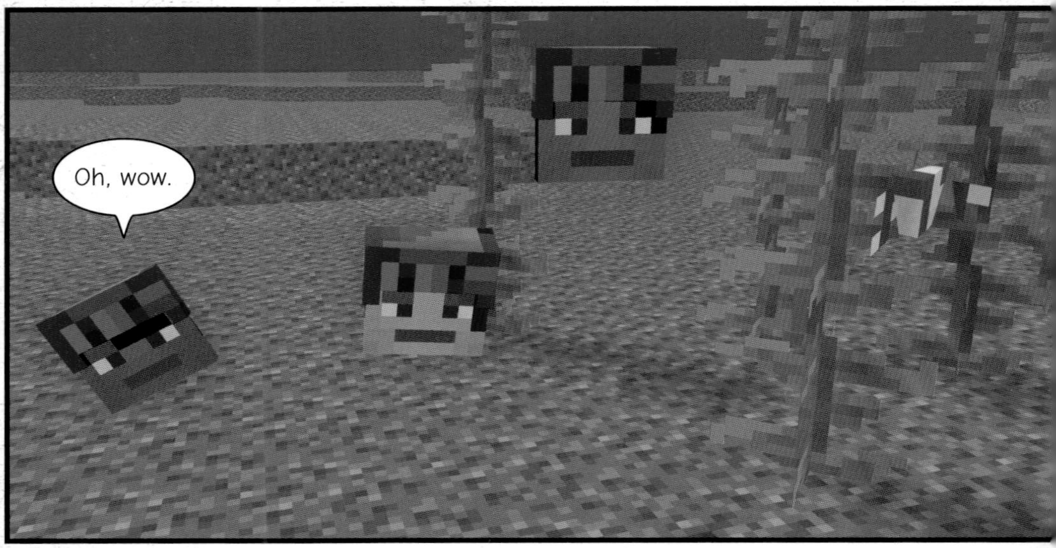
Oh, wow.

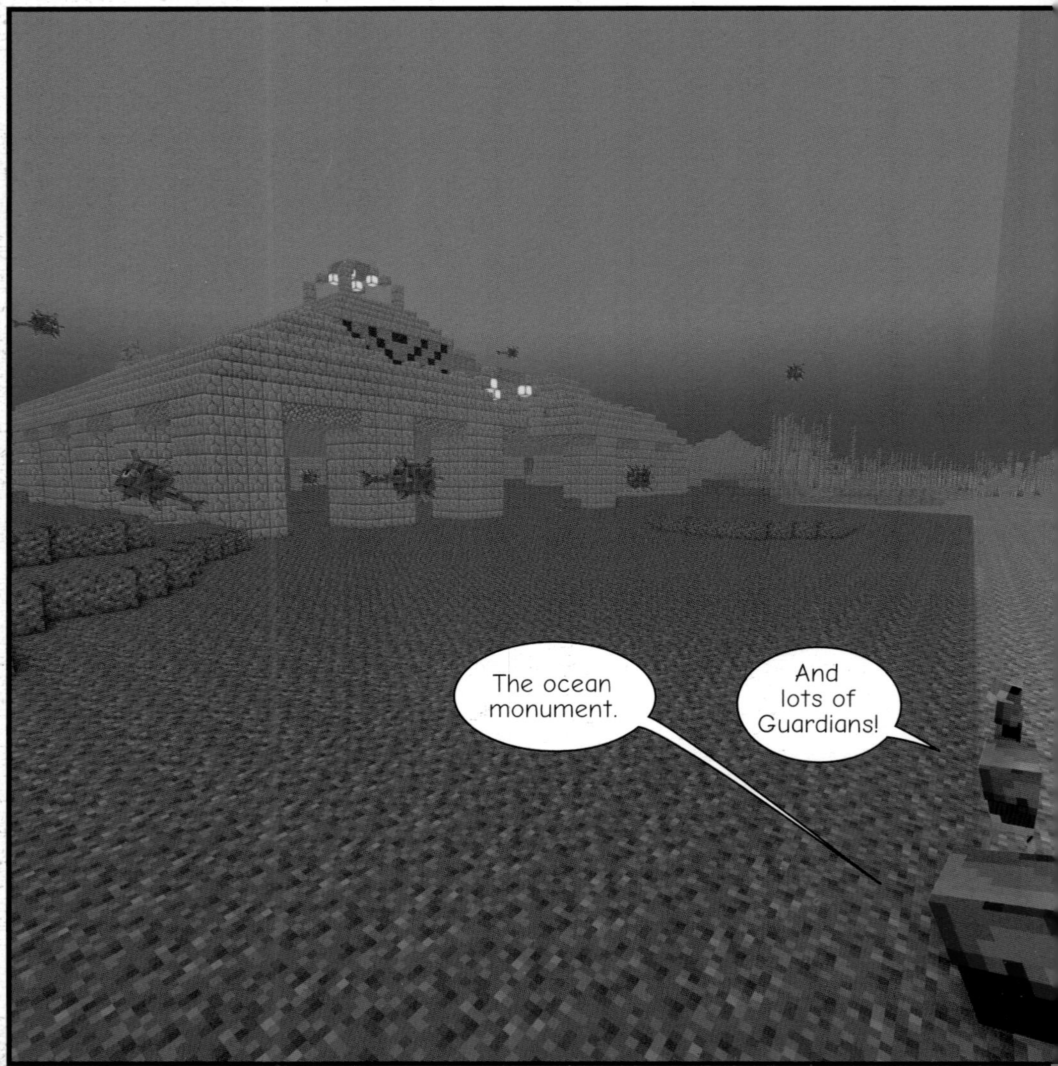
The ocean monument.
And lots of Guardians!

Chapter 6
Orvar and Odger

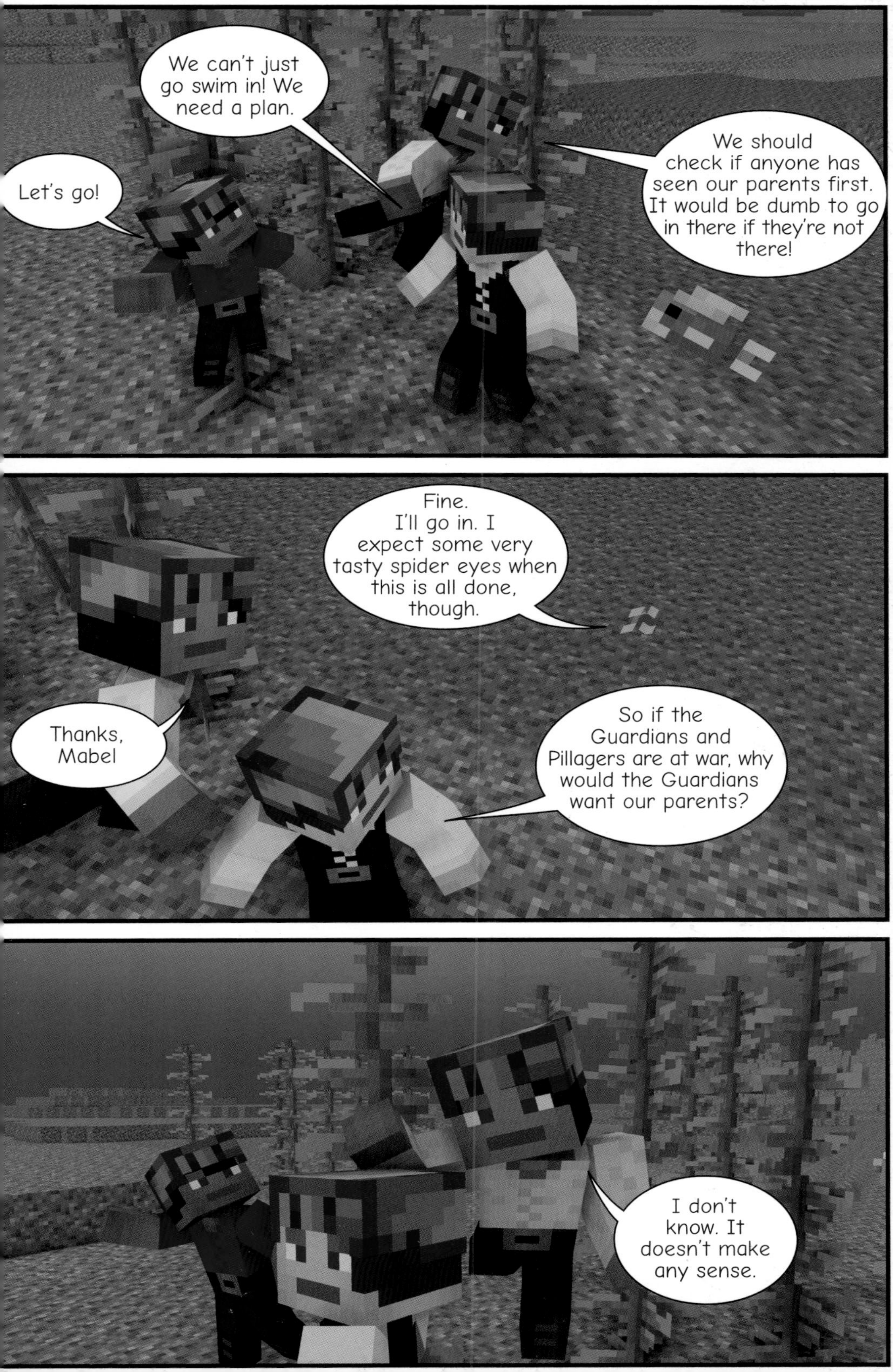
Let's go!
We can't just go swim in! We need a plan.
We should check if anyone has seen our parents first. It would be dumb to go in there if they're not there!
Fine. I'll go in. I expect some very tasty spider eyes when this is all done, though.
Thanks, Mabel
So if the Guardians and Pillagers are at war, why would the Guardians want our parents?
I don't know. It doesn't make any sense.

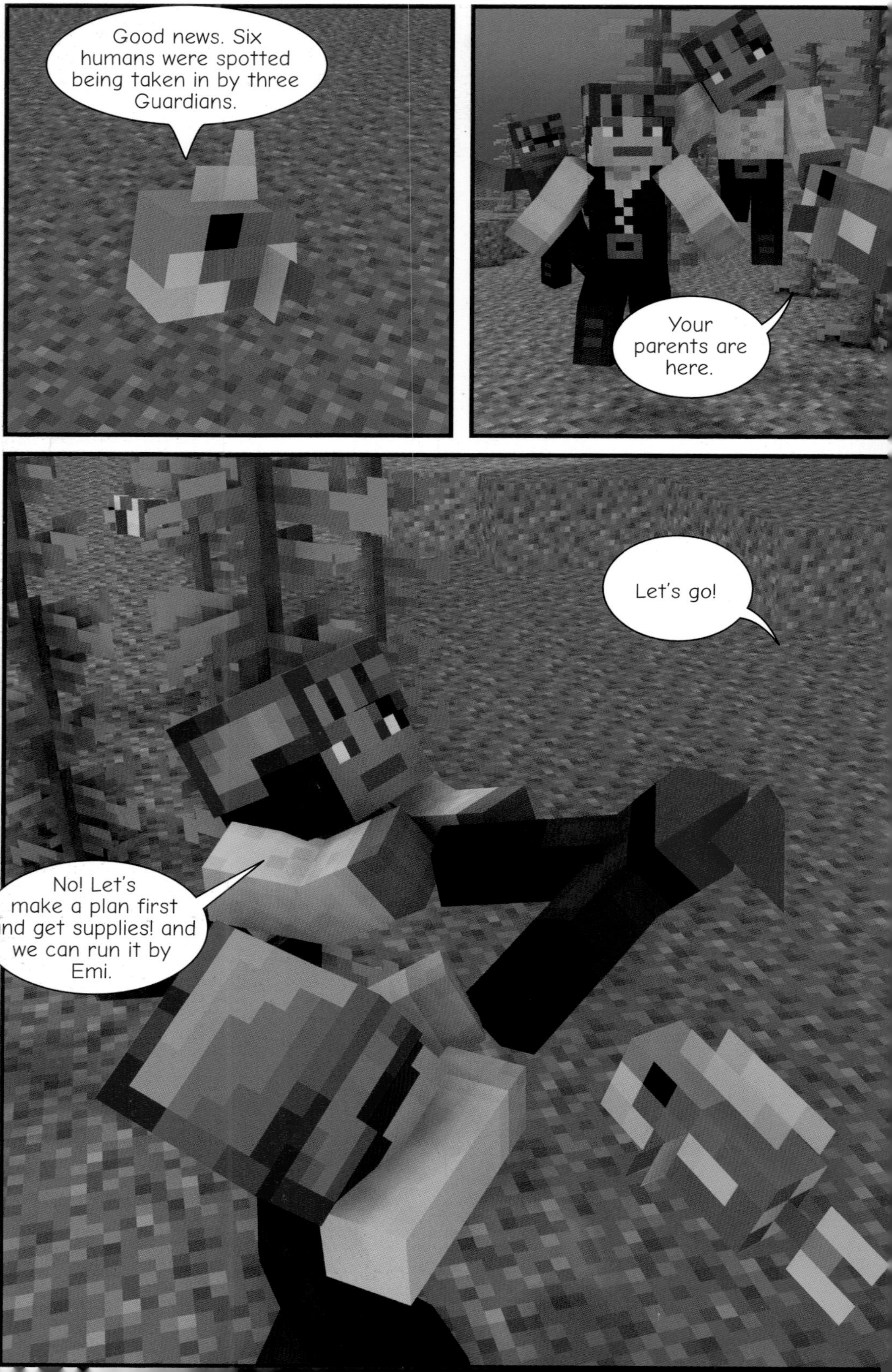
Good news. Six humans were spotted being taken in by three Guardians.
Your parents are here.
Let's go!
No! Let's make a plan first and get supplies! and we can run it by Emi.

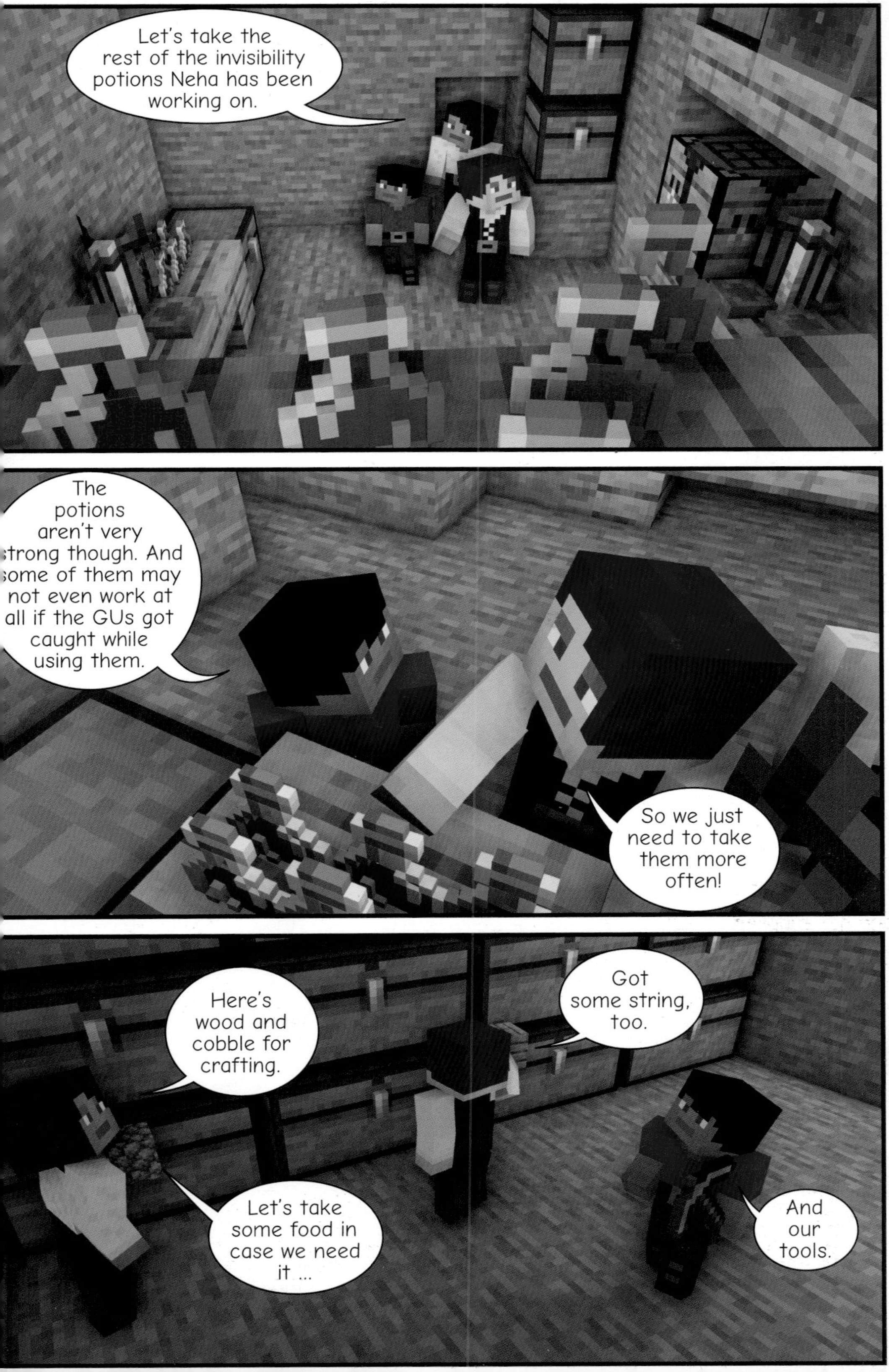
Let's take the rest of the invisibility potions Neha has been working on.
The potions aren't very strong though. And some of them may not even work at all if the GUs got caught while using them.
So we just need to take them more often!
Here's wood and cobble for crafting.
Got some string, too.
Let's take some food in case we need it ...
And our tools.

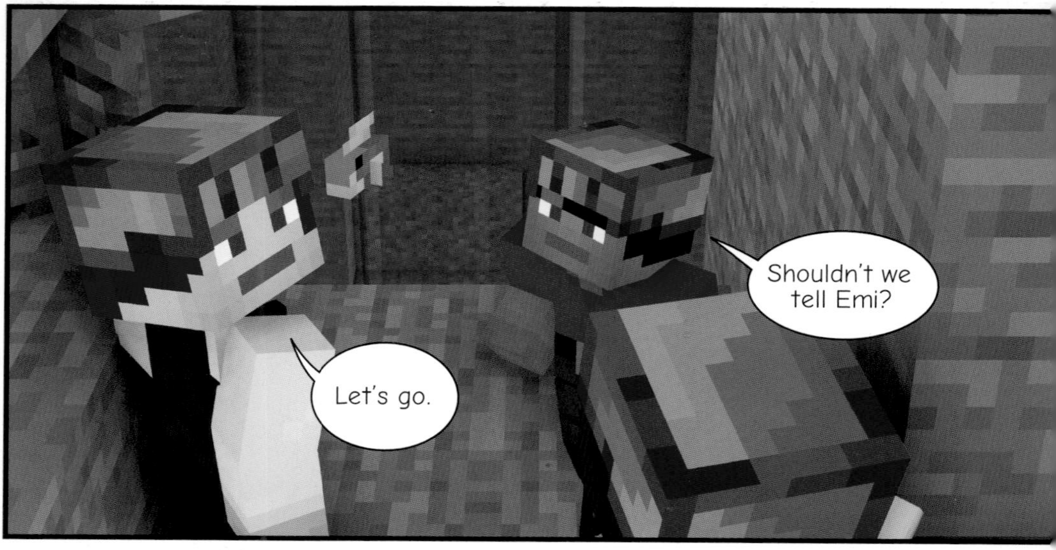
Shouldn't we tell Emi?
Let's go.

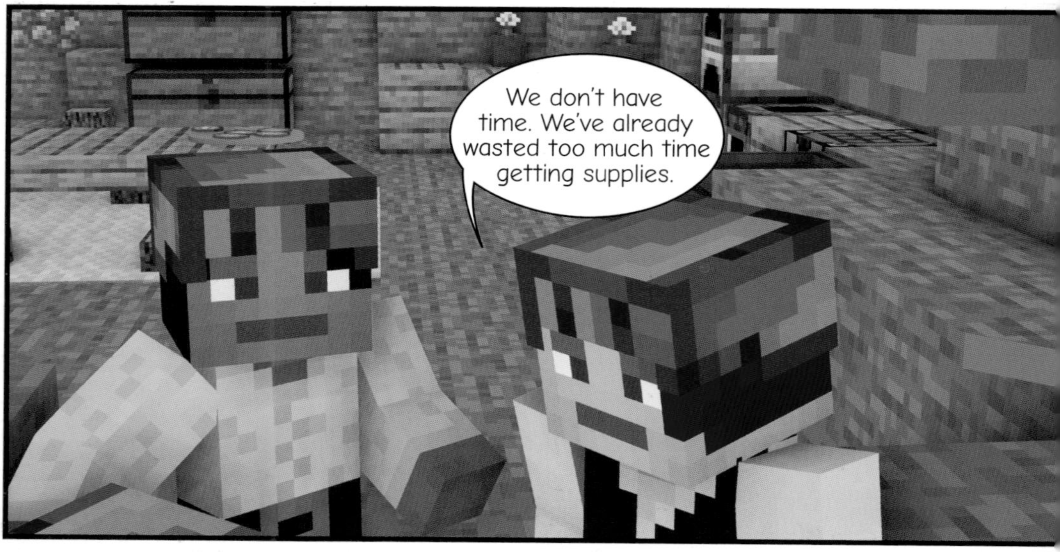
We don't have time. We've already wasted too much time getting supplies.

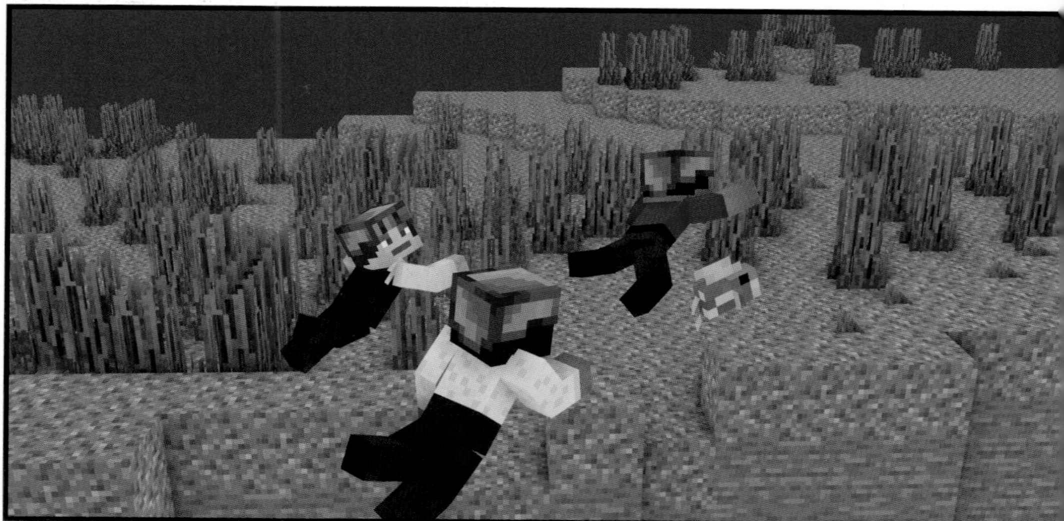

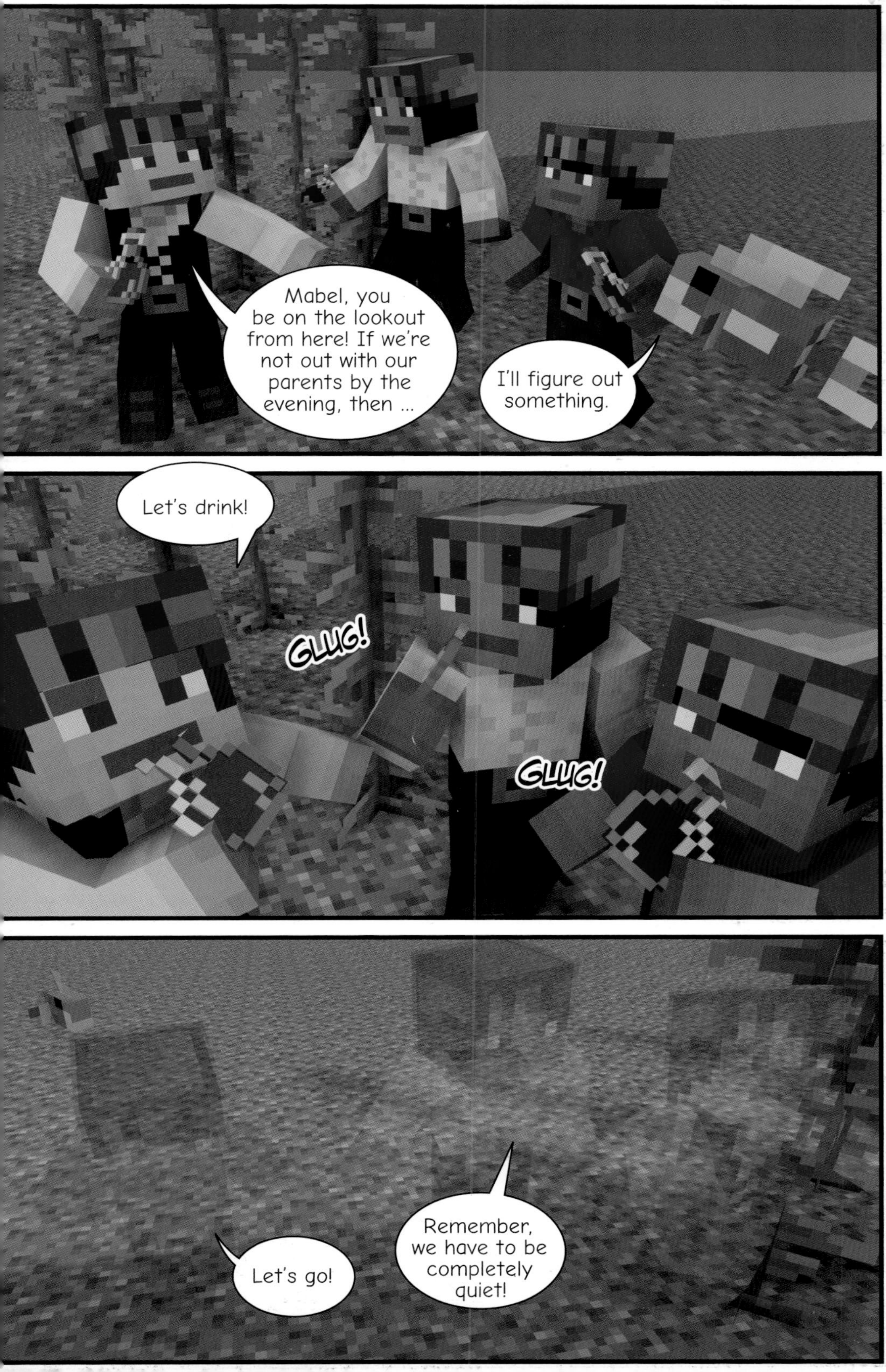
Mabel, you be on the lookout from here! If we're not out with our parents by the evening, then ...
I'll figure out something.
Let's drink!
GLUG!
GLUG!
Let's go!
Remember, we have to be completely quiet!

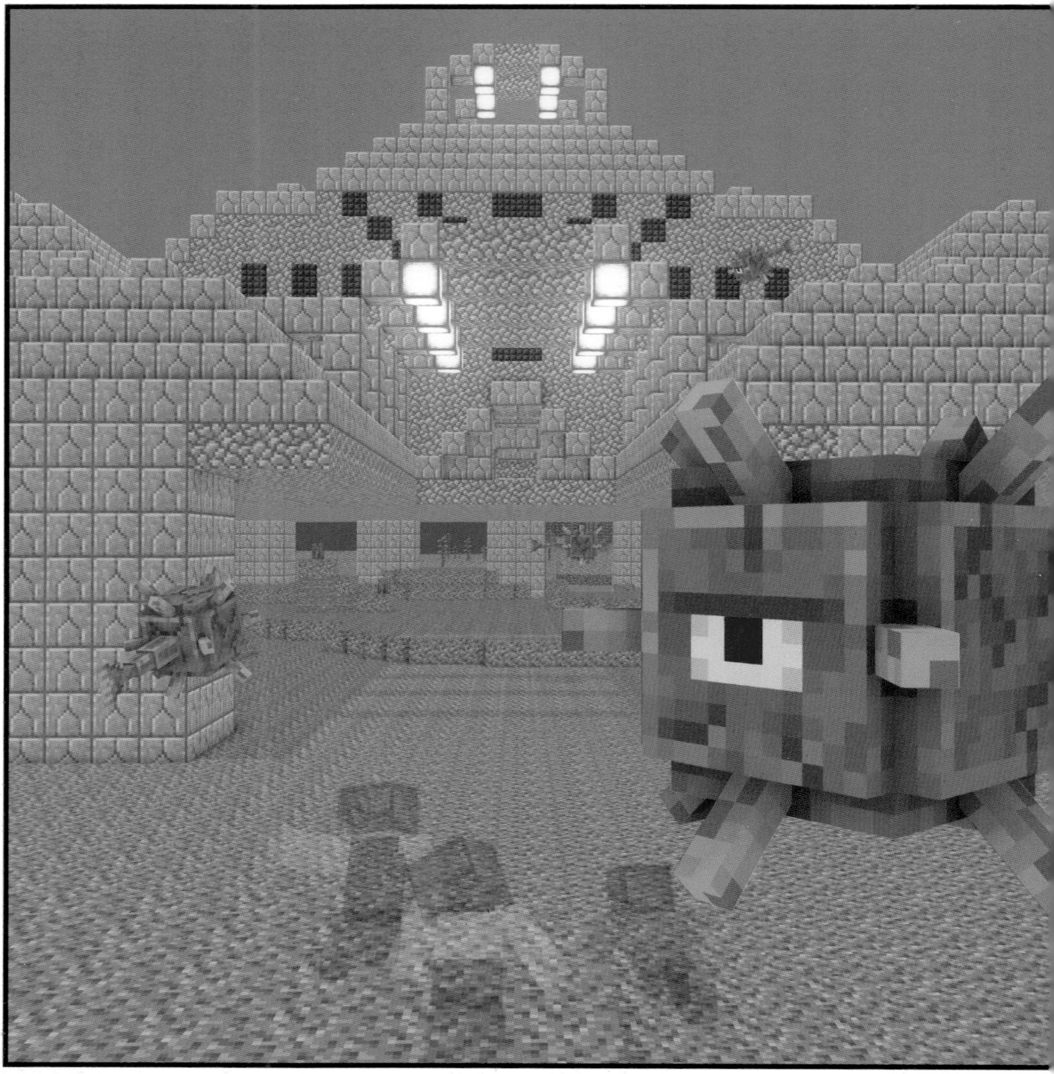

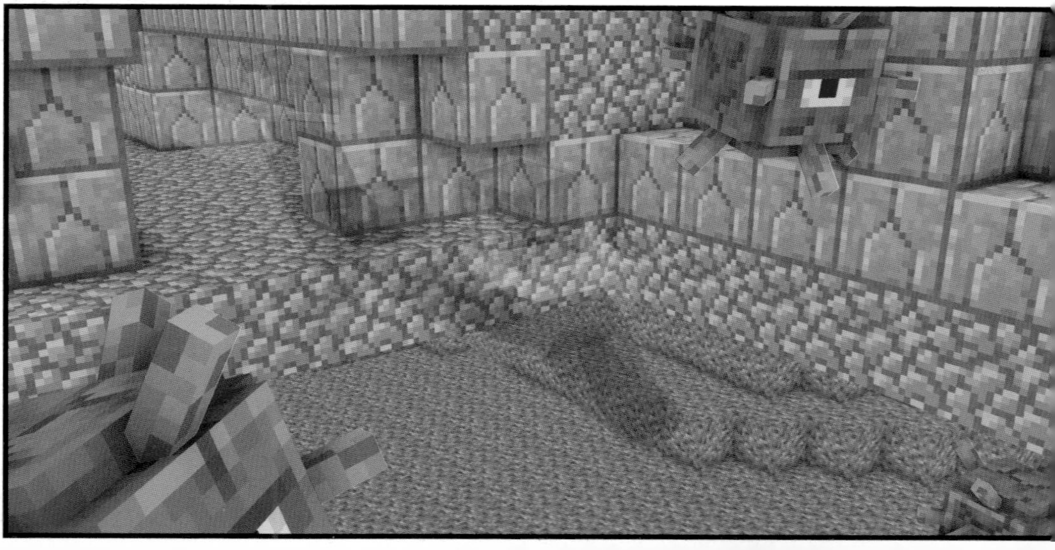

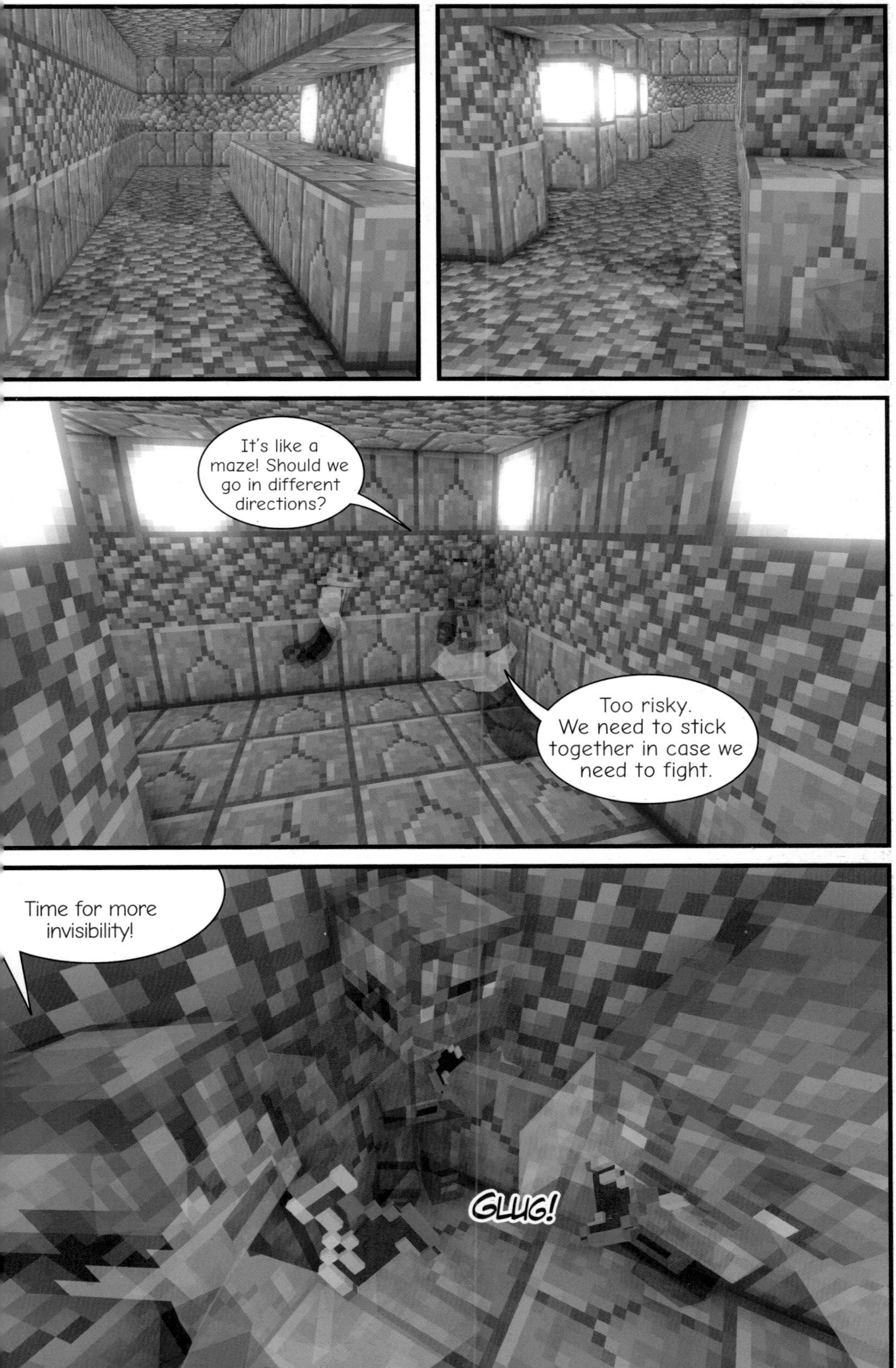
It's like a maze! Should we go in different directions?
Too risky. We need to stick together in case we need to fight.
Time for more invisibility!
GLUG!

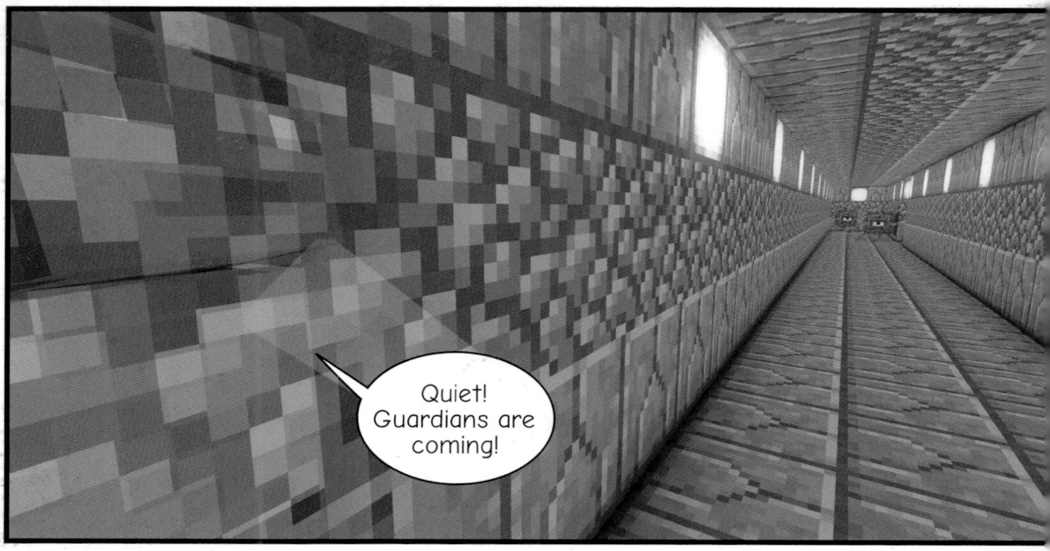
Quiet! Guardians are coming!

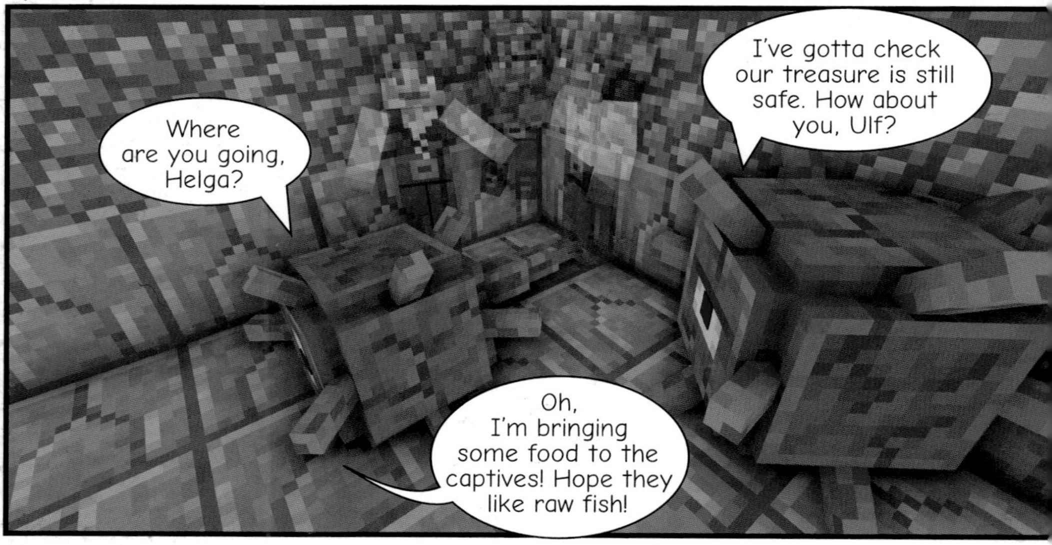
Where are you going, Helga?
I've gotta check our treasure is still safe. How about you, Ulf?
Oh, I'm bringing some food to the captives! Hope they like raw fish!

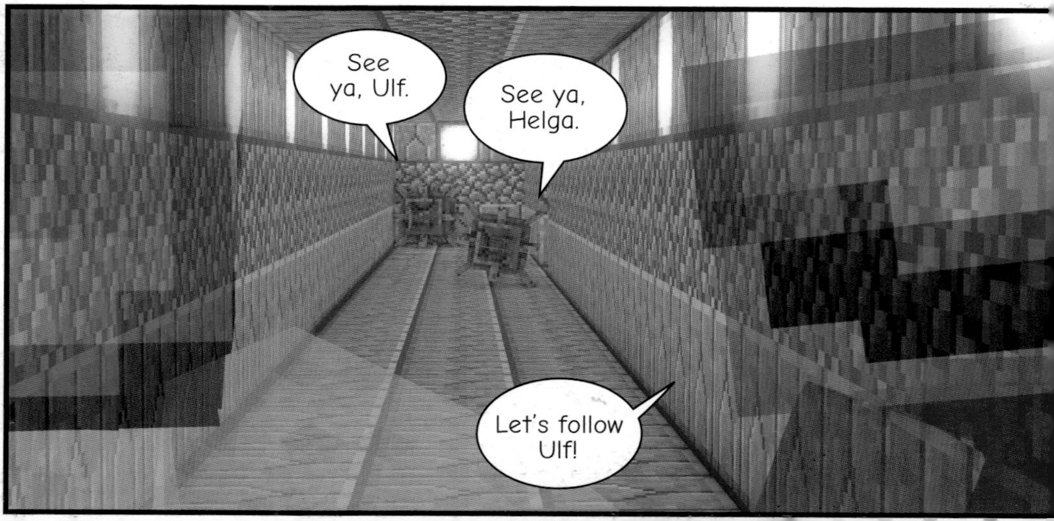
See ya, Ulf.
See ya, Helga.
Let's follow Ulf!

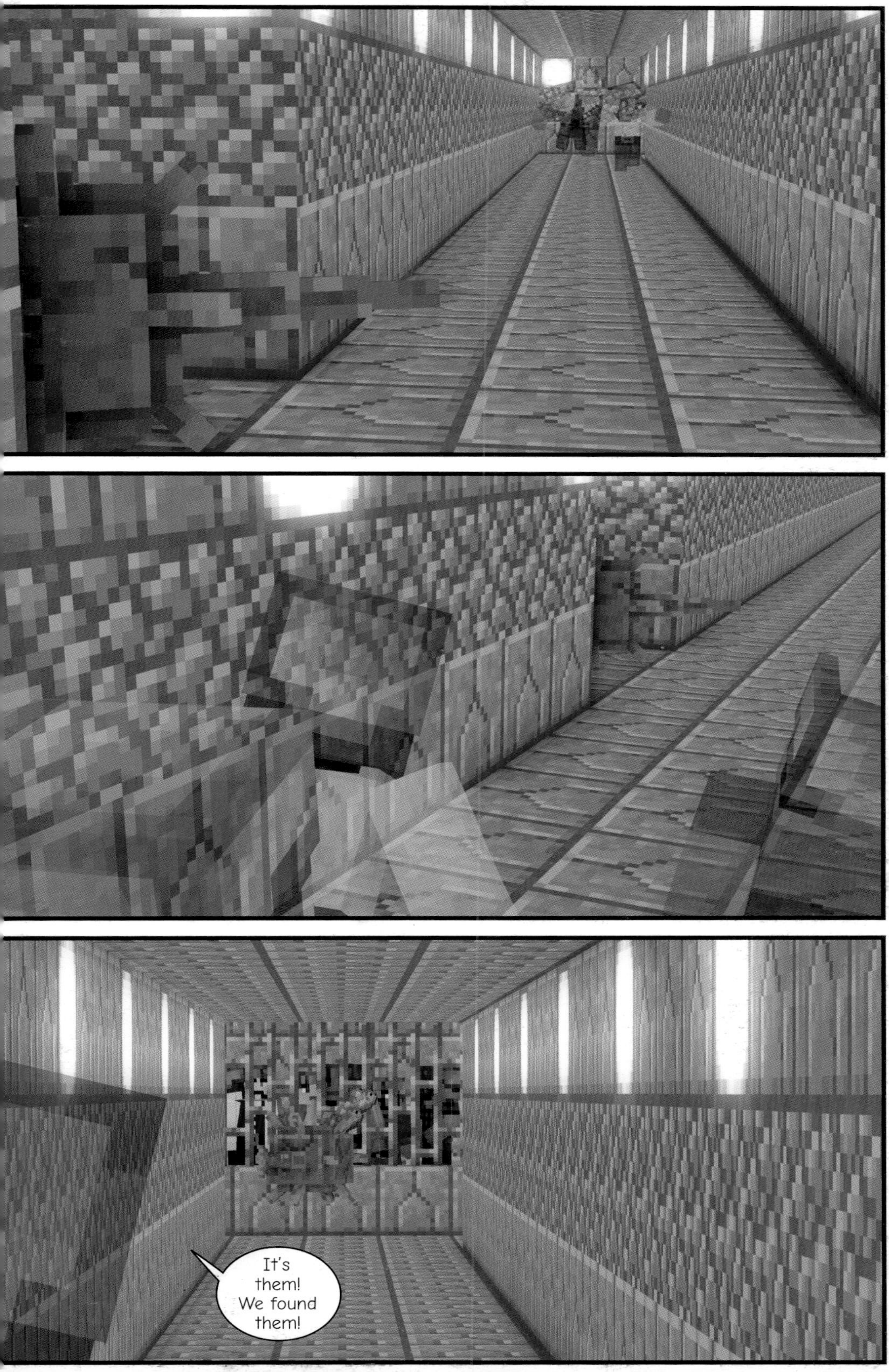
It's them! We found them!

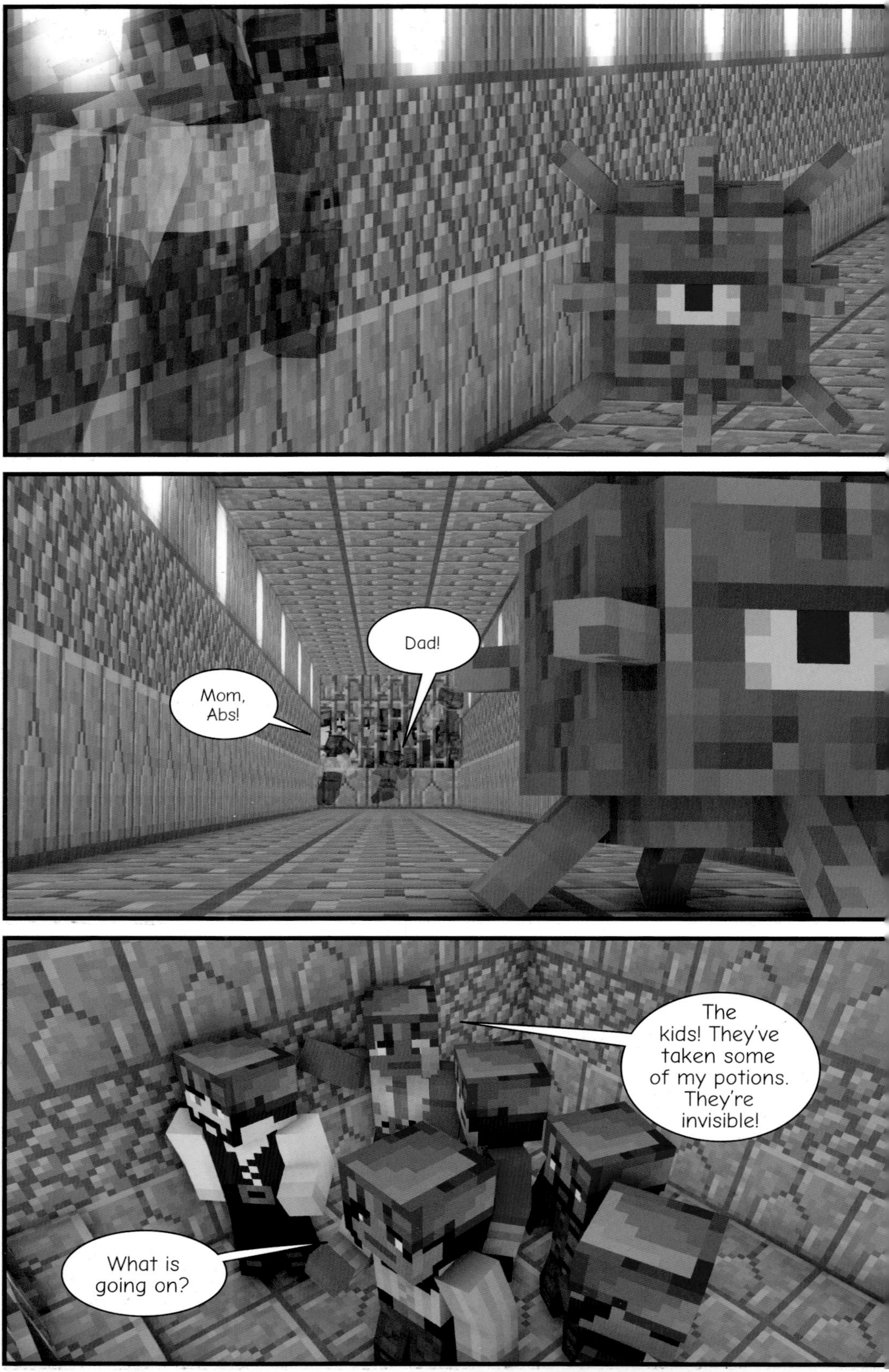
Mom, Abs!
Dad!
The kids! They've taken some of my potions. They're invisible!
What is going on?

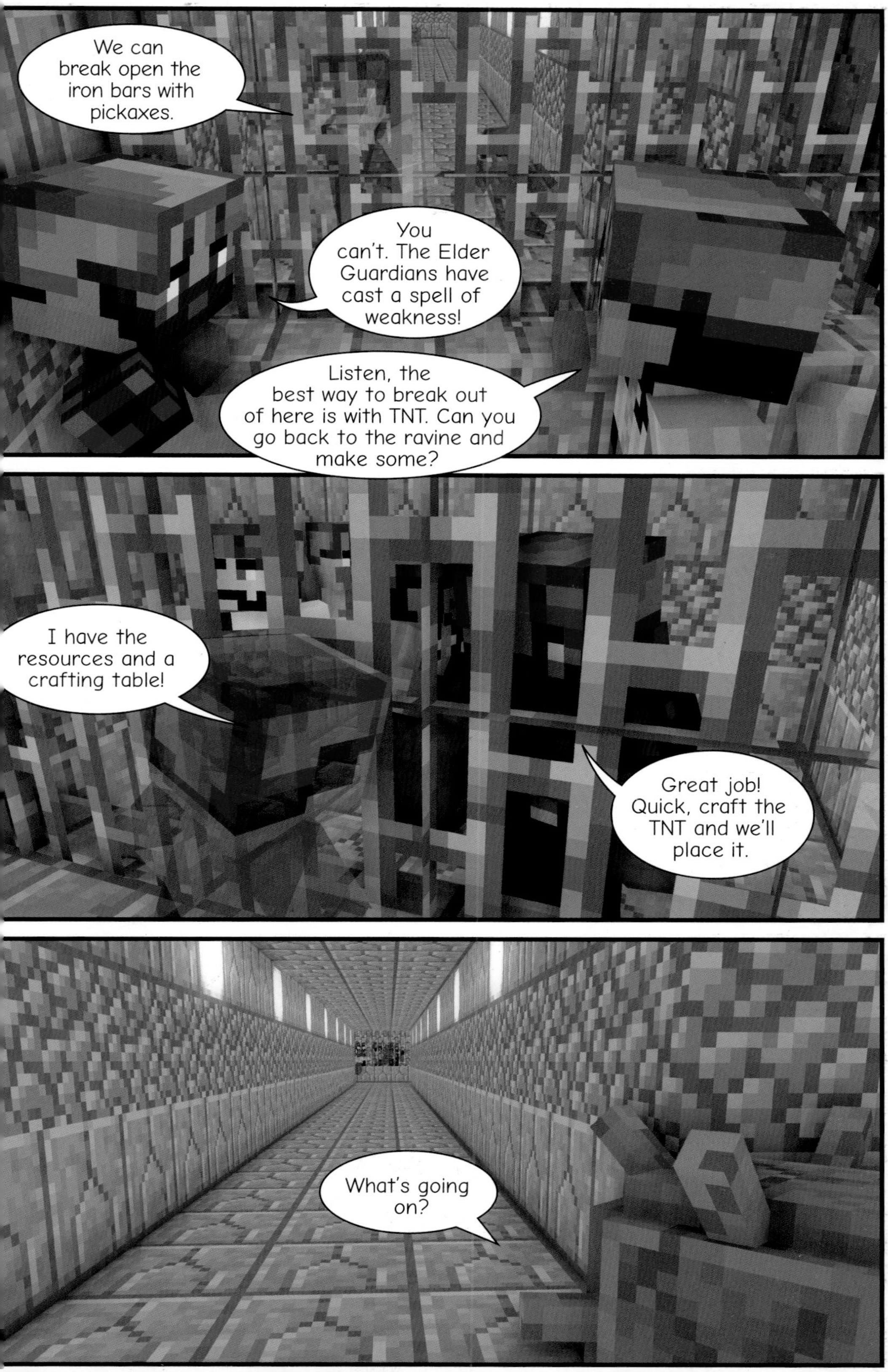
We can break open the iron bars with pickaxes.
You can't. The Elder Guardians have cast a spell of weakness!
Listen, the best way to break out of here is with TNT. Can you go back to the ravine and make some?
I have the resources and a crafting table!
Great job! Quick, craft the TNT and we'll place it.
What's going on?

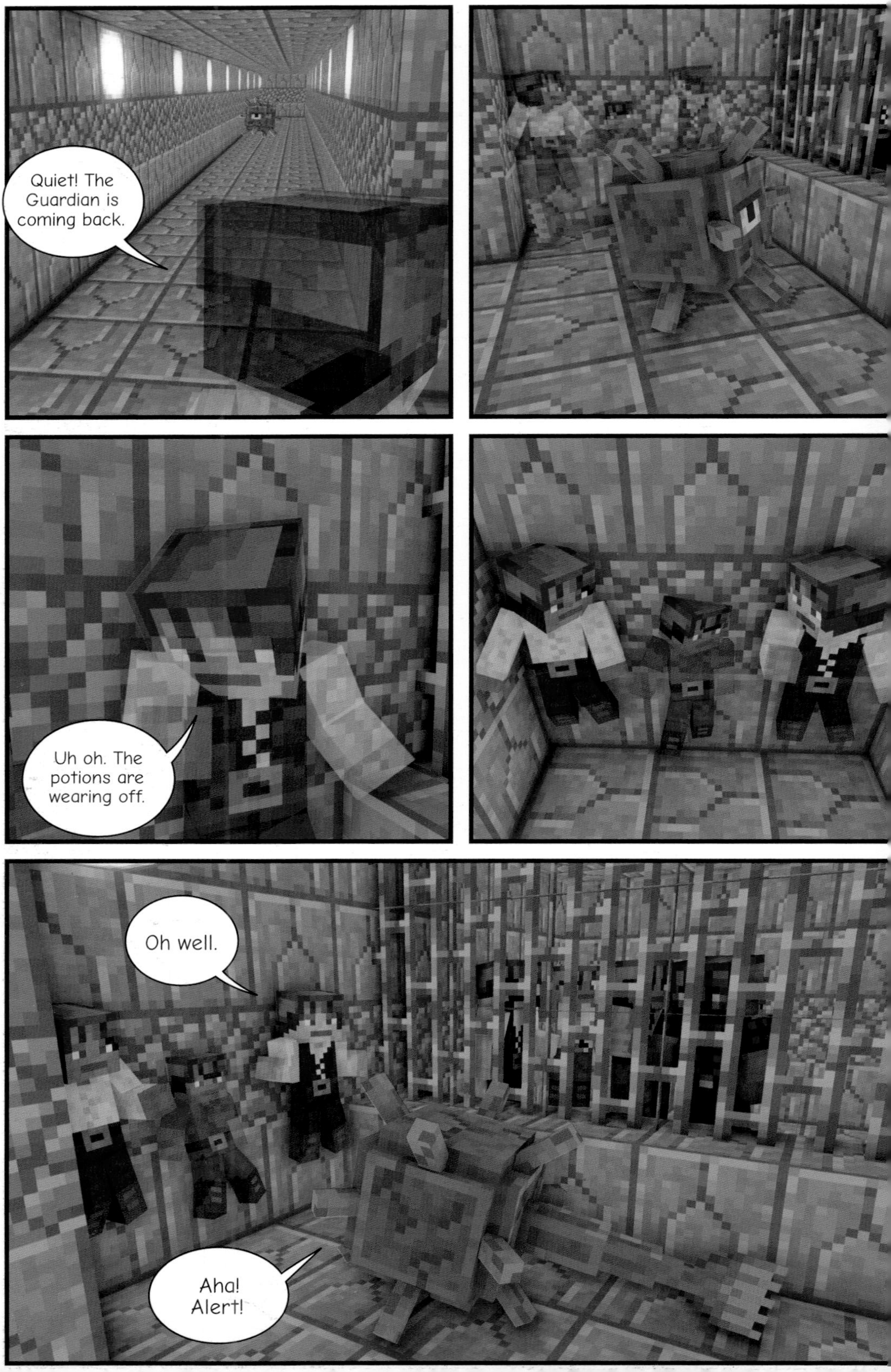
Quiet! The Guardian is coming back.
Uh oh. The potions are wearing off.
Oh well.
Aha! Alert!

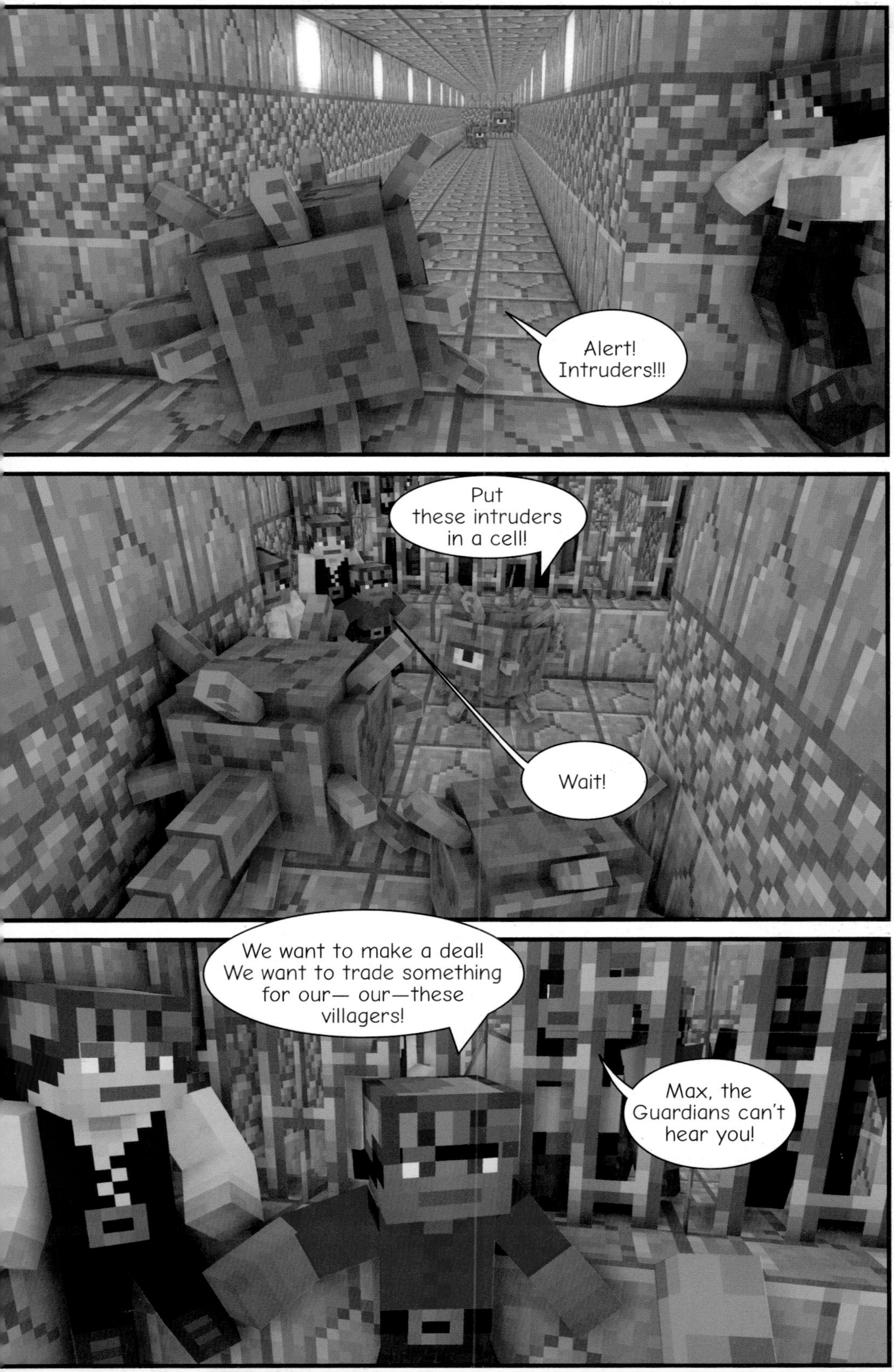

Alert! Intruders!!!
Put these intruders in a cell!
Wait!
We want to make a deal! We want to trade something for our— our—these villagers!
Max, the Guardians can't hear you!

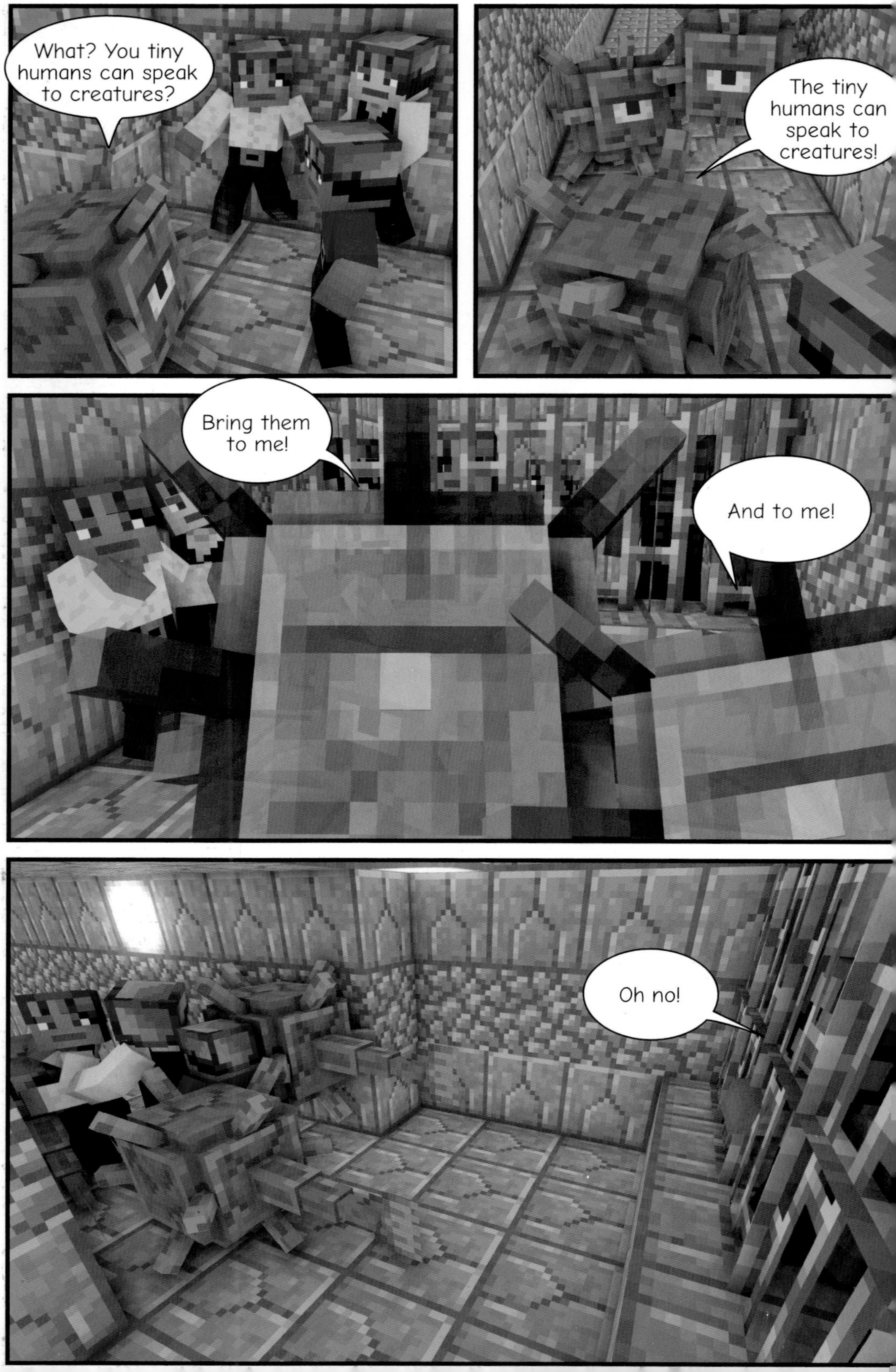
What? You tiny humans can speak to creatures?
The tiny humans can speak to creatures!
Bring them to me!
And to me!
Oh no!

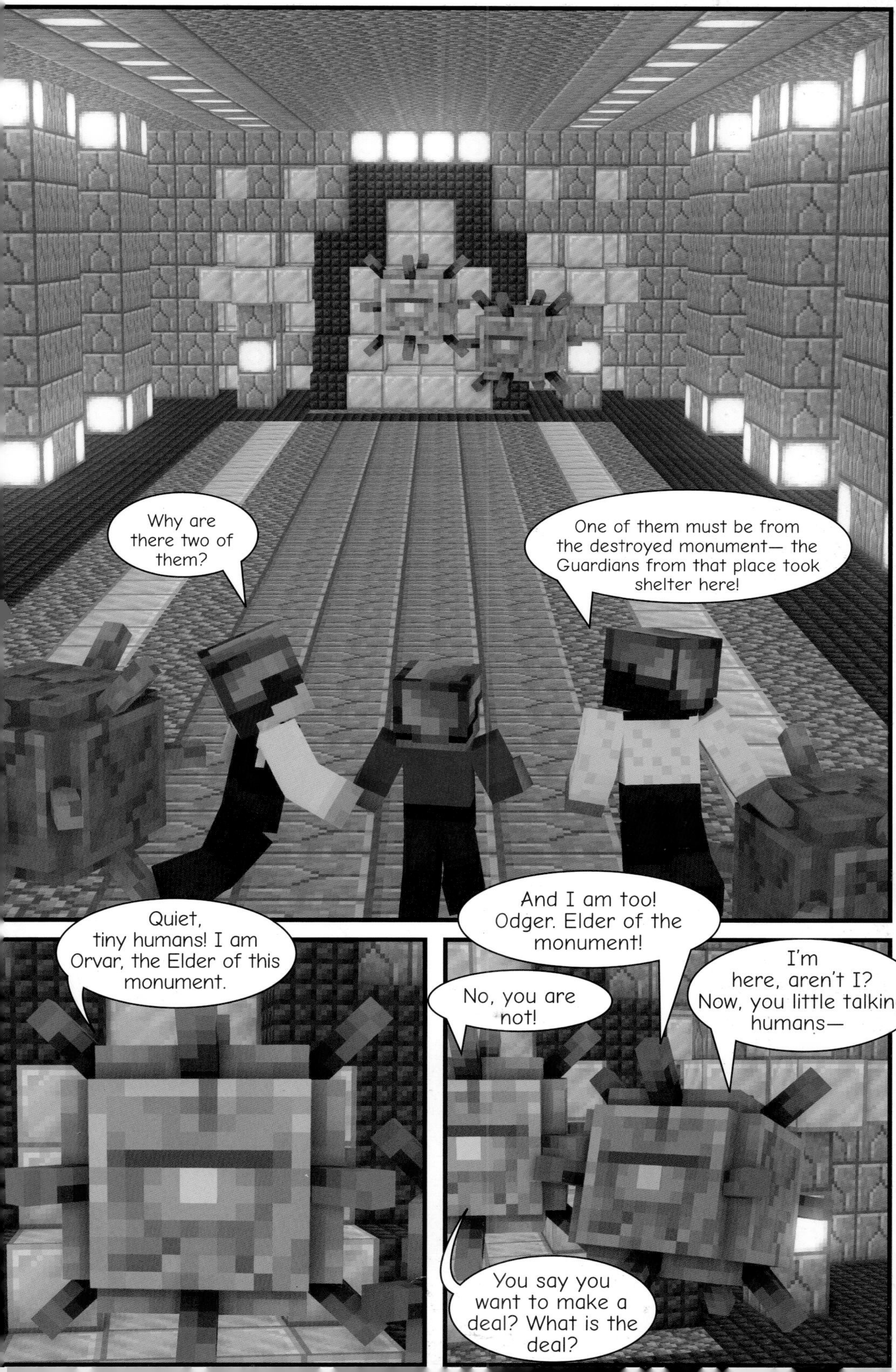
Why are there two of them?
One of them must be from the destroyed monument— the Guardians from that place took shelter here!
Quiet, tiny humans! I am Orvar, the Elder of this monument.
And I am too! Odger. Elder of the monument!
No, you are not!
I'm here, aren't I? Now, you little talking humans—
You say you want to make a deal? What is the deal?

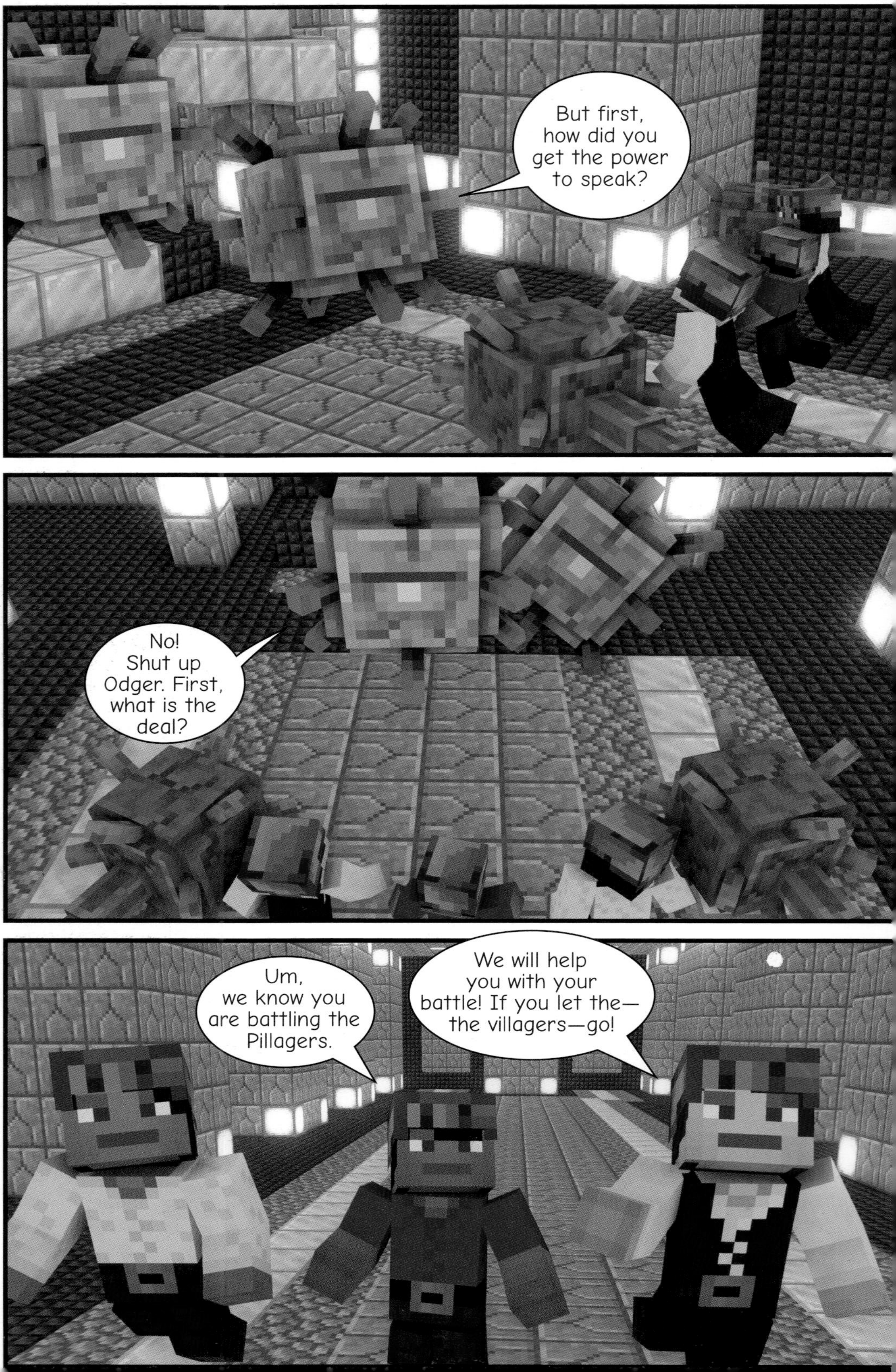
But first, how did you get the power to speak?
No! Shut up Odger. First, what is the deal?
Um, we know you are battling the Pillagers.
We will help you with your battle! If you let the— the villagers—go!

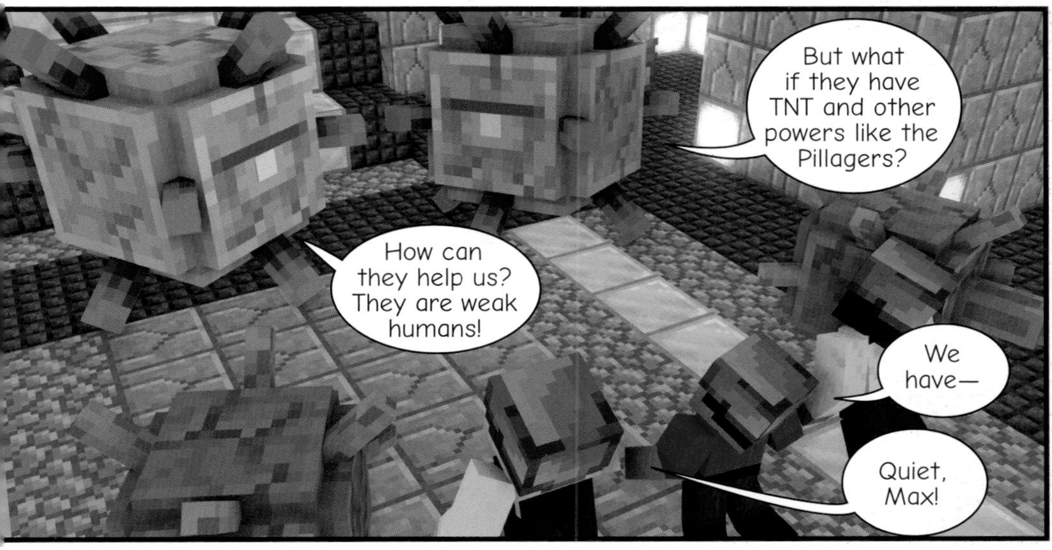
But what if they have TNT and other powers like the Pillagers?
How can they help us? They are weak humans!
We have—
Quiet, Max!

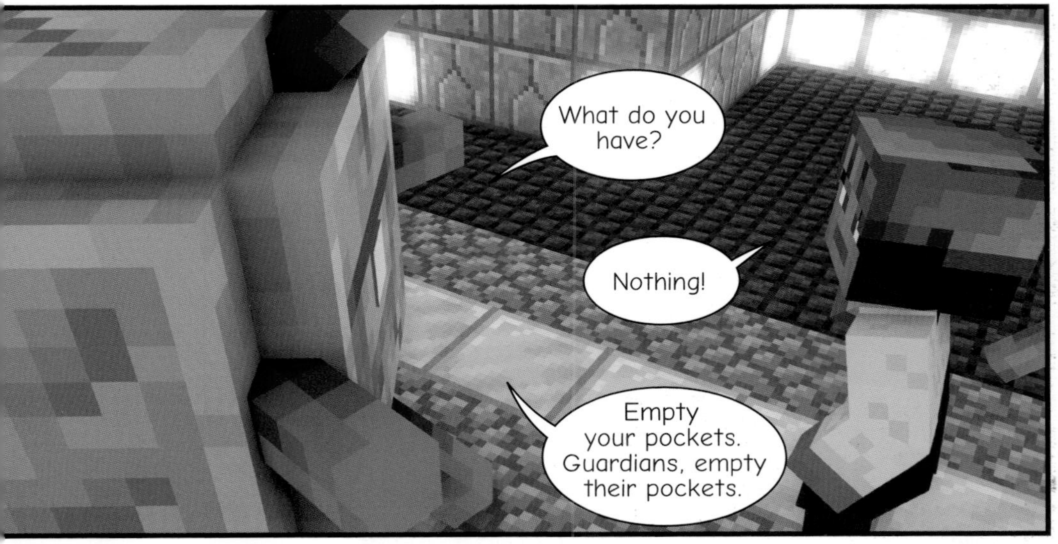
What do you have?
Nothing!
Empty your pockets. Guardians, empty their pockets.

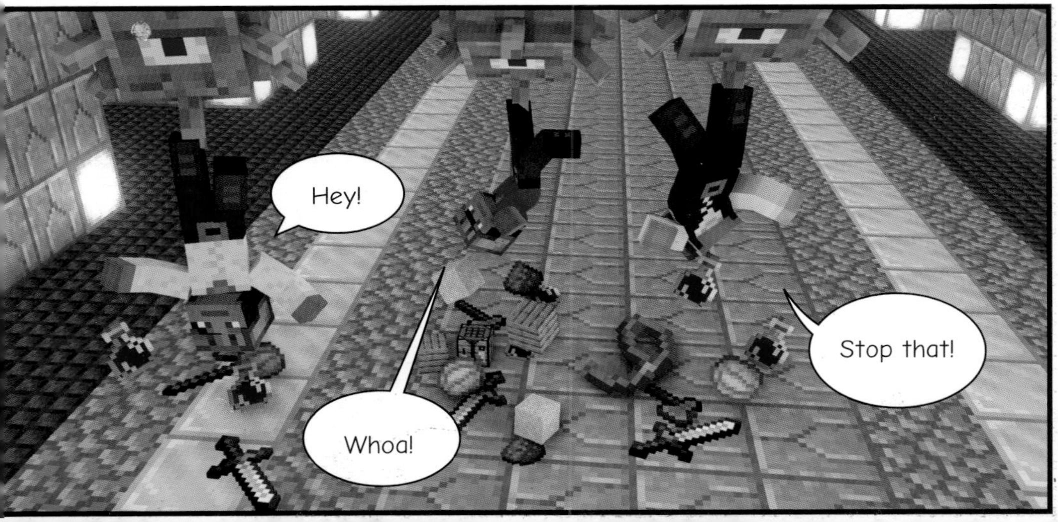
Hey!
Whoa!
Stop that!

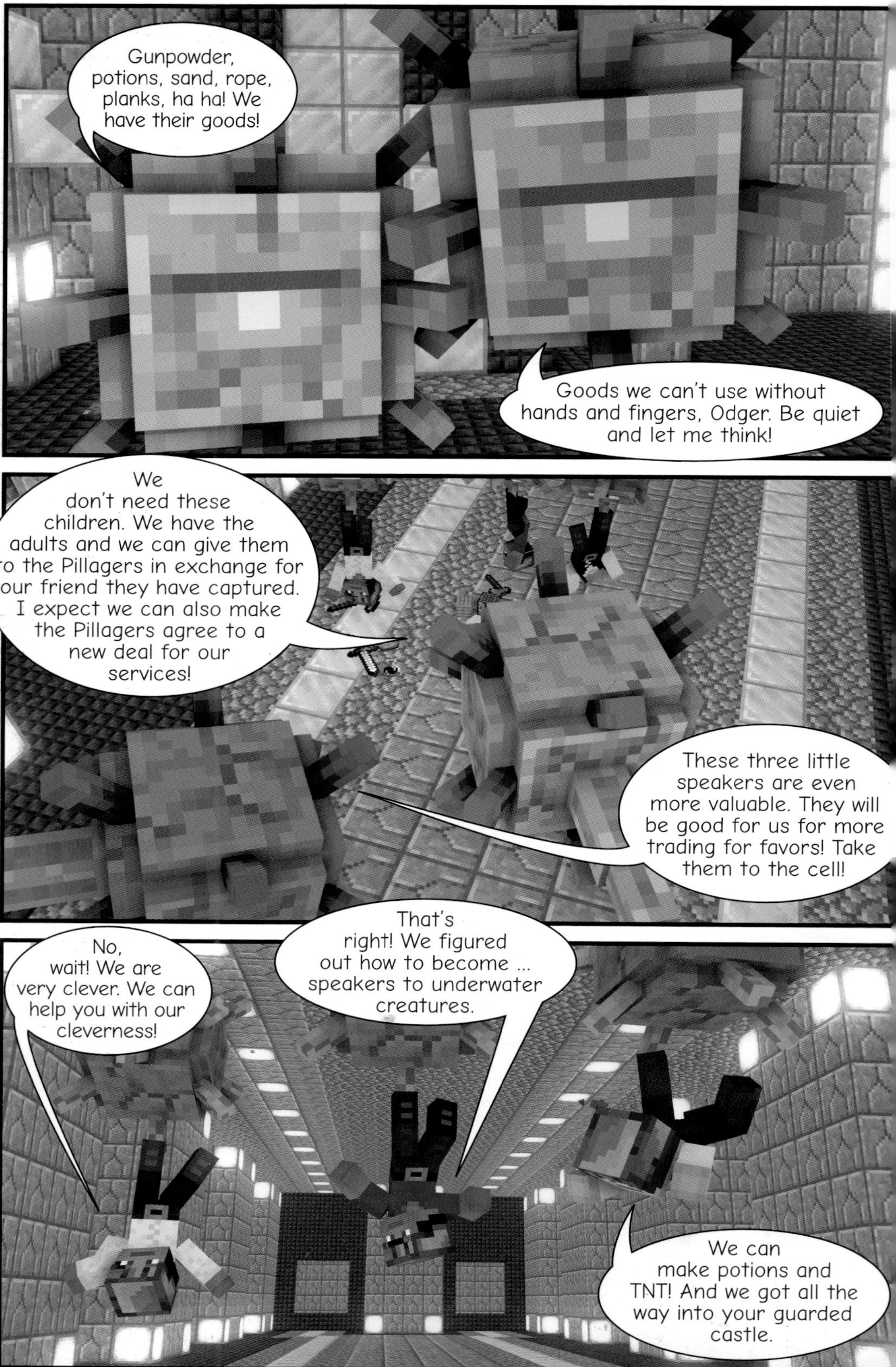
Gunpowder, potions, sand, rope, planks, ha ha! We have their goods!
Goods we can't use without hands and fingers, Odger. Be quiet and let me think!
We don't need these children. We have the adults and we can give them to the Pillagers in exchange for our friend they have captured. I expect we can also make the Pillagers agree to a new deal for our services!
These three little speakers are even more valuable. They will be good for us for more trading for favors! Take them to the cell!
No, wait! We are very clever. We can help you with our cleverness!
That's right! We figured out how to become ... speakers to underwater creatures.
We can make potions and TNT! And we got all the way into your guarded castle.

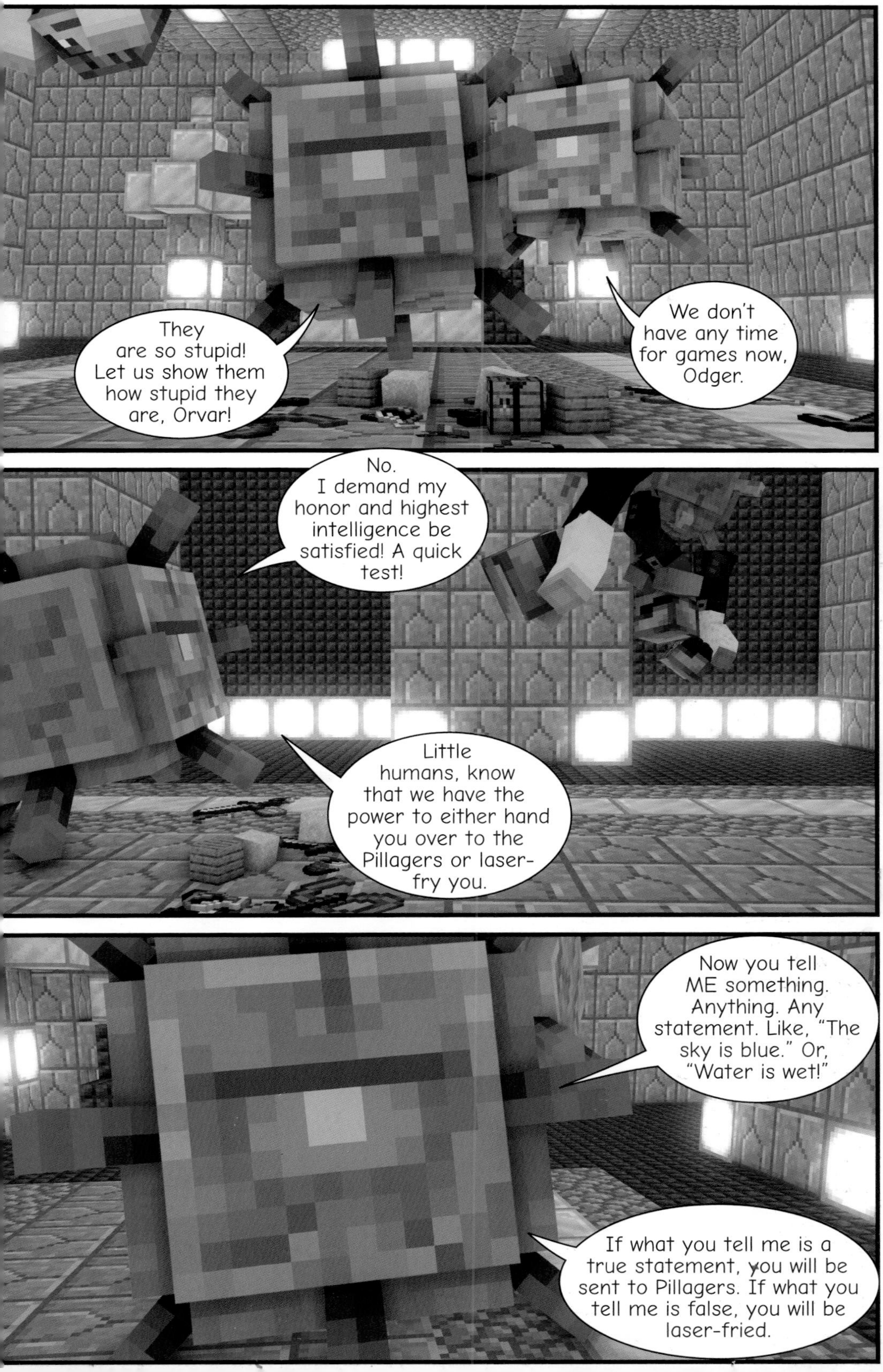
They are so stupid! Let us show them how stupid they are, Orvar!
We don't have any time for games now, Odger.
No. I demand my honor and highest intelligence be satisfied! A quick test!
Little humans, know that we have the power to either hand you over to the Pillagers or laser-fry you.
Now you tell ME something. Anything. Any statement. Like, "The sky is blue." Or, "Water is wet!"
If what you tell me is a true statement, you will be sent to Pillagers. If what you tell me is false, you will be laser-fried.

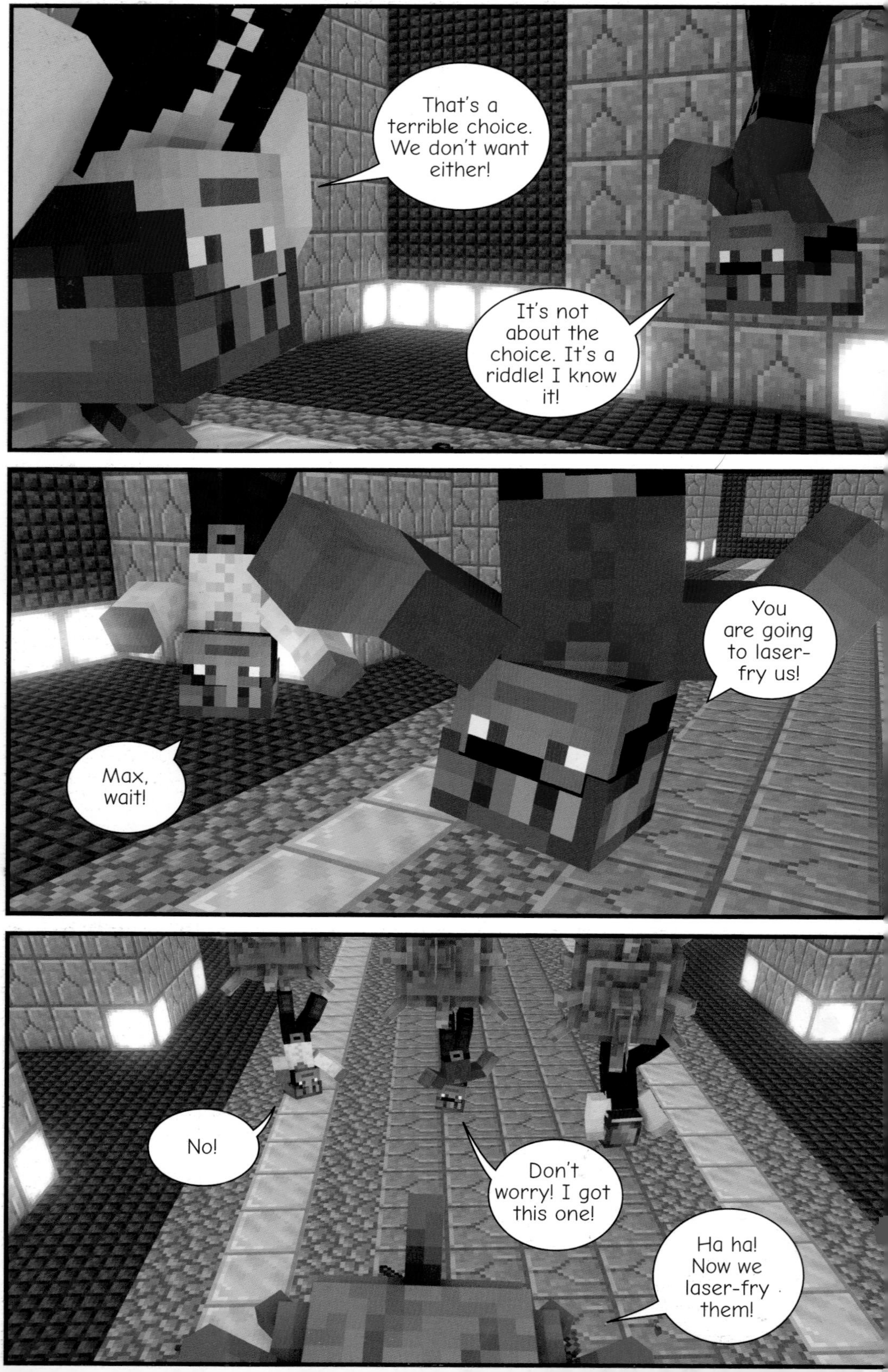
That's a terrible choice. We don't want either!
It's not about the choice. It's a riddle! I know it!
You are going to laser-fry us!
Max, wait!
No!
Don't worry! I got this one!
Ha ha! Now we laser-fry them!

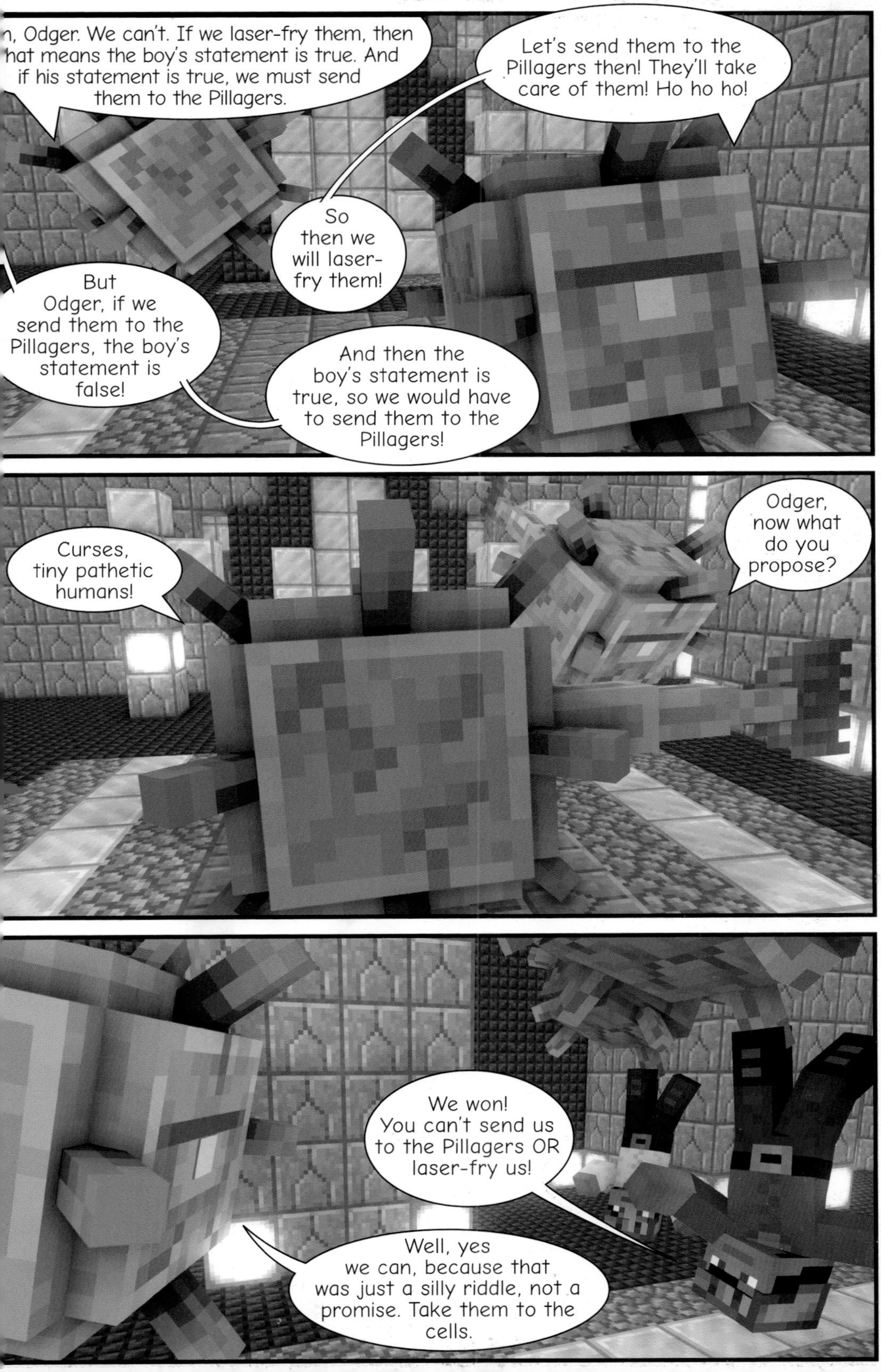
n, Odger. We can't. If we laser-fry them, then hat means the boy's statement is true. And if his statement is true, we must send them to the Pillagers.
Let's send them to the Pillagers then! They'll take care of them! Ho ho ho!
So then we will laser-fry them!
But Odger, if we send them to the Pillagers, the boy's statement is false!
And then the boy's statement is true, so we would have to send them to the Pillagers!
Curses, tiny pathetic humans!
Odger, now what do you propose?
We won! You can't send us to the Pillagers OR laser-fry us!
Well, yes we can, because that was just a silly riddle, not a promise. Take them to the cells.

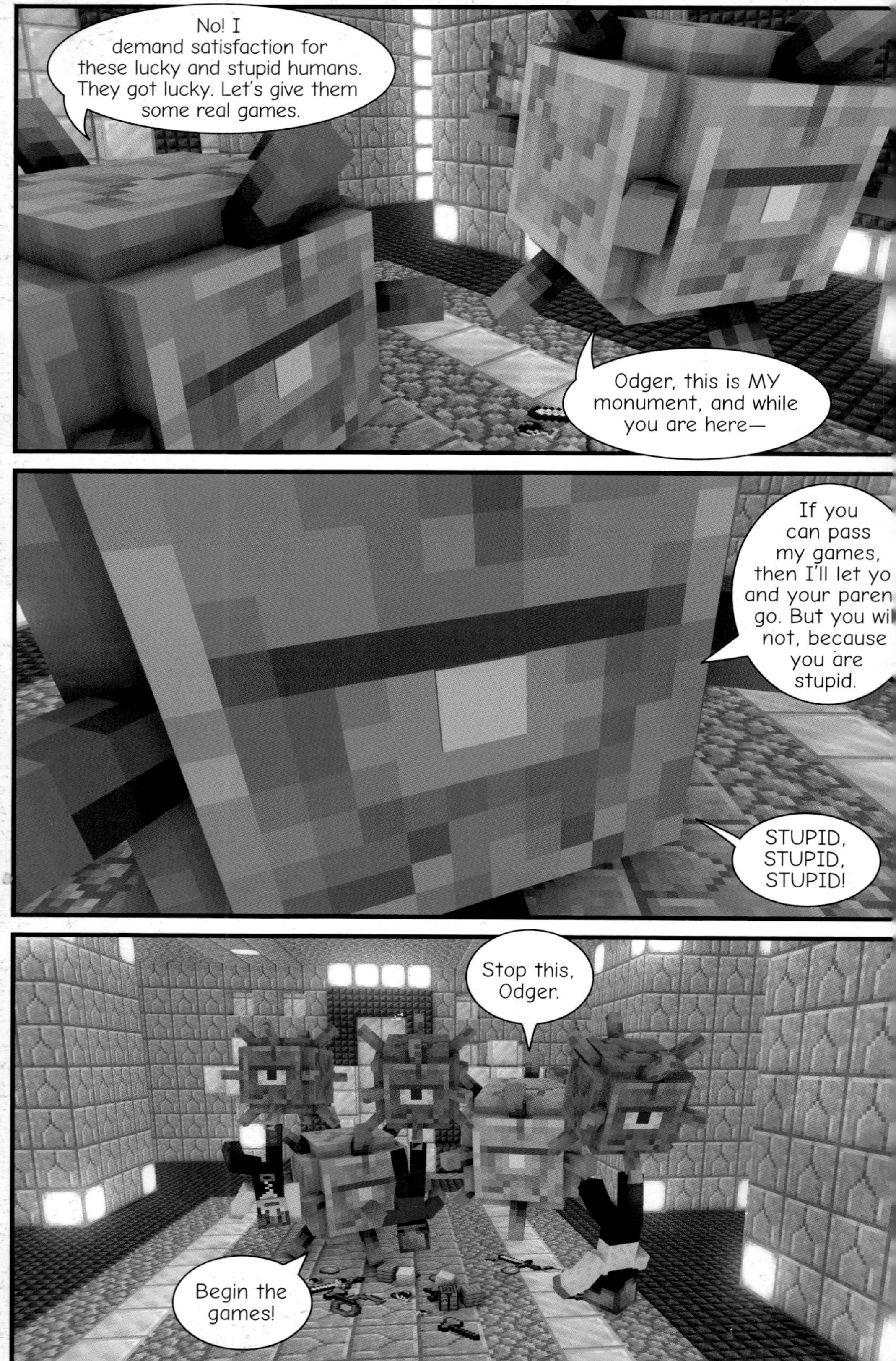
No! I demand satisfaction for these lucky and stupid humans. They got lucky. Let's give them some real games.
Odger, this is MY monument, and while you are here—
If you can pass my games, then I'll let yo and your paren go. But you wi not, because you are stupid.
STUPID, STUPID, STUPID!
Stop this, Odger.
Begin the games!

Chapter 7
Escape from the Skeletons

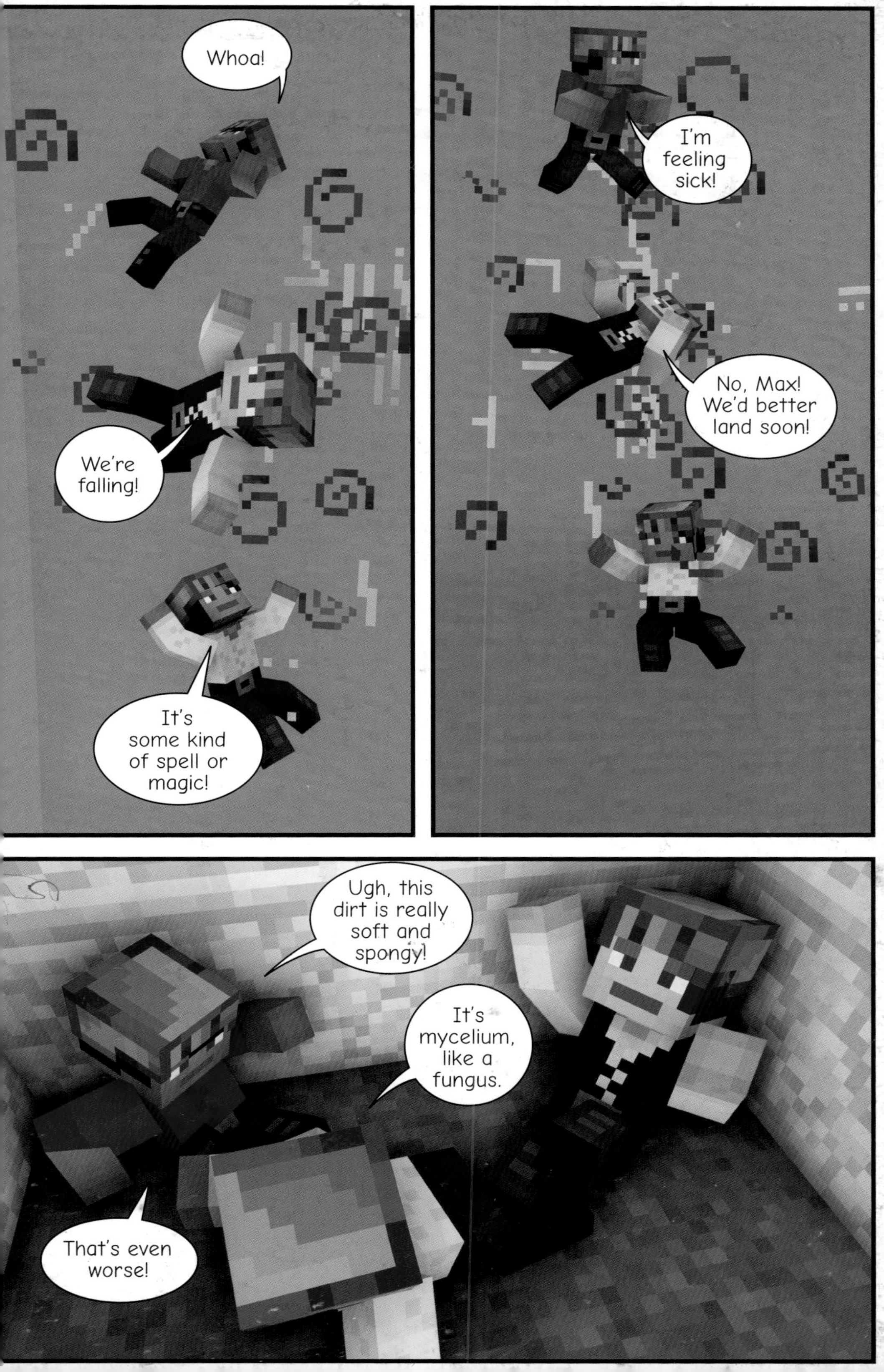
Whoa!
We're falling!
It's some kind of spell or magic!
I'm feeling sick!
No, Max! We'd better land soon!
Ugh, this dirt is really soft and spongy!
It's mycelium, like a fungus.
That's even worse!

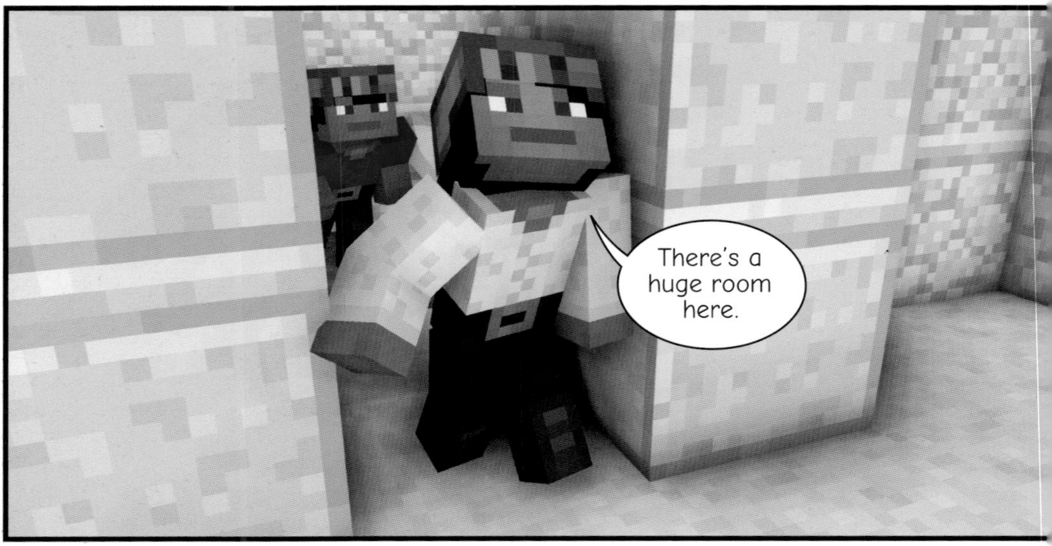
There's a huge room here.

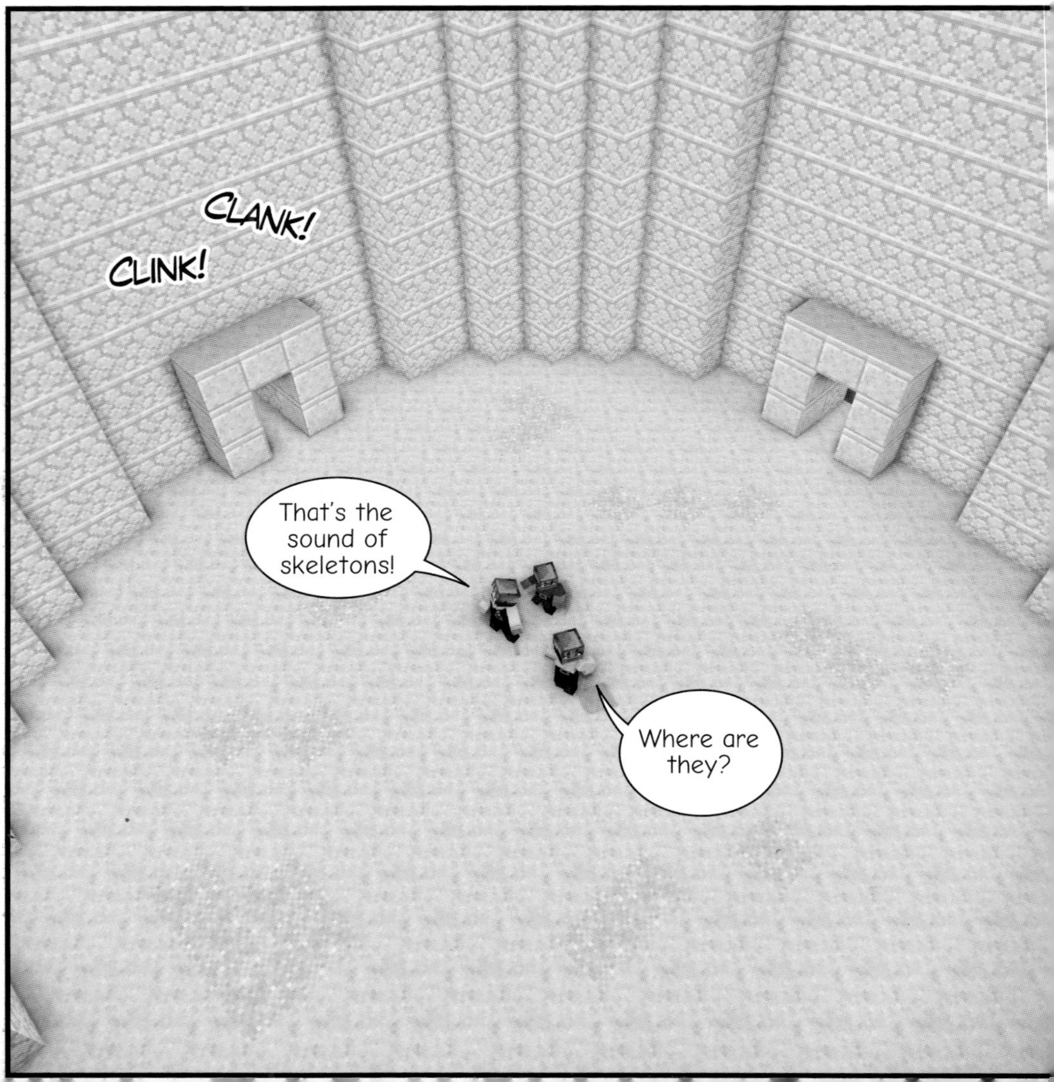
CLANK!
CLINK!
That's the sound of skeletons!
Where are they?

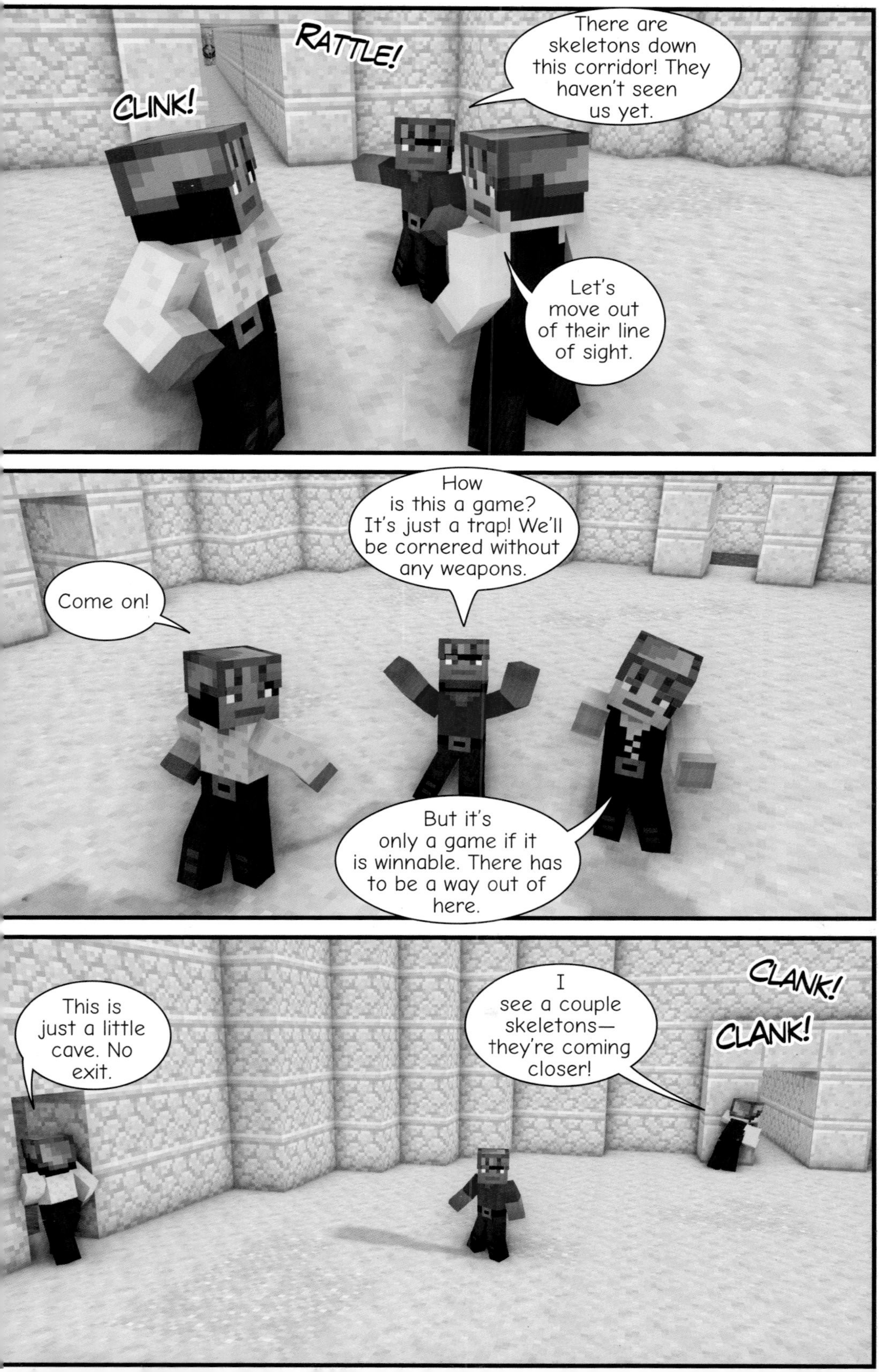
CLINK!
RATTLE!
There are skeletons down this corridor! They haven't seen us yet.
Let's move out of their line of sight.
Come on!
How is this a game? It's just a trap! We'll be cornered without any weapons.
But it's only a game if it is winnable. There has to be a way out of here.
This is just a little cave. No exit.
I see a couple skeletons— they're coming closer!
CLANK!
CLANK!

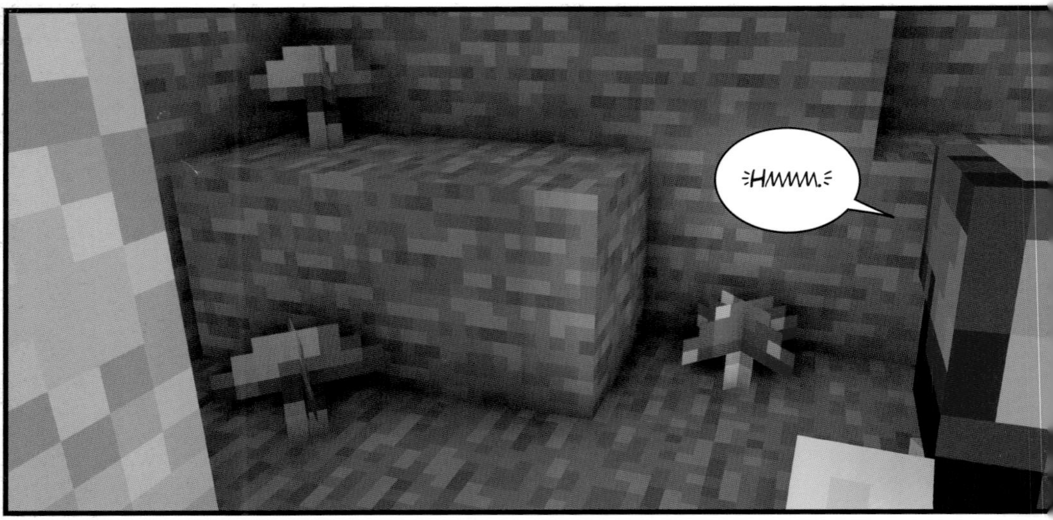
HMMM.

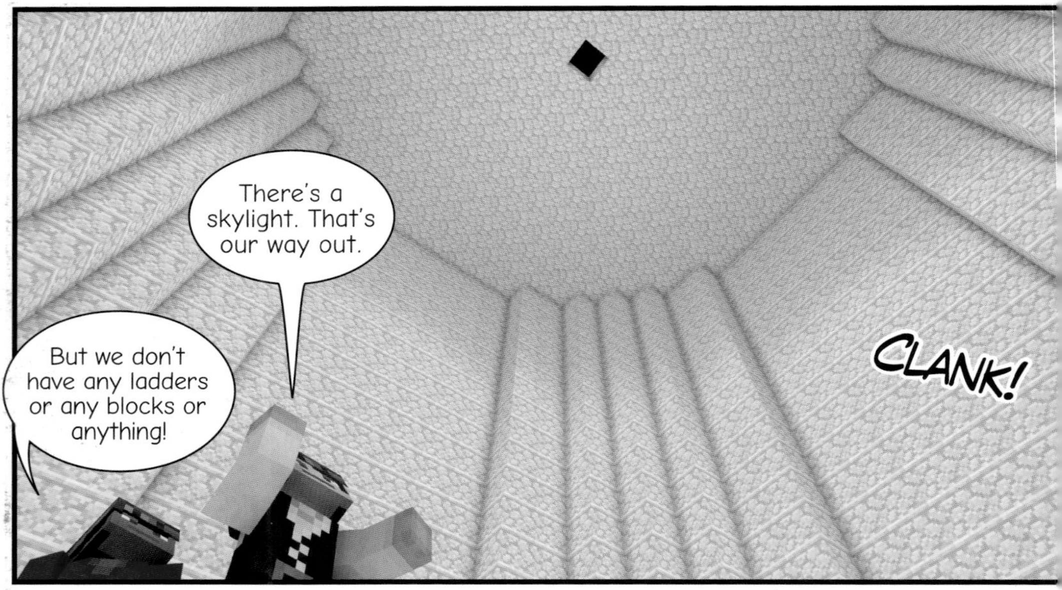
There's a skylight. That's our way out.
But we don't have any ladders or any blocks or anything!
CLANK!

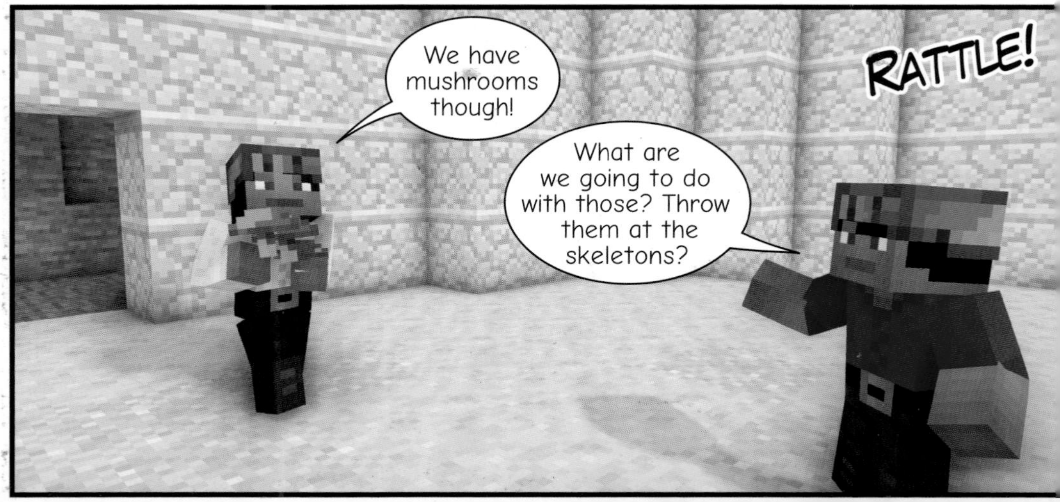
RATTLE!
We have mushrooms though!
What are we going to do with those? Throw them at the skeletons?

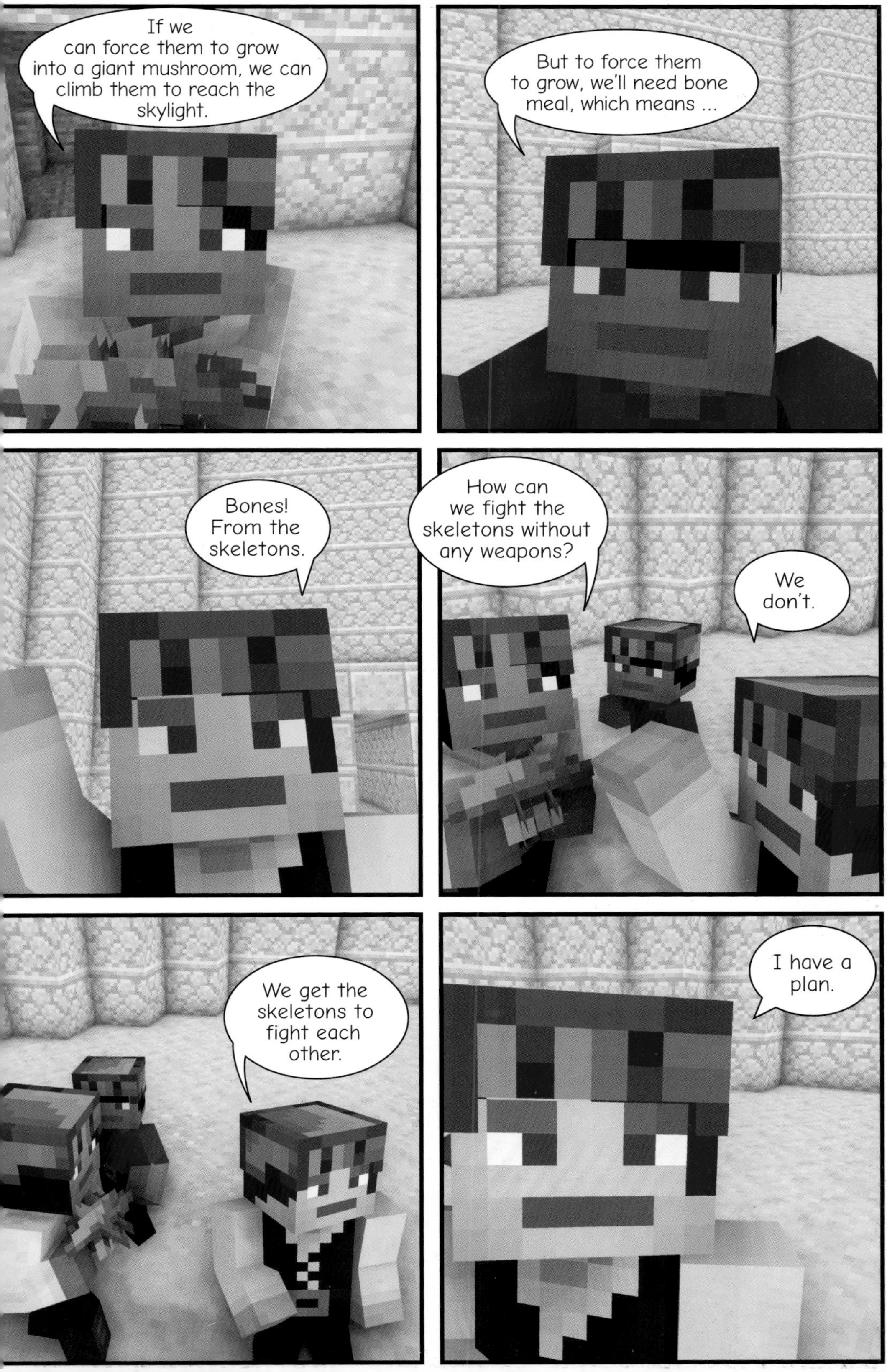
If we can force them to grow into a giant mushroom, we can climb them to reach the skylight.
But to force them to grow, we'll need bone meal, which means ...
Bones! From the skeletons.
How can we fight the skeletons without any weapons?
We don't.
We get the skeletons to fight each other.
I have a plan.

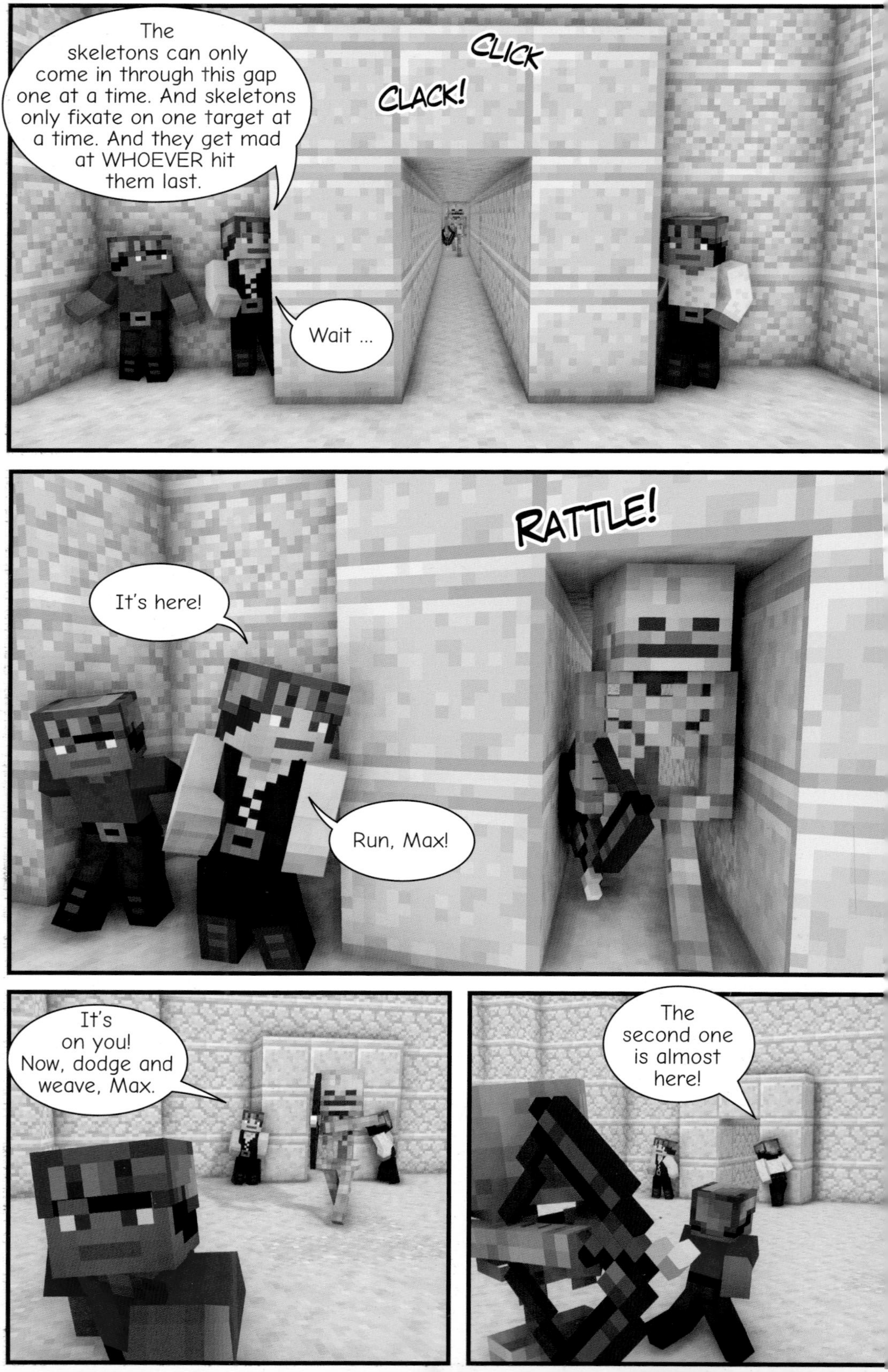
The skeletons can only come in through this gap one at a time. And skeletons only fixate on one target at a time. And they get mad at WHOEVER hit them last.
CLICK
CLACK!
Wait ...
RATTLE!
It's here!
Run, Max!
It's on you! Now, dodge and weave, Max.
The second one is almost here!

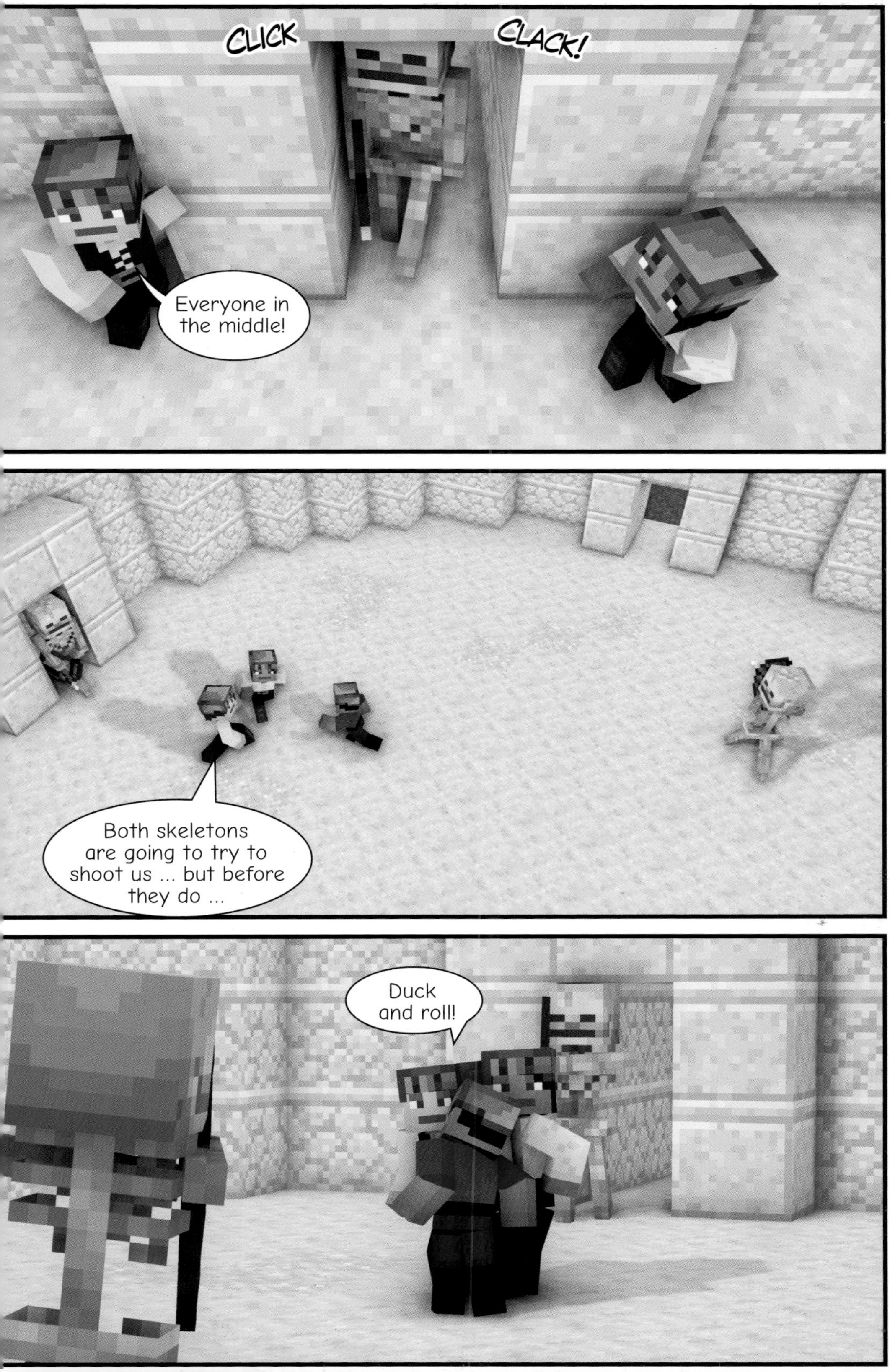
CLICK
CLACK!
Everyone in the middle!
Both skeletons are going to try to shoot us ... but before they do ...
Duck and roll!

THWACK!
PEW!
It worked!
PEW!
THWACK!
PEW!
PEW!
POOF!
POOF!

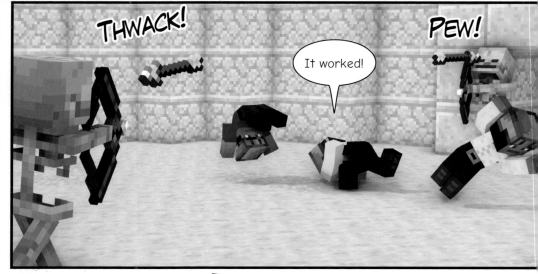

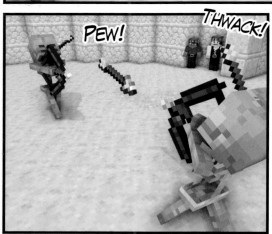

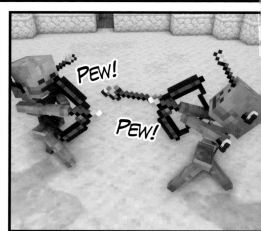

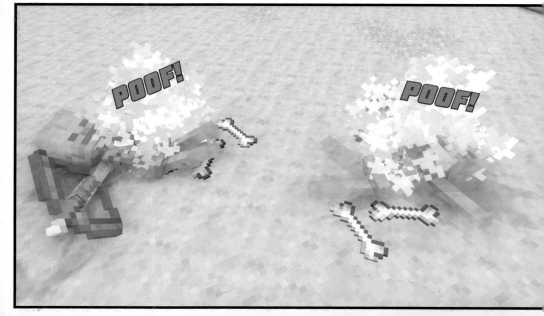

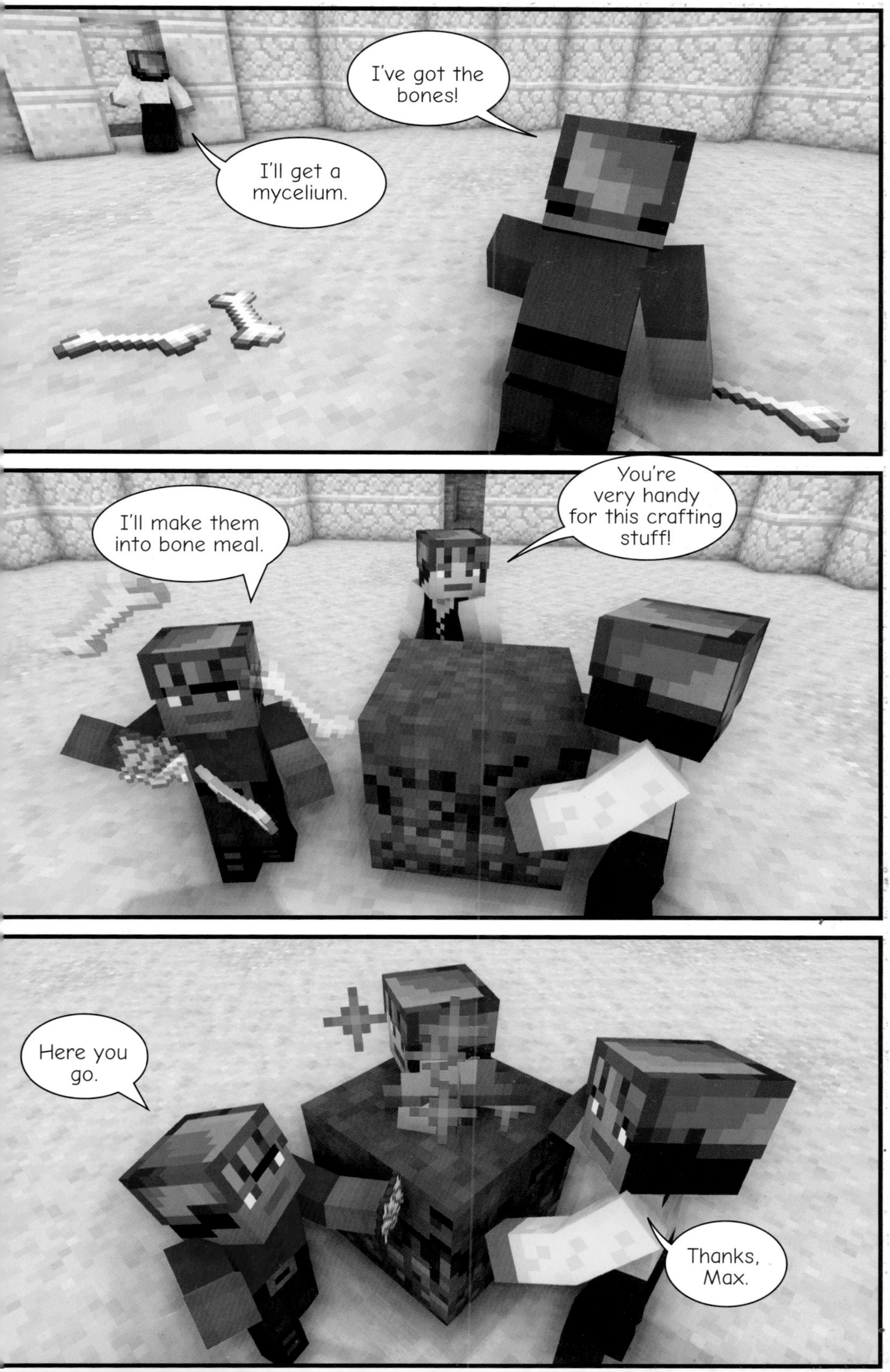
I've got the bones!
I'll get a mycelium.
I'll make them into bone meal.
You're very handy for this crafting stuff!
Here you go.
Thanks, Max.

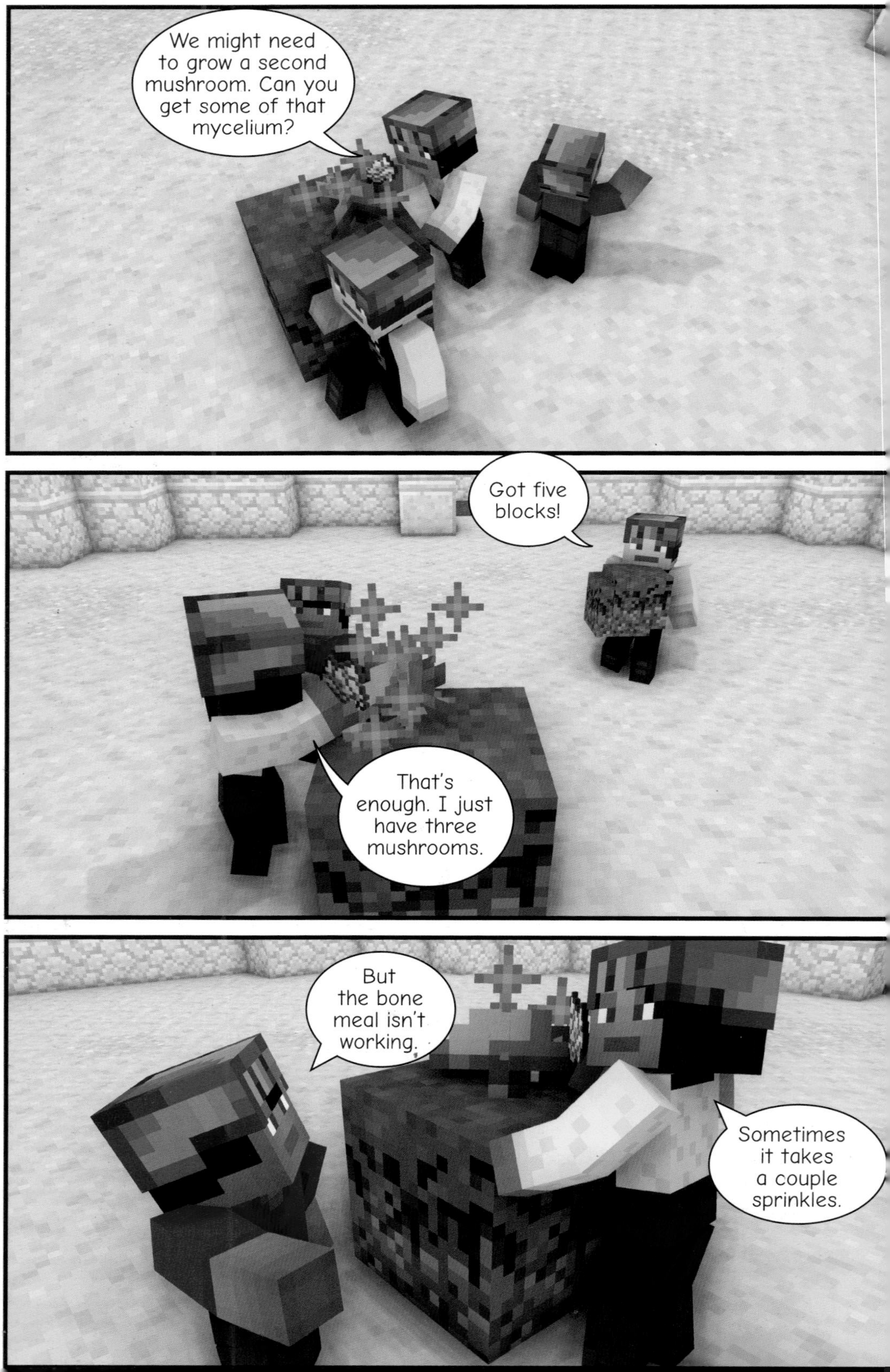

We might need to grow a second mushroom. Can you get some of that mycelium?
Got five blocks!
That's enough. I just have three mushrooms.
But the bone meal isn't working.
Sometimes it takes a couple sprinkles.

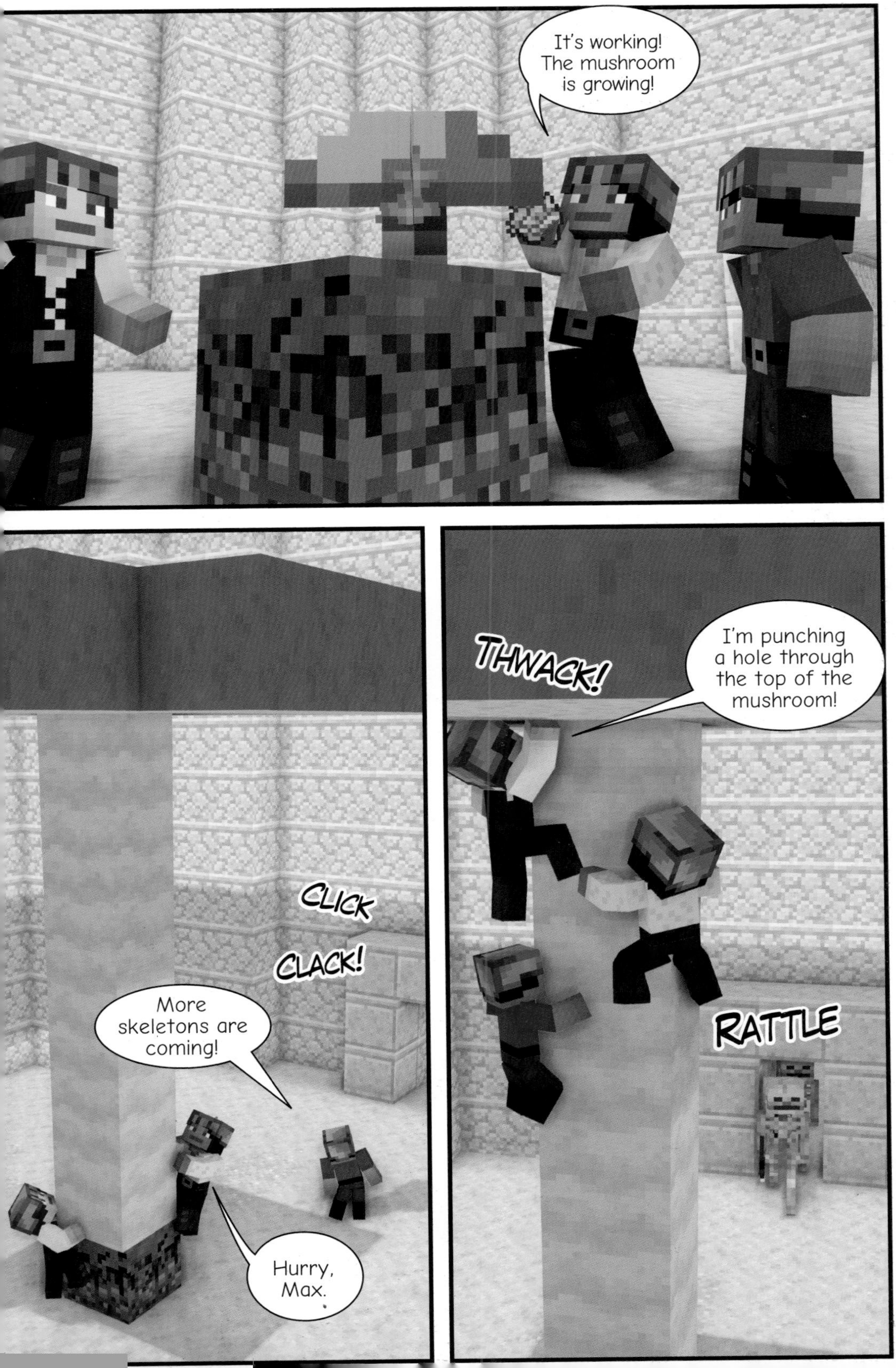
It's working! The mushroom is growing!
More skeletons are coming!
CLICK
CLACK!
Hurry, Max.
THWACK!
I'm punching a hole through the top of the mushroom!
RATTLE

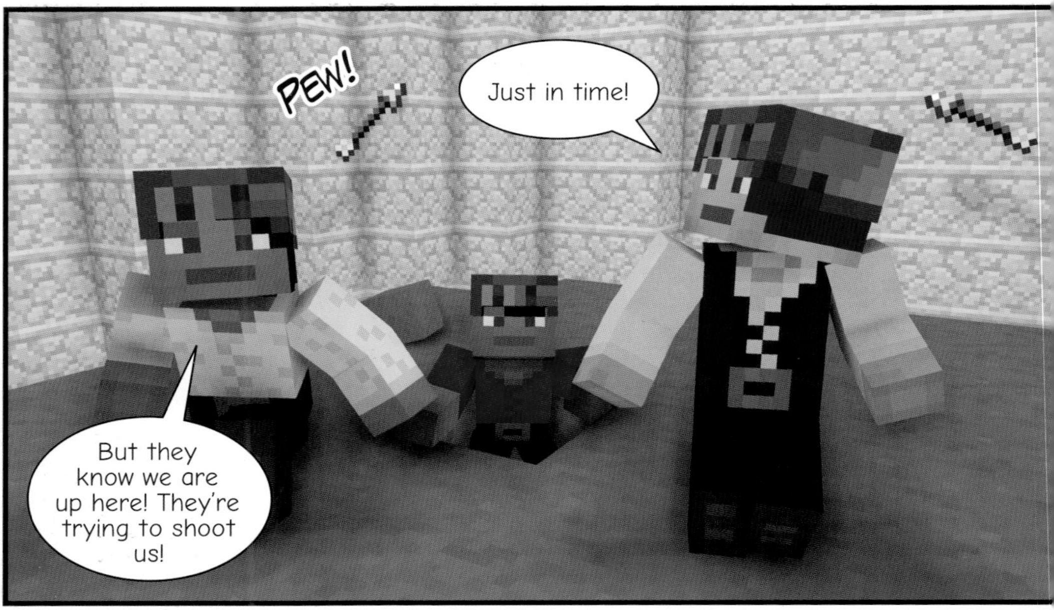
PEW!
Just in time!
But they know we are up here! They're trying to shoot us!

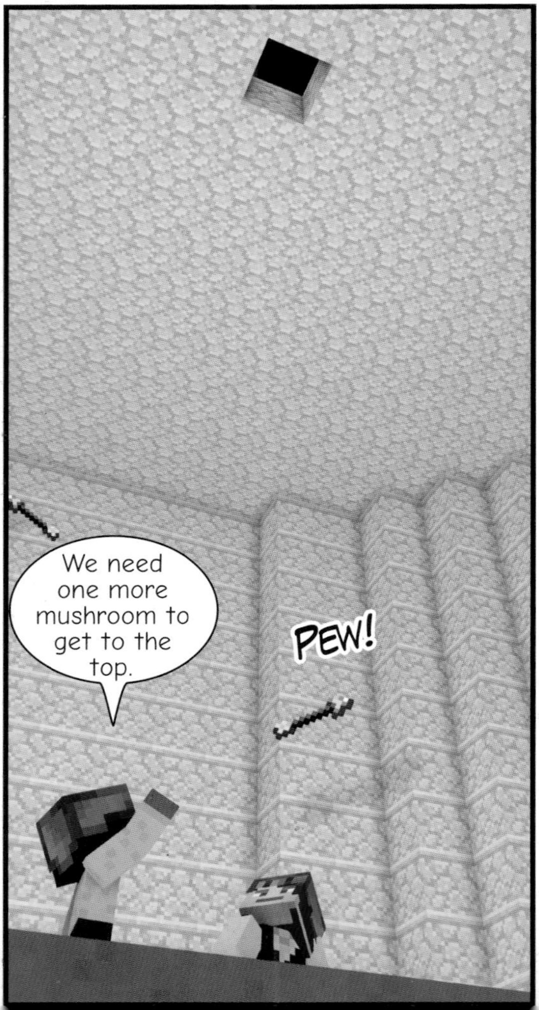
We need one more mushroom to get to the top.
PEW!

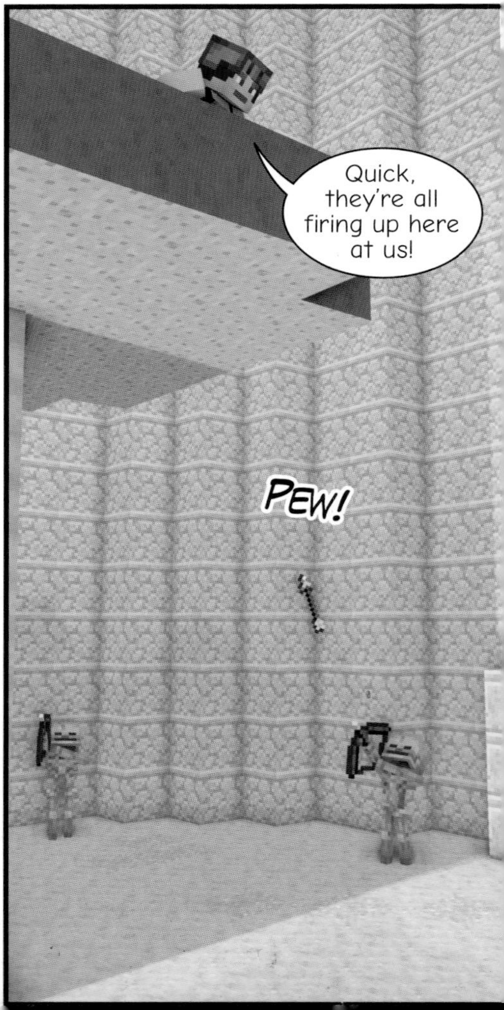
Quick, they're all firing up here at us!
PEW!

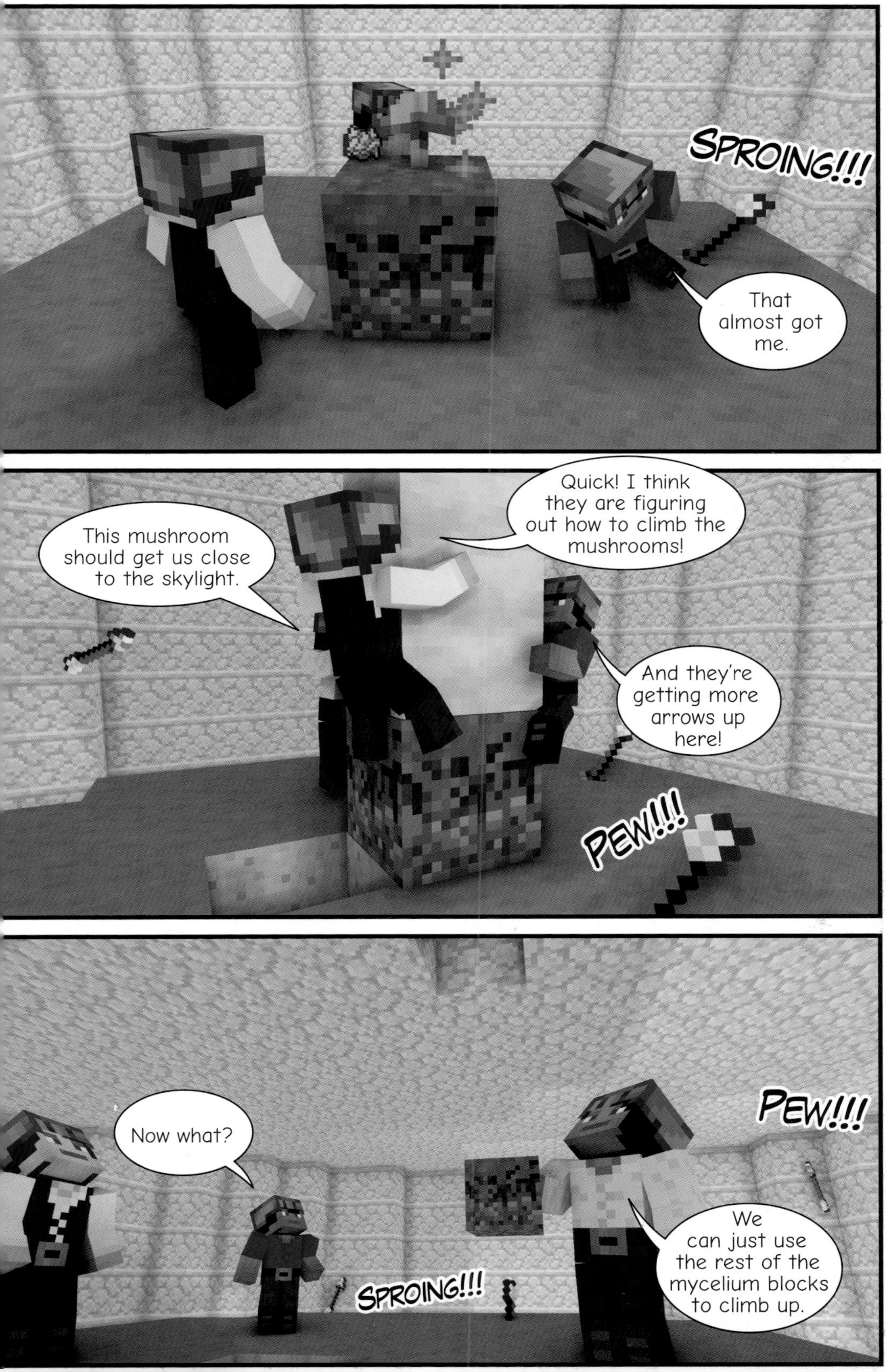
SPROING!!!
That almost got me.
This mushroom should get us close to the skylight.
Quick! I think they are figuring out how to climb the mushrooms!
And they're getting more arrows up here!
PEW!!!
Now what?
PEW!!!
SPROING!!!
We can just use the rest of the mycelium blocks to climb up.

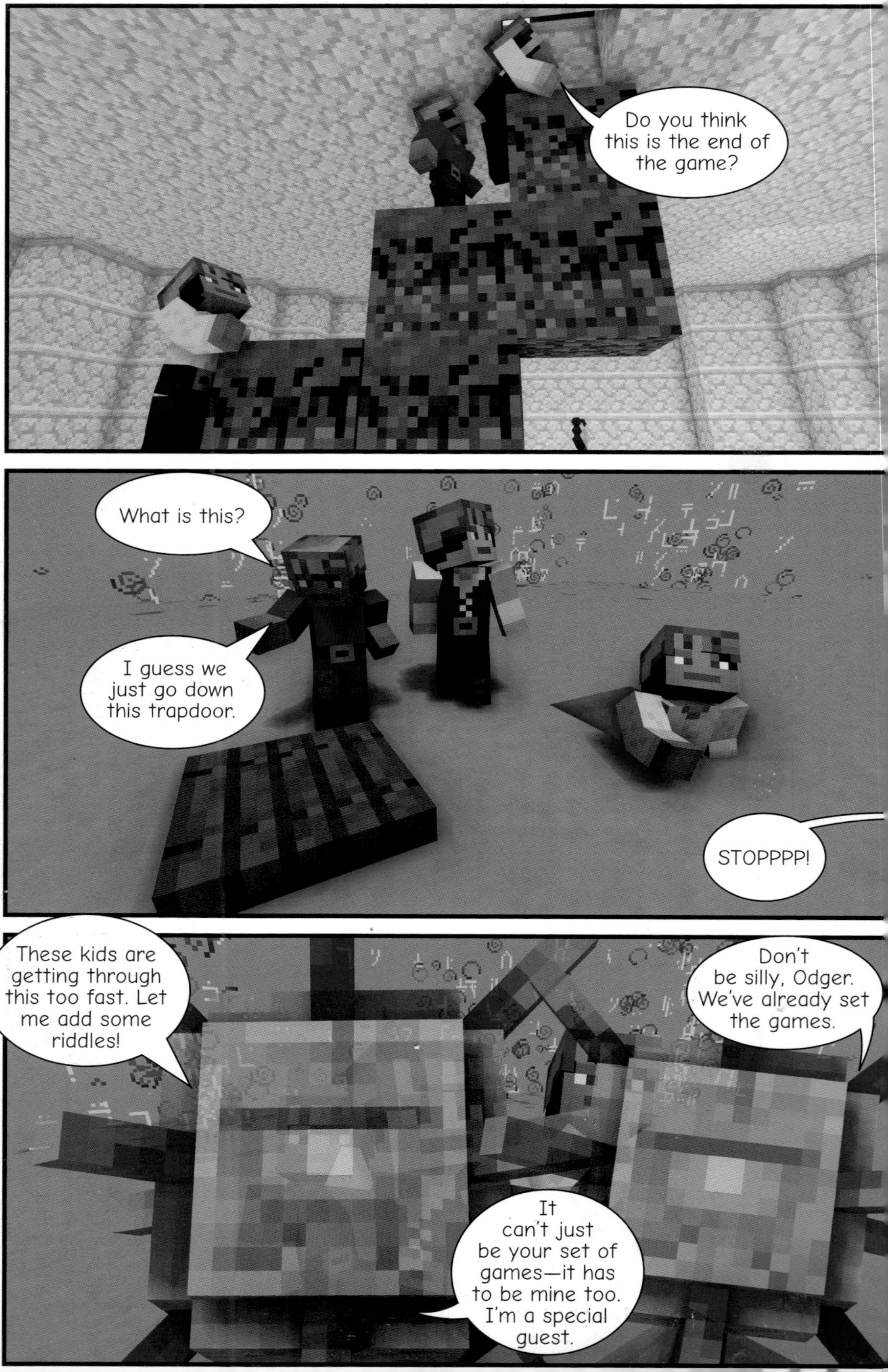

Do you think this is the end of the game?
What is this?
I guess we just go down this trapdoor.
STOPPPP!
These kids are getting through this too fast. Let me add some riddles!
Don't be silly, Odger. We've already set the games.
It can't just be your set of games—it has to be mine too. I'm a special guest.

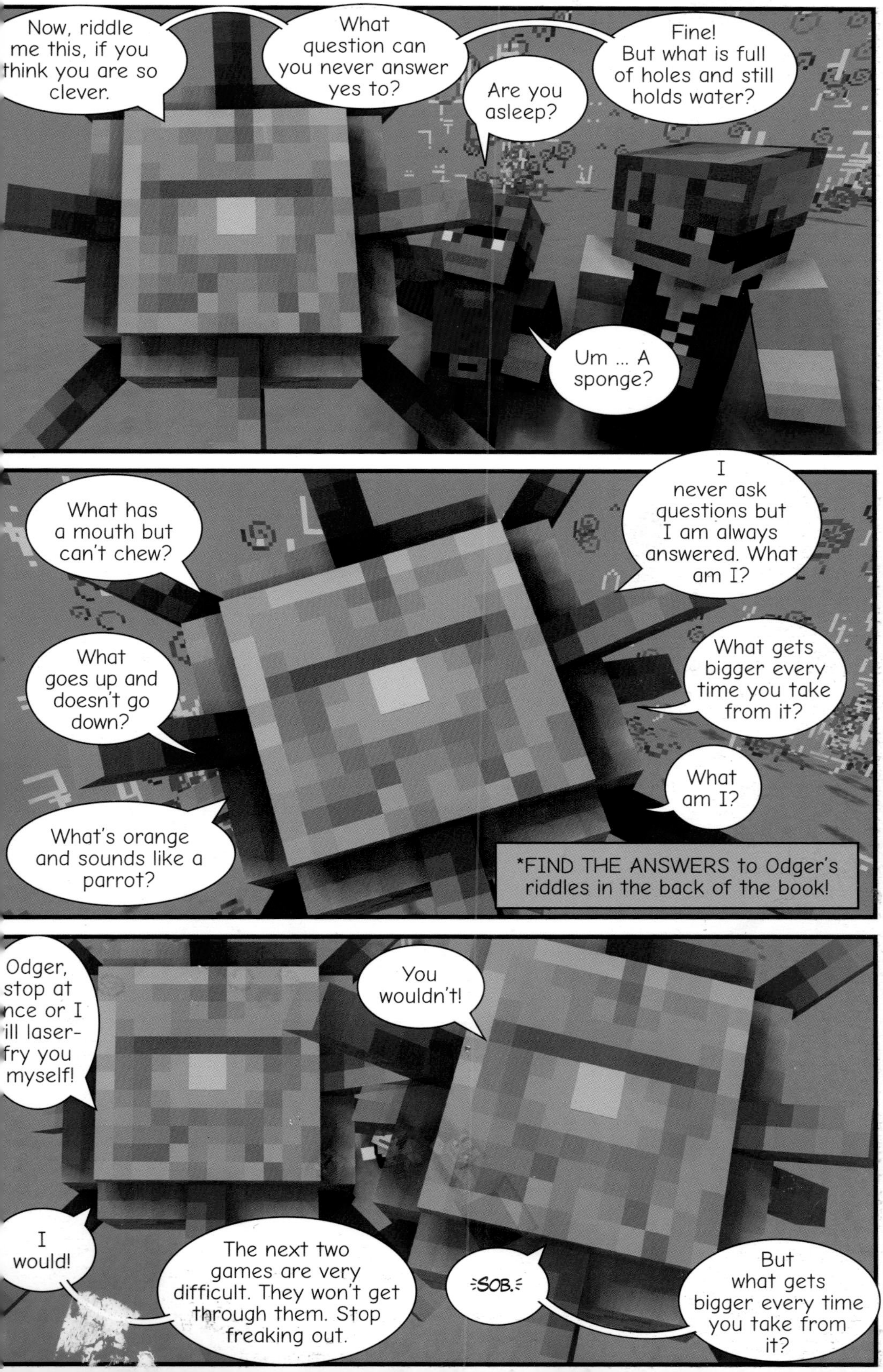
Now, riddle me this, if you think you are so clever.
What question can you never answer yes to?
Are you asleep?
Fine! But what is full of holes and still holds water?
Um ... A sponge?
What has a mouth but can't chew?
I never ask questions but I am always answered. What am I?
What goes up and doesn't go down?
What gets bigger every time you take from it?
What am I?
What's orange and sounds like a parrot?
*FIND THE ANSWERS to Odger's riddles in the back of the book!
Odger, stop at nce or I ill laser-fry you myself!
You wouldn't!
I would!
The next two games are very difficult. They won't get through them. Stop freaking out.
SOB.
But what gets bigger every time you take from it?

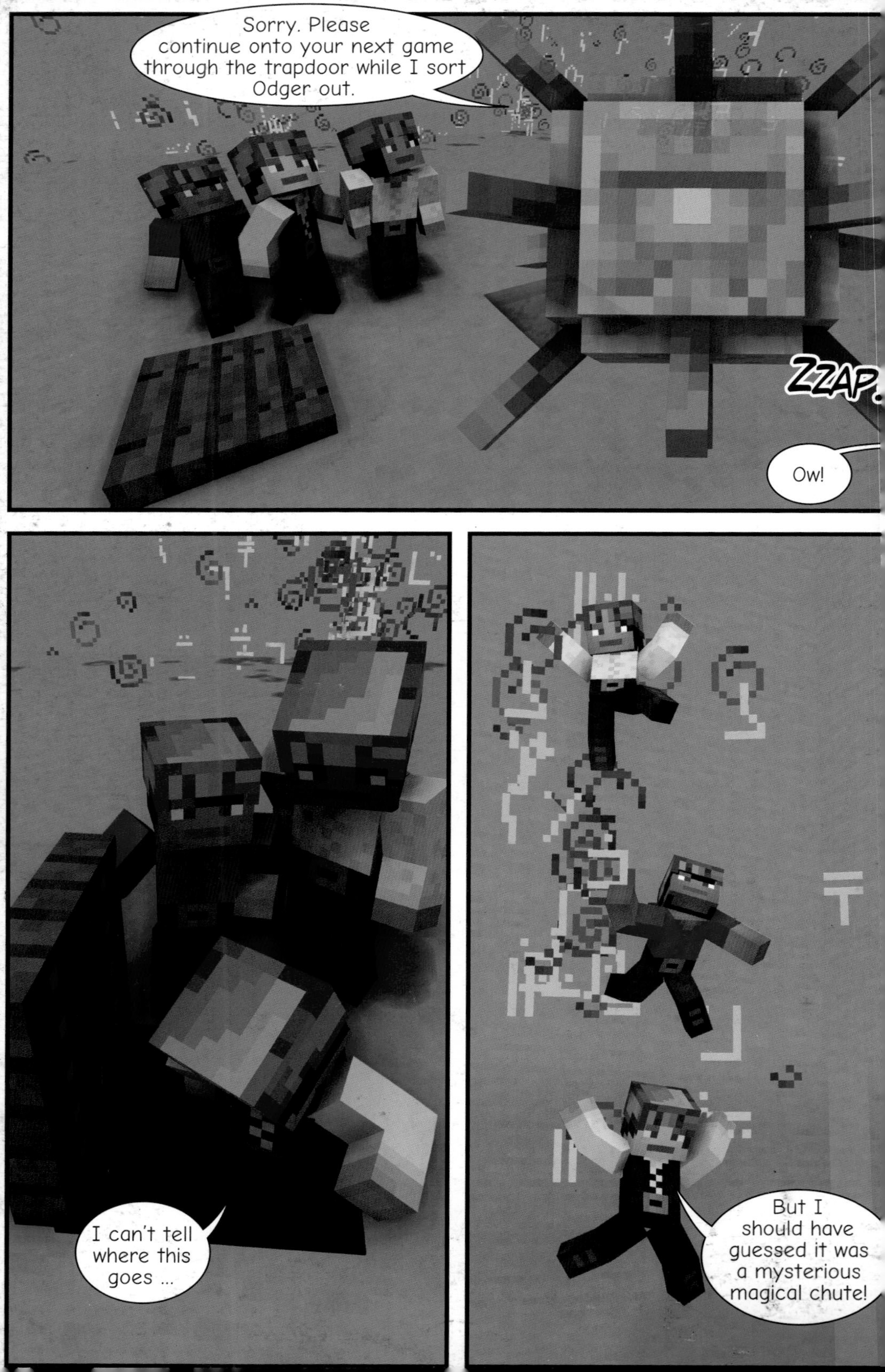
Sorry. Please continue onto your next game through the trapdoor while I sort Odger out.
ZZAP!
Ow!
I can't tell where this goes ...
But I should have guessed it was a mysterious magical chute!

Chapter 8
A Squid, a Fish, and a Baby Guardian

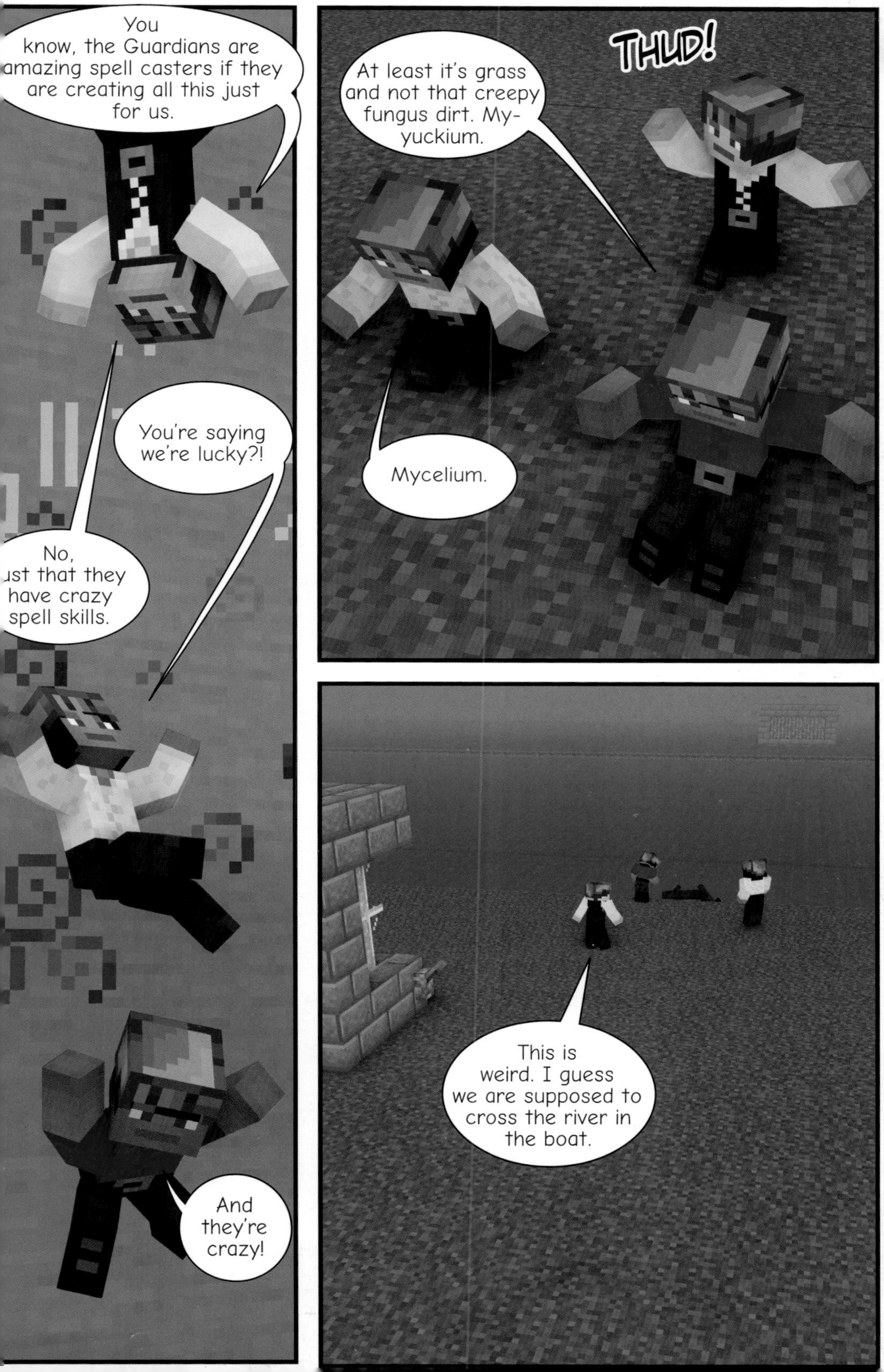
You know, the Guardians are amazing spell casters if they are creating all this just for us.
You're saying we're lucky?!
No, ust that they have crazy spell skills.
And they're crazy!
THUD!
At least it's grass and not that creepy fungus dirt. My-yuckium.
Mycelium.
This is weird. I guess we are supposed to cross the river in the boat.

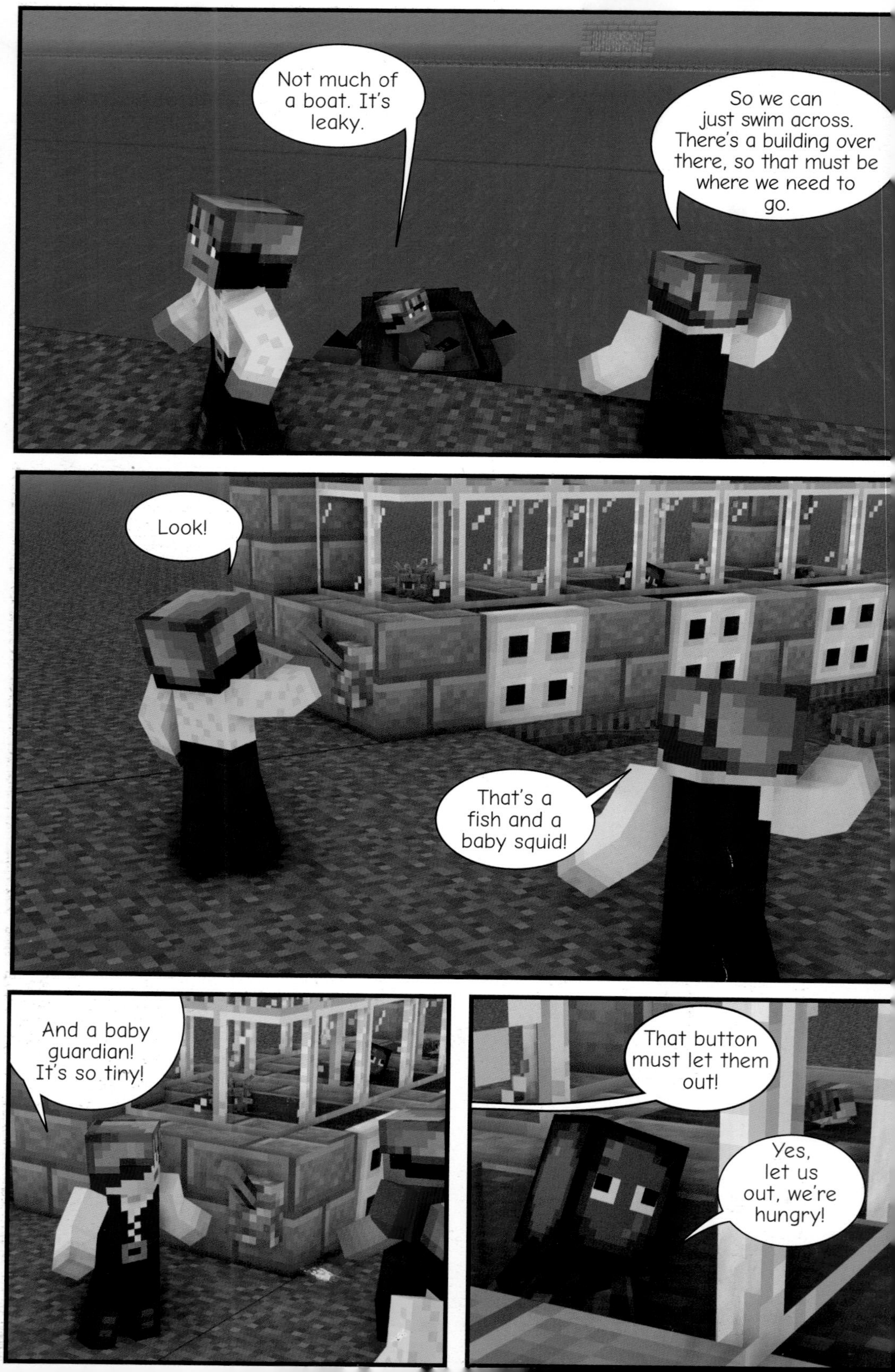
Not much of a boat. It's leaky.
So we can just swim across. There's a building over there, so that must be where we need to go.
Look!
That's a fish and a baby squid!
And a baby guardian! It's so tiny!
That button must let them out!
Yes, let us out, we're hungry!

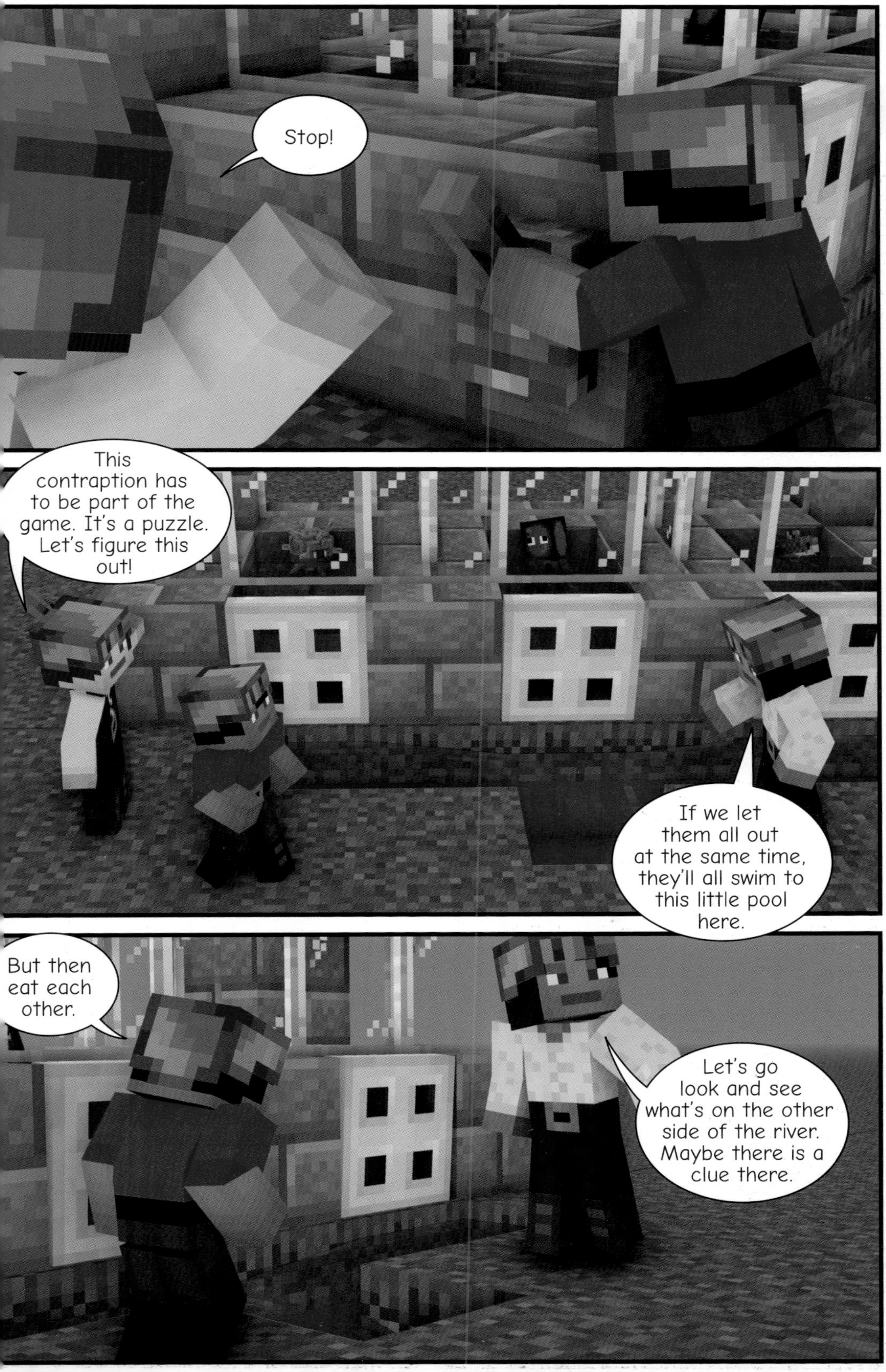
Stop!
This contraption has to be part of the game. It's a puzzle. Let's figure this out!
If we let them all out at the same time, they'll all swim to this little pool here.
But then eat each other.
Let's go look and see what's on the other side of the river. Maybe there is a clue there.

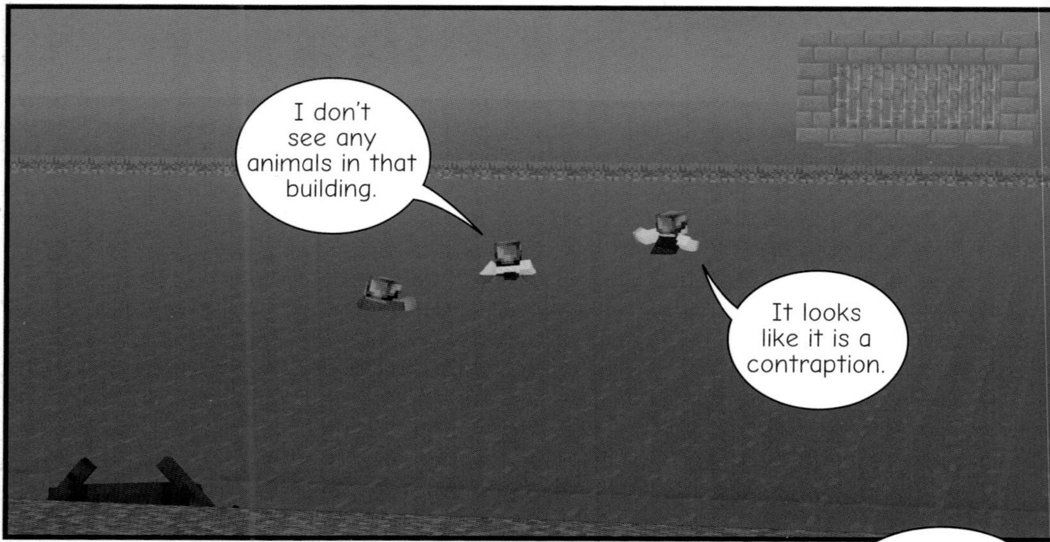
I don't see any animals in that building.
It looks like it is a contraption.

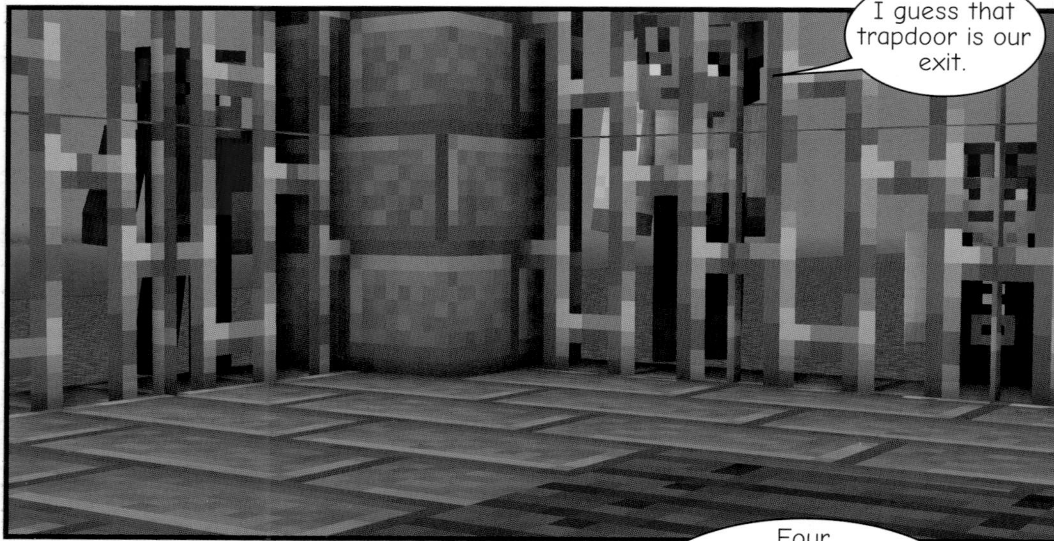
I guess that trapdoor is our exit.

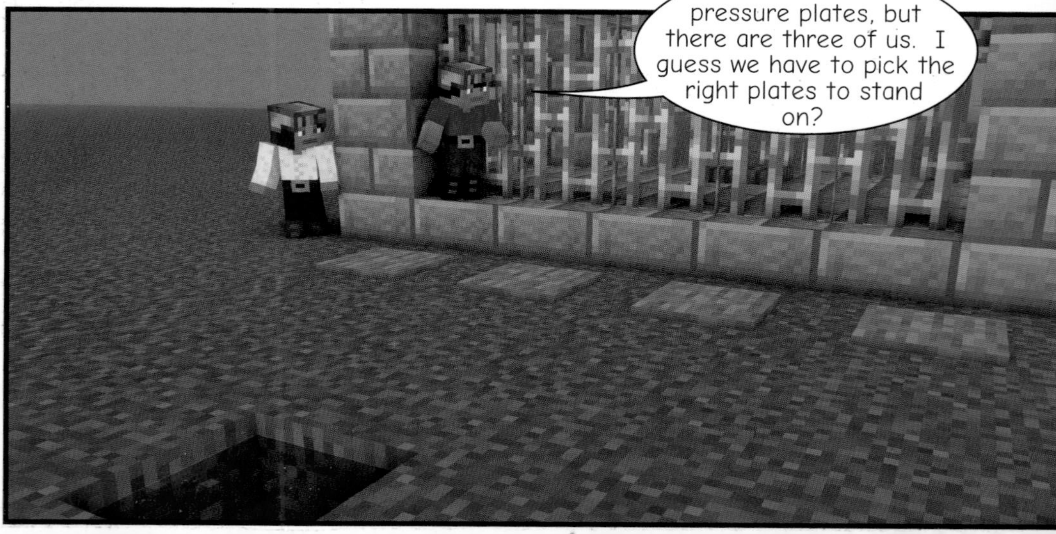
Four pressure plates, but there are three of us. I guess we have to pick the right plates to stand on?

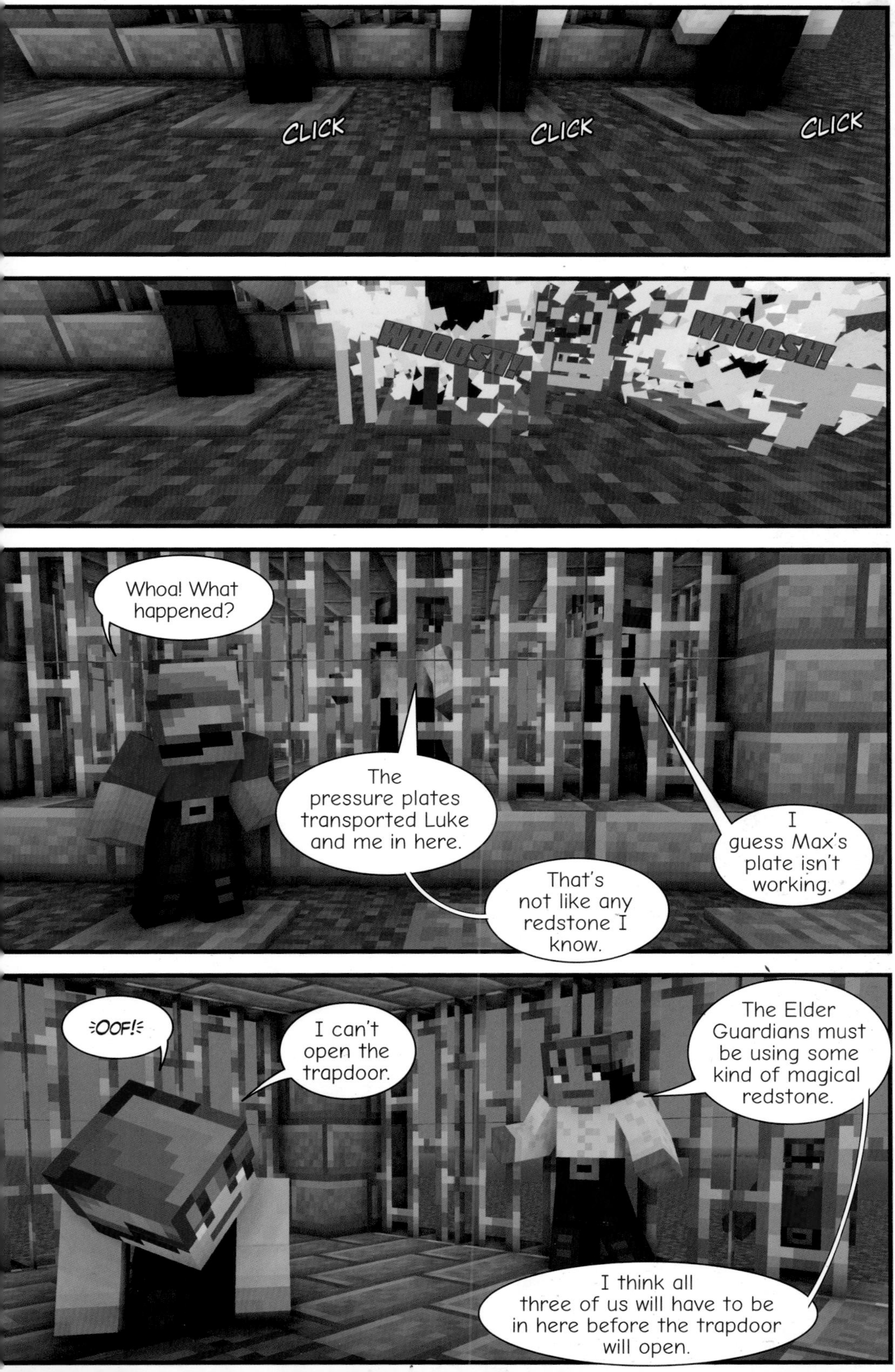
CLICK
CLICK
CLICK
WHOOSH!
WHOOSH!
Whoa! What happened?
The pressure plates transported Luke and me in here.
That's not like any redstone I know.
I guess Max's plate isn't working.
OOF!
I can't open the trapdoor.
The Elder Guardians must be using some kind of magical redstone.
I think all three of us will have to be in here before the trapdoor will open.

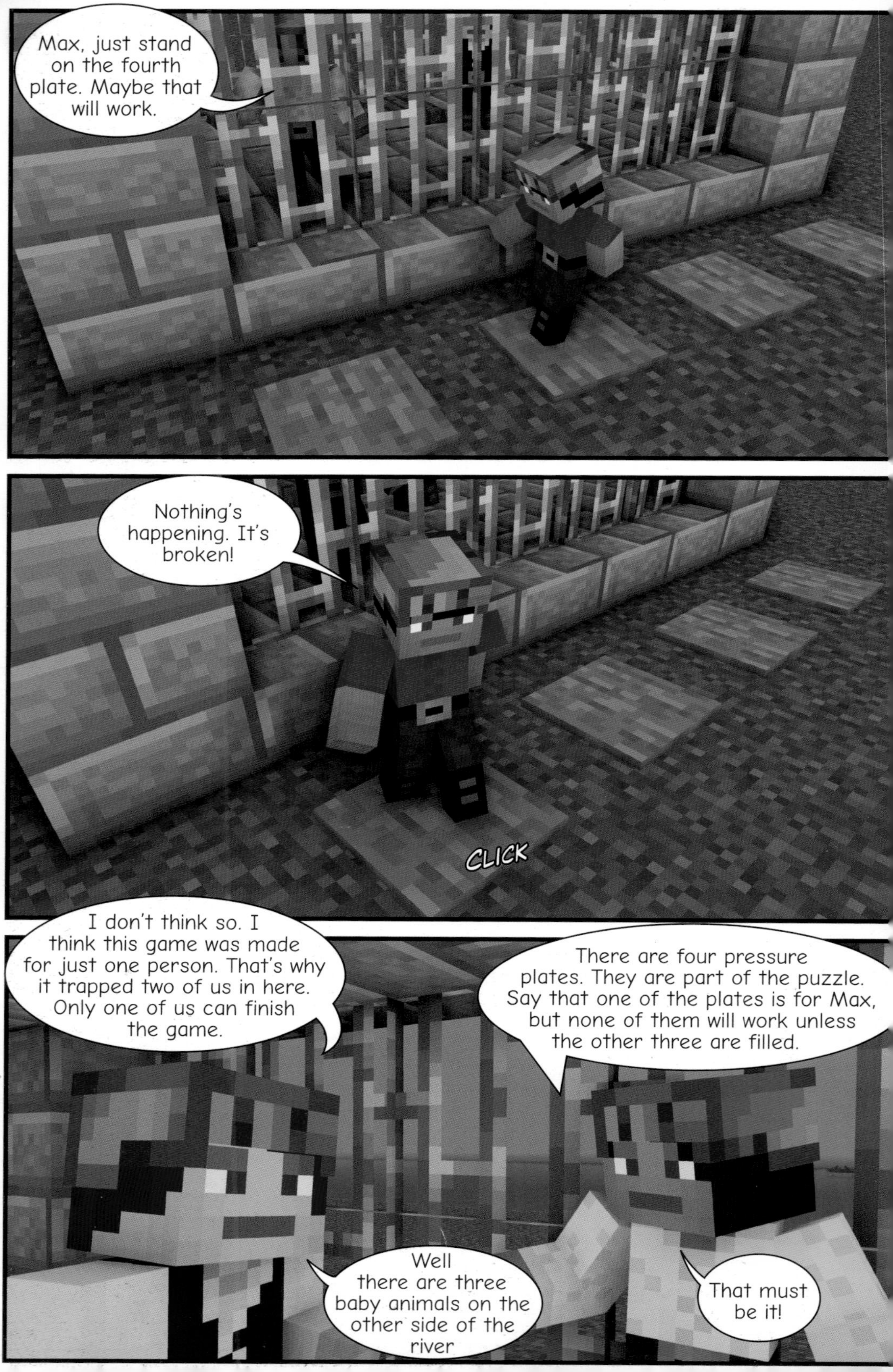
Max, just stand on the fourth plate. Maybe that will work.
Nothing's happening. It's broken!
CLICK
I don't think so. I think this game was made for just one person. That's why it trapped two of us in here. Only one of us can finish the game.
There are four pressure plates. They are part of the puzzle. Say that one of the plates is for Max, but none of them will work unless the other three are filled.
Well there are three baby animals on the other side of the river
That must be it!

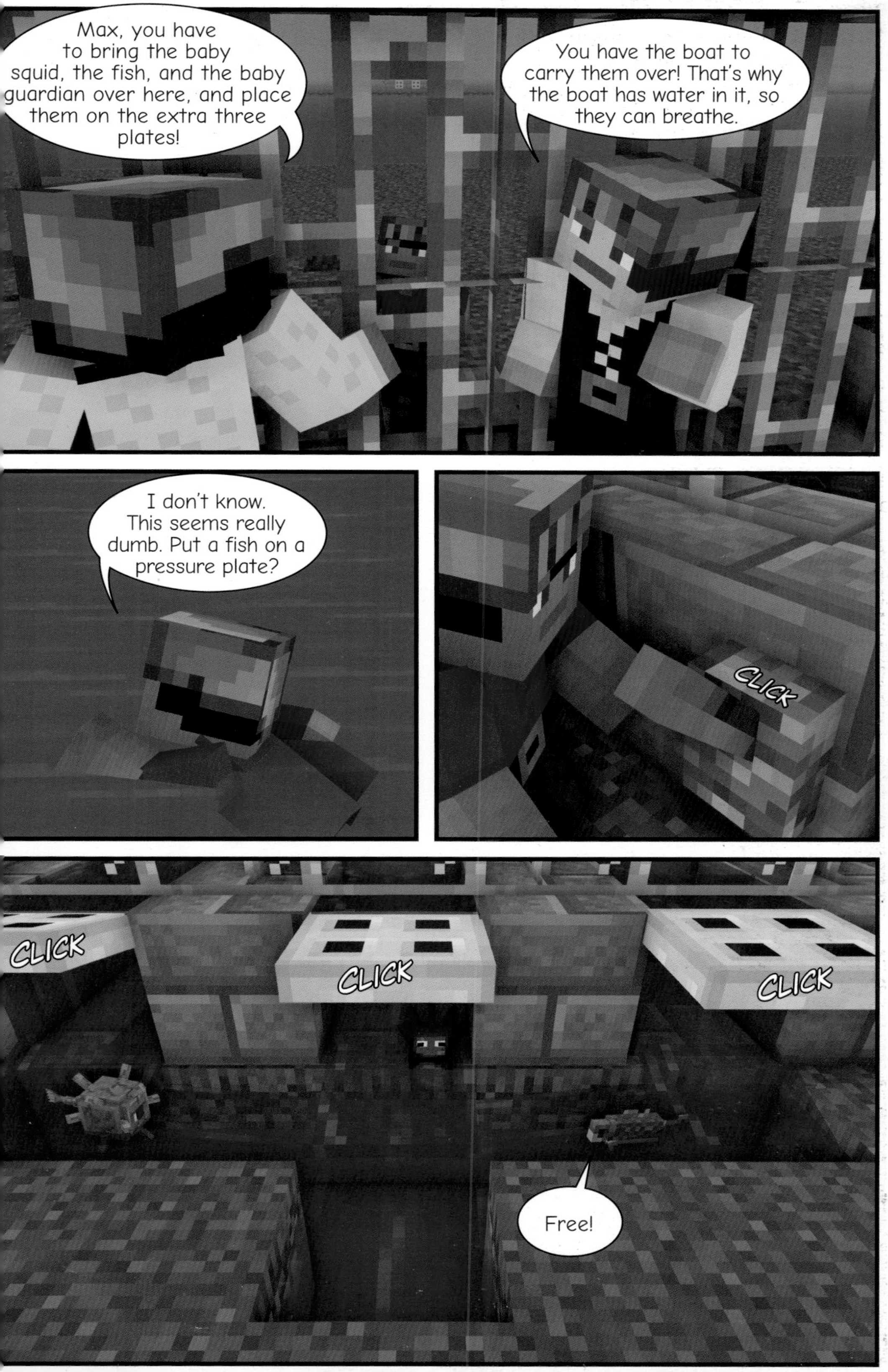
Max, you have to bring the baby squid, the fish, and the baby guardian over here, and place them on the extra three plates!
You have the boat to carry them over! That's why the boat has water in it, so they can breathe.
I don't know. This seems really dumb. Put a fish on a pressure plate?
CLICK
CLICK
CLICK
CLICK
Free!

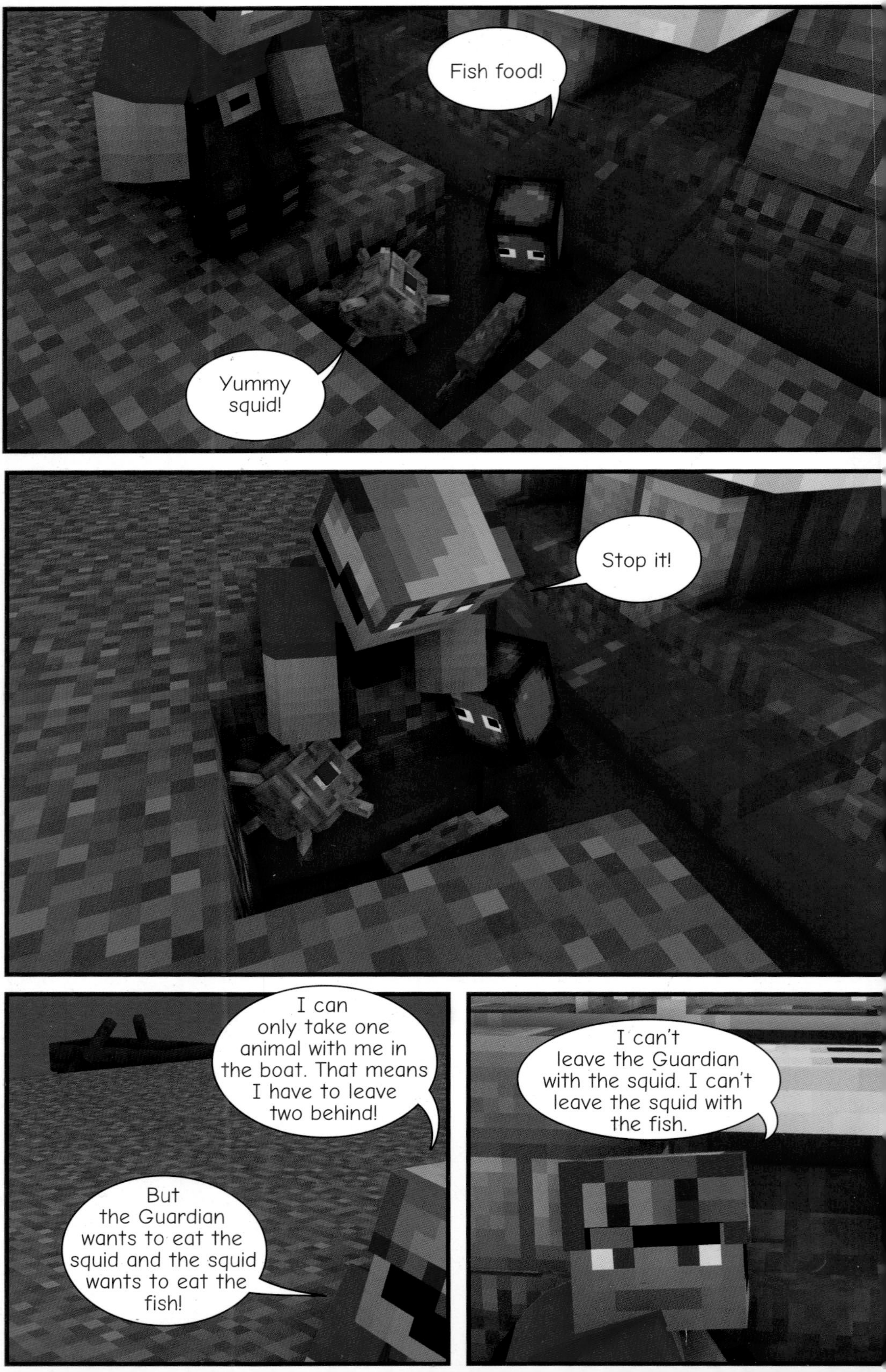
Fish food!
Yummy squid!
Stop it!
I can only take one animal with me in the boat. That means I have to leave two behind!
But the Guardian wants to eat the squid and the squid wants to eat the fish!
I can't leave the Guardian with the squid. I can't leave the squid with the fish.

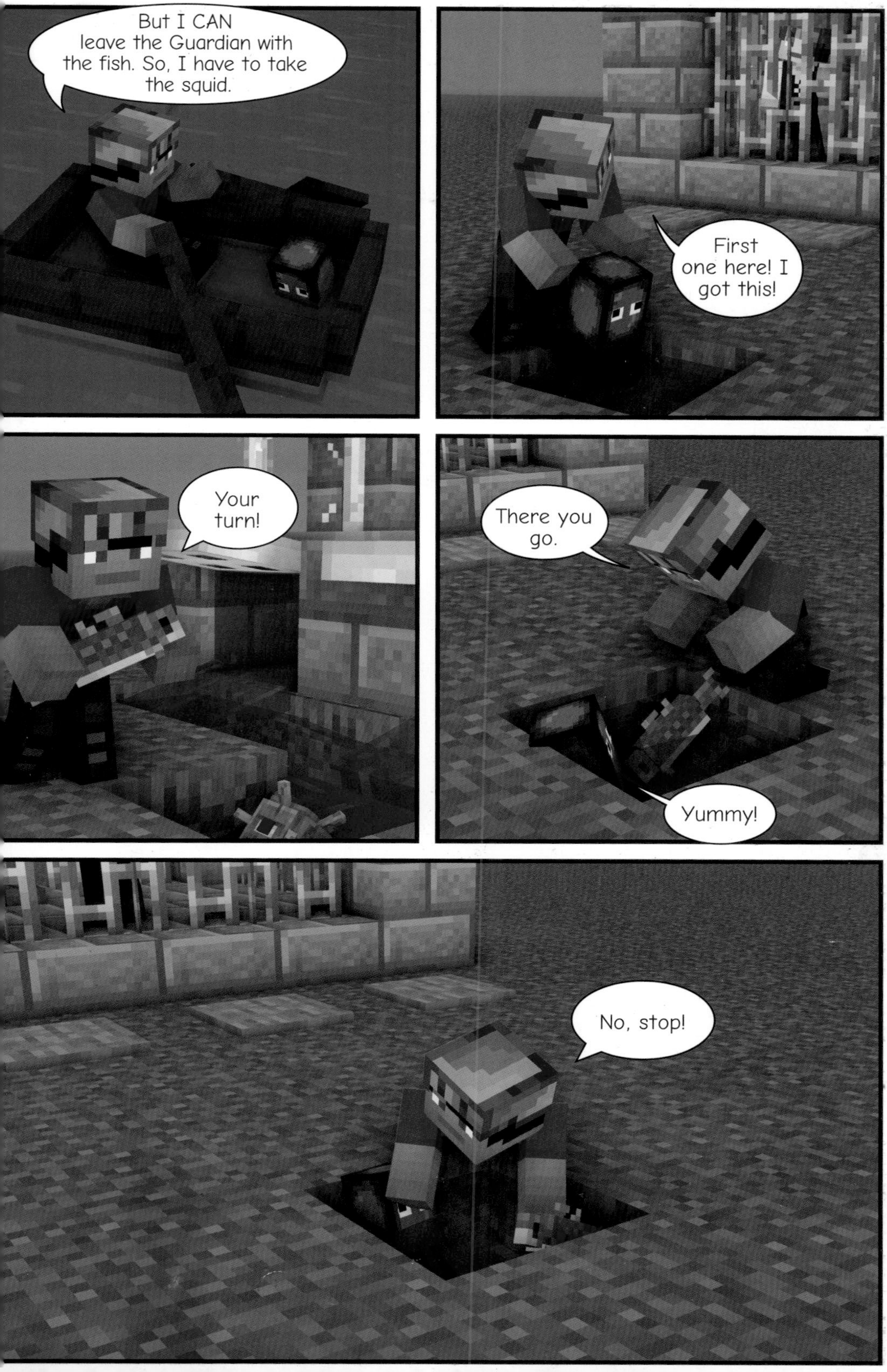

But I CAN leave the Guardian with the fish. So, I have to take the squid.
First one here! I got this!
Your turn!
There you go.
Yummy!
No, stop!

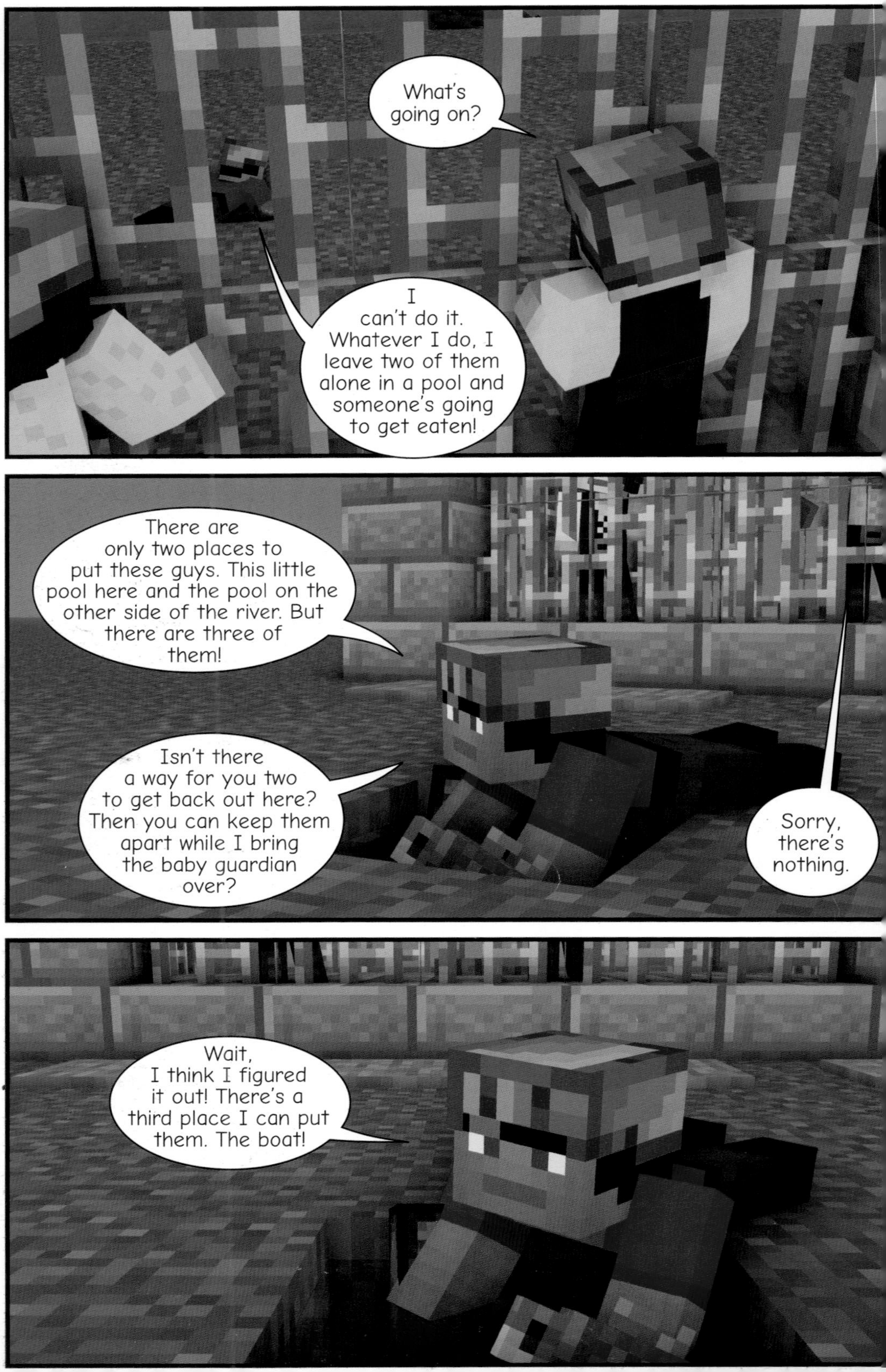
What's going on?
I can't do it. Whatever I do, I leave two of them alone in a pool and someone's going to get eaten!
There are only two places to put these guys. This little pool here and the pool on the other side of the river. But there are three of them!
Isn't there a way for you two to get back out here? Then you can keep them apart while I bring the baby guardian over?
Sorry, there's nothing.
Wait, I think I figured it out! There's a third place I can put them. The boat!

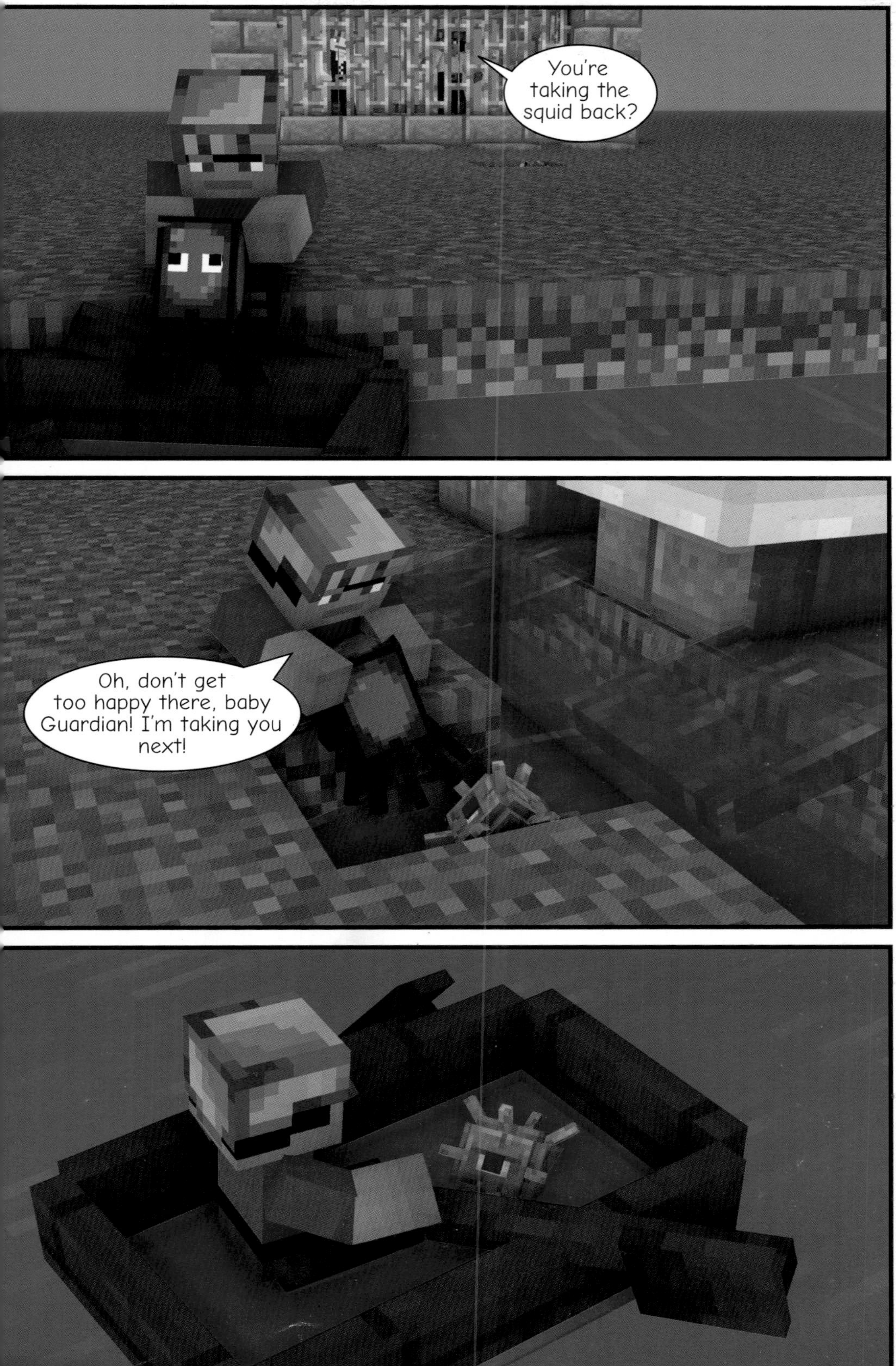
You're taking the squid back?
Oh, don't get too happy there, baby Guardian! I'm taking you next!

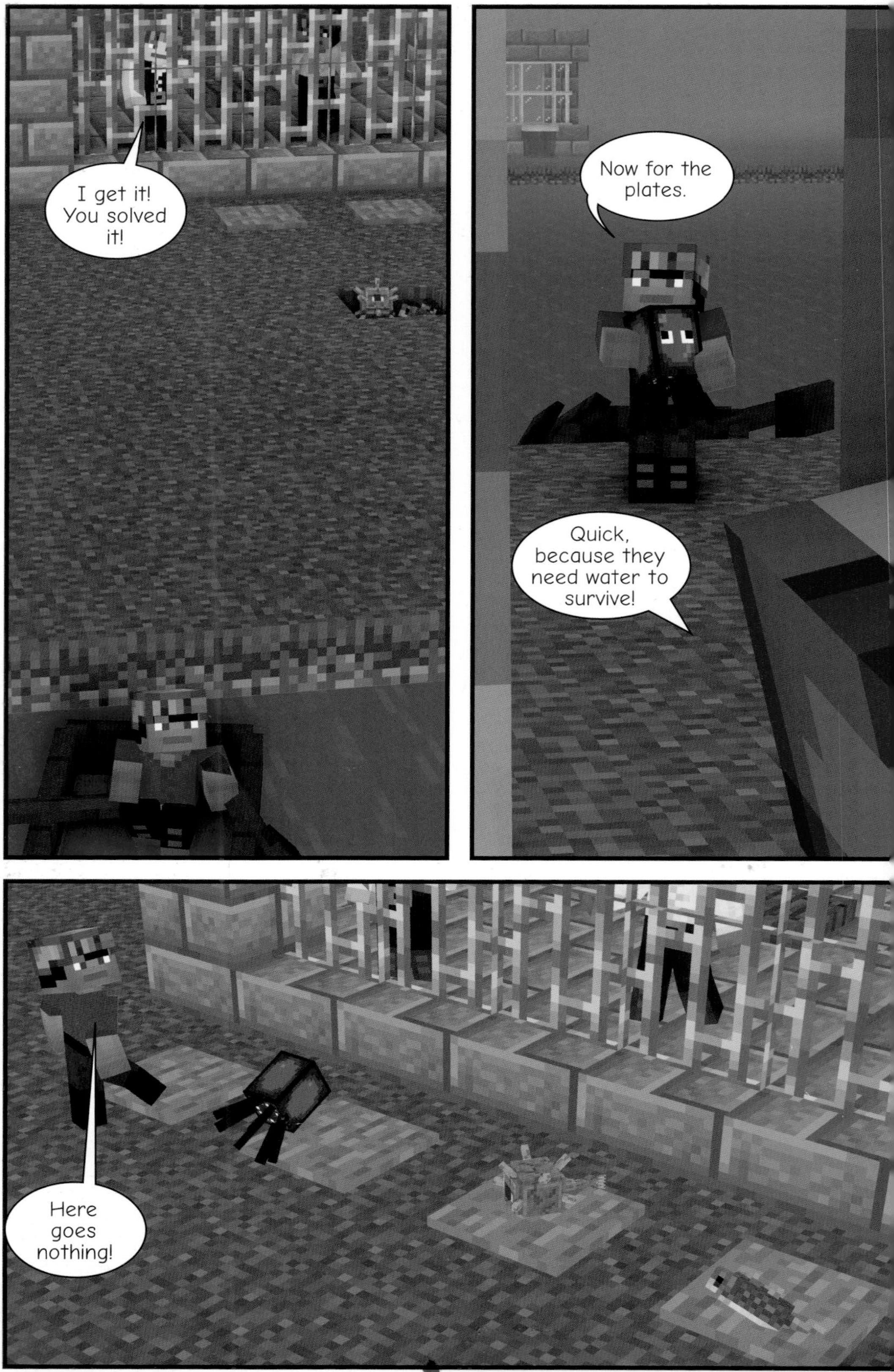

I get it! You solved it!
Now for the plates.
Quick, because they need water to survive!
Here goes nothing!

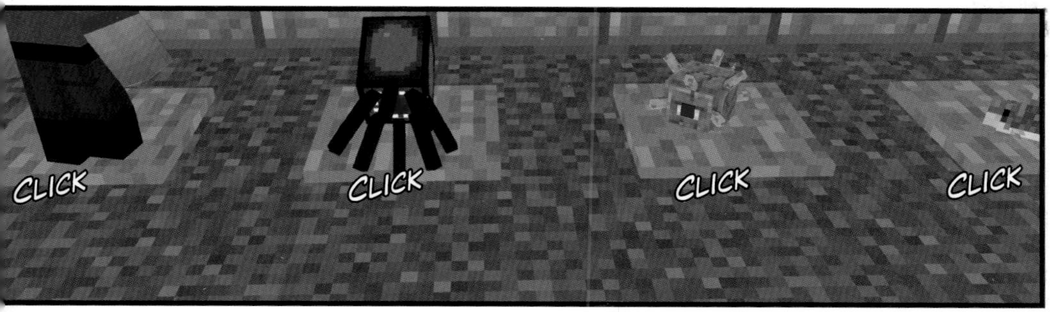
CLICK
CLICK
CLICK
CLICK

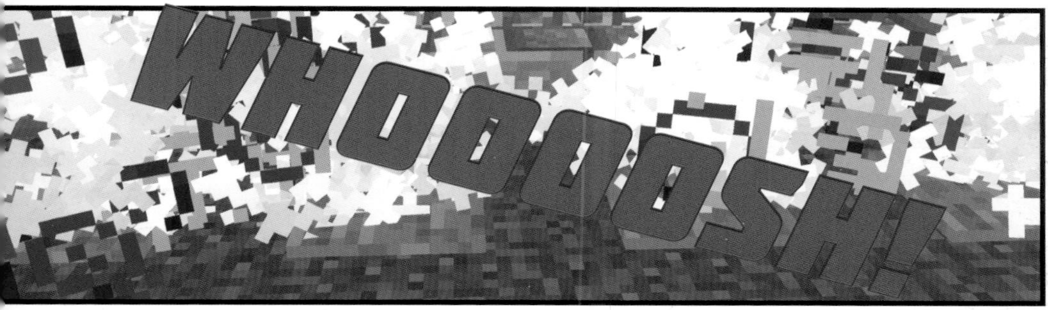
WHOOOOSH!

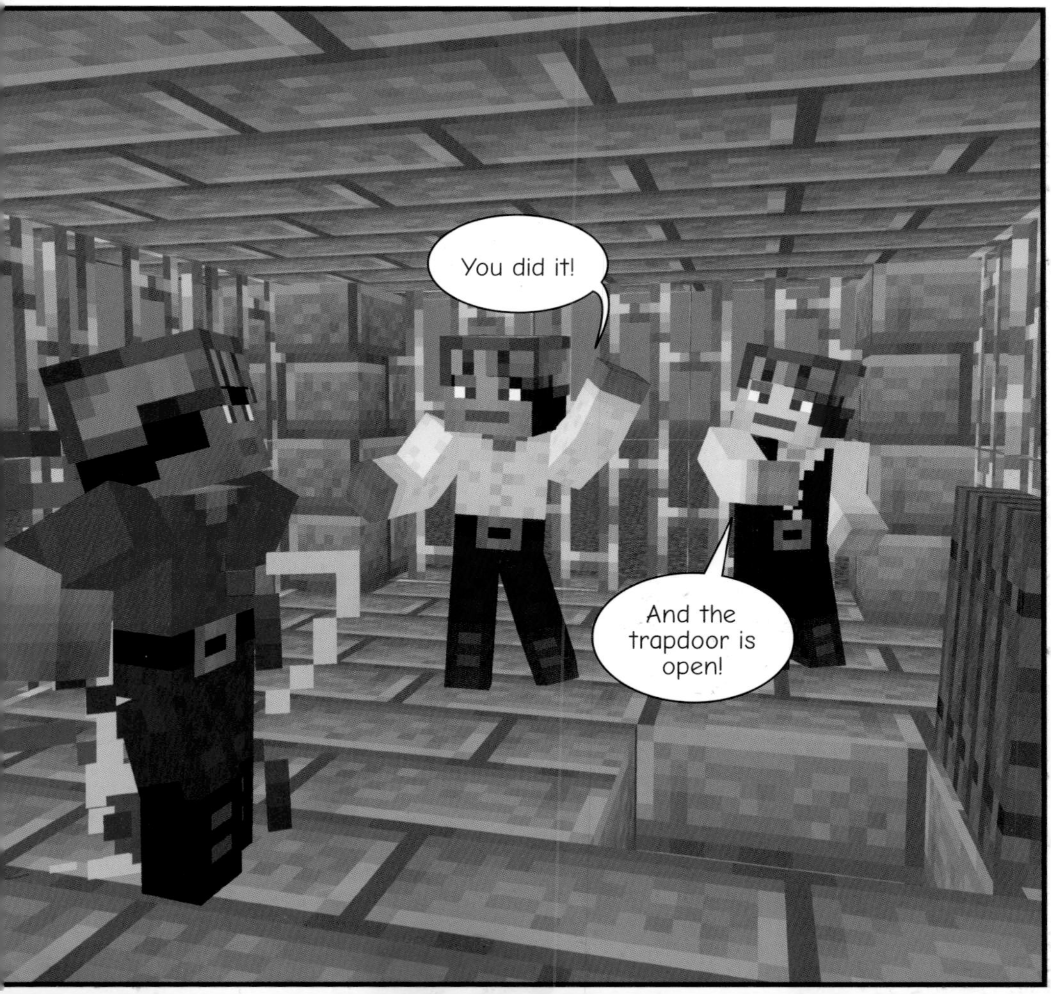
You did it!
And the trapdoor is open!

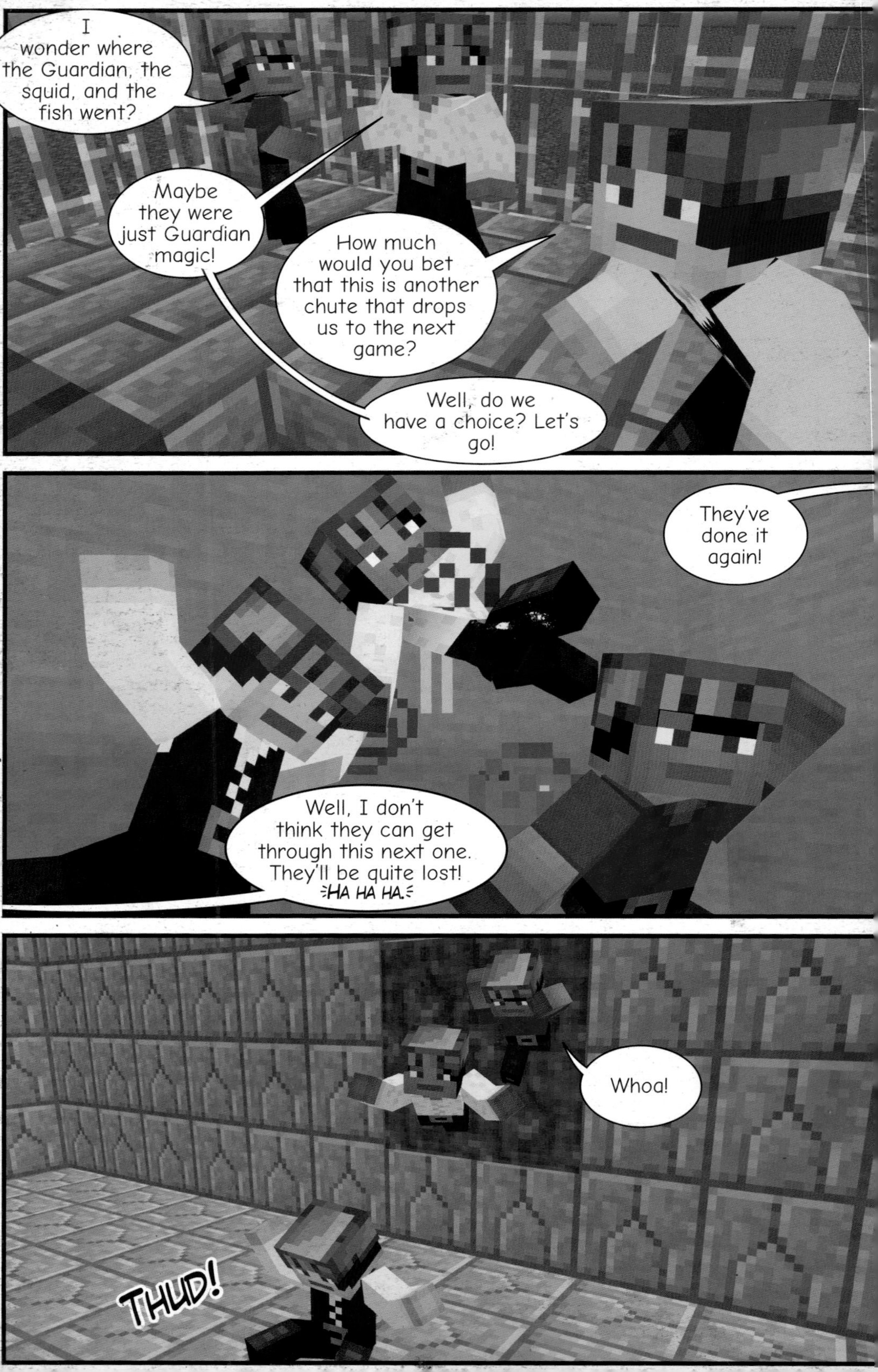
I wonder where the Guardian, the squid, and the fish went?
Maybe they were just Guardian magic!
How much would you bet that this is another chute that drops us to the next game?
Well, do we have a choice? Let's go!
They've done it again!
Well, I don't think they can get through this next one. They'll be quite lost! HA HA HA.
Whoa!
THUD!

Chapter 9
The Maze

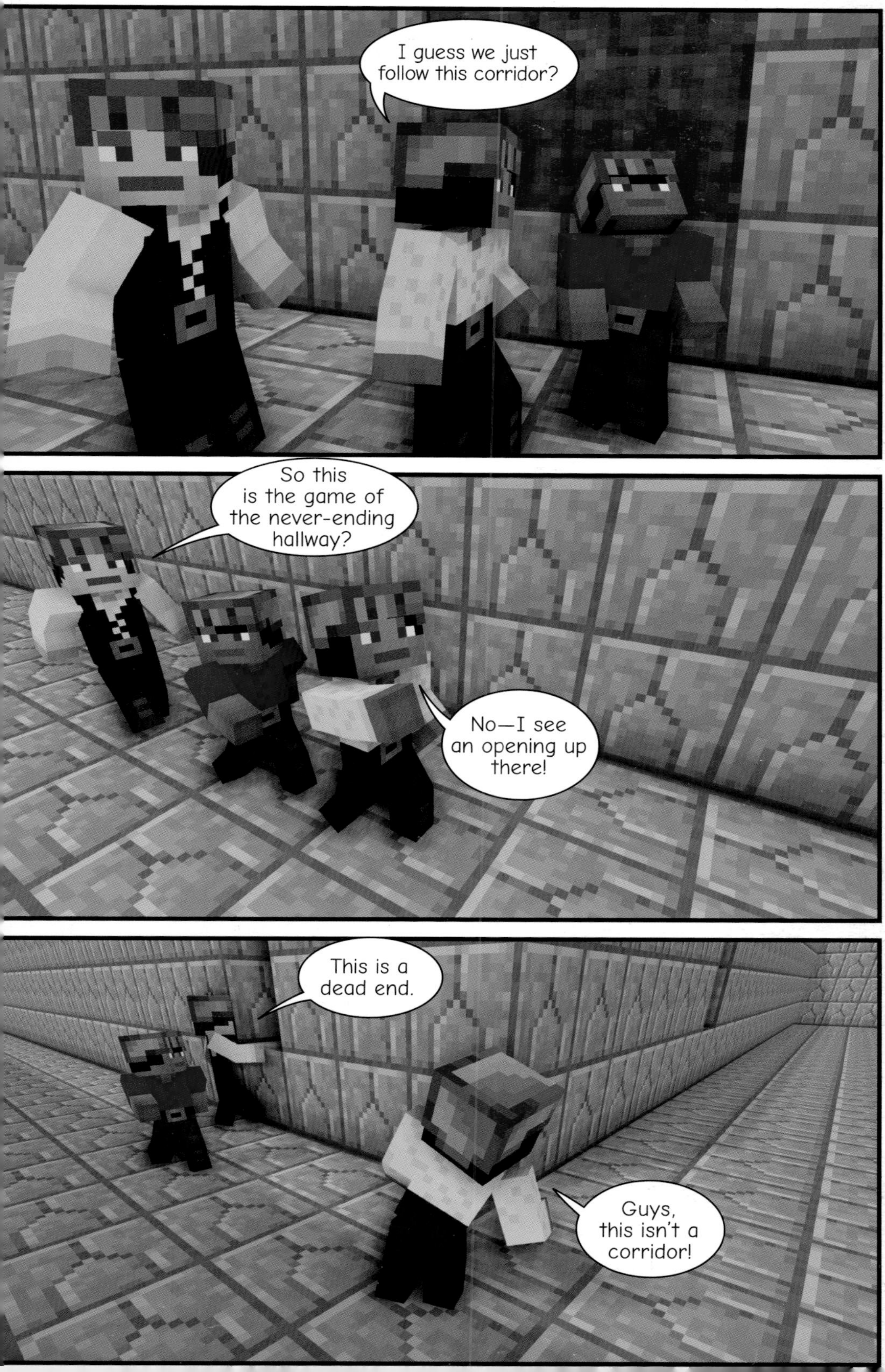

I guess we just follow this corridor?
So this is the game of the never-ending hallway?
No—I see an opening up there!
This is a dead end.
Guys, this isn't a corridor!

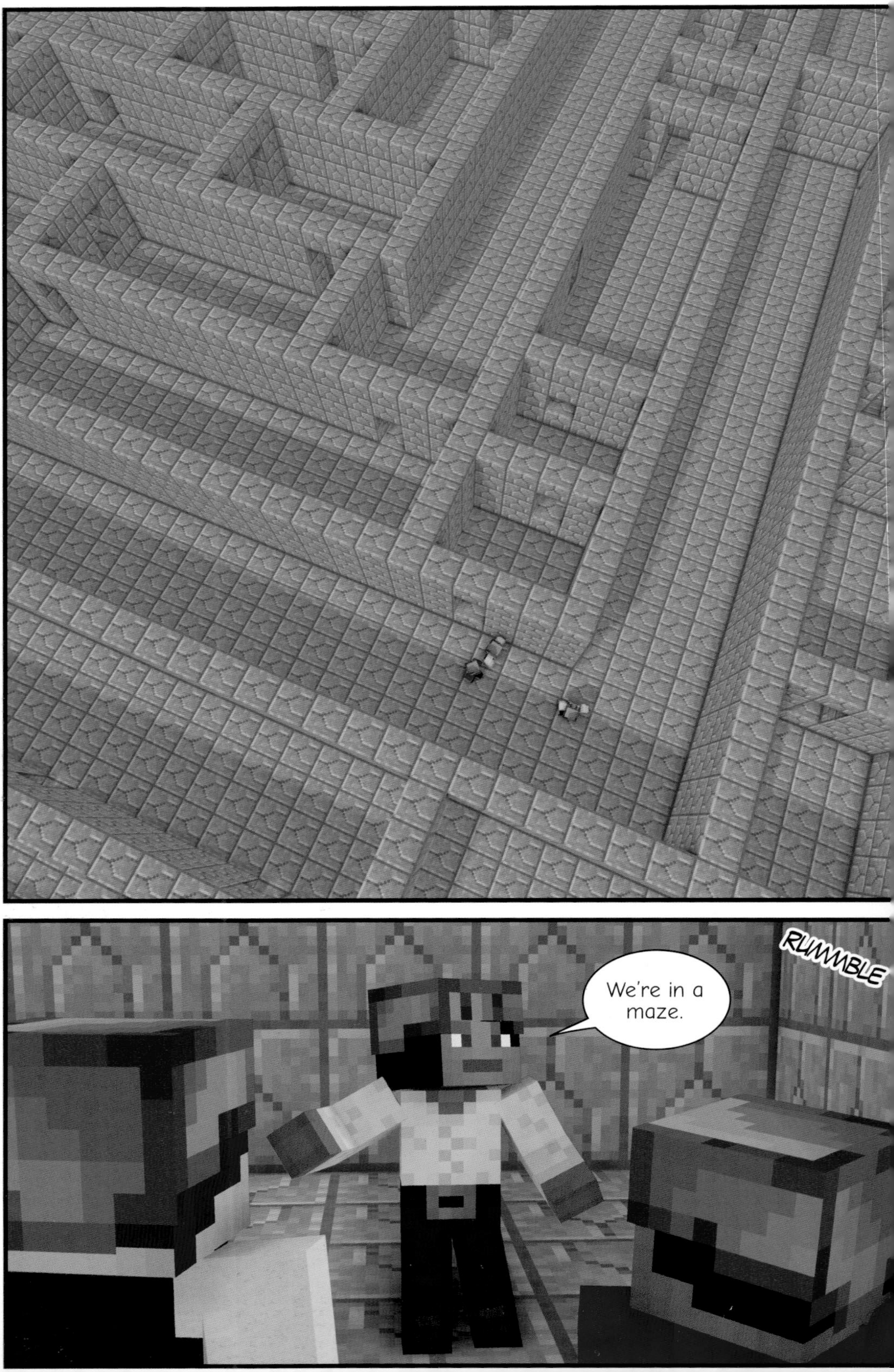
RUMMBLE
We're in a maze.

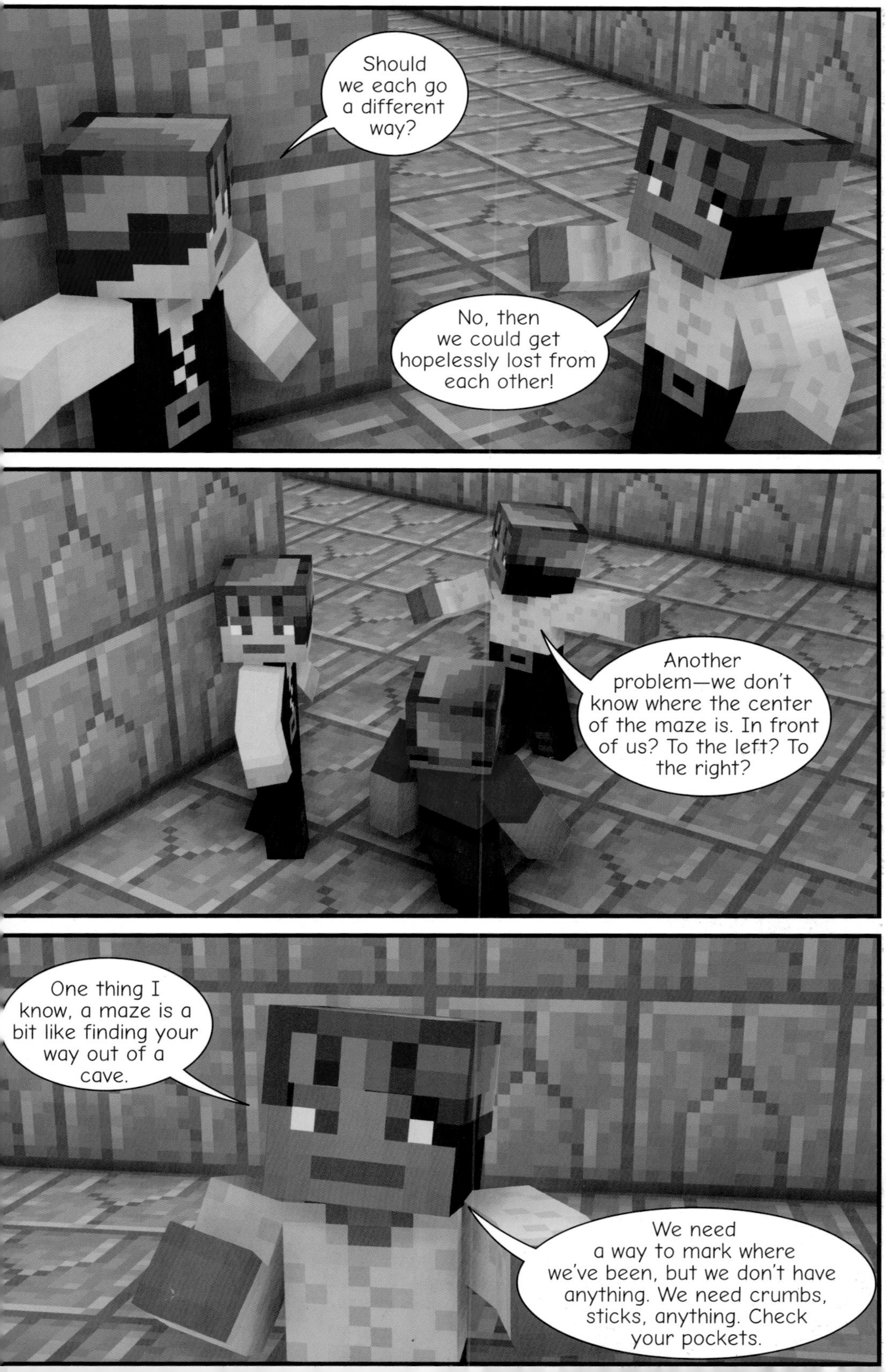
Should we each go a different way?
No, then we could get hopelessly lost from each other!
Another problem—we don't know where the center of the maze is. In front of us? To the left? To the right?
One thing I know, a maze is a bit like finding your way out of a cave.
We need a way to mark where we've been, but we don't have anything. We need crumbs, sticks, anything. Check your pockets.

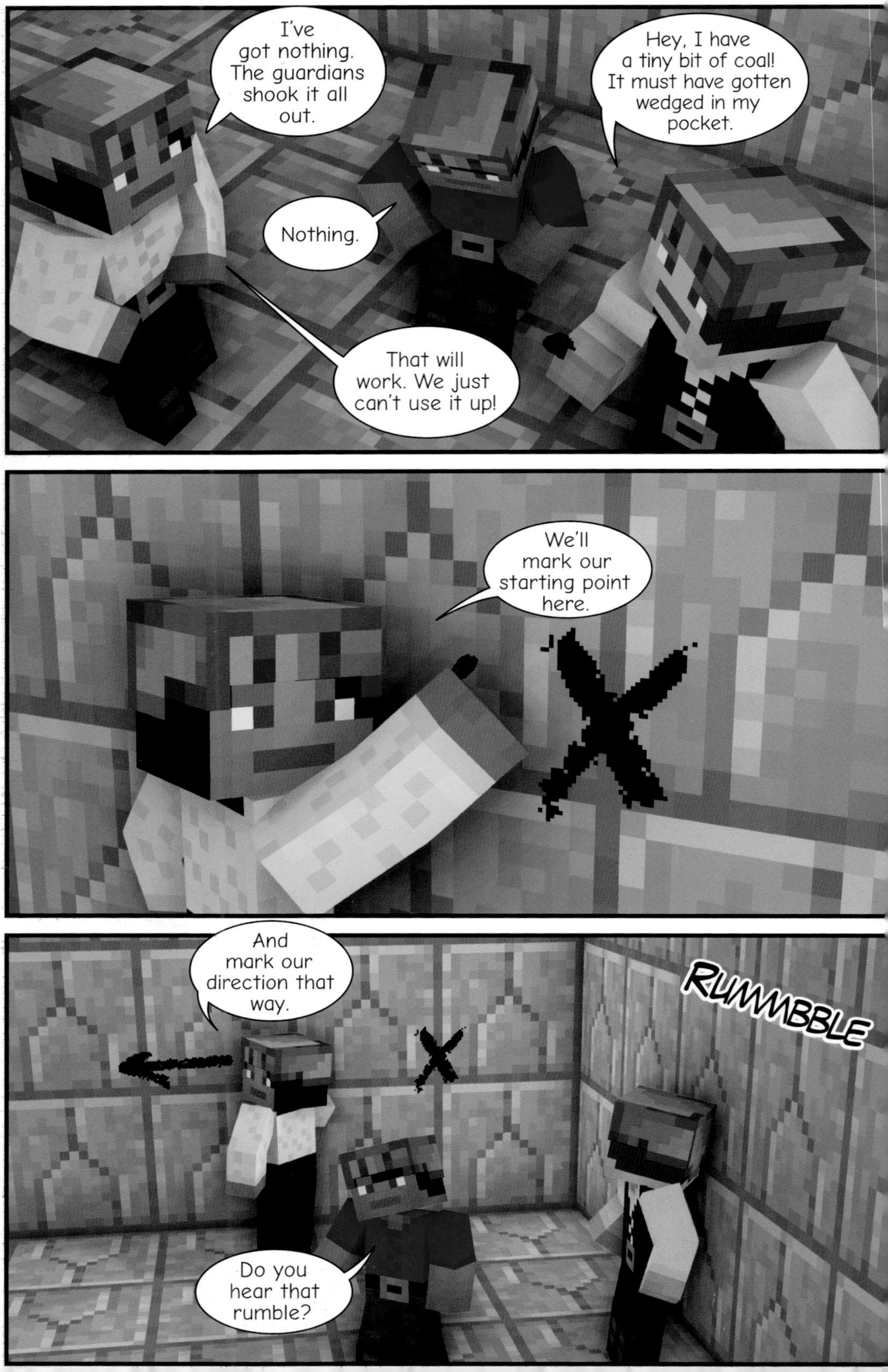
I've got nothing. The guardians shook it all out.
Hey, I have a tiny bit of coal! It must have gotten wedged in my pocket.
Nothing.
That will work. We just can't use it up!
We'll mark our starting point here.
And mark our direction that way.
RUMMBBLE
Do you hear that rumble?

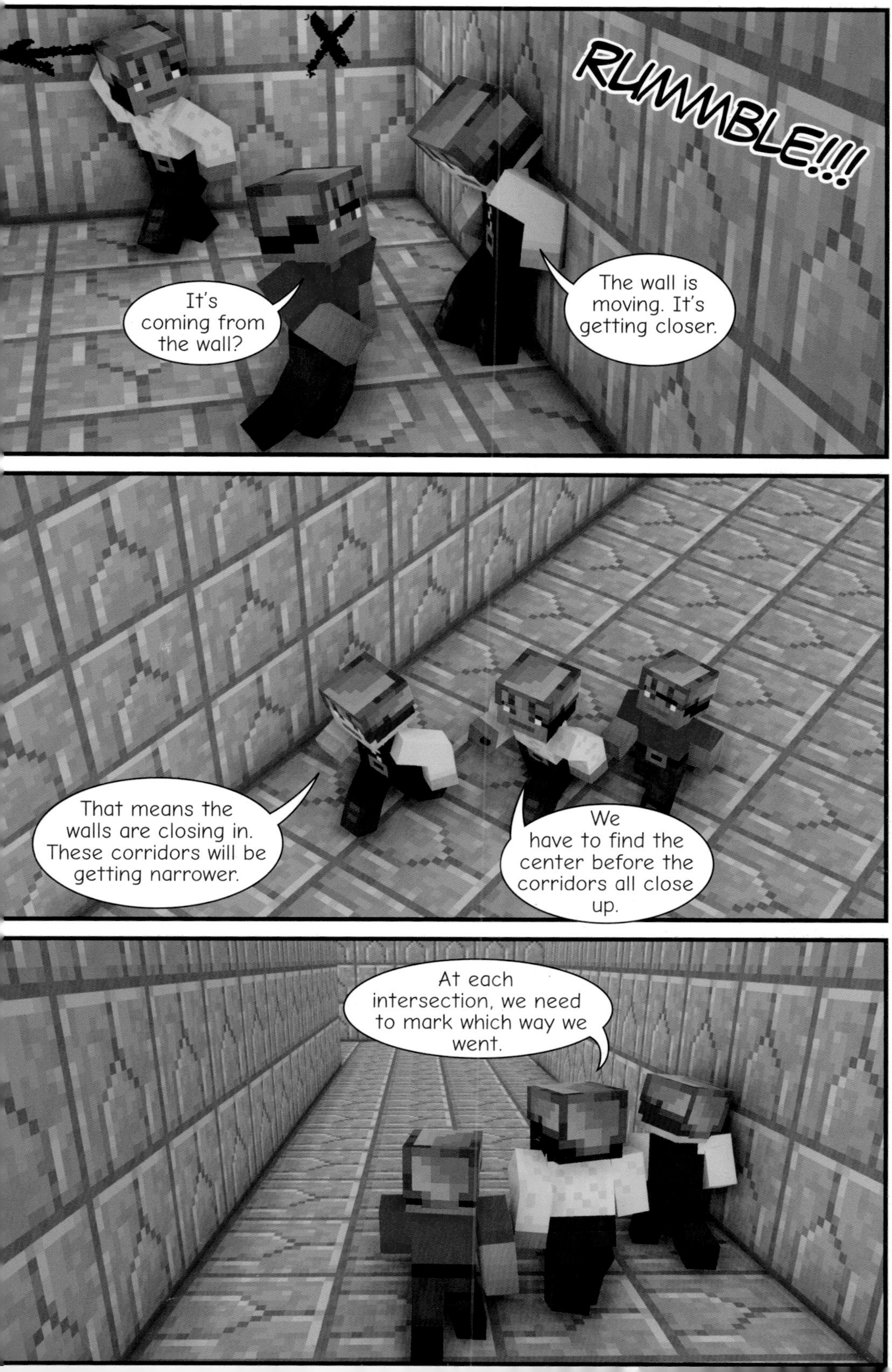
RUMMBLE!!!
It's coming from the wall?
The wall is moving. It's getting closer.
That means the walls are closing in. These corridors will be getting narrower.
We have to find the center before the corridors all close up.
At each intersection, we need to mark which way we went.

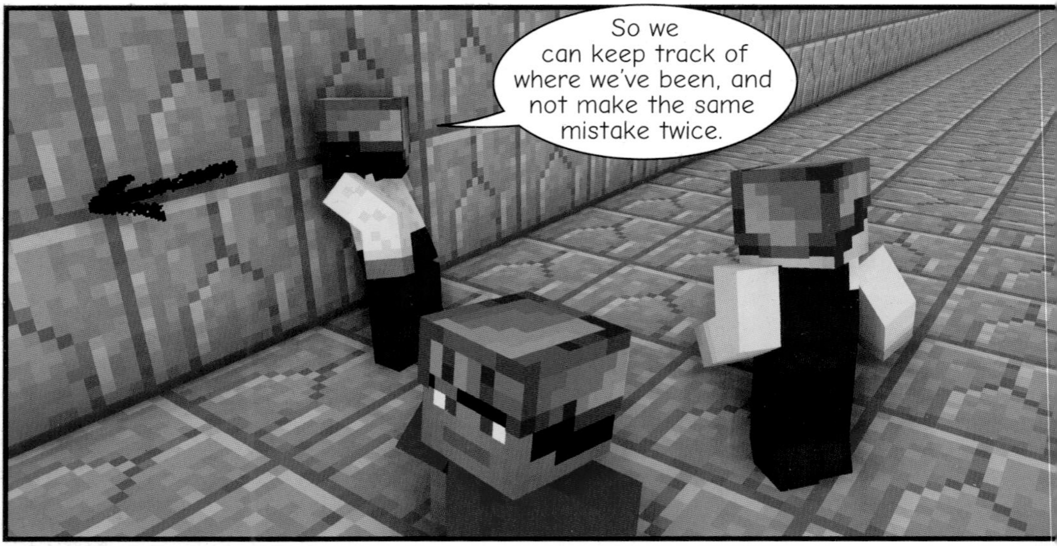
So we can keep track of where we've been, and not make the same mistake twice.

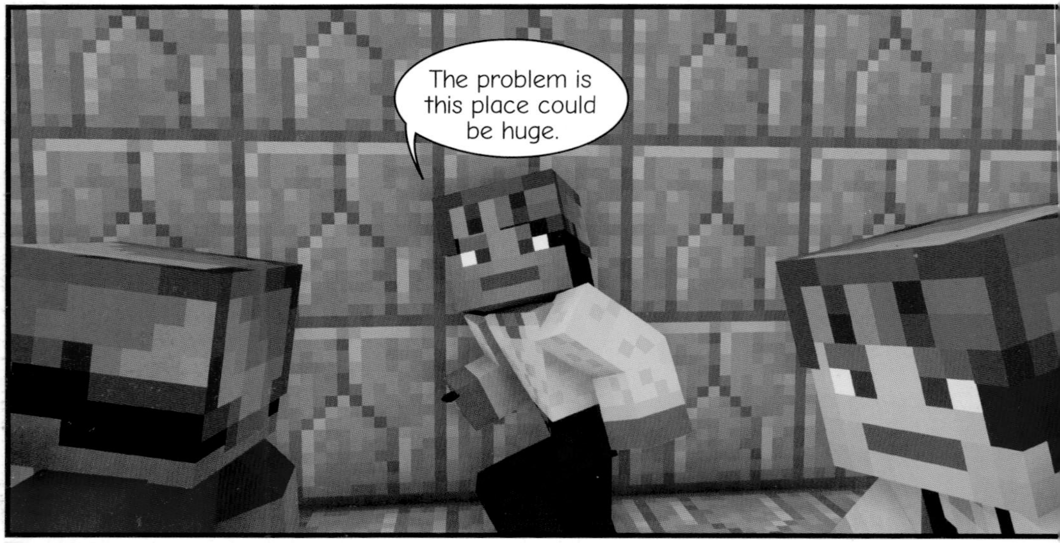
The problem is this place could be huge.

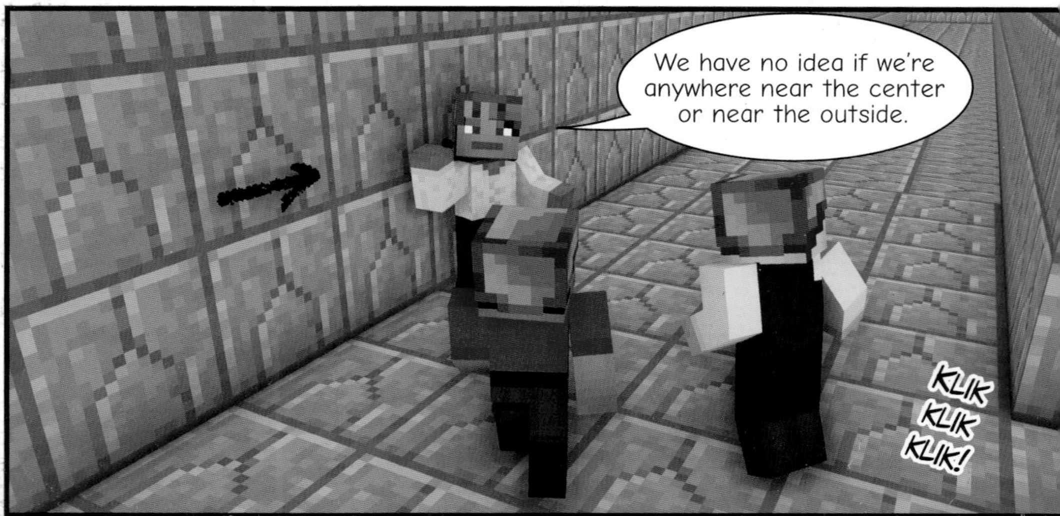
We have no idea if we're anywhere near the center or near the outside.
KLIK
KLIK
KLIK!

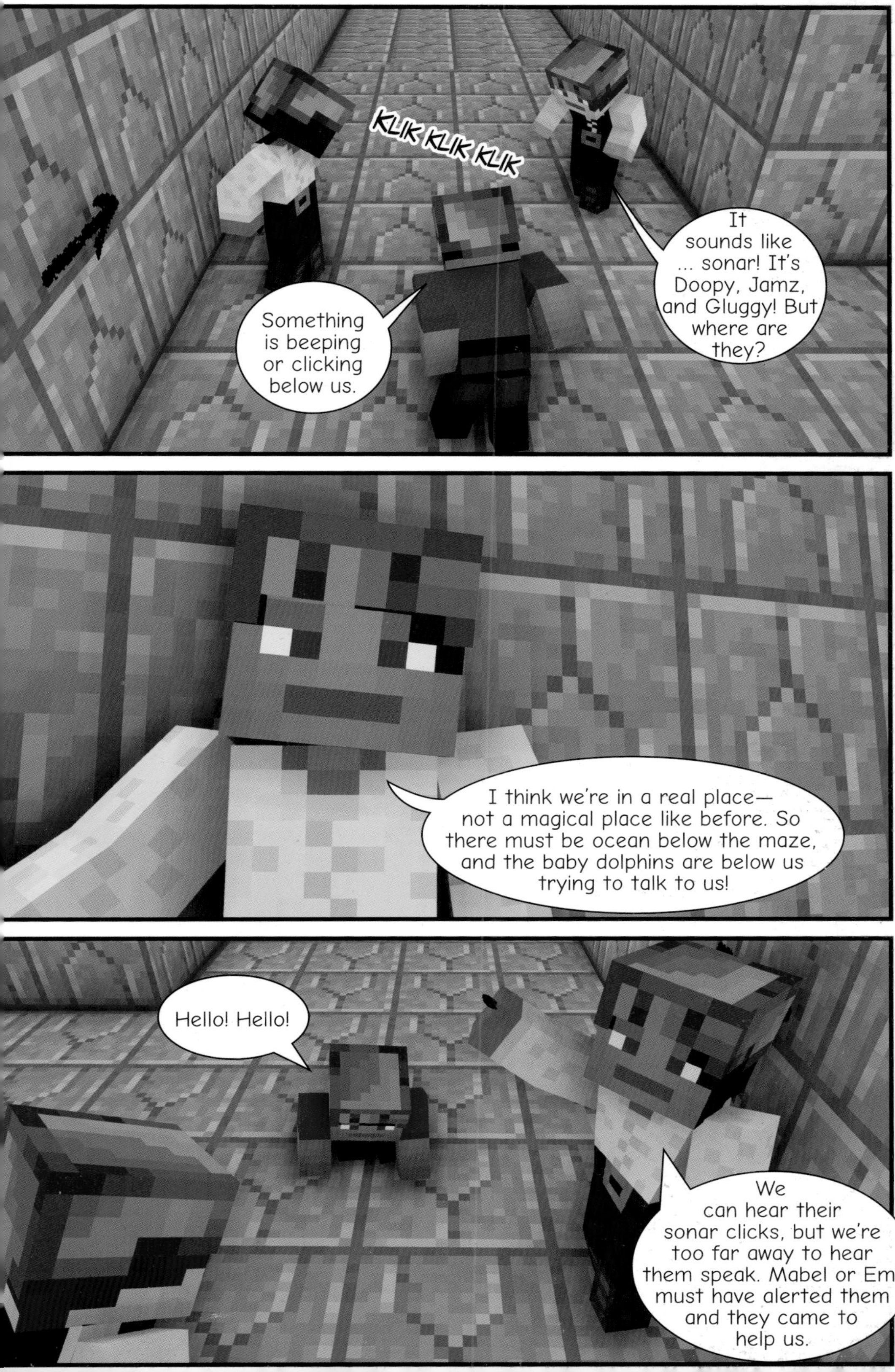

KLIK KLIK KLIK
It sounds like ... sonar! It's Doopy, Jamz, and Gluggy! But where are they?
Something is beeping or clicking below us.
I think we're in a real place—not a magical place like before. So there must be ocean below the maze, and the baby dolphins are below us trying to talk to us!
Hello! Hello!
We can hear their sonar clicks, but we're too far away to hear them speak. Mabel or Emi must have alerted them and they came to help us.

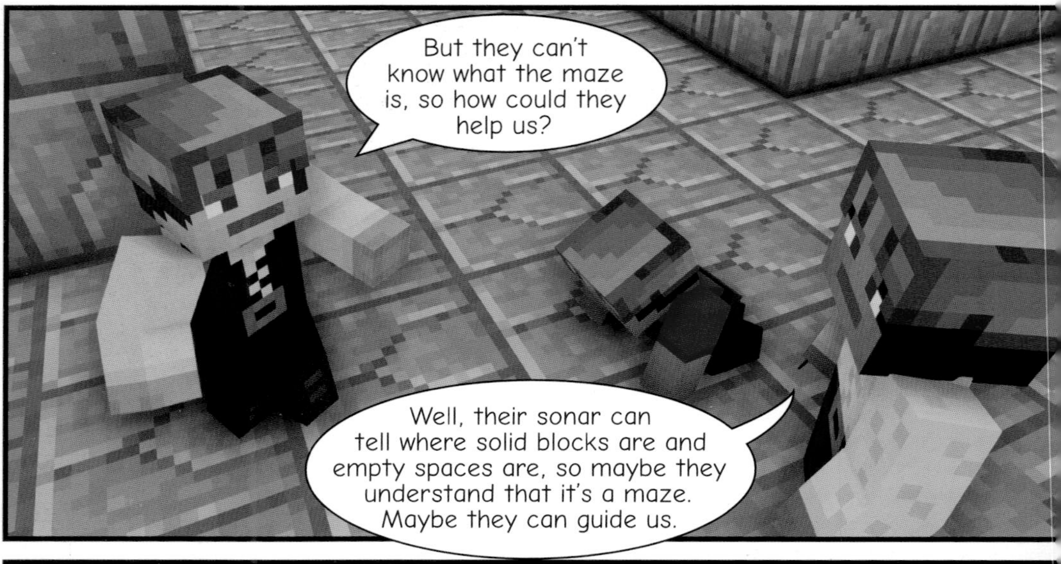
But they can't know what the maze is, so how could they help us?
Well, their sonar can tell where solid blocks are and empty spaces are, so maybe they understand that it's a maze. Maybe they can guide us.

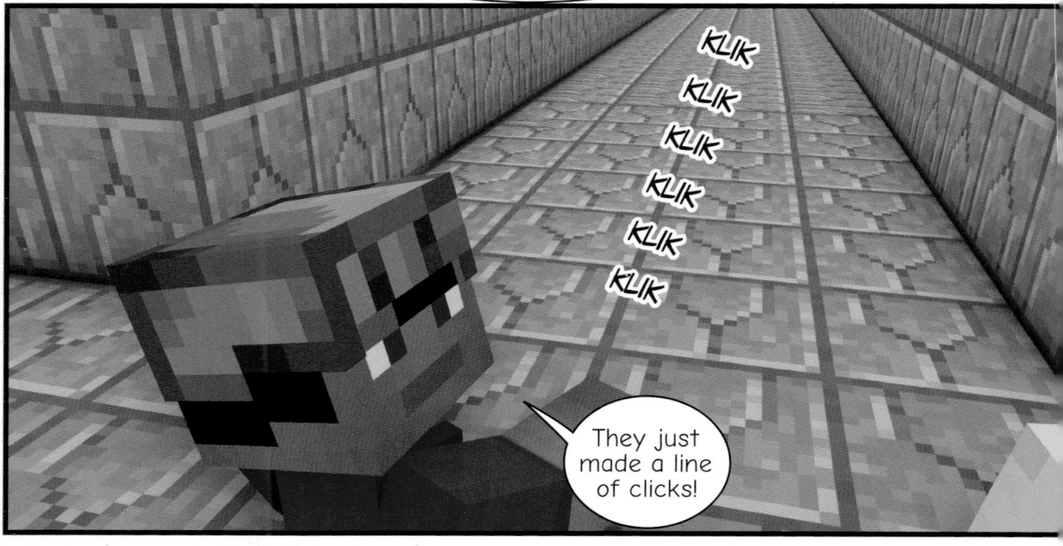
KLIK
KLIK
KLIK
KLIK
KLIK
KLIK
They just made a line of clicks!

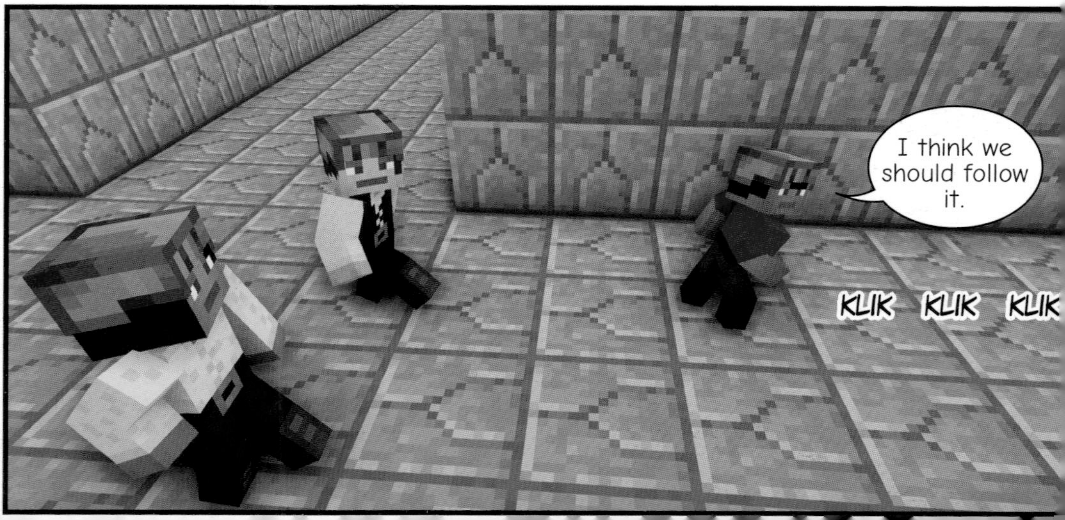
I think we should follow it.
KLIK KLIK KLIK

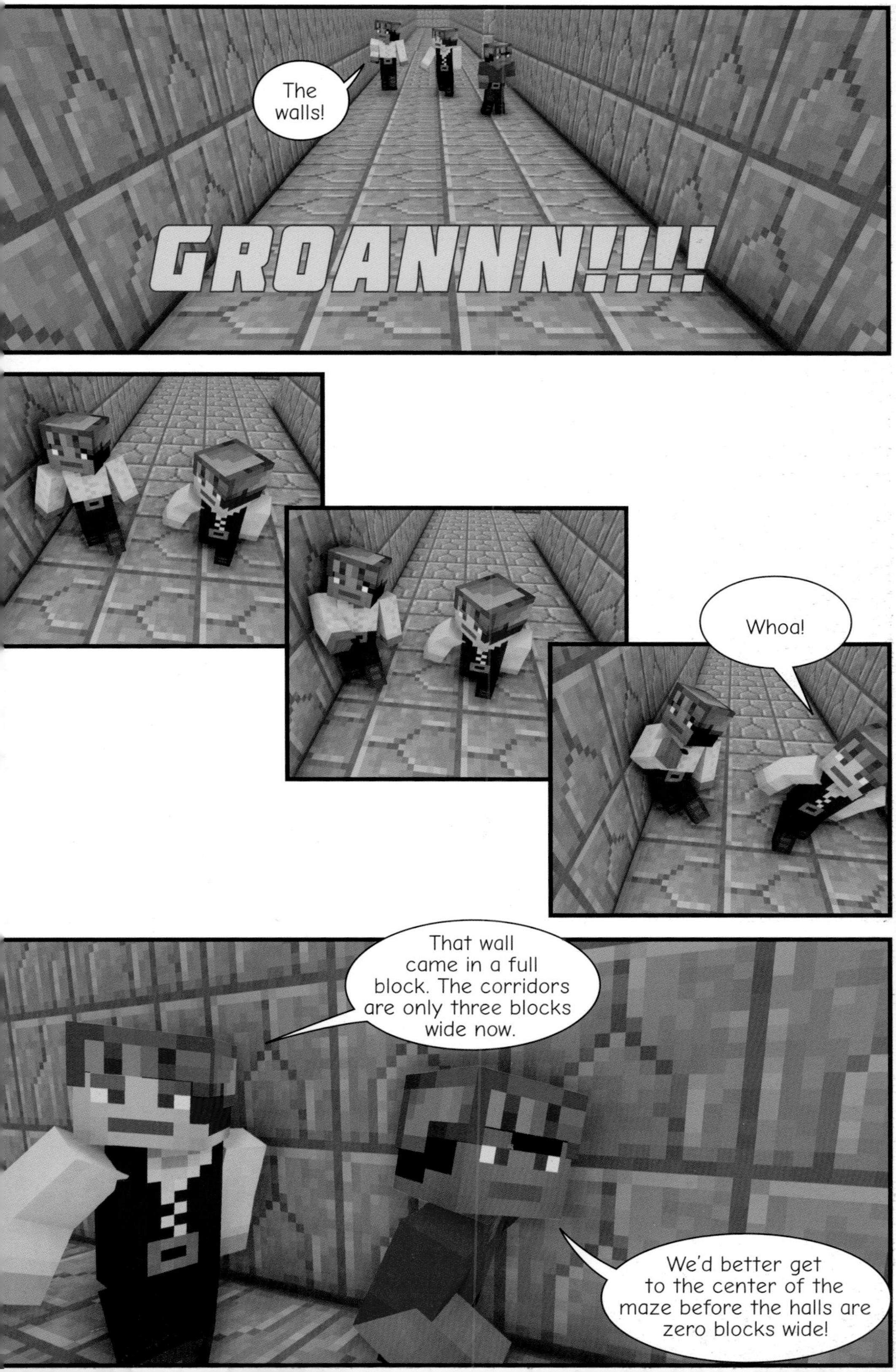
The walls!
GROANNN!!!!
Whoa!
That wall came in a full block. The corridors are only three blocks wide now.
We'd better get to the center of the maze before the halls are zero blocks wide!

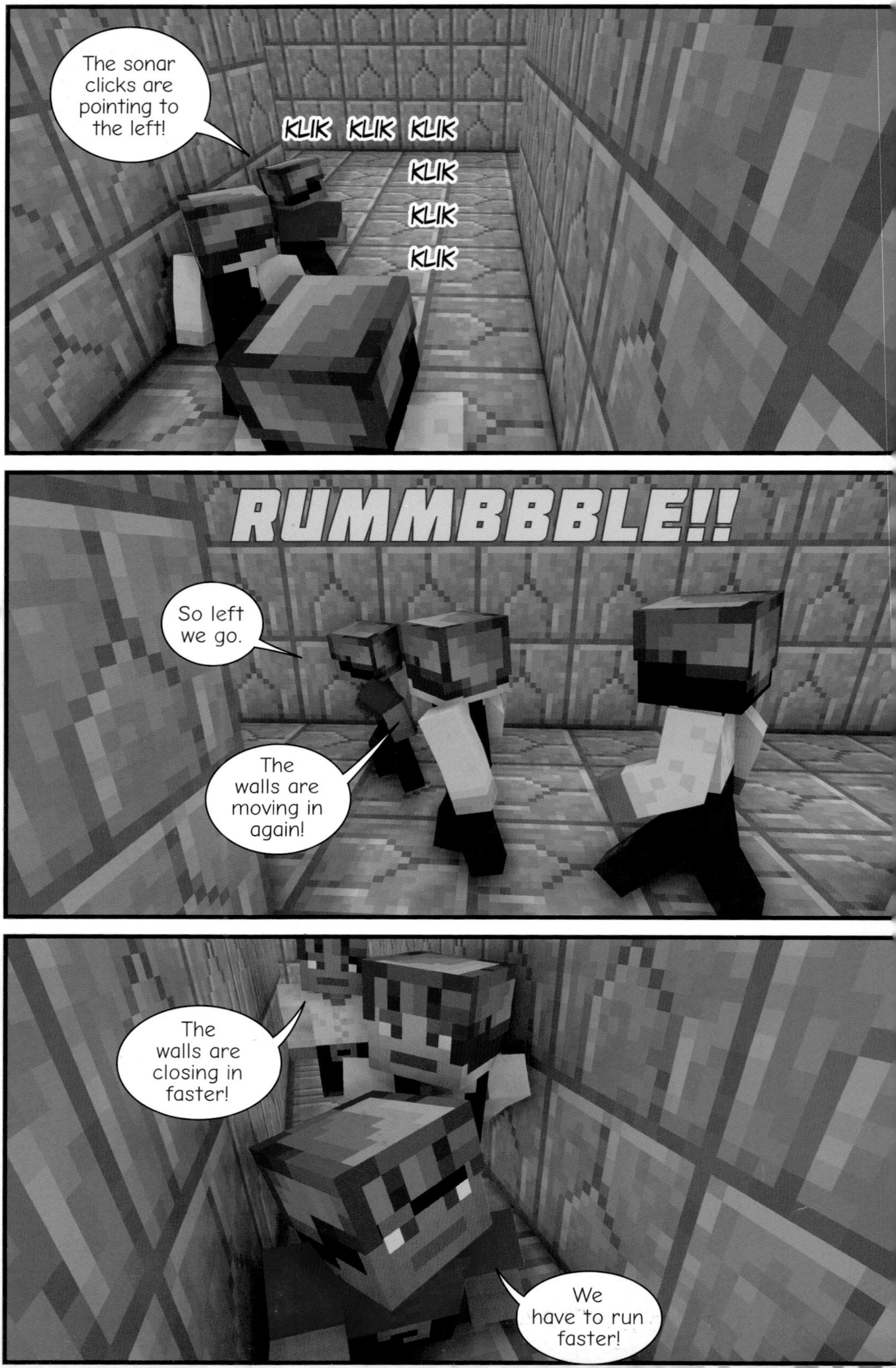
The sonar clicks are pointing to the left!
KLIK KLIK KLIK
KLIK
KLIK
KLIK
RUMMBBBLE!!
So left we go.
The walls are moving in again!
The walls are closing in faster!
We have to run faster!

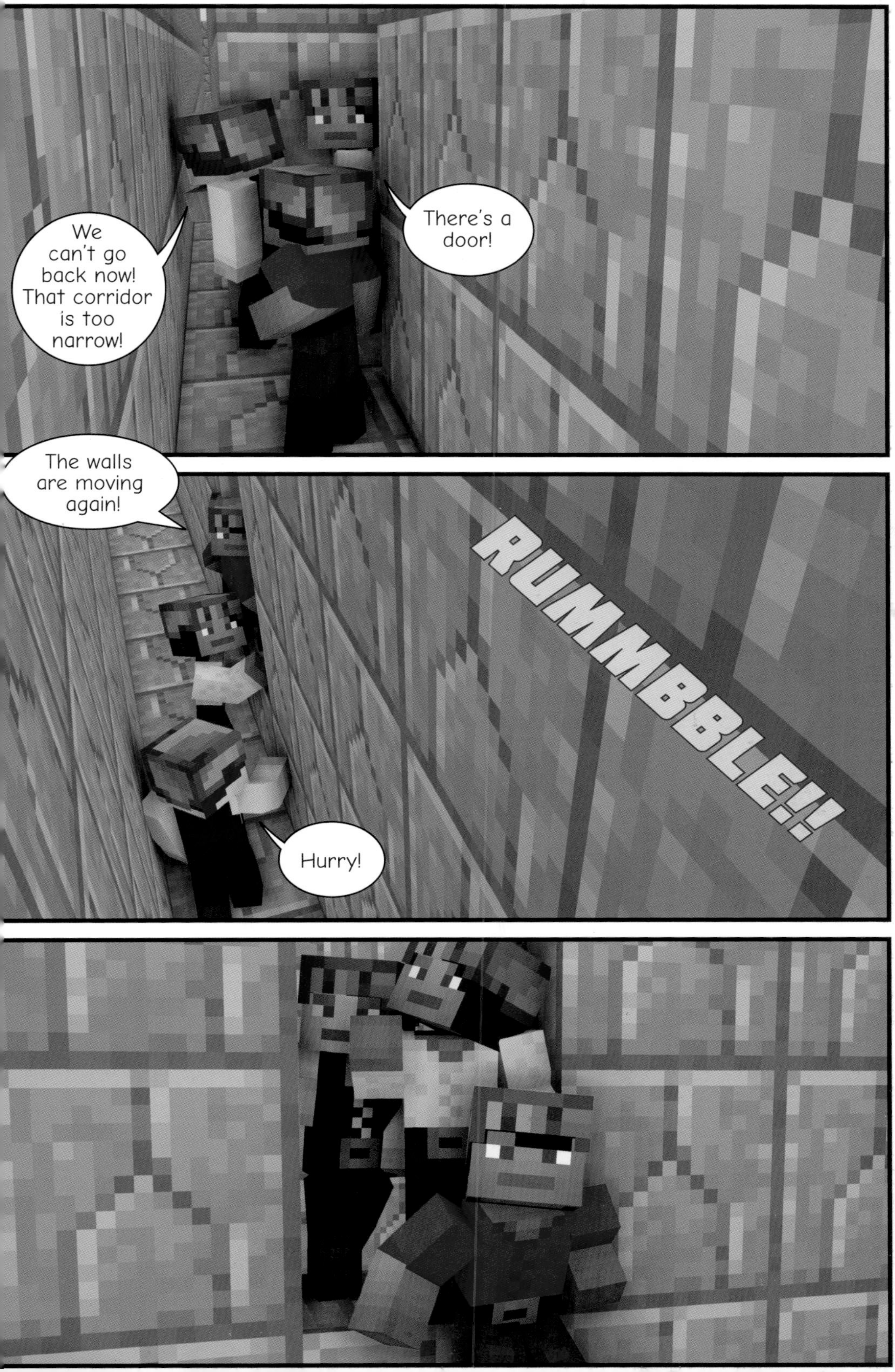
We can't go back now! That corridor is too narrow!
There's a door!
The walls are moving again!
RUMMBBLE!!
Hurry!

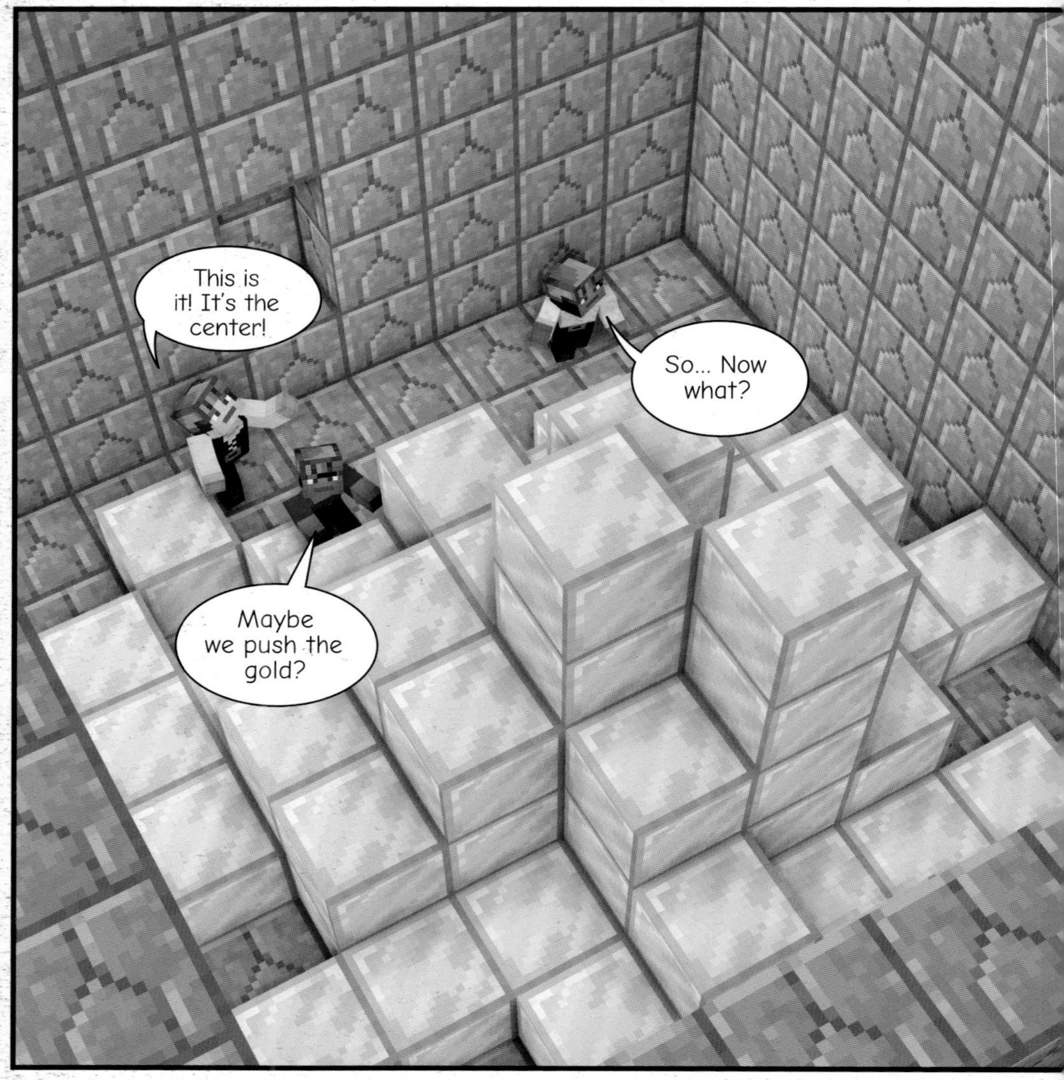
This is it! It's the center!
So... Now what?
Maybe we push the gold?

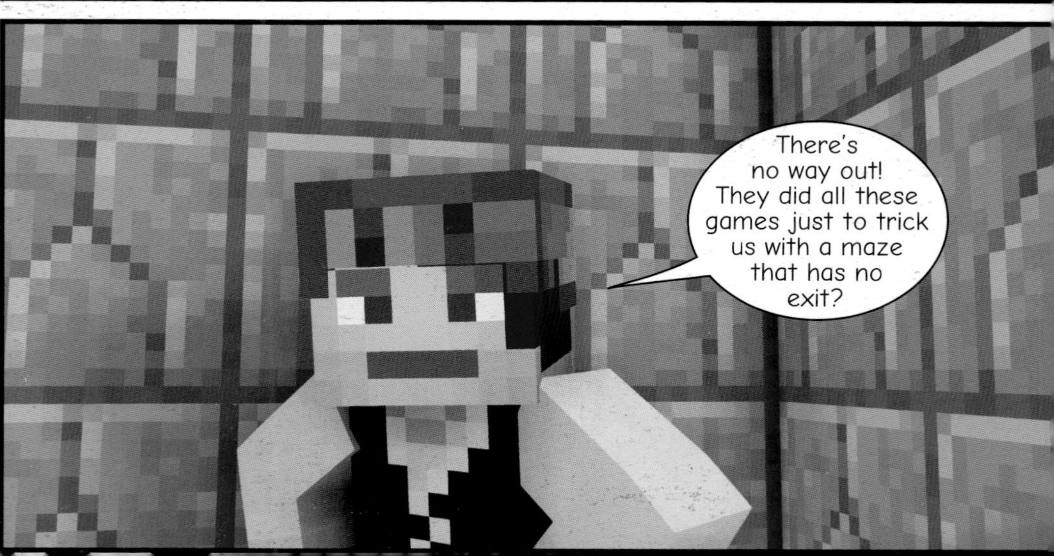
There's no way out! They did all these games just to trick us with a maze that has no exit?

Chapter 10
One Last Riddle

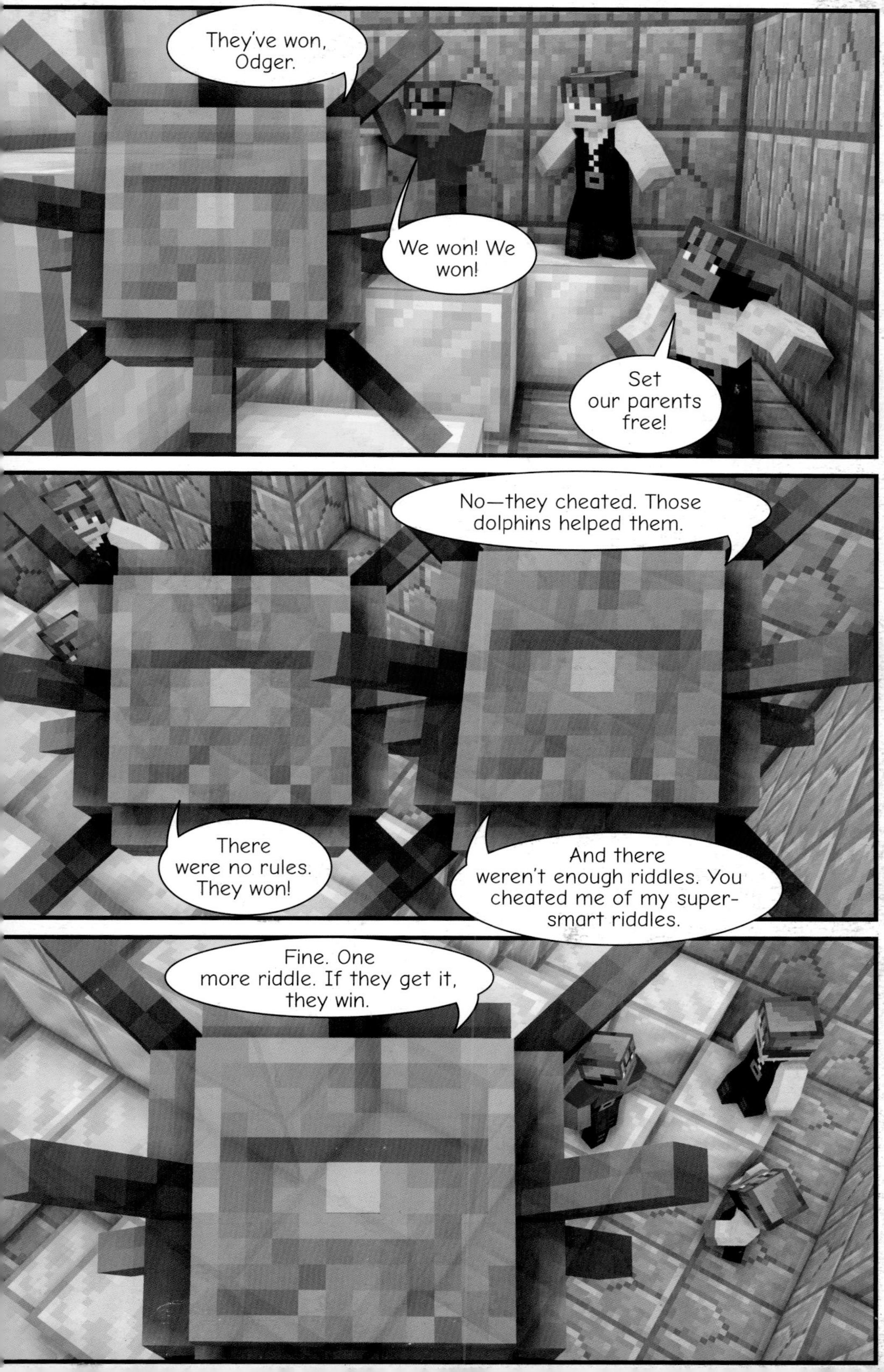
They've won, Odger.
We won! We won!
Set our parents free!
No—they cheated. Those dolphins helped them.
There were no rules. They won!
And there weren't enough riddles. You cheated me of my super-smart riddles.
Fine. One more riddle. If they get it, they win.

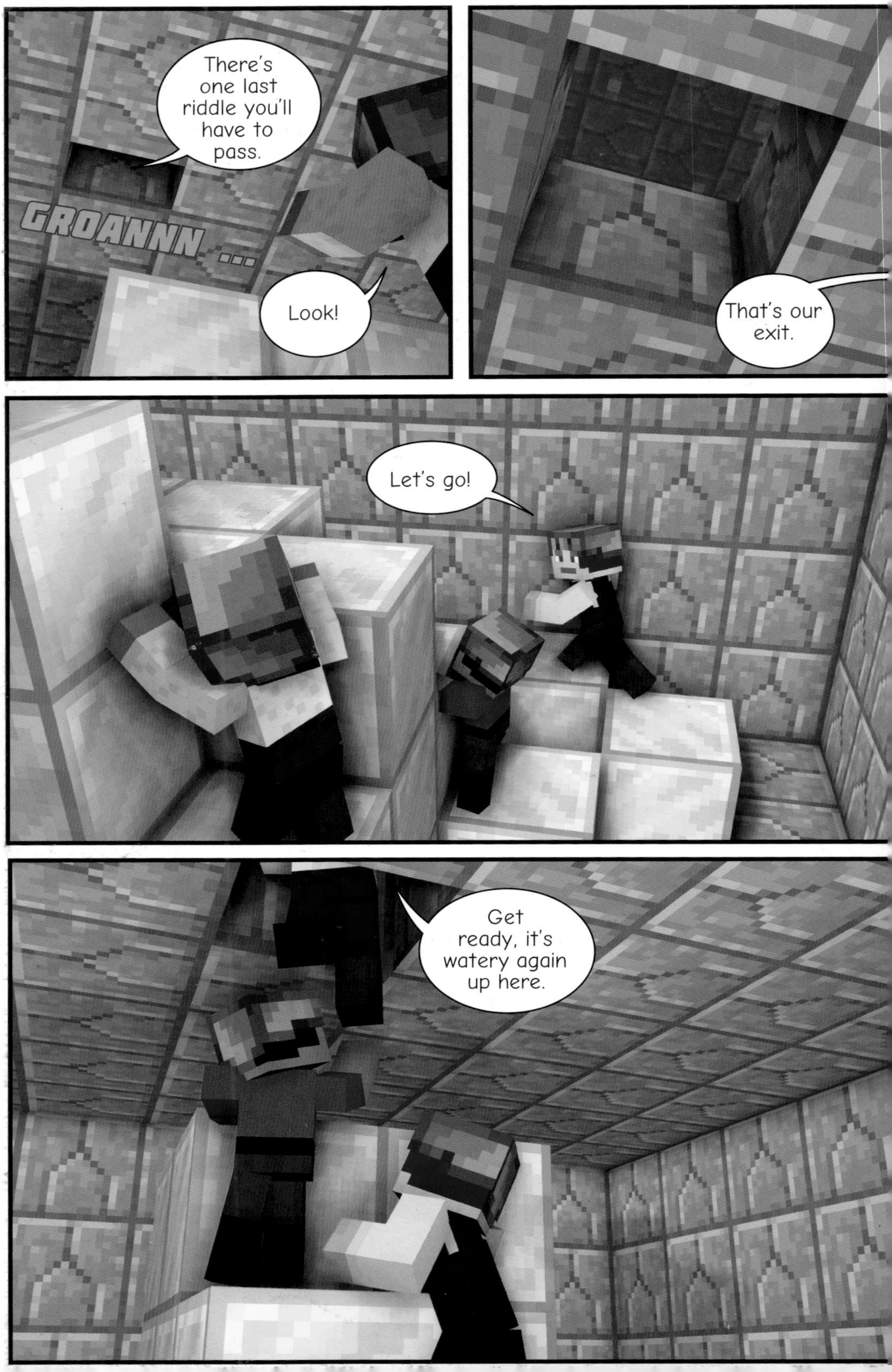
There's one last riddle you'll have to pass.
GROANNN ...
Look!
That's our exit.
Let's go!
Get ready, it's watery again up here.

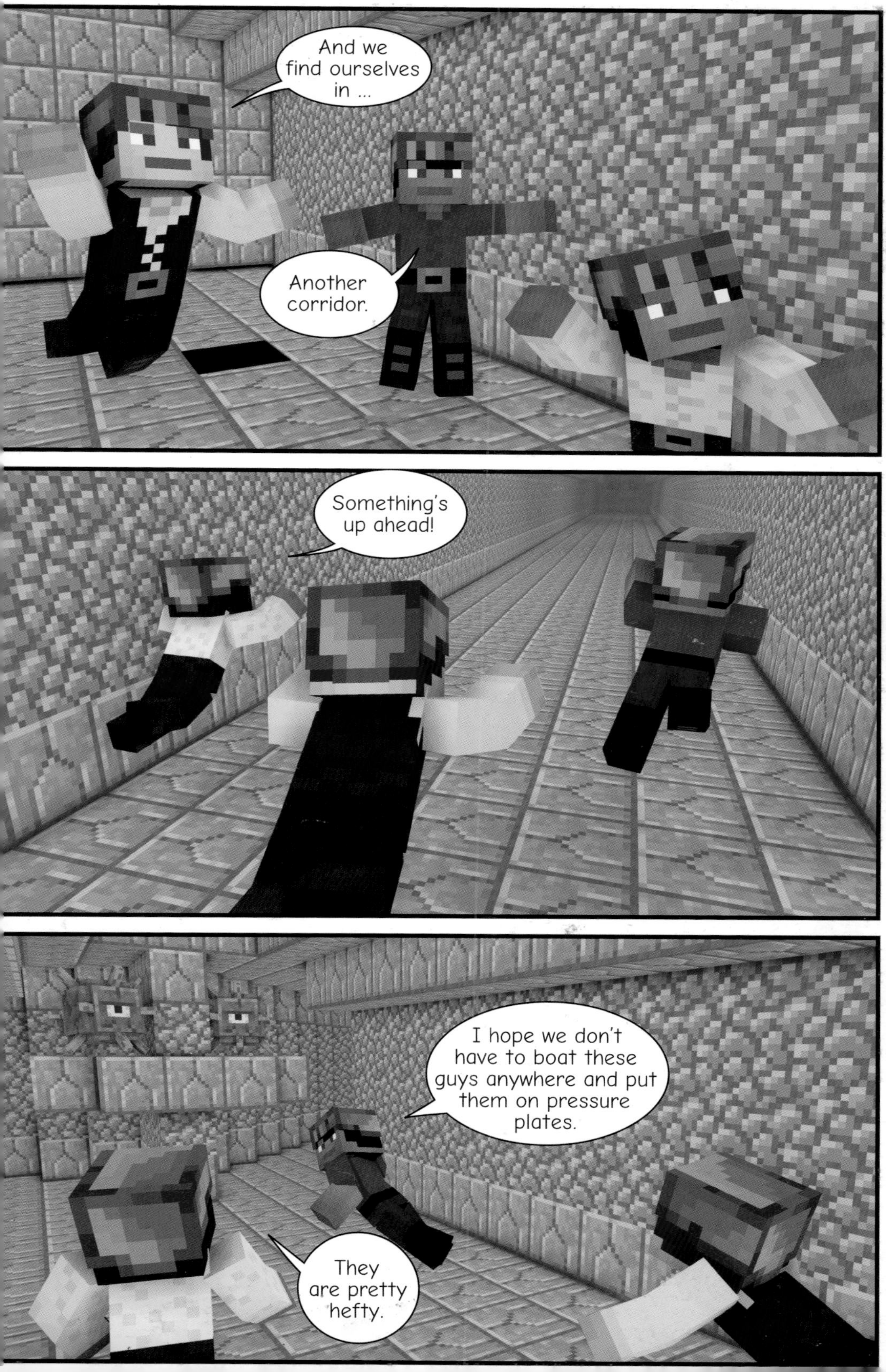
And we find ourselves in ...
Another corridor.
Something's up ahead!
I hope we don't have to boat these guys anywhere and put them on pressure plates.
They are pretty hefty.

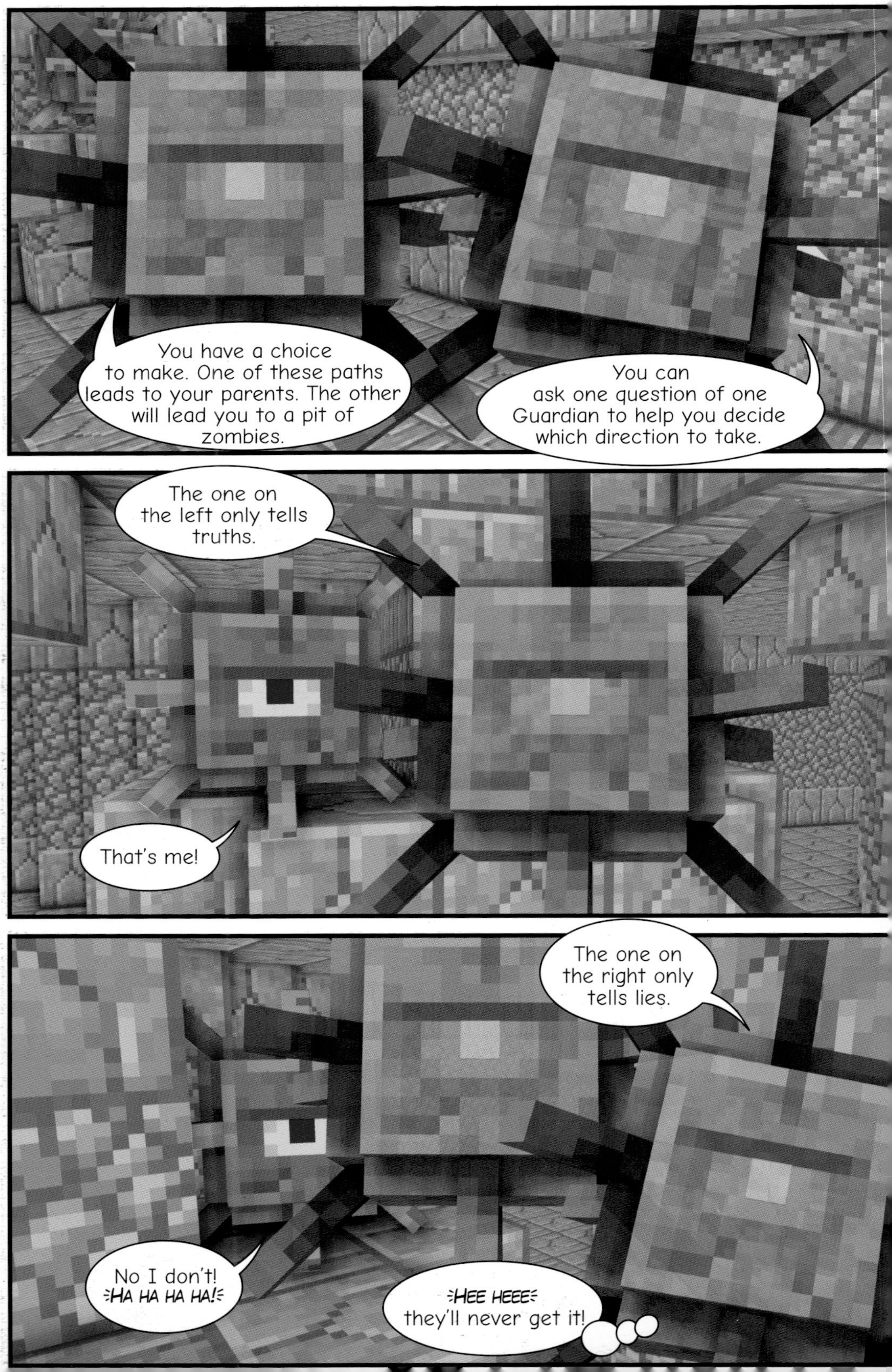
You have a choice to make. One of these paths leads to your parents. The other will lead you to a pit of zombies.
You can ask one question of one Guardian to help you decide which direction to take.
The one on the left only tells truths.
That's me!
The one on the right only tells lies.
No I don't! HA HA HA HA!
HEE HEEE they'll never get it!

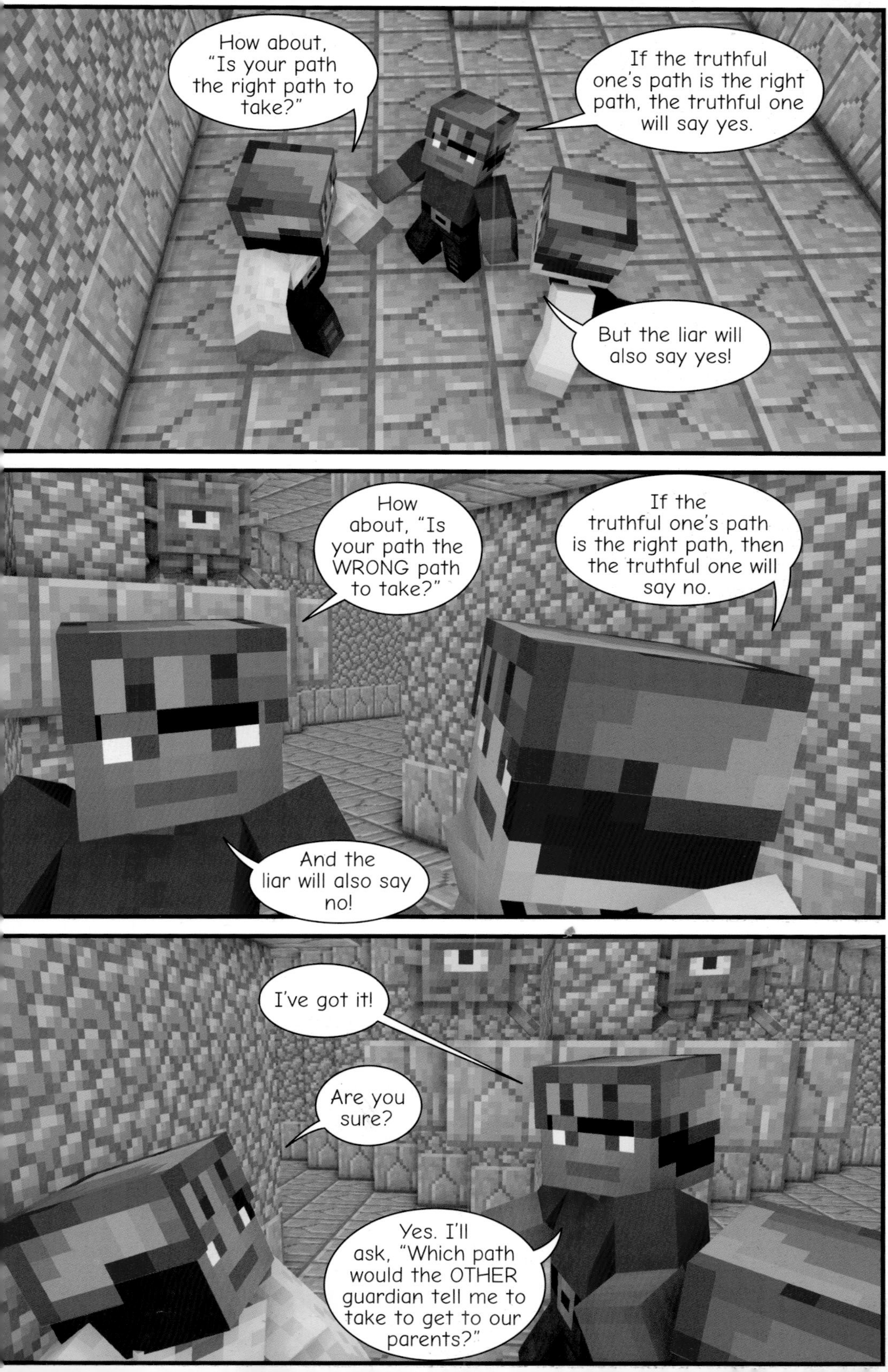
How about, "Is your path the right path to take?"
If the truthful one's path is the right path, the truthful one will say yes.
But the liar will also say yes!
How about, "Is your path the WRONG path to take?"
If the truthful one's path is the right path, then the truthful one will say no.
And the liar will also say no!
I've got it!
Are you sure?
Yes. I'll ask, "Which path would the OTHER guardian tell me to take to get to our parents?"

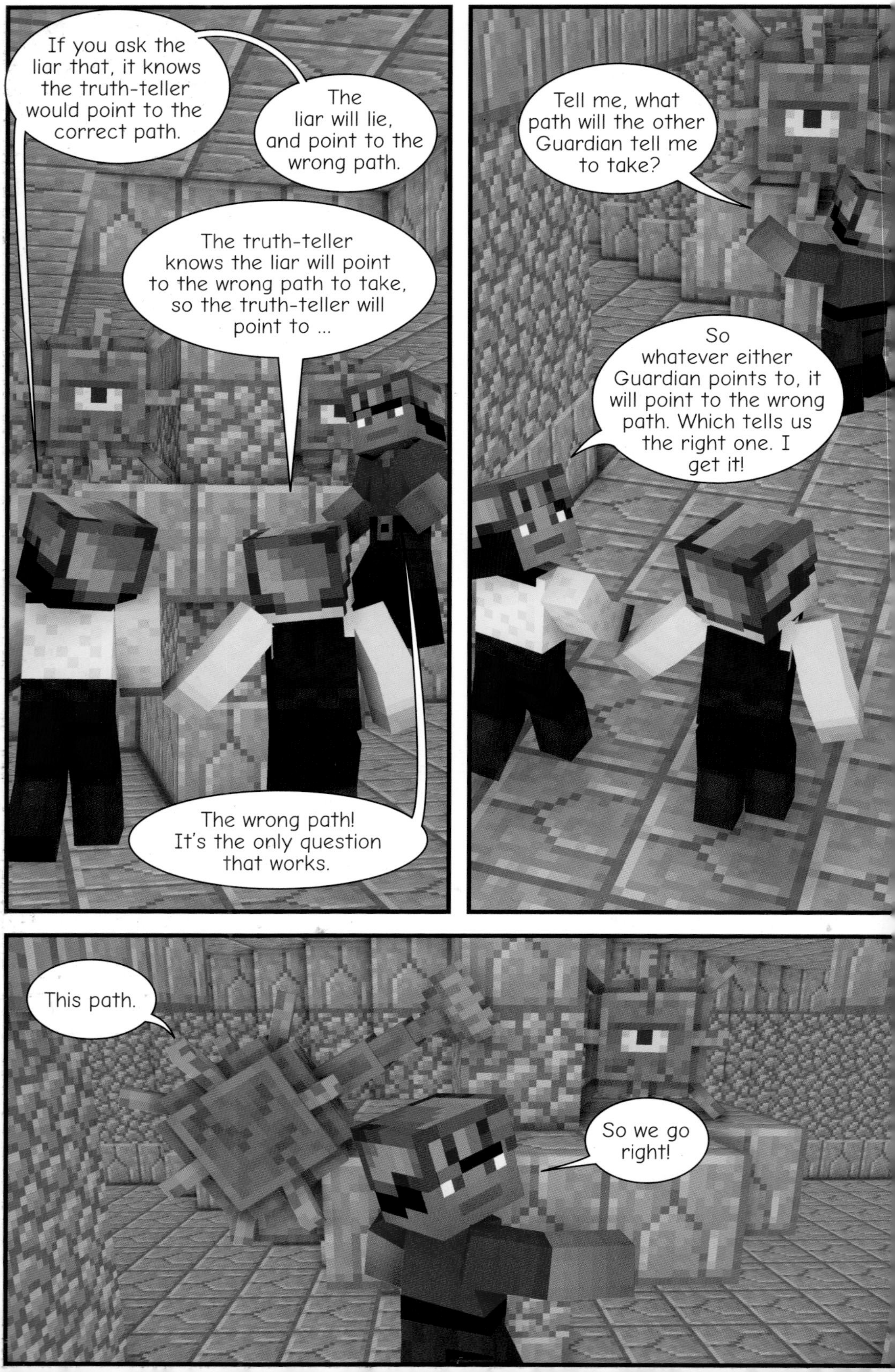
If you ask the liar that, it knows the truth-teller would point to the correct path.
The liar will lie, and point to the wrong path.
The truth-teller knows the liar will point to the wrong path to take, so the truth-teller will point to ...
The wrong path! It's the only question that works.
Tell me, what path will the other Guardian tell me to take?
So whatever either Guardian points to, it will point to the wrong path. Which tells us the right one. I get it!
This path.
So we go right!

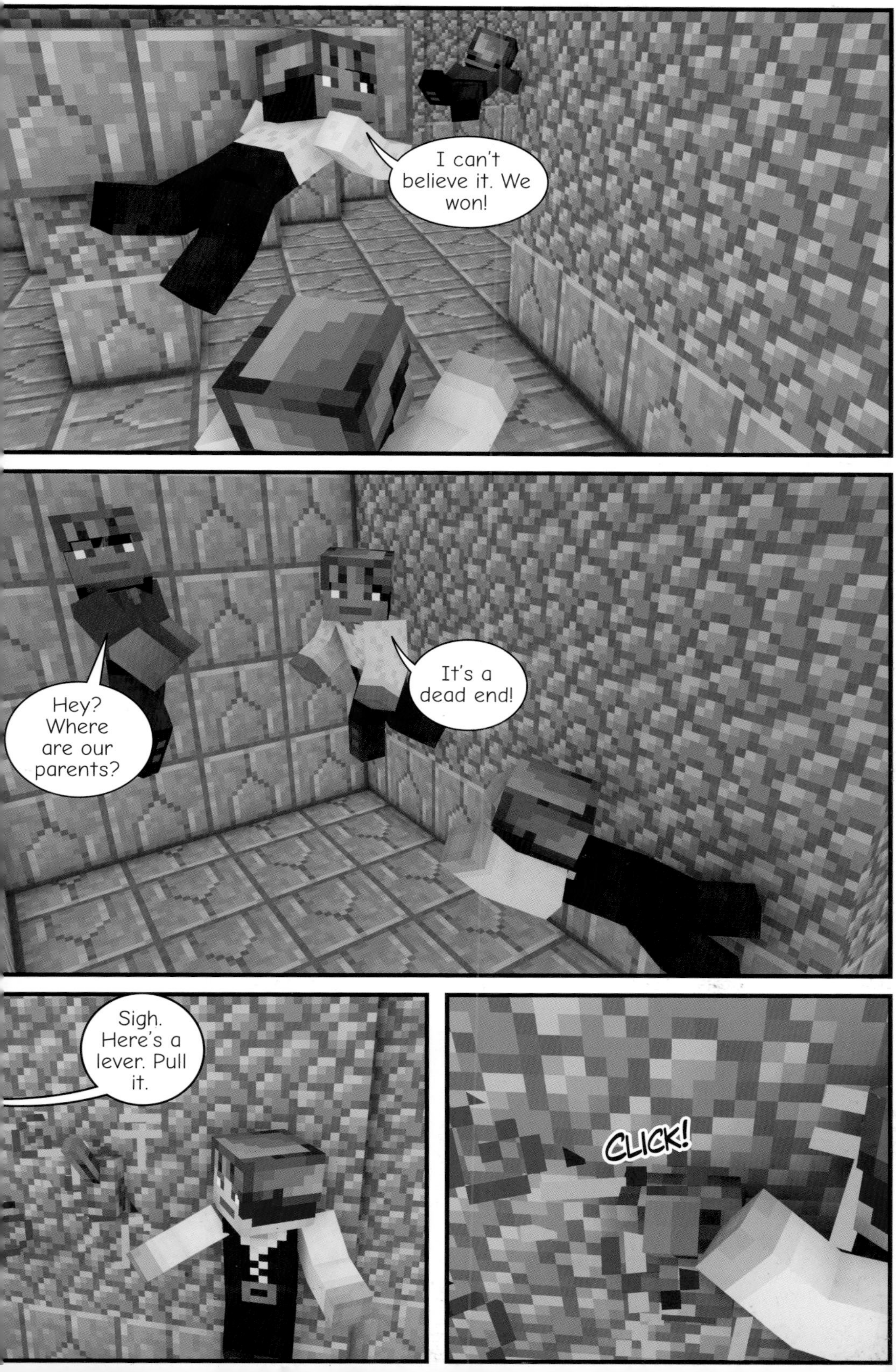
I can't believe it. We won!
Hey? Where are our parents?
It's a dead end!
Sigh. Here's a lever. Pull it.
CLICK!

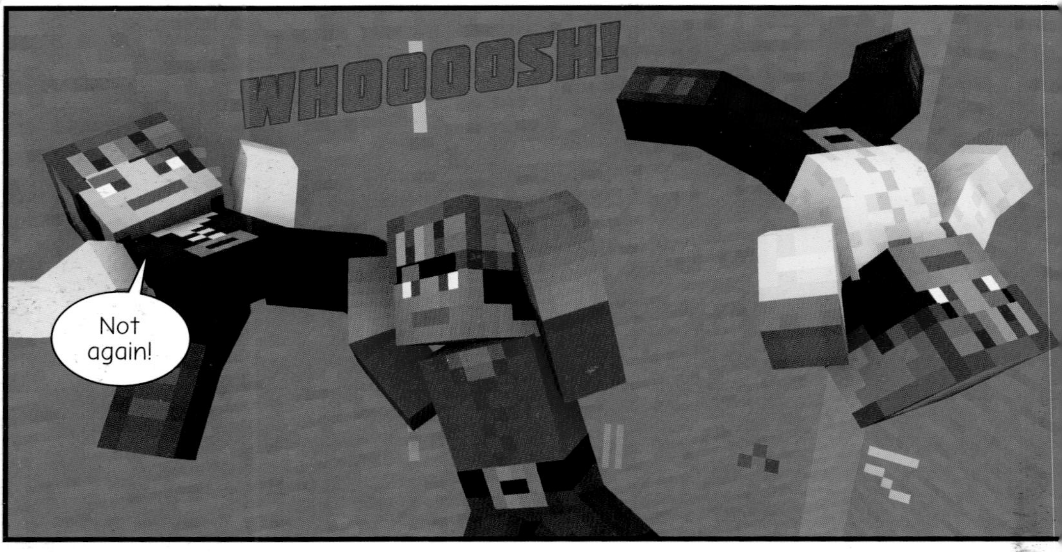
WHOOOOSH!
Not again!

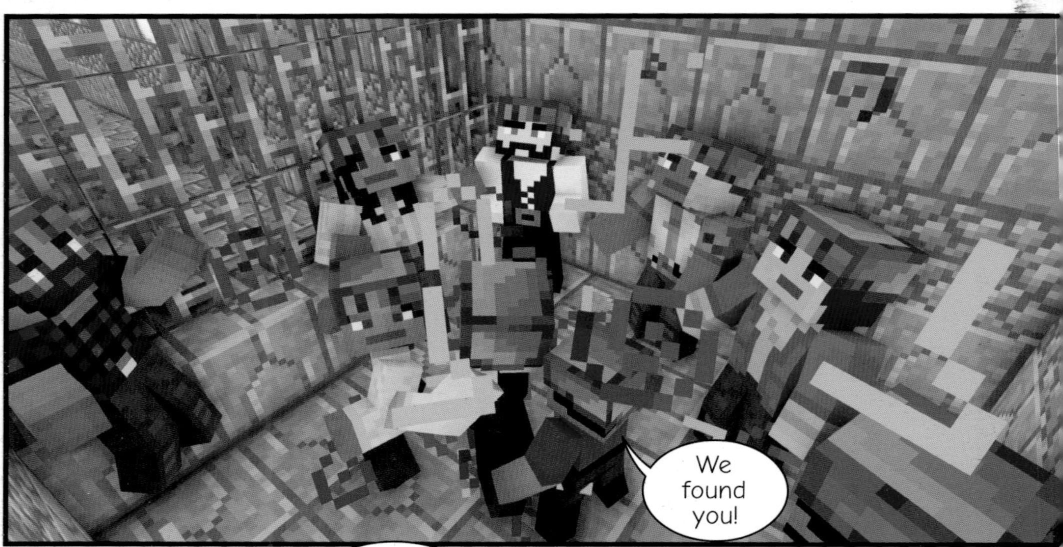
We found you!

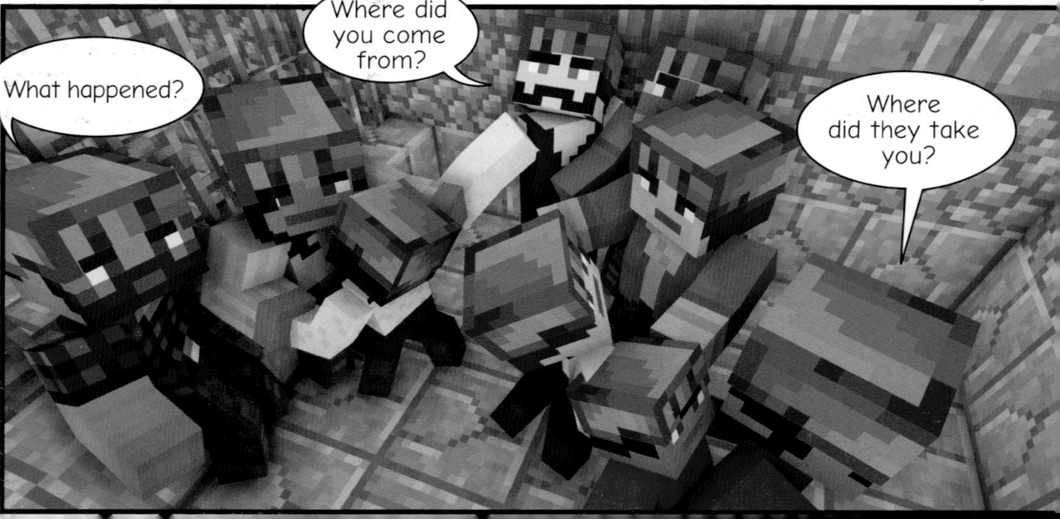
What happened?
Where did you come from?
Where did they take you?

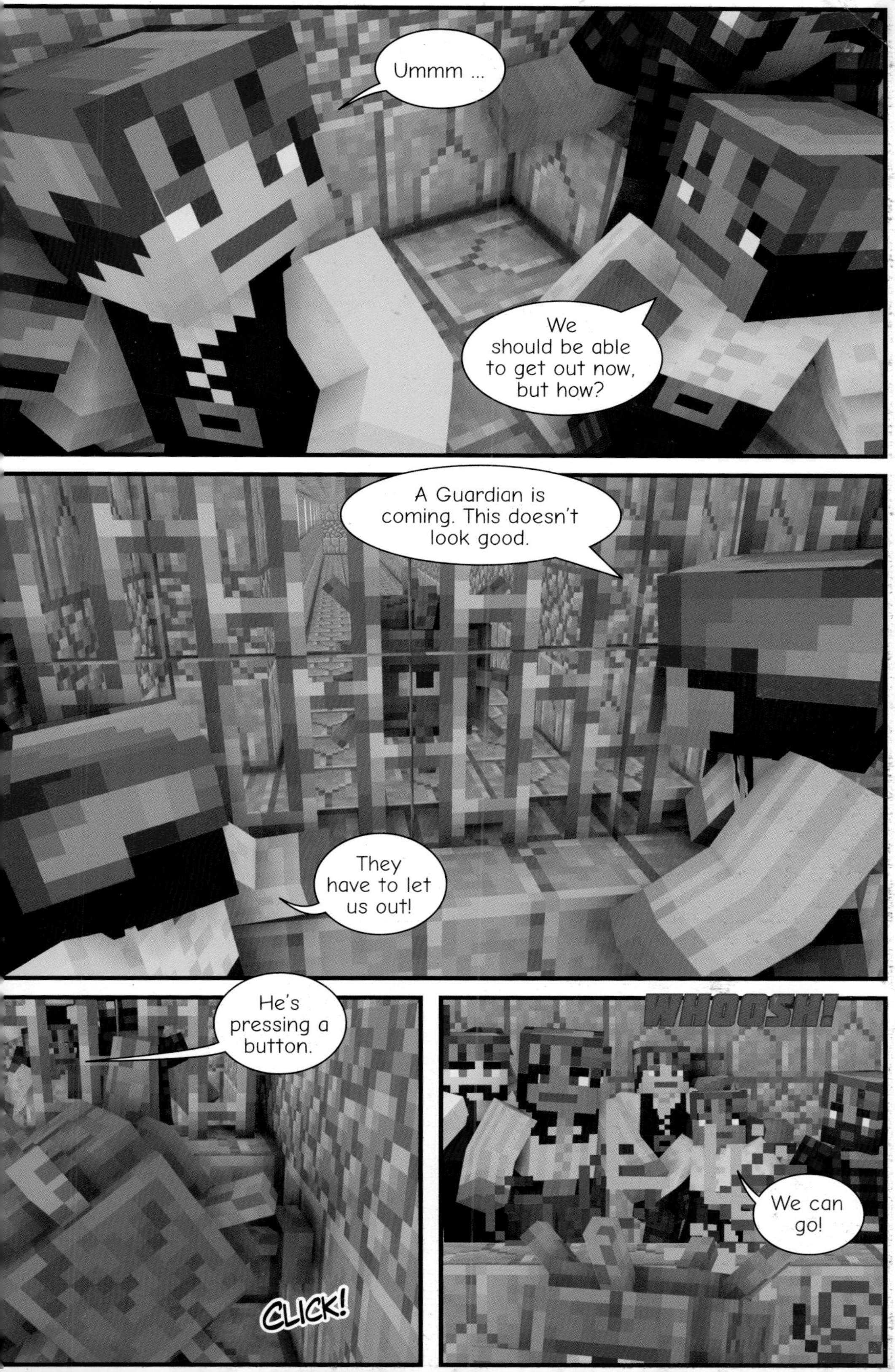
Ummm ...
We should be able to get out now, but how?
A Guardian is coming. This doesn't look good.
They have to let us out!
He's pressing a button.
CLICK!
WHOOSH!
We can go!

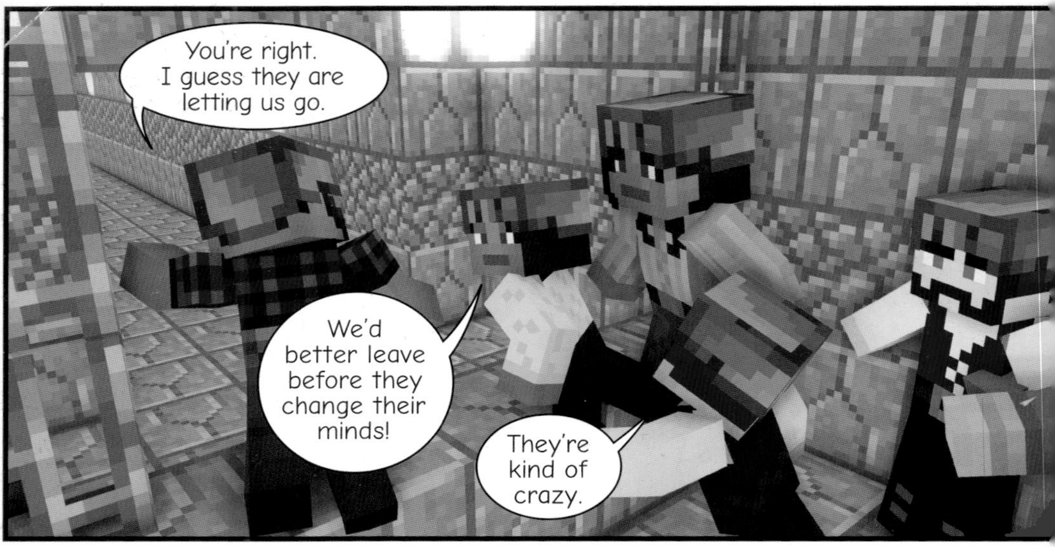
You're right. I guess they are letting us go.
We'd better leave before they change their minds!
They're kind of crazy.

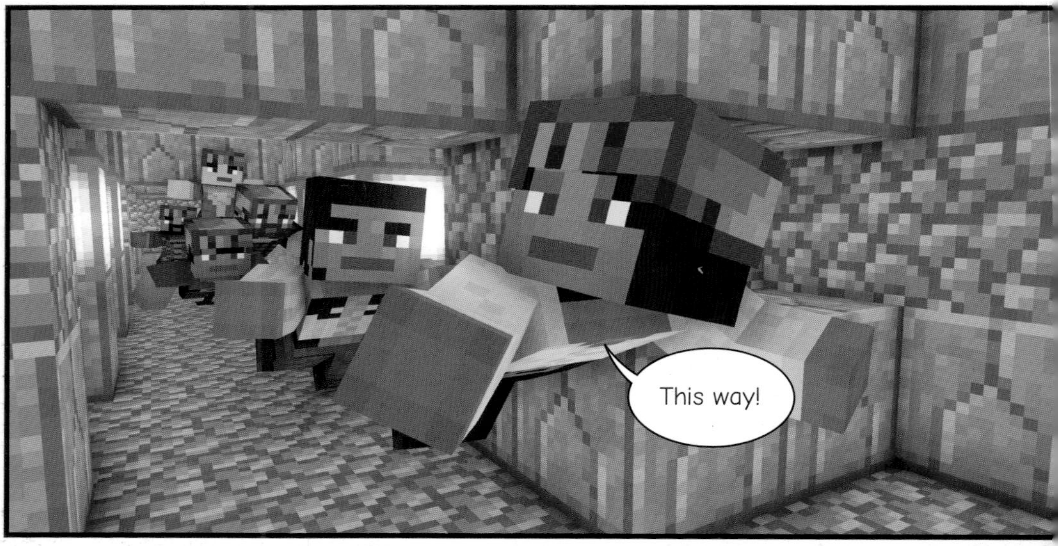
This way!

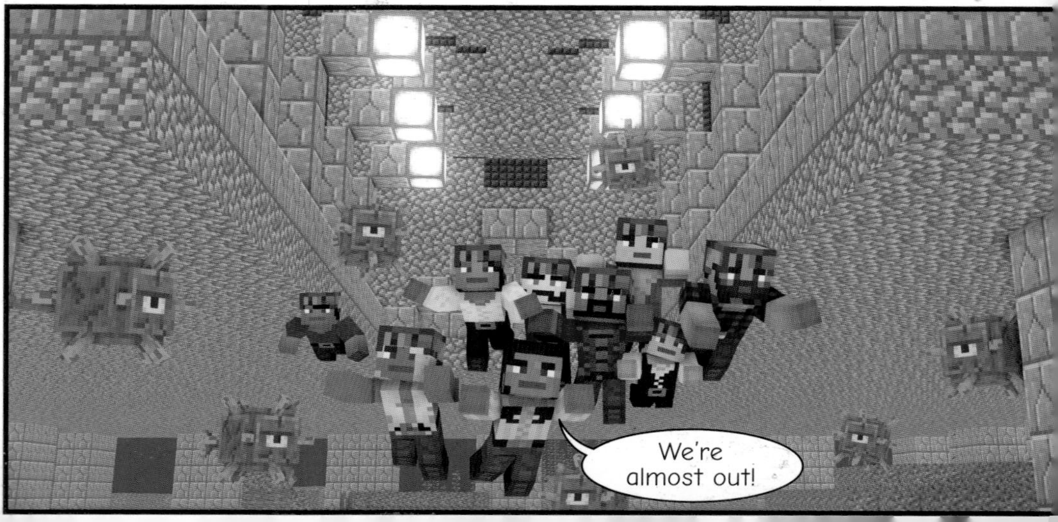
We're almost out!

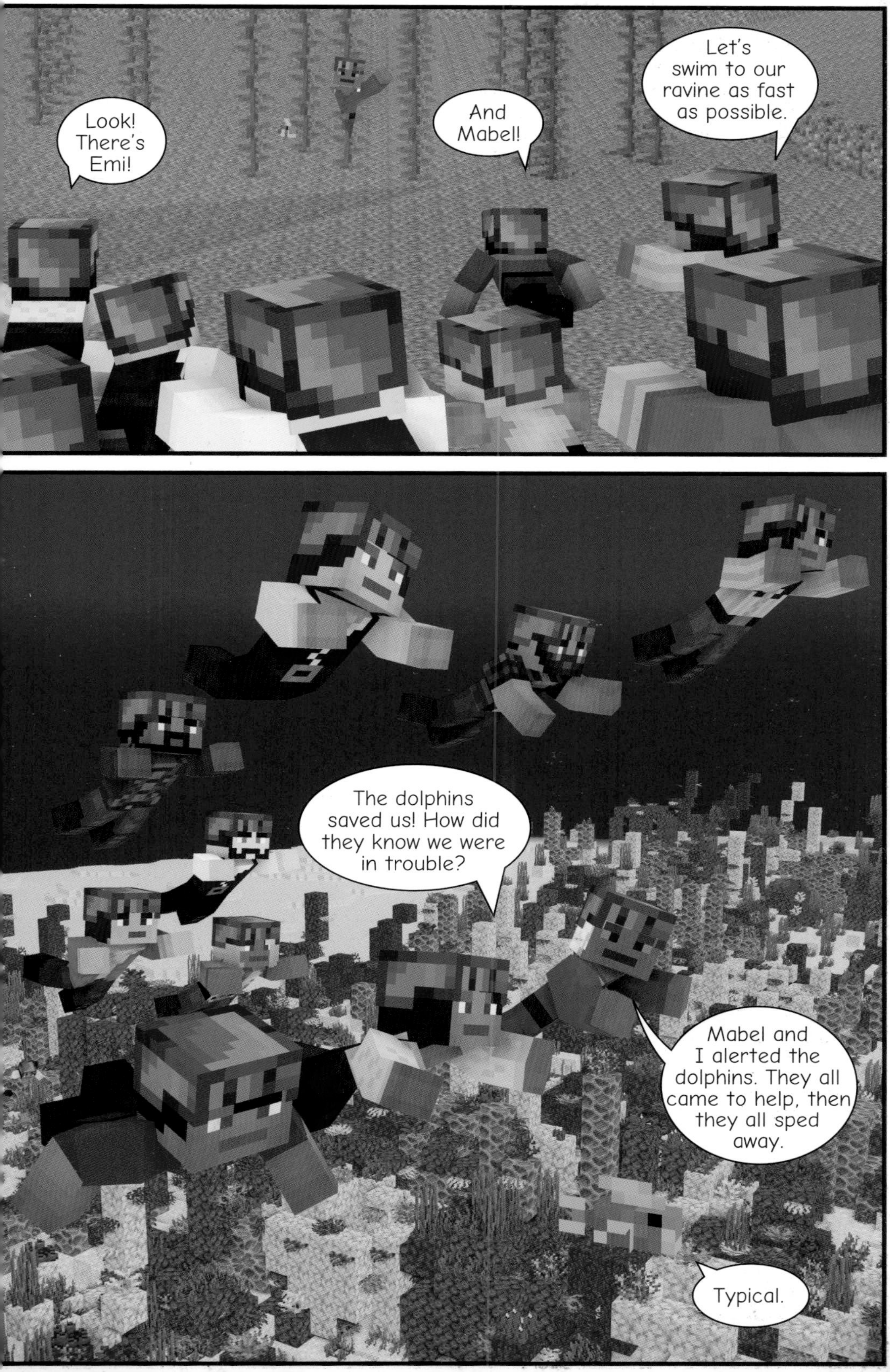

Look! There's Emi!
And Mabel!
Let's swim to our ravine as fast as possible.
The dolphins saved us! How did they know we were in trouble?
Mabel and I alerted the dolphins. They all came to help, then they all sped away.
Typical.

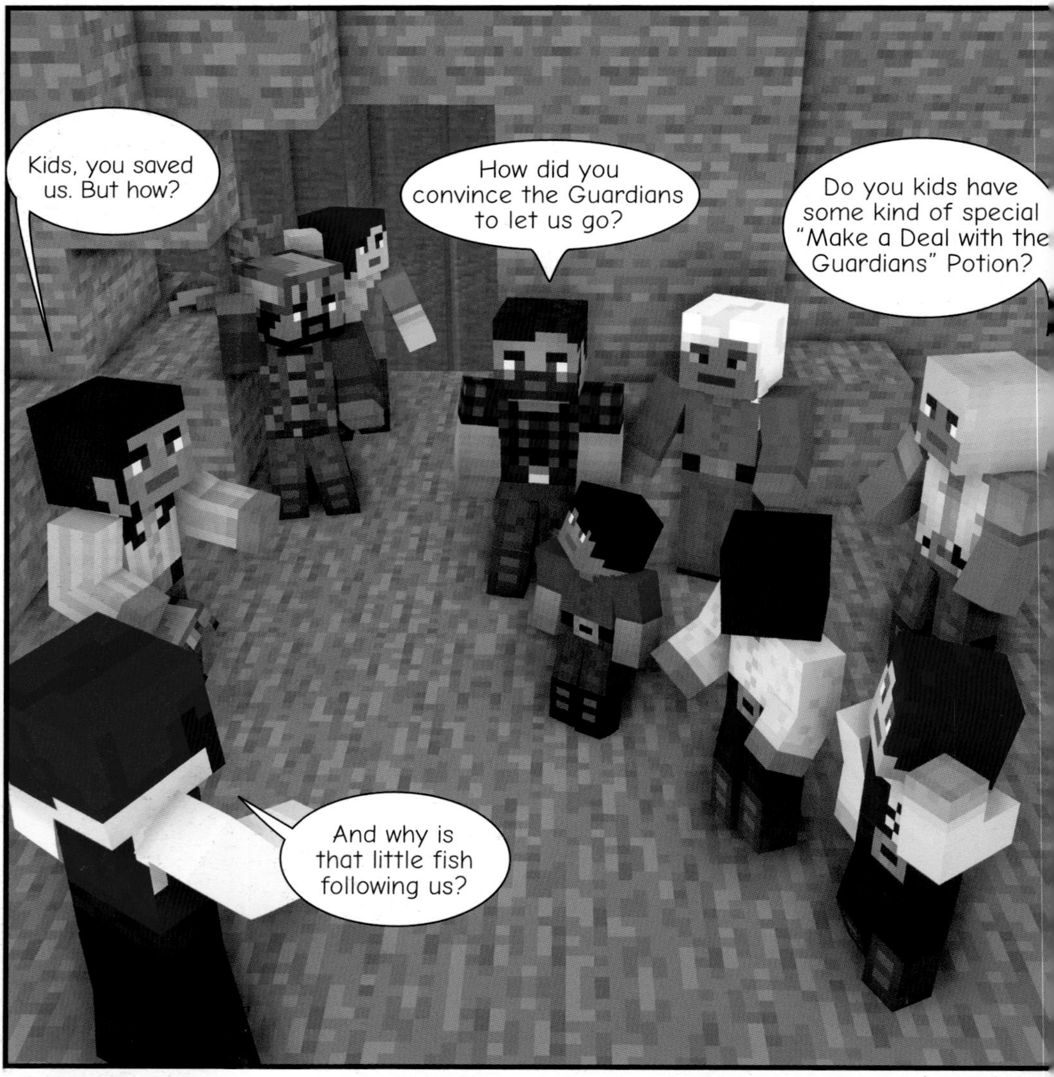
Kids, you saved us. But how?
How did you convince the Guardians to let us go?
Do you kids have some kind of special "Make a Deal with the Guardians" Potion?
And why is that little fish following us?

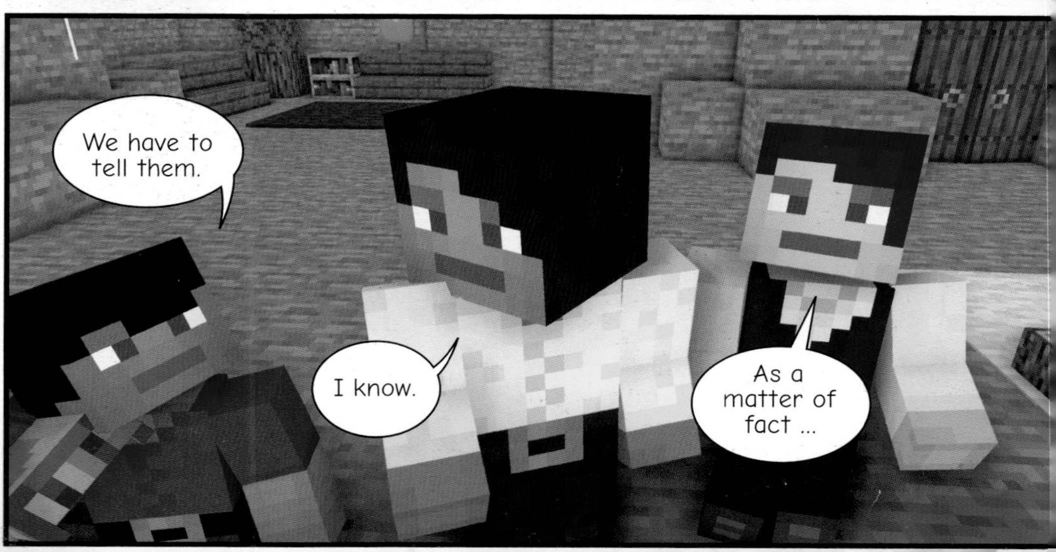
We have to tell them.
I know.
As a matter of fact ...

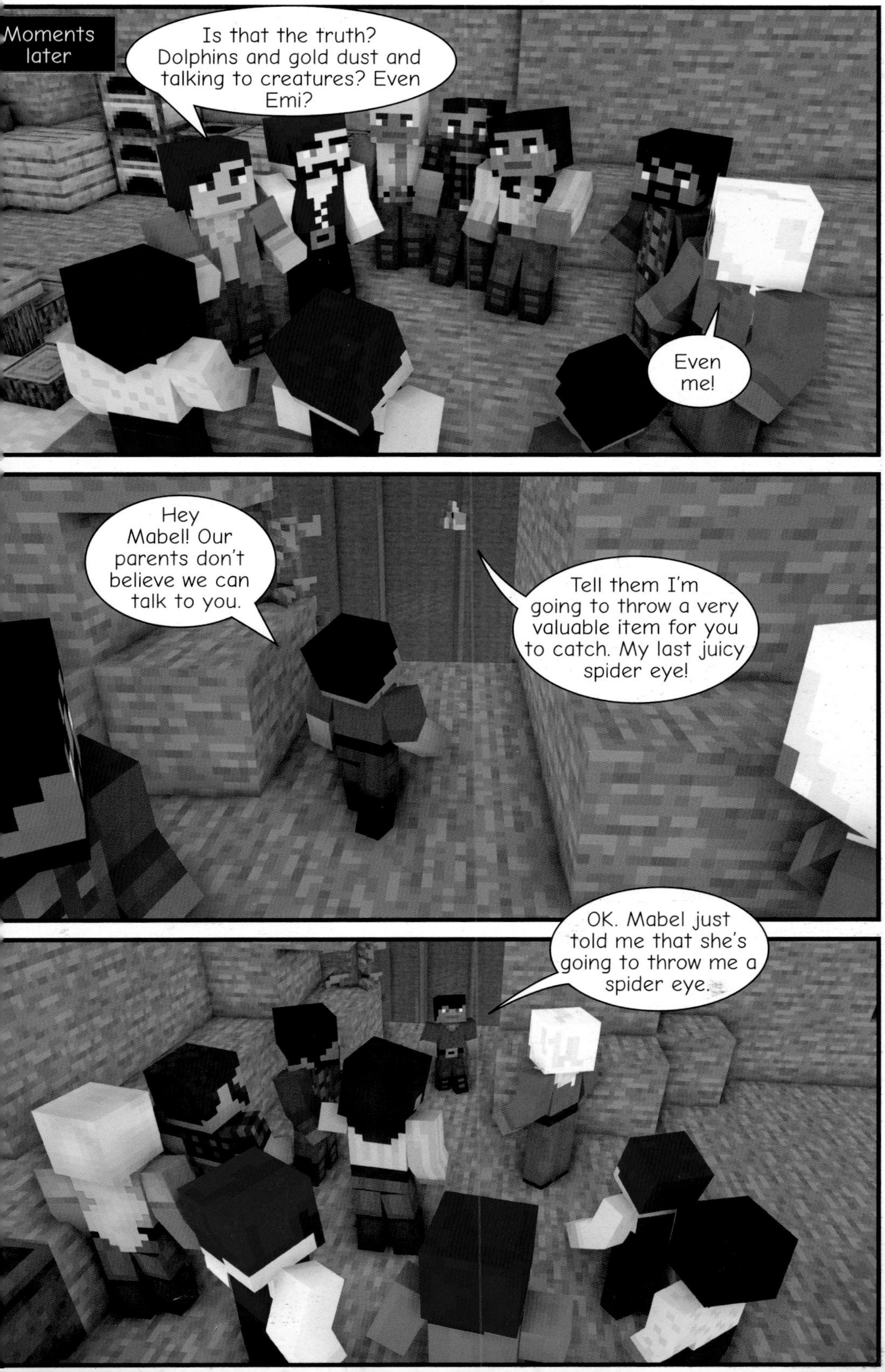
Moments later
Is that the truth? Dolphins and gold dust and talking to creatures? Even Emi?
Even me!
Hey Mabel! Our parents don't believe we can talk to you.
Tell them I'm going to throw a very valuable item for you to catch. My last juicy spider eye!
OK. Mabel just told me that she's going to throw me a spider eye.

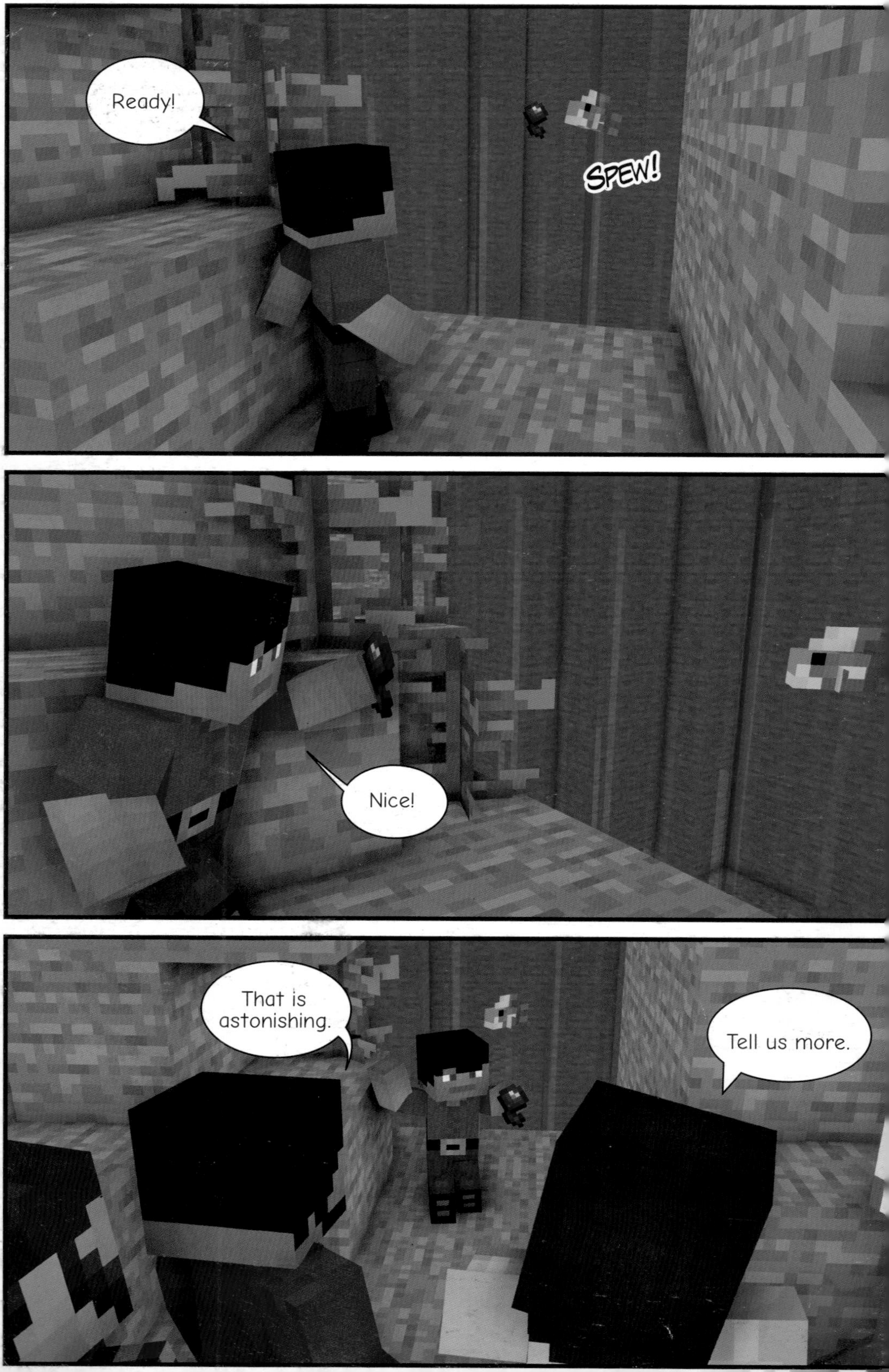
Ready!
SPEW!
Nice!
That is astonishing.
Tell us more.

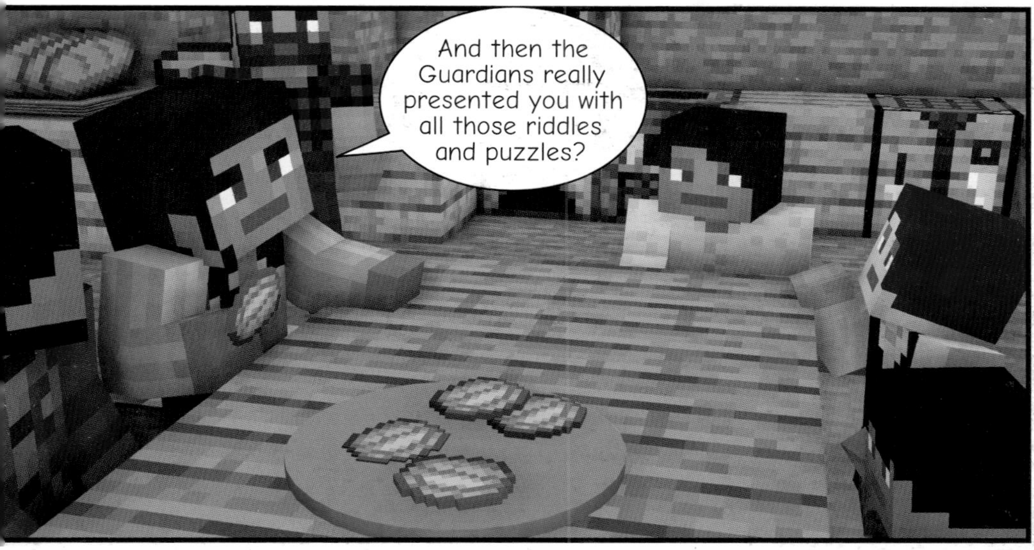
And then the Guardians really presented you with all those riddles and puzzles?
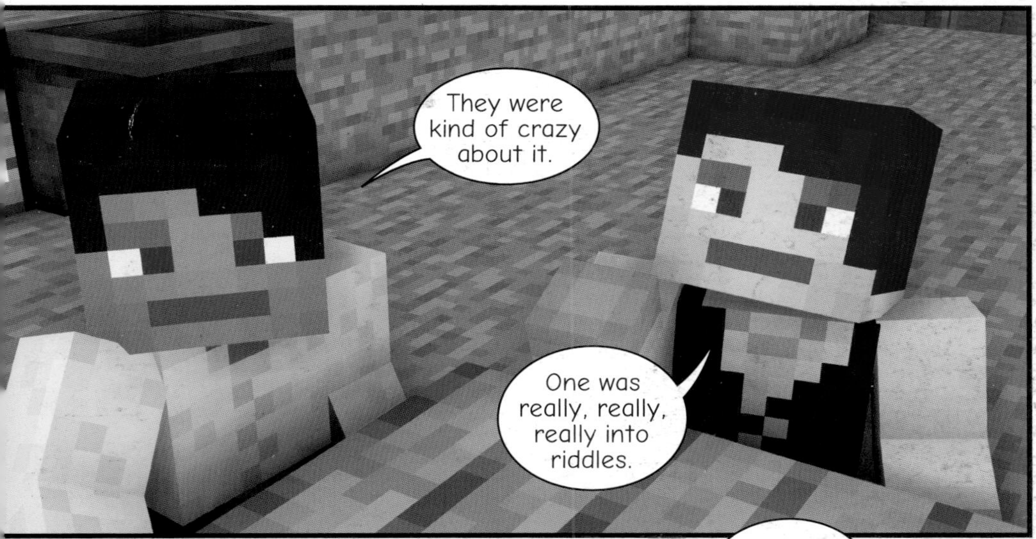
They were kind of crazy about it.
One was really, really, really into riddles.
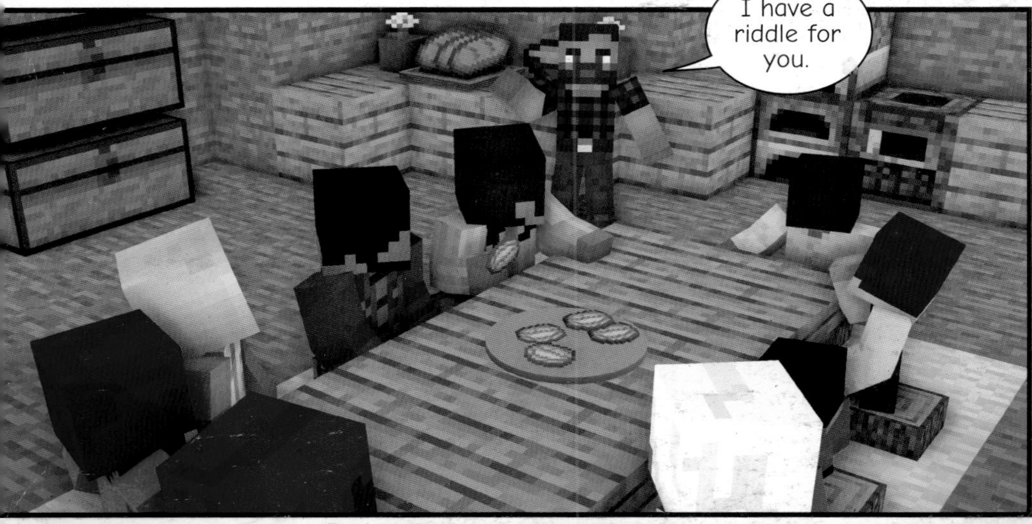
I have a riddle for you.

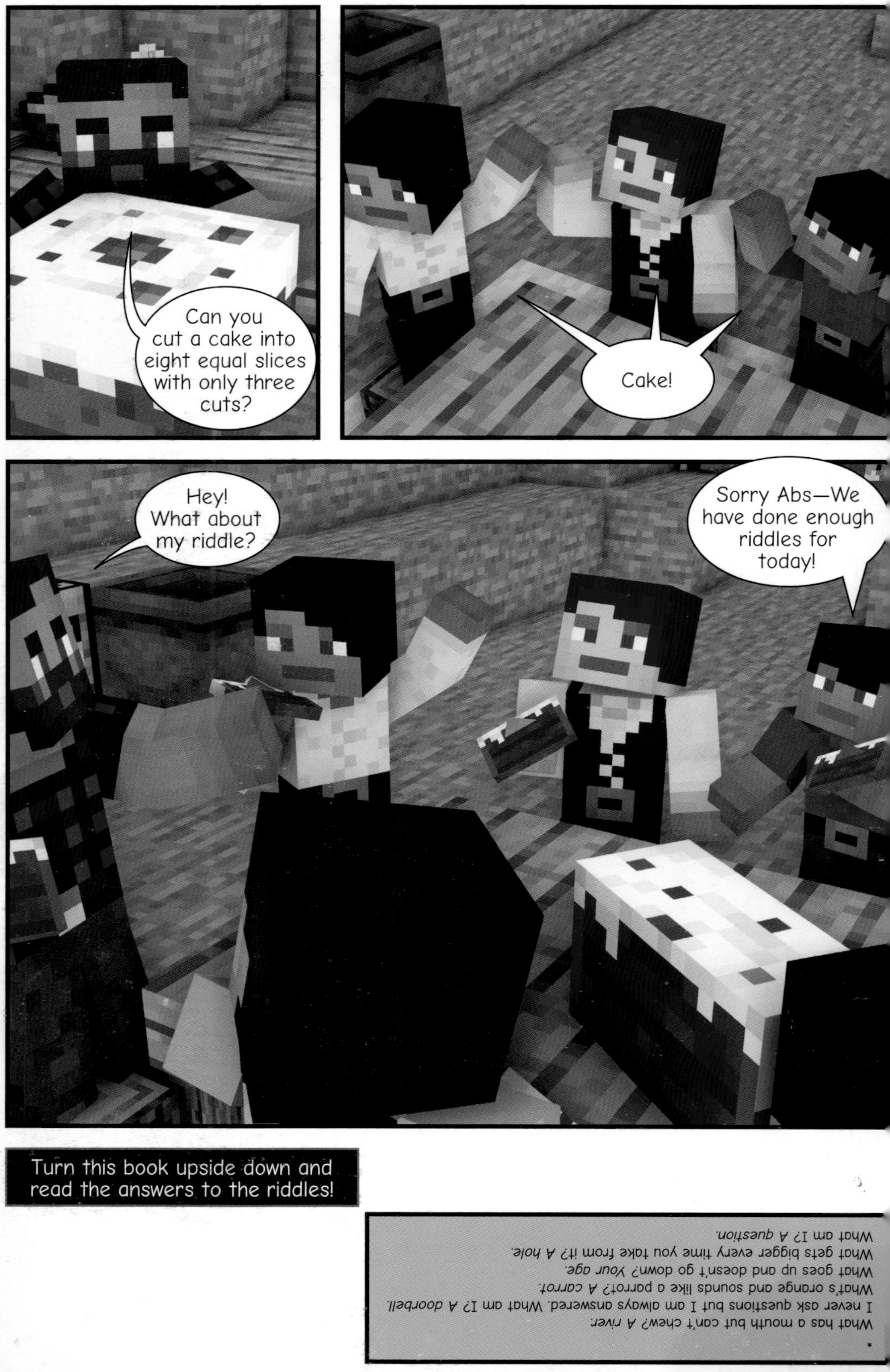
Can you cut a cake into eight equal slices with only three cuts?
Cake!
Hey! What about my riddle?
Sorry Abs—We have done enough riddles for today!

Turn this book upside down and read the answers to the riddles!

What has a mouth but can't chew? *A river.*
I never ask questions but I am always answered. What am I? *A doorbell.*
What's orange and sounds like a parrot? *A carrot.*
What goes up and doesn't go down? *Your age.*
What gets bigger every time you take from it? *A hole.*
What am I? *A question.*